Becoming Benedict Arnold

Lauren,

Thank you so
much for your
kindness during
my interview!
Carpe Diem,
Steve

BECOMING BENEDICT ARNOLD

A Traitor's Tale

STEPHEN YOCH

ISBN 13: 978-1-63489-642-9
Library of Congress Catalog Number has been applied for
Printed in the United States of America
First Printing: 2023
28 27 26 25 24 23   5 4 3 2 1

Image on book cover courtesy of the National Archives, No. 148 GW 0617.
Cover art, design, and all maps by Isabel Lieb.
Interior design by Ryan Scheife / Mayfly Design and typeset in the Arno Pro and
    1820 Modern typefaces

Wise Ink Creative Publishing
807 Broadway St. NE
Suite 46
Minneapolis, MN 55409

For my parents, who taught me the gift of a classical education is only the beginning of lifelong learning.

Table of Contents

Historical Note

This is a work of historical fiction, with an emphasis on the word *historical*. Every person in this book was part of Benedict Arnold's life. Even among highly respected historians, there are significant inconsistencies in the descriptions of Arnold's life. This book takes into account the evolving scholarly view of Arnold and the growing understanding of the challenges he faced, while not excusing his behavior. I have chosen a version of events I believe is the most likely. The extended author's notes at the back of this book identify and discuss controversial topics or note discrepancies among historians concerning Arnold's life.

Much of the dialogue in this book is the result of supposition. Where possible, I have used actual documents to inform the content of conversations. When presenting historical quotations, I have purposely included the incorrect spelling and creative capitalization that characterized the correspondence of the period. Letters accurately quote the original text, subject only to minor modifications and shortening to improve readability.

Finally, I have also included terms such as *Indians, savages, slaves,* and *negroes*, all of which are inappropriate in our time. Nevertheless, they were the words Benedict Arnold and his contemporaries used in daily speech. Eighteenth-century syntax and word choice can also be awkward to the modern ear; I have attempted to maintain the flavor of the speech while keeping the book readable.

INDEX OF MAPS AND IMAGES

MAPS

IMAGES

Arnold's Revolutionary War
1775 - 1780

CANADA

MAINE

QUEBEC

CHAUDIÈRE

ST. LAWRENCE

DEAD

VERMONT

RICHELIEU

KENNEBEC

MONTREAL

ST. JOHN

VALCOUR ISLAND

LAKE CHAMPLAIN

FERRIS BAY

FT. CROWN POINT

LAKE GEORGE

FT. TICONDEROGA

SKENESBOROUGH

NEWBURYPORT

BOSTON

SARATOGA

FT. STANWIX

MOHAWK

ALBANY

HUDSON

NORWICH

NEW YORK

DANBURY

NEW HAVEN

WEST POINT

RIDGEFIELD

MORRISTOWN

NEW YORK

ATLANTIC OCEAN

TRENTON

PHILADELPHIA

N

100 Mi

BATTLE LOCATION

xi

Prologue

London, England – January 6, 1801

They say over time pain loses its sharp edge like sea glass. Yet I still feel the wounds of all I have lost like it was yesterday.

I pick up my pen because the world knows the story of the "Father of His Country"—the remarkably unremarkable George Washington.

What of my story? I was the man who *truly* loved his country, who shed his *own* blood for the Cause.

Days, weeks, and years flow by in a jumble of people, places, work, sleep, happiness, and sadness, and yet there are pivotal moments that make us who we are and give life meaning. Here is my story. My truth.

As you see events unfold, I ask you, fair reader, to consider whether you could have done otherwise. As Providence drove others to exalted heights, so it also destined me to this unhappy place and time—unloved and mislabeled a "traitor" when I was the one betrayed.

PART I
My Rise

Chapter 1

Spanish Colony, Belize Town - June 17, 1766

The *Sally* showed the wear and tear of an arduous voyage as we glided into Belize Town. For a captain, maintaining discipline and unloading cargo while the men hear the siren call of rum and women ashore is especially taxing.

As was the tradition in foreign ports, I was invited by the senior British commander to join the other ship captains for dinner; however, I was so busy that I forgot to deliver my written regrets. Recognizing my mistake, the following morning, I donned my finest uniform and was rowed to Captain Croskie's ship to apologize in person. While his vessel was larger and more heavily armed than mine, it revealed a lack of discipline. I was escorted by a slovenly sailor to the captain's filthy cabin. Before I could open my mouth to speak, the red-eyed British captain snapped, "You are a damned Yankee, destitute of good manners or of those of a gentleman!"

I felt my face flush but said nothing in reply; instead, I calmly removed my gloves and handed them to Croskie, challenging him to a duel. As I returned to my ship, I thought I had shown great control in not drawing my sword.

The next day, I waited on the east side of the island across the bay from the fort. As the sun rose over an emerald sea, not even a hint of a breeze welcomed the day. I had the choice of either staying in the shade near the jungle to avoid the heat and being attacked by swarms of mosquitoes, or standing closer to the shore and roasting in the sweltering glare. I removed my fine wool captain's coat with gold buttons and epaulets and neatly hung it on a tree at the edge of the teeming jungle. I could feel sweat moving down my spine, my fine silk shirt sticking to my back.

Croskie was late. Standing on a deserted isle with my second and a surgeon, part of me simply wished to return to my ship. However, if I were to leave only for him to arrive later, I could be branded a coward for abandoning the field of honor. So, I remained, sweaty hands clasped behind my back, and waited.

It has been a long road to this distant shore, I thought. *I have fought too hard and done too much to abandon my honor now.* My mind drifted back to another stifling day . . .

Chapter 2

Canterbury, CT - August 17, 1753

"*Audens*." Professor Cogswell's pointer, and sometimes his whipping cane, moved to the next word on the chart at the front of the room. The boys in his boarding school read in unison: "*Audentis, audenti, adentem*."

Dr. Cogswell was a Yale-educated minister and my mother's kinsman. It was only through her good graces that I was being educated like a gentleman. At age twelve, I understood that learning Latin was necessary, but as the pointer continued its journey across the chart, I sat in the summer heat and longed to be outside.

As we stepped through the balance of the declensions, Dr. Cogswell's wife appeared at the door. She had always been incredibly kind to the boys, acting as a surrogate mother for many of us as we struggled being away from home. However, recent events had transformed her from an angel to a messenger of death. Yellow fever was raging in Connecticut—her presence now was an ominous portent.

As she quietly opened the door, a dozen boys gave a collective gasp. It was as though the innocence of youth were being sucked out of the room as each boy slumped in his seat, hoping to disappear and avoid the pointing, bony finger beckoning the unlucky out into the common room.

I slid further down in my chair, heart pounding, as Mrs. Cogswell's eyes landed on me. Silently, I willed them to move on—but instead, she confirmed my worst fears with a weary nod. I wished more than anything to continue the Latin lessons I had loathed mere moments before. Mrs. Cogswell placed a gentle hand on my shoulder as I crossed the threshold, then pointed to a chair and sat next to me, setting a letter in my lap. She and the headmaster read all incoming and outgoing correspondence, so she already knew its contents. I looked down and tried to control my reaction.

My Son,

For 3 or 4 days past we looked on Mary as one just stepping off ye banks of time, and to all appearances, Hannah just behind. What God is about to do with us I know not that God should smite your sisters and spare you as yet. Pray improve your time and beg of God to grant his spirit, or death may overtake you unprepared. For his commission seems sealed for a great many, and, for aught you know, you may be one of them. My dear, fly to Christ. If ye don't know ye way, tell him. His guidance of ye Holy Spirit to guide you to that only shelter from death eternal. For, death temporal, we must all try, sooner or later. Farewell.

Your distressed mother.

When I had finished reading, Mrs. Cogswell took the letter from me. I struggled unsuccessfully to fight back the tears; she said nothing as she held my hand.

I was permitted only a few minutes to compose myself. Excessive wailing or remonstration was not tolerated, as it showed both lack of self-control and, more importantly, an implicit questioning of God's will. A good Christian would return to class with the understanding that this plague was all a part of the Lord's plan. As I forced down my sobs, Mrs. Cogswell put her arm around me, and then led me back into the room.

Shortly thereafter, I learned my father, mother, and sister Hannah had survived, but my other sisters Mary and Elizabeth were dead. Once the fever had cleared, I was sent home—not to commiserate, but because we could no longer afford even the discounted tuition. I returned to our gambrel-roof white clapboard house, with its dozen ample rooms, eight fireplaces, and mature elm trees surrounding our five-acre lot. Now, however, I realized that the house was threadbare—many pieces of furniture had been sold, and those that remained required repair.

My mother directed me into the parlor. As if reading my mind, she said, "You see, dearest, your father was a successful ship captain, assessor, and selectman, but it is the war—or I should say the lack of war. He benefitted greatly from a series of wars between Spain, Britain, and France, but now most of the wars are over, and his business has suffered much. We have substantial debt. That is why you had to come home from school."

With the innocence of a boy who was only beginning to understand that his life had changed, I asked, "Is that why father spends his time at Peck Tavern and his ships remain moored at the Chelsea Wharf?"

She nodded silently.

"I can help. I could work on the ships."

Placing a consoling hand on my arm, she replied, "I know you can, dear, but I am afraid all we can do is pray and place our fate and faith in the hands of the Lord."

With little to do and my father's star falling rapidly, I sought distraction with my chums in town. One day a nearby barn caught fire, and I ran out with my friends to watch the inferno. I do not know what possessed me, but I climbed to the top of the slanted, burning roof and held out my hands for balance, as I had seen circus performers do in Norwich. I proceeded to transit the burning roof, surrounded by smoke and flames.

Bored and unhappy, I also slipped out of town to explore the surrounding lands. I met Chief Benjamin Uncas, who presided over two hundred Mohegan Indians in the nearby hills. Uncas taught me to fish, paddle a canoe, stalk a deer, and move through the woods with the stealth and strength of a savage. My later success guiding men through the wilderness is entirely attributable to him and those he led.

I was of middling height, five feet five inches tall; broad in the shoulders and legs, equal to many men who worked on the docks. I was not a bully and didn't tolerate those who were. My strong sense of justice drew boys to me, as I would stand up for what I believed was right.

None of the lads mentioned the humiliating fact that my drunken father on several occasions had been consigned to debtor's prison. From the time he was first incarcerated, my anger was always there, clawing behind my eyes, scratching to be let out in fits of violence if anyone crossed me or impugned our family honor.

Most days, I saw my mother only in the morning as I grabbed a quick snack. She was either praying in the parlor or on her way to church. In the evenings, I inhaled whatever meager food she could put on the table. One evening, after I'd spent the day carousing with my friends, she stopped me with a rare half smile. "Benedict, I have good news for you. I know you were disappointed to have left Mr. Cogswell's school." I felt a flush of both embarrassment and anger. By implicit mutual consent, we never again mentioned my shame of leaving school.

"There is nothing for your father's businesses but debt," she continued. "But I am pleased to say that, nevertheless, the Lord has blessed us. I have spoken with Daniel Lathrop. He is a graduate of Yale College and trained as a physician in London. Indeed, he is the only reputable apothecary between Boston and New York, and he is a relation of ours." I had heard his name from time to time, but never met him in person.

"I met with him today, and his lovely wife, Jerusha. I have signed articles of apprenticeship." I almost stood in outrage, but she held my arm. "Let me be clear, Benedict: This is your last and perhaps only chance to make something of yourself. Your father, God help me for saying so, has failed us. The Lathrops are kind, well educated, and prosperous. You will be bound to them until your twenty-first year; in the interim, I hope you will learn much." There were no tears. Nevertheless, her voice broke as she said, "It is time for you to leave. I wish I did not have to do this, but it is the only way I can see for you. Hannah and I will get by somehow."

Guilt instantly replaced my anger. I recognized that I would be leaving my penniless mother and sister behind as I went to make my way. Their bad situation was only going to become worse. Belatedly, I realized that throughout the conversation, Hannah had been standing in the shadows, saying nothing; now she too met my gaze with tear-filled eyes. I placed my hand on top of my mother's and said, "Thank you. I will do my best for you, Hannah, and our entire family."

Two days later, we gathered my meager belongings and walked down to the Lathrops' riverfront mansion. The fine white house stood just north of the intersection of Town and Washington Streets. It faced the village green's back, filled with long, gracious gardens. The contrast between the squalor and deprivations caused by my father's depravity and the gentility of the Lathrop home was so profound that it lit a fire inside of me. I vowed never to fail like my father.

Mr. Lathrop put me to work, and I relished the opportunity. The more responsibility he gave me, the greater my effort. I was no longer repeating mindless phrases on a chalkboard. I was now learning about business and the wider world. While her husband taught me the ways of businessmen, Mrs. Jerusha Lathrop taught me how to be a gentleman. She was tall, graceful, and dignified, with fair skin, expressive blue eyes, and delicate features. The daughter of a governor, she knew how to manage both the household and its slaves. All three of her children had died of yellow fever, and she treated me like a son.

My beleaguered and loving mother died on August 15, 1759. Now eighteen, I needed to ensure that Hannah could care for our now invalid father and arrange for our mother's Christian burial. I wrote on our mother's headstone: "She was a pattern of piety, patience, and virtue." The loss of our siblings and now our one responsible parent only pushed Hannah and me closer together. We shared our father's shame and knew that we could only depend upon each other.

Shortly thereafter, I began going on voyages to Canada, the Caribbean, and Great Britain. On Dr. Lathrop's ships, I learned the fundamentals of trading and seamanship. I also worked carefully to assist the Lathrops in their business ventures and acted as bookkeeper, recording in ledgers their apothecary and trading enterprises.

After one long voyage, I was busy unloading the ship when I looked over the rail to see a stone-faced Hannah standing on the dock, arms wrapped tightly about herself. I strode up to her, and we silently embraced. At some level, I was hoping she would tell me our father had finally passed, but I knew she would not be as upset if that were the case. Dispensing with any pleasantries, I asked, "What has he done now?" Years of jointly shared humiliation allowed us to speak frankly and truthfully, if only with each other.

"He is with the constable. They are holding him for drunkenness. He was down at the wharf again."

Nodding in resignation, I went back to the ship to get my hat and purse. I felt the eyes of everyone following us. The death of my mother had unhinged my father's last connections to decency. I am mortified to admit that he became a wharf drunk, ridiculed by all. Many in Norwich seemed to revel in seeing someone once respected fall from grace.

Looking straight ahead to avoid meeting anyone's eyes as we walked, Hannah continued in a flat tone, "The First Church has publicly admonished Father. They are going to excommunicate him."

I stopped for a second—Hannah stopped as well, and then we both resumed our walk. Matching her tone, I asked, "Has it occurred yet?"

"No. I spoke with the reverend. I reminded him of Mother and her support of the Church in better days."

With a nod of grateful agreement, I said, "Well done."

We arrived at the constable's office and found our father semi-conscious, covered in his own filth. When I glared at the constable, he retorted, "Listen here, young Mr. Arnold. They pay me to pick up drunkards like your father. They don't pay me to wash them down. That is your responsibility."

I paid the fine for his release and stepped into the cell. He was mumbling to himself as I grabbed him hard under his arms and easily lifted him to his feet. I had grown strong while he had grown weak. I think he barely recognized me as I dragged him out onto the street and toward home, again trying to ignore the judging stares.

Many children experience their father's strength and violence, strong hands striking small bones and supple skin. In a strange way, I longed for a father with the vitality to take control. Instead, I was presented with weakness, tears, and drink. Some men became violent when they drank. My father blubbered more like a toddler than a man. I loathed the sight of him and the dishonor he placed on me.

Finally, eighteen months later, he died, leaving nothing but debt and a stain on our good family name. As his plain casket was lowered into the ground, I resolved that I would rehabilitate our family and its fortunes. I would continue to respect my superiors and be courteous to my lessers, but I would *never* allow our family name or my honor to sink any further.

Chapter 3

Norwich, CT - January 15, 1762

I t was one of those rare midwinter days when the wind comes gently from the south and the snow has largely melted. All know it is only a brief respite, but our thick New England blood makes us believe we can walk about without a coat and imagine spring is coming soon.

As Hannah and I strolled back home after a lovely dinner, I pointed to a bench overlooking Norwich's famous green. Church towers pierced the sky, reaching above handsome oaks. The town was the picture of domestic tranquility and contentment, yet so much of it represented only embarrassment and torture for us. Those lofty houses of worship were the source of much of our unhappiness.

Hannah rarely smiled, but we were both in a good mood. "Well, Brother, it has been quite a twenty-four hours for you—your birthday and the release from your apprenticeship."

I had been mulling over what to do next, but I had not yet shared my plans with her. "The Lathrops have been so good to me," I said. "They were only required to give me two secondhand sets of clothes and pocket change. Instead, they gave me £500 and letters of introduction for both Connecticut and London merchants."

Hannah's smile turned to an open-mouthed gape. Twisting on the bench seat to face her, I continued, "We need to leave this town. Everyone hates us because of Father. We need a fresh start. The Lathrops have encouraged me to consider New Haven to open an apothecary shop. With Yale College and the town's population doubling every few years, there is a real opportunity. It has a port and no apothecary to speak of." Pausing to look her squarely in the eye, I added, "I want to be clear; I could never leave without you. You are part of my plans, the only person in the world I trust."

While she tried to remain impassive, I could see her eyes flare with excitement. A life of disappointment had made her careful. Returning to her default taciturn expression, she said in her typical flat tone, "Pray tell me, what will I do in New Haven? I don't have much of a life here, but it is something."

"Why, you will run my business on Chapel Street, of course. I am going to buy ships and own a fleet by the time I am thirty."

As her head cocked in confusion, I continued, "I have already signed a lease. I am having a sign made." I held up my hands, displaying the imaginary sign in the air. "Of course, we must have a Latin motto. All those years with Dr. Cogswell had to be good for something. It shall be 'Sibi Totique,' which means 'For Himself and for Everybody.' We can pattern the store after the Lathrops. We will provide herbs and medicines like Francis's Female Elixir, James's Fever Powder, Turlington's Balsam of Life, and Spirits of Scurvy Grass. My emporium will also carry various fineries for the growing town, such as books, maps, cosmetics, and jewelry."

Hannah's implacability gave way to a closemouthed grin, which slipped into a broad smile. "As usual, Benedict, you have it all figured out. When do we leave?"

"I have to go to London to buy supplies, but you will settle our affairs here and move to our temporary lodging, which I have arranged for us in New Haven. By the time I get back with a ship full of goods, I am confident you will have the store arranged and our household in order. Then we can start a new life with better people."

She wrapped her shawl around her as we stood. The cold was beginning to creep in, but our mood was too ebullient to let it ruin the moment. "A new life indeed, Benedict," she said, as she hooked her arm through mine and we strode into the future.

Chapter 4

New Haven, CT - January 14, 1763

O ver the next year, I looked for ways to improve my standing in the community by volunteering for local activities. I also made an effort to get to know my customers through discussions about not only their health (which I treated with various medicines), but also what they were reading. I had read virtually every book I purchased and sold, including classics like Shakespeare, Ovid, Plutarch, and Homer. As my business continued to thrive, I moved to a large storefront on Water Street. Some New Haveners began to refer to me as "Doctor Arnold," yet my gaze was directed toward the sea, where the merchants and shippers called me "Captain Arnold."

I made an imposing physical impression at that time in my life. I had the distinctive aquiline "Arnold nose," a high forehead, a prominent chin, unruly thick black hair, and piercing gray eyes—suffice it to say I did not go unnoticed by the ladies. I was solidly built, blessed with strength, endurance, and some grace of movement. My confident manner and strong, deep voice generally made me a natural leader among men. I recognize that at times I was perceived as somewhat overbearing; still, I quickly learned that it is better to risk being arrogant and have men obey than to be deferential and chance being perceived as weak.

I repurchased my family home in Norwich from the Lathrops. I viewed this as a message to the Norwich neighbors who maltreated us; having made my point, I turned around and sold the home at a considerable profit just six months later, simultaneously demonstrating my success and restoring some of our family honor. I then bought Hannah a new home in New Haven in early 1764. She ran the store there and grew the business while I was off on trading voyages. I was, quite rightly, deeply protective of my sister. A year younger than me, she was tall and blonde, with blue-gray eyes. She was graceful, witty, and pretty, at all times a gentle woman of refinement, dignity, intelligence, and more than an ordinary sense of sound judgment.

While she ran the store, I owned three ships that sailed the Atlantic. I drove hard bargains, seized opportunities, paid my creditors slowly, and ensured my debtors paid me on time. I bought low and sold high. I did not suffer fools, but I readily profited from them. Life was good and my prospects endless as I set off for Central America.

Chapter 5

Spanish Colony, Belize Town – June 18, 1766

A fter four years of struggles and hard work, I was standing on a deserted beach, ready to risk my entire fortune to guard my honor against a captain who had insulted me.

Finally, I saw Captain Croskie's boat in the distance. It confirmed my suspicion. He had delayed, hoping to find me gone.

A half dozen burly natives accompanied the captain and his second. Realizing it was an ambush, I felt my fear depart. I strode the shoreline without putting on my coat. I had received a fine brace of Wogdon & Barton dueling pistols as part of an exchange for unpaid goods while in Canada. I flipped open the box and quickly loaded them. Out of the corner of my eye, I saw my second frantically loading his weapon as well.

Moving forcefully to the edge of the waterline, I cocked both pistols and aimed them at Croskie and his second just as they reached the surf. In a voice somewhere between a growl and a roar, I declared, "By Christ's blood, if a single savage exits that boat, you two will be the first to die."

Looking down the barrel of my gun, a wide-eyed Croskie mumbled some incomprehensible response. He slowly and carefully got out of the boat with his second while the savages rowed away.

I was surprised to realize that despite his age and seniority, I was the one in control. I had just forced all his allies to leave, and now he stood on an empty beach, facing me. He only briefly looked up, but never met my eye; instead, he kept glancing at his second. After some further hesitation, his second approached mine, and they began to perform their duties to allow us to proceed.

Calmly handing one of my pistols to my second, I strolled

unhurriedly to my coat and carefully recomposed myself. I then walked back to Croskie and faced him.

As the man challenged, Croskie had the privilege of the first shot. Even with thirty feet of sand, rocks, and ankle-high saw grass separating us, I could see his hands were shaking; I knew he would miss. Nevertheless, I prudently turned sideways to minimize my profile while looking him directly in the eye for the first time as he took aim. Like a rabbit freezing under a hawk's shadow, I held perfectly still.

There is a suspension of time as a man raises a gun and points it at your head. An eternity passed from the click of the flint to the flash of the powder and the sound of the ball screaming above my head. I am proud to say that I did not flinch.

I let out the breath I had been holding impossibly long—knowing it might be my last. When I inhaled, it was like the first gasp of a newborn. I felt the surge of a life lost and now returned. I radiated the fury of a baby drawn from the safety of the womb into a cold world.

My gun was already loaded and at my side. I raised it and pointed at the quivering Croskie. Killing a British captain would not enhance my reputation, though I had not a shadow of doubt that I *could* kill him. Instead, I aimed carefully and fired. I hit him precisely where I intended: the outer edge of his shoulder.

As the surgeon hastily bandaged Croskie's wound, I faced the captain and bellowed, "I give you notice! If you miss this time, I shall kill you!"

In response, I saw him reach into his pocket and wipe his pox-marked face with a handkerchief.

I believed I had the measure of the man, and I was proven right. A moment later, Croskie's second scurried over to him and a brief exchange occurred; shortly after, the second bade me and my own second to approach. After further discussion, Croskie walked over to me. Instead of meeting my eye, he looked at my gun, which I still held firmly in my hand, and said, "You have behaved honorably, Captain Arnold. I regret the insult."

I could have demanded a more complete apology, but Honor had been satisfied, and I had no appetite for further dueling.

I shifted my pistol to my left hand and extended my right; his gun had already been set aside. He took my hand with an audible sigh of relief, inviting me back to his ship to share a drink. I gladly accepted. We departed friends. I returned to New Haven with my reputation—and more importantly, my honor—defended and elevated.

Chapter 6

New Haven, CT - December 12, 1766

L ater that year, I sat in the parlor of Samuel Mansfield, the high sheriff of New Haven and a fellow Mason. After hearing about my purchase of yet another ship and the growing prosperity of my apothecary, he suggested I meet his daughter, Margaret. I was at an age and position where acquiring a wife, especially a well-connected one, was expected and, indeed, desirable.

Margaret was dressed in a lovely yellow gown with a high collar and matching shoes. The obvious expense of her attire reflected the importance of this meeting—while we had previously been introduced and had subsequently met on several occasions, we both understood the formality of this encounter. Accordingly, I wore a fine suit with sterling buttons and polished buckles on my shoes.

After a perfunctory introduction, Margaret's father took his leave with the doors left open. She was seated at rigid attention before the hearth as a maid brought in tea. I found her a bit too thin for my taste, lacking much of a bosom or hips. She was one of those wiry women who could not seem to eat enough to burn off some internal tension. Her eyes were downcast and her mouth was naturally straight, neither smiling nor frowning. Her tightly closed lips hinted at some thought or word that was being withheld. When I had seen her smile in the past, she'd had straight white teeth. I was pleased to see upon closer examination that she possessed a clear complexion and regular features, which made her attractive if not beautiful.

I understood it was my duty to speak first. "Your home is lovely—as is your dress."

Without looking up, she said flatly, "It is my father's house. The dress is new, and I thank you."

Silence lingered. At that point I would have expected a question or comment directed to me, but either she could think of nothing to say or she was indifferent to the conversation. I found myself getting irritated, but I forced a calming breath, understanding that this was a good match. "My suit is new too. I had it made for me on my most recent trip to London on my newest ship."

Again, no comment, eyes down. I decided to reveal my growing frustration. "What, pray, do you do with your time, when not being forced to sit with the likes of me?"

A look of both fear and horror fluttered across her face. She stammered, "Oh, Captain Arnold, I am sorry. I very much enjoy being with you. It is my father's will, which of course I honor, but I am also pleased to be in your company."

So she is just quiet and shy. "No. Not at all. So tell me, what do you enjoy? I like the sea and running my businesses, but what of you?"

She now looked up for the first time, with a flushed complexion and fetching large eyes. "I knit. I do needlework." Then, sitting a bit straighter (if that were possible), "I can read and write." With that, the energy went out of her, and she again defaulted to silence.

Recognizing that she was not going to ask a question, I decided again to take control. "You know I am a captain of ships, but what else can I tell you about myself?"

Looking at me only briefly, she said, "I know of your store, and I have met your sister. I am told you are from Norwich." With that last comment, her hands twisted slightly in her lap.

There it is. The family reputation. Norwich and New Haven are only sixteen leagues apart. Too close to escape my family's past. I must hit this head-on. "You may have heard that my father fell on hard times and brought embarrassment to our family." I paused to see if she had any questions. She stared back blankly, clearly waiting for me to continue. I then repeated what I had told many prominent men about town: "I am the sixth of my name. The first of my line sailed from England in 1635 and landed in Massachusetts. They left a year later with Roger Williams to help found Rhode Island. The first of my name became a wealthy landowner and was elected governor ten times. The second served on Rhode Island General Court and became speaker of the House of Deputies. The third had a large family but was not as prosperous. His son, my father, was the fourth Benedict. He moved to Norwich, became involved in shipping, prospered, and was a leader in town. The fifth Benedict died just ten months after his birth, and I was the sixth of the name. When trade suffered after the war, so did my father's prospects."

She waited for me to continue with that same flat look, lacking sympathy or accusation.

"He lost my family fortune and his way. I was a bit of a wild boy. However, with the help of my mother and other good relations, I worked hard and regained our fortune and position. I now own the forty-ton, single-masted *Fortune*, the thirty-ton *Sally*, and the twenty-eight-ton *Three Brothers*. We travel throughout the Caribbean, New England, and Canada. I have holdings in livestock, Spanish gold, molasses, pork, grain, salt, and cotton." I knew I was being excessively detailed, but I wanted to impress upon her my substantial and growing wealth.

She nodded. "I understand." There were no words of comfort, appreciation, or even recrimination—just an acceptance of a conclusion which had probably already been pronounced by her father. She stood and pointed to the door without enthusiasm. "Would you like to see the gardens?"

The courtship continued the appropriate amount of time, and we were wed on February 22, 1767, at the First Church of New Haven. Our initial days were warm, and Margaret seemed to soften as three healthy sons were born in succession. But the longer I spent at sea, the colder and more distant she became—rarely writing me despite my entreaties for updates on her and our children.

PART II

The Revolutionary

Chapter 7

New Haven, CT - December 23, 1773

O ver the next half dozen years, my mercantile business, shipping, and reputation all grew. I became an active member of the community when I was in port. More than that, I was a growing voice for justice in the face of British oppression. Infringement upon freedoms of any sort did not sit right by me—and when those infringements directly impacted my purse, they were all the more intolerable. Parliament had passed the Tea Act, showing favoritism to well-known royal families in America who received low-cost direct tea shipments from India, harming merchants like me.

While the adverse impact of Parliament's actions on my wallet were a strong encouragement for me to support the Sons of Liberty, fundamental issues of American sovereignty, taxation without representation, and the right to protest were also at the front of my mind. I was truly appalled when I learned soldiers had fired into a crowd of American tax protestors in Boston, killing four and injuring scores. I wrote friends that I was not only "very much shocked" by the loss of American lives, but disappointed by my countrymen's failure to rise in protest. "Good God! Are the Americans all asleep and tamely giving up their glorious liberties, or are they all turned philosophers, that don't take immediate vengeance on such miscreants?"

After a local loyalist, Reverend Samuel Peters, spoke out against the Boston Tea Party, I decided to take matters into my own hands. I led a group of the Sons of Liberty to his New Haven home at ten o'clock at night. When our group arrived, I shouted for Peters to open his gate. He responded, "The gate shall not be opened this night, but on pain of death!"

The mob cried as a group, "Doctor Arnold, break down the gate, and we will follow you, and punish the Tory Peters!"

I roared back, "Bring an axe and split down the gate."

Peters, cocking his gun, responded, "Arnold, so sure as you split the gate, I'll blow your brains out."

Years of experiencing life and death at sea allowed me to quickly recognize the determination in the terrified man's voice. When I did not proceed, one of my cohort yelled, "Coward!"

I turned and said, "I am no coward, but I know Dr. Peters's disposition and temper. He will fulfill every promise he makes. I have no wish for death at present."

At that point, I was still unwilling to risk actual violence with my neighbors. True violence was restricted to innocent civilians murdered by British regulars in Boston. Our goal was to dramatize the seriousness of our purpose, not to kill Puritan loyalists.

Chapter 8

Philadelphia, PA - September 8, 1774

Silas Deane
Engraving by B. L. Provost of painting by Du Simitière.
Courtesy of the Library of Congress #2001699813

"**B**y Christ's blood!" I barked as my shoulder banged into the side of the carriage. I slammed my book closed in frustration.

Silas Deane sat across from me in his comfortable carriage, a smile spread across his smooth face. With his hands crossed on his chest, he looked like he was about to doze, except for the sharp eyes that remained fixed and focused. He murmured, "I'll confess, Benedict, that I thought if anyone could read in a carriage, it would be you. A ship's captain is used to being knocked about on the waves."

"The waves in the ocean are different; they are predictable. I can write and read with ease, except in the roughest seas. At some level, my body begins to anticipate how the ship and the water are moving. You cannot do it in this confounded carriage." As Deane's right eyebrow rose at my comment, I realized I had potentially insulted him. "I do beg your pardon, Silas—this is a lovely carriage, and I know it has the best possible springs. It is just—"

Deane politely interrupted me with a wave of the hand. "—The roads. I understand, Benedict. No offense taken. These so-called roads are often little more than two ruts cut through a continuous path of mire and fallen trees. It would have been easier to go by sea, but this meeting of the Continental Congress in Philadelphia is a poorly kept secret. We would run the risk of being intercepted by the Royal Navy. Thus, we get to take the more scenic route." As he spoke, he pointed out the window at a farmer working in his fields and covered in filth.

I laughed out loud, and Silas joined in. "I do not want to sound ungrateful," I told him. "It was kind of you to include me, and more importantly, I appreciate your help in introducing me to the members of the Committees of Correspondence. I know it is you, as much as anyone, who was responsible for getting me elected to go to Philadelphia."

"No, it was your leadership and enthusiastic support of the Sons of Liberty that led you here. Besides, this is a great opportunity for both of us. I am going to Philadelphia because of my ability to scratch out a useful word or two. You, my intrepid friend, are a man of action. If this revolution is going to succeed, they will need us both."

Of course, Silas was right. In the nine months since the Boston Tea Party, I had become enthralled with the political transformation that was occurring throughout the colonies. The growing fervor also changed how people viewed me. Whereas my willingness to use violence had been detested by many, it was now seen as bravery. Whereas my supreme confidence had been lamented as arrogance, it was now seen as decisiveness. I was counted among the leaders of Connecticut to meet the other great men of the Colonies.

"There is an ancient concept that comes from the Orient—I believe the Chinese call it yin and yang. Opposites complement each other. I am small, weak, and soft. You are tough, vital, and strong." He held up his hand to stifle my protest. "You are a man of action, and I am a man of letters." Deane's father had not suffered the same reversals as mine, so Silas had been educated at Yale College in New Haven, where he'd graduated in 1758 and begun practicing law. He later received his master of arts. "And yet we both have a similar drive for success in business and a desire to lead our communities. I am pleased we are friends and have done business together. I believe we can also make a meaningful difference in the cause of liberty."

I nodded in agreement, and we lapsed into comfortable silence. Not talking always felt more natural for me than it did for the loquacious Deane. Unable to hold his tongue any longer, he inquired, "How is your family? Are they well?"

"My wife, Margaret, is fine. We have three strong sons. My parents, as you know, are with the Lord. My sister Hannah helps run my businesses while I am at sea. Frankly, I don't know what I would do without her."

Silas was now fully engaged. "You will forgive me for my directness, my friend, and I do again apologize that I missed your wedding, but normally your bride would be assisting you in looking after the business. It seems . . ."

Knowing he was searching for a tactful way to ask, I interrupted him. "Unusual?"

"Come, come. We have known each other for over a decade. You may rely on my discretion."

With a shrug, I decided to tell him the truth. "She is not communicative or interested in my business or me. She rarely writes me when I travel, and when I am home, she is often dour."

I did not share my deepest sadness: that she'd never really loved me. Indeed, as time went by, the internal light that animated her spirit faded like a cloud darkening a sun-dappled ocean.

Silas nodded in understanding. "You married her for sound reasons, correct? I know her father; he is a worthy gentleman."

I shrugged in agreement.

"And she is neither disobedient nor abusive of you or your children, correct?"

Again I inclined my head.

"I will tell you the advice I was given when I got married. All a man can hope for is an obedient and fertile wife. If love is part of the equation, all the better. From the sound of it, what your wife lacks, your sister is able to provide, as far as your business is concerned."

I nodded again without speaking.

Deane leaned forward across the carriage, grabbed my knee, and shook. "Be happy. You have one of the finest homes in town and are rightly respected. Your wife has provided you with three strong sons. If the good Lord gave us everything, we would have nothing to strive for."

Initially, I did not smile, but Deane kept shaking my leg. I said, "Stop that."

He shook it all the more and replied, "Not until you smile, my taciturn friend. Come on—smile!"

I'll confess that my first instinct was to throttle the little man, but his good humor and kindness were so infectious that I found myself smiling and laughing. "All right, all right. You win, and you are right. I have much for which to thank the Lord."

"The Lord be damned," Silas interjected, although somewhat quieter so his driver and coachmen wouldn't hear the blasphemy. "It is our hard work and perseverance that put us in this carriage on our way to Philadelphia today. The Lord helps those who help themselves."

"Amen," I said in a full voice as he finally let go of my knee. "And how go your own family and business?"

He sat back with a satisfied grin. "We are landlubbers, as you well know. Our mercantile business continues to grow. Where you have your sister Hannah, I have my brother Barnabas. My first wife, may God rest her soul, brought me to the business. My second wife's family allowed us to use political and financial connections to grow it. As a side benefit, my wife and I are well suited to each other."

Silas was a good friend, trying to downplay his good fortune in having a loving wife when I did not. Sensing my unease, he changed the subject. "We shall take Philadelphia by storm. Yin and yang."

Smiling, I replied, "You know more about many of these personalities than I do. I was at sea while you were meeting and corresponding with many of them."

"Yet another opportunity for me to bore you to tears as we share the scenery."

True to his word, Silas and I discussed each of the representatives from the various colonies and how we intended to deal with them.

Once we arrived, my fellow delegates and I visited the famous Jersey markets on High Street and the insane asylum at the stately Pennsylvania Hospital. Deane and I went to a series of political caucuses, dinners, luncheons, and coffees. Much of the planning of the Continental Congress involved informal meetings held throughout the week before the formal sessions began. Leading Philadelphians were happy to host these well-read men from around the Colonies, whom they had not previously met in person. In particular, the Shippen family, led by Judge Edward Shippen, hosted many dinners with their three beautiful daughters.

Finally, at the end of September 1774, representatives of all the Colonies had arrived for the Congress. We ultimately met in Carpenters' Hall, a small, handsome building with an adequate meeting room and library to discuss, protesting England's actions. At that time, we did not see war as inevitable; instead, we were hoping to reconcile with the Crown peacefully. The New Englanders were the most radical in the group; Virginia and Pennsylvania were decidedly more circumspect. We continued to hear rumors and information regarding the British ill-treatment of Boston. As we met, the redcoats continued to drill nearby to intimidate our members.

Chapter 9

New Haven, CT - March 17, 1775

O ver one hundred men met in the green at the center of town in New Haven, less than five months after the meeting of the Continental Congress. My voice boomed as I stood on a crate to elevate myself above the crowd. "Here it is, gentlemen!" I cried, shaking the large copy of Connecticut's declaration. "The king says we are in rebellion. The Crown proclaims that blows will decide whether we are free men or slaves to his tyranny. Well, by God, Connecticut has given him our answer!" A cheer went up as I punched the air. "We have the right to self-government, self-policing, and self-taxation, but most of all, self-defense!" With my other hand, I reached down and lifted the rifle I had placed at my feet. A tremendous shout went out from the men as I shook the gun over my head. "The General Assembly has asked us to form the Governor's Second Company of Guards, to be known as the Foot Guard. I tell every man here that I will do my part and help others to bear arms to make our company the finest in New England!"

My friend and local distillery owner, Eleazer Oswald, was standing at my feet. We had already spoken about what I wanted to happen next. When there was a lull, he shouted, "We need to elect a captain. It should be Benedict Arnold!" With that, I shrugged and stepped down from my temporary pedestal to be replaced by Oswald, who continued, "He is the obvious man to lead. He has been to Philadelphia—he is a leader in the Sons of Liberty and a ship captain. He will put his money where his mouth is, and he is a man of honor. Is there any other man who will stand against him?"

As he surveyed the assembled group, I was pleased that no name came forward. With a broad grin he intoned, "All those in favor of electing Benedict Arnold as our captain of the Foot Guard, raise your hand and say aye."

A chorus of ayes went up, and suddenly there were hands slapping me on the back and shaking my shoulders. I was fairly hoisted back up onto the box. "Thank you, gentlemen. I am honored by your confidence, but we will be more than a regiment in name only. I will require all those who sign up to train regularly and behave with military discipline, respecting the orders of their officers. We are not a rabble. We will show the king what free men can accomplish when the yoke of oppression is removed from their backs."

I spent large amounts of my own money to ensure that, unlike many militia companies, we were well fitted, clad in scarlet and blue uniforms. As the commanding officer, I wore a coat trimmed with silver-coated buttons and buff-colored lapels, collar, cuffs, and facings, with a ruffled shirt, waistcoat, breeches, and black leggings.

The Connecticut General Assembly ordered the militia to train for twelve days in April 1775, and set pay at double the normal rate to encourage day laborers to join. Six other Connecticut militia regiments were organized—almost six thousand men. Fast ships went to the West Indies to obtain weapons and gunpowder. Anyone suspected of loyalty to the king—or worse, disloyalty to the radical cause—was run out of the militia with the assistance of the Sons of Liberty.

Chapter 10

New Haven, CT – April 20, 1775

O n April 19, 1775, one thousand British soldiers marched out for Lexington and Concord and were opposed by swarms of American militia. As news of the three hundred British dead and wounded spread throughout the colonies, all knew war had arrived.

In response, I assembled the Foot Guard and argued we should travel to Boston and stand with that beleaguered city. The overwhelming majority agreed we would depart immediately. I knew I was leaving my family and making a tremendous financial sacrifice—but I also deeply loved my country and believed in the Cause.

The city of New Haven had not yet authorized our regiment to march to Massachusetts; indeed, its initial resolution was to stay neutral. The timid "leaders" of the city did not want to get caught up in the passion sweeping the colonies, known as the *rage militaire*. I had no patience for civic leaders unwilling to do their patriotic duty. The powder and shot we required were in the city's hands. We all understood ammunition was needed far more in Boston than it was in New Haven.

Early the next morning, I led my wife and three sons down the street. Militia members scrambled from their homes and pulled on their uniforms as they fell in behind me. I had arranged my militia in neat rows by the time this parade reached the town green, where we were cheered by a growing crowd.

When I finished reviewing the Foot Guards, I ordered the men to march out in column to the nearby Hunt's Tavern. New Haven's leading citizens peeked out from the tavern's windows. After a few long moments, sixty-five-year-old David Wooster opened the door and stepped out to meet me, standing in front of my troops. I knew Wooster well as a fellow Mason, but our cordial relations would not stop me from doing my duty.

I declared, "These finest of men, the Foot Guards of this Colony, demand the weapons and powder to secure our nation's liberty." I then held out my hands, demanding keys to the town's powder house.

Wooster responded, "This is Colony property."

I nodded in agreement, continuing to implacably hold out my hand.

With a shake of his head, Wooster said, "We cannot give it up without regular orders from those in authority."

My calm demeanor vanishing, I bellowed just feet away from the elderly man, "Regular orders be damned!"

He tried to buy time, stuttering, "The selectmen need to discuss the further fighting in Lexington and Concord. They have not decided whether it is prudent to send militia to Massachusetts."

Now fully animated, I repeated, "Orders be damned! Our friends and neighbors are being mowed down by redcoats! Give us powder or we will take it!"

Wooster began to speak, but I interrupted, "None but Almighty God shall prevent my marching!" Turning to my men, I declared, "We shall rip the door of the powder house from its hinges." My men cheered and started to move in the direction of the building.

For a moment, Wooster raised his hands to stop us; then, recognizing refusal was futile, he nodded in agreement and went to recover the keys.

Chapter 11

New Haven, CT – April 24, 1775

In just a matter of days, we organized the Foot Guards to head north. We were still a relatively undisciplined force, yet we were well outfitted and had weapons and ammunition as we began our 135-mile march to Massachusetts. Each volunteer brought his own food and money.

With huzzahs and good wishes, we left town, Connecticut's colony flag proudly proclaiming "Qui Transtulit Sustinet" ("He who transplanted us hither will support us") emblazoned in gold. Along the way, we wrote a covenant to govern our behavior as soldiers. "Driven to the last necessity, and obliged to have recourse to arms in defense of our lives and our liberties," we promised to "conduct ourselves decently and inoffensively as we marched, both to our countrymen and one another." We renounced "drunkenness, gaming, profaneness, and every other vice of that nature," as we were "serving in so great and glorious a cause." My men also agreed "to submit on all occasions to such decisions as shall be made and given by the majority of the officers we have chosen." We traveled north, absolutely certain in the rectitude of our actions and resolved to fight tyranny even at the cost of our lives.

Most of the Colonies were not yet at war, yet the country felt like a lid shaking atop a boiling pot. Everywhere we looked, people were arming to fight the British or their loyalist neighbors. The cauldron was ready to spill in Boston. I knew it was only a matter of time before the entire country was on fire.

I had scarcely left New Haven when we ran into Colonel Samuel Parsons, with whom I was well acquainted. He was heading south. I dismounted from my horse and gave him a friendly wave as he alighted from his carriage in a colonel's uniform. "My dear Colonel Parsons, what a pleasure to see you. I believe you are heading in the wrong direction. We need your leadership in the north."

My attempt at humor fell flat when I saw the grave look on his face. As he drew within half a rod of me, he bowed formally and said, "I am pleased you are heading north, Captain Arnold. Your regiment will be welcomed. For my part, I have already been to Boston. I am going to Hartford to meet with other leaders of the Cause."

Several of my officers had now joined us; we all surrounded Colonel Parsons as I asked, "Indeed, what can you tell us of the conditions there? What will we see when we arrive?"

"You will find the center of the city occupied by the British and surrounded by patriots. The British have fortified the peninsula and are well supplied by ship. Our men are in desperate need of supplies, particularly artillery. We have gone so far as to paint logs to look like guns to keep the British at bay."

At the word *artillery*, my mind jumped immediately to my trips north along Lake Champlain into Canada. Without a pause, I said, "I know where we can get cannon." Ignoring the look of surprise on Parson's face, I continued, "There are huge numbers of cannon at Forts Ticonderoga and Crown Point along Lake Champlain. I have seen it myself. The forts are in tremendous disrepair, and if my past experiences are any indication, they are protected by the worst sort of men. They will provide little resistance to anyone who comes to take the cannon. A few hundred men could overpower the guard and bring the cannon, shot, and no doubt large amounts of powder back to Boston to attack the British."

To my surprise, Parsons seemed indifferent to my idea. Merely shrugging, he said, "Be that as it may, I am heading in the other direction. My most sanguine desire is to send more troops north to join you in Boston shortly." We exchanged farewells and moved on.

I was later outraged to learn that Parsons had stolen my plan. When he arrived in Hartford, he gave me no credit, and dispatched Captain Edward Mott to head an expedition to capture the cannon with the help of the Green Mountain Boys.

Meanwhile, my properly attired soldiers caused quite a sensation when we marched with precision into Cambridge on April 29, 1775. We were immediately given the honor of escorting the body of a British soldier mortally wounded at Concord through the lines to the British headquarters. When I saw, for the first time, the organization and professionalism of the British camp, I was in awe. The British held the port of Boston, while the Americans were relegated to a makeshift tent city located across the river. The disorganized, trash-filled, rotting camp held by the Americans was a disappointment to the men of Connecticut after our long journey north. The Americans had surrounded the British in Boston Harbor, but we had no hope of capturing the city without cannon.

Chapter 12

Cambridge, MA - April 30, 1775

I had my men comfortably billeted in the abandoned mansion of Andrew Oliver, a recently departed Royalist and the lieutenant governor of Massachusetts. Having completed this important task, I sought out Dr. Joseph Warren, a fellow Mason and member of the Massachusetts Committee of Safety, the de facto governing body controlling the army. I shared my plan for capturing the guns at Ticonderoga and Crown Point, emphasizing to Warren that I believed the New York forts would be lightly defended and contain abundant small arms and military stores.

Appearing before the Massachusetts Committee of Safety, I requested men and supplies to take Fort Ticonderoga, indicating,

Gentlemen:

You have desired me to state the number of cannon, etc. at Ticonderoga. I have certain information that there were at Ticonderoga 80 pieces of heavy cannon, 20 brass guns, from 4 to 18 pounders, and 10 to 12 large mortars. At Skenesborough, on South Bay, there are 3 or 4 brass cannon. Fort Ticonderoga is in ruinous condition and has not more than 50 men at the most. There are large numbers of small arms and considerable stores and a British sloop of 70 or 80 tons on the Lake. The place could not hold out an hour against a vigorous onset.

In response to my convincing presentation, on May 2, General Artemas Ward and the Massachusetts Provincial Congress commissioned me as a colonel and gave me money, horses, and supplies. They sent me north on my "secret service" with their full confidence in my "judgment, fidelity, and valor." I was charged with taking "possession of cannons, mortars, stores, etc., upon the lake" and returning all "serviceable" weaponry to Cambridge. While I was only given £100 in cash, I was authorized to draw on a letter of credit "suitable for provisions and stores for the army." Unfortunately, while I had the "support" of Massachusetts, I was required to recruit *new* soldiers as I traveled. I left behind my trusted aide Eleazer Oswald to find troops and follow as quickly as possible.

I was unhappy to be leaving the Foot Guard, which I had built into a respectable force. Still, I was genuinely excited about the possibility of leading this new mission. At that point, I did not know that others were on the same expedition I had envisioned.

I rode hard to Bennington, Vermont. Upon arrival, I was directed to an unpainted building simply known as Fay's, which had become the Green Mountain Boys' unofficial headquarters. A sad mix of stale beer, urine, and men in need of a bath wafted out into the street. The rough-hewn and slightly askew tavern door moaned like an angry cow as I pushed it open.

Filthy men's shouts, songs, and laughter filled the room. All went silent as I stood just inside the door, ramrod straight in my scarlet jacket.

Someone yelled, "A redcoat!" Men grabbed their tomahawks and raced for their guns.

Feigning complete indifference, I held my orders high in the air and said in the booming voice of an experienced ship captain, "Gentlemen! I am Colonel Benedict Arnold. I hold here orders signed by the State of Massachusetts and endorsed by His Excellency George Washington. I am charged with taking Fort Ticonderoga and will welcome brave men to join me in the battle."

None moved. Silence stretched.

Finally, one of the men began to guffaw, and the whole room exploded in laughter, returning to their revelry. After a couple of minutes, a red-faced, grime-covered, emaciated man in his thirties sauntered up to me. He had surprisingly intelligent eyes and possessed the easy demeanor of a man who spends too much time in taverns. "You see here, Colonel, these are Green Mountain Boys. We take orders from no one, except our elected officers and our main man, the mighty Ethan Allen. He has already beaten you to the punch. While you are carryin' around papers signed by a bunch of fellas down in Boston who don't know their head from a handbasket, he's already attacking the fort." Pointing at the door, he continued, "Now, if you get on your horse, you might catch them in Castleton. That's about fifty miles from here."

With that, he gave the knowing nod of a man who had done a good deed, but felt the pull of drink. He returned to his chair without waiting for my response; for my part, I spun on my heels, found a rough bed, grabbed a few hours' sleep, and headed north.

Chapter 13

Castleton, *VT* - *May 8, 1775*

I arrived in the hamlet of Castleton on a spent, rangy bay mare. While arranging to have my mount fed and rubbed down, the stable boy told me that "a bunch of muckety-mucks and mayhap Colonel Allen were meeting down the street." As he said Allen's name, the lad involuntarily removed his hat; he then directed me down a dirt-covered road.

A group of lazy men were sprawled around a small makeshift tavern. Knowing this must be the location for the "meeting," I walked in without slowing my stride. Once again, the room fell silent. However, this time I saw a man in a makeshift uniform. Again, I repeated my introduction. The uniformed man answered indignantly, "I am Captain Mott. I have been dispatched by the people of Connecticut and am working in conjunction with Colonel Allen. Your interference will frustrate the whole design." He was flanked by two ridiculous little men I later learned to be James Easton and John Brown, who would prove to be thorns in my side for years to come.

Looking Mott square in the eye, I handed him my papers. "You will see, *Captain*"—which I took pains to emphasize, given my colonelcy—"that I have titular command here. Do you have any such papers from the State of Connecticut? Does your vaunted *Colonel* Allen have any such proper authority?"

When he delayed in answering, I decided to take a more conciliatory tone. "Captain Mott, you are obviously a lettered man who could read and understand these orders. We are not a mob. We are part of an organized army resisting the British."

Mott glanced uncomfortably at the two men standing behind him. His gaze downcast, he said in a tone more pleading than strident, "You must understand, Colonel, we have all suffered under British tyranny. The men are resolved to be commanded only by their own officers."

I knew I had him. His defiance was gone, and now he was blaming the "men."

Putting the papers back into my pocket, I said quietly but in a firm and matter-of-fact tone, "The men need to be led. We need to provide examples. They will follow your lead. In any event, we need to get to Mr. Allen to finalize these issues and commence the attack. What information do you have about the fort and its status?"

Mott pointed to another man, who stood, took a step forward, and bowed in acknowledgment of my authority. "I am Captain Noah Phelps. I have reconnoitered the fort and confirmed that the walls are in ruins and the gates are open. We intend to use a number of small boats on the lake to move up the shoreline and seize the fort."

"It sounds like a very solid plan, Captain. Thank you very much. Gentlemen, I have been given a commission by the Committee of Safety in Massachusetts that I am in overall command of the expedition."

Mott seemed to have regained a little of his composure and will. Shaking his head so violently it was almost comic, he said, "We just cannot agree, Colonel. That is not how it works up here, and we have made promises."

Recognizing that we had reached an impasse, I still knew I had the upper hand. "Very well—I will be heading north to the fort. I would like you and your men to come with me and resolve these issues once and for all." I had phrased the request as a command. I knew that if they obeyed, I would begin to take the necessary control.

Shrugging in acknowledgment, the men began to collect their belongings. I was confident that when I met Ethan Allen, I would be in a strong position to lead the charge on Ticonderoga.

Chapter 14

Lake Champlain, VT - May 9, 1775

The following day, in an open field sloping down to Lake Champlain, Ethan Allen and I finally stood face to face. I presented my orders to him and explained that I was in command.

I was not only a foot shorter, but narrower in the shoulders than the burly Allen, who was clad in a massive green uniform with oversized gold epaulets, shiny brass buttons, and yellow breeches. Three years my senior, and certainly more physically imposing, he stared at me stony eyed for almost a full minute; then, he turned and, in a voice that boomed across the field like a cannon to his men, said "What shall I do with this damned rascal—put him under guard?"

I did not take my eyes off Allen when one of his men shouted from behind me, "We should take this macaroni dandy in a redcoat's uniform and string him up proper!"

Years at sea taught me how to handle a bellicose man like Allen. As I stared at him with an unblinking gaze that came from the unchallenged command of a ship's captain, I saw him blanch. "Colonel Allen, I have the legal authority and the endorsement not only of the State of Massachusetts, but that of His Excellency George Washington. Do you?" I knew the comment about Washington was a stretch, but Allen did not.

Reading over my papers, Allen recognized that they were all in order and that he had no real authority besides the loyalty of his men. With exaggerated resignation, the towering man flung his hands up in the air and turned to them. "I am sorry, boys! I guess I can't lead you no more. This fancy fella is your new commander."

In unison, his men began stacking their guns or throwing them over their shoulders and meandering away. A couple shouted, "We won't serve under no officer that we ain't elected."

Feigning sympathy, Allen merely shrugged his shoulders as the exodus began.

After a minute or so, Allen's lieutenant slid in next to me. "You know, Colonel," he said quietly, "we have the same goal. We both want to take the fort." He offered what was clearly Allen's intent: "Perhaps you could go side by side."

As word passed of this suggestion, Allen's men yelled, "We ain't joined the Green Mountain Boys to be led by some lobsterback from Boston." It didn't seem the time to note that I was neither a redcoat nor from Boston.

Allen now took a step toward his men, his arms open wide. "Now boys, I know you are upset, but this here colonel is just doin' what he is told. We hate the Brits, don't we?"

The men roared with approval.

"Do you really want to walk away and let those sons of bitches sit up there in Ticonderoga?"

His troops began inching toward him, yelling, "No!"

I had to admit he was a very effective leader of men.

"All you fellas listen well. I am going to lead this here battle"—he paused and pointed his thumb over his shoulder—"with the help of Colonel Arnold. We are going to go up and kill some British bastards. Do you want to go home and tell your wives and sweethearts that I asked you for your help and you slinked back home?" A number of the soldiers shook their heads.

With an almost fatherly, comforting tone, he continued, "My Green Mountain Boys are braver than that. This fella here"—he nodded his head toward me with no small amount of contempt—"ain't goin' to stop us from doin' what we already was plannin' on doin'. Let's let him join us and take the god-damned fort."

As his men cheered and shook their guns in the air, Allen turned to me with a self-satisfied smile and nod. I knew from the beginning, notwithstanding his size and eloquence, that he was a cracked bell ringing a note that sounded false.

He and I agreed that he would lead his men and I would lead the

Massachusetts men—such as they were. To confirm our agreement, Allen handed me a blunderbuss to supplement my pistol and saber.

Chapter 15

Lake Champlain, VT - May 10, 1775

Allen had sent a raiding party to get a loyalist boat at Skenesborough and bring it to 250 men who had assembled along the eastern shore of Lake Champlain at Hand's Cove. The men did not find the loyalist double-masted schooner, which was cruising to the north; they had to settle for a thirty-three-foot bateau.

It was three o'clock in the morning when Allen's men and their stolen bateau finally arrived at Hand's Cove. Forty men climbed into the badly overloaded boat. In a drenching rain, white caps breaking over the gunwales, we endured a ninety-minute trek across the mile-wide lake, bailing water the entire way. When we reached the opposite shore, the boat went back to pick up another group of forty men.

An hour later, the soaked black sky yielded to a gray morning as the second boat disembarked. Eighty-three men stood a quarter mile east of the fort. I turned to Allen, who had been sitting on a log watching the progress, and said, "We cannot wait here any longer, Colonel. We'll lose the initiative sitting here, waiting for another boat."

Allen nodded in agreement. He stood, arched his back, and laced his fingers together, inverting his hand and cracking his knuckles as he reached for the sky. I do not believe I hid my irritation about the delay as I suffered his gyrations.

We approached the men, who were sitting or standing, all looking at us for direction. I said, "I want your guns primed, but not cocked. An accidental firing will be our undoing."

I'd never been one for long patriotic speeches, but Allen couldn't help himself. In a voice so loud that it made me concerned the British might hear him, he said, "We must this morning either quit our pretensions to valor, or possess ourselves of this fortress in a few minutes. In that this is a desperate attempt, none but the brave should undertake it. I do not urge to proceed any contrary to his will." We all knew the men, having already ferried across the lake, were volunteers—no one would turn around at this point. Nevertheless, Allen had his intended effect when he added, "If you be ready, form in three ranks and have your muskets primed, your chests out, and your eyes on me." As one, the men lined up and were ready.

With the assistance of a local youth named Nathan Beeman, who had grown up playing with children of the British garrison, we were able to creep slowly uphill from the lake to the fort. Years of neglect had allowed the forest and heavy brush to approach close to the fort, so we remained invisible in the diffuse morning light. We advanced through the brush as silently as we could, walking on tiptoe, trying to prevent our bags and guns from making any noise. Our group crawled up the cliff from the fort's eastern curtain wall while skirting the corner bastion.

We then made our way toward the main gate along a narrow path between the fortress wall and Lake Champlain, which lay at the bottom of a sheer hundred-foot drop to our left. I gestured for everyone to pause at the edge of the tree line; the lightening sky framed the fort's imposing walls, with the barracks roofs and gables peeking above. The entrance stood thirty yards away, which seemed an impossible distance for us to traverse without being seen. The main gate was locked with a heavy iron-bound oak door; however, to our relief, a smaller door, known as a wicket gate, was open and just big enough to accommodate a single man. A lone guard sat dozing on a chair he had leaned against the wall next to the open door.

Allen and I gave the order to move. As one, we silently traversed the open area toward the gate. We got within ten yards before the sentry noticed us. For a split second, the guard stood agape, unwilling or unable to process the sight of eighty armed men approaching him. However, after the initial pause, he reached for his gun. At that moment, Allen growled, "Now!"

All the men broke into a full voiceless sprint—still hoping not to wake up the rest of the garrison. Our bags and boots now jangled and pounded as we raced toward the shocked sentry.

Allen and I began the charge together. I was faster—by the time we reached the gate, Allen was a dozen feet or more to my rear. The guard raised his gun and yelled "Halt!" as we charged straight at him, but when he pulled the trigger of his gun, it merely clicked. I knocked him to the ground as we burst through the door.

As we passed through the wicket gate into the interior courtyard, Allen's idiot Green Mountain Boys gave an Indian war whoop, shouting, "No quarter!"—thus alerting every other man in the fort to our presence and eliminating any further chance of surprise. Nevertheless, securing the fort was not taxing, as the garrison's muskets were neatly stacked outside the barracks, where over forty British soldiers slept.

As we surged toward the east wall, a second sentry appeared. This time, Allen reached him first. The redcoat fired high and rushed with his bayonet—Allen sidestepped and swung his heavy saber but refrained from delivering a death blow, instead cutting the side of the soldier's head, resulting in the man's immediate surrender. We hauled the guard to his feet and demanded that we be taken to the commandant's quarters as our men poured into the fort. The stunned sentry pointed to the left stairway of the west barracks, where the commandant's quarters filled the second floor.

Allen bounded up the stairway. He stood waving his sword and roaring at the closed door, "Come out this instant, you damn skunk, or I'll sacrifice the whole garrison!" This ungentlemanly behavior irritated me, but I held my tongue.

A flustered and half-dressed Lieutenant Jocelyn Feltham responded through the door, "I endeavored to make them hear me, but it was impossible."

Allen looked over at me, nonplussed by this confusing response, and bellowed once again through the closed door, "I must have immediate possession of the fort, and all the effects of George III!"

Feltham timidly opened the door and asked, "By what authority do you demand it?"

His face inches from Feltham's, Allen screamed, "In the name of the Great Jehovah and the Continental Congress!"

When the lieutenant merely looked puzzled, Allen drew his sword over his head. With maniacal fervor, he screamed, "If there is a single shot fired, neither man, woman, nor child should be left alive in the fort!"

Worried that he might be losing control of himself, I interjected in a calmer tone, "Give up your arms, and you'll be treated like gentlemen."

Commander Delaplace then stepped past Feltham and said in words that were stronger than his tone, "Damn you, what . . . what . . . what does this mean?"

Continuing calmly, I replied, "Commander, we are representatives of the Massachusetts Committee of Safety. We are in control of this fort and require your immediate surrender to avoid the effusion of blood."

Allen had begun to calm down, but interjected, "You will surrender now, by God."

The commander looked at Lieutenant Feltham, who shrugged and nodded in agreement. "Very well. The fort is yours if you can guarantee the safety of my men."

Like a child who was bored with the conversation, preferring to leave the unpleasantries to the grown-ups, Allen bolted away to his men, yelping, "We have won. Don't kill no one else, but help yourself to the fort, boys!"

In less than ten minutes, we had the British and their families safely secured. All forty-four British soldiers were taken prisoner, along with twenty-four women and children. In perhaps his last act of decency and command, Allen made arrangements for the prisoners to be sent off by two different routes to Connecticut, separating officers and common soldiers. That done, he turned to the spoils—the fortress held 120 iron cannon, fifty swivels, two ten-inch mortars, ten tons of musket balls, three cartloads of flints, thirty gun carriages, shells, ten casks of powder, material for boat building, two brass cannon, pork, flour, and other valuable prizes of war.

What followed was a complete lack of military discipline and organization. The Green Mountain Boys ran hither and thither, entirely out of control. Allen's men immediately helped themselves to ninety gallons of rum in the supply room, taking any clothing or goods that struck their fancy. Outraged with their behavior, I wrote to the Massachusetts Committee of Safety, "There are here at present near 100 men who are at greatest confusion and anarchy, destroying and plundering private property, committing every enormity and paying no attention to public service." I went on to say, "Colonel Allen is a proper man to head his own wild people, but entirely unacquainted with military service."

I tried to have Allen's men respect private property. This demand irritated them to the point that men began firing shots in my direction, and at least one placed a gun barrel against my chest and threatened to blow a hole through me unless I admitted that Ethan Allen was the sole commander of the fort. Recognizing the man for what he was—a drunken scoundrel—I stared him in the eyes until he backed down and walked away. On at least two other occasions over the following days, drunken Green Mountain Boys continued to take potshots at me.

Nevertheless, I wrote further, "The power is not taken out of my hands and I am not consulted, nor do I have a voice in any matters. As I am the only person who has been legally authorized to take possession of this place, I am determined to insist on my right, and I think it is my duty to remain here against all opposition, until further orders." I kept myself in the face of these boors.

After several days of abuse at the hands of Allen and his men, I was pleased and indeed thrilled to see a friendly face. Silas Deane sent his brother Barnabas as part of an inspection tour to ascertain the condition of the fort and Connecticut troops. Sitting down on the edge of the lake, having completed his inspection, Barnabas said, "Benedict, I am amazed by all you have accomplished here. Even more so, as Allen's men apparently don't care about the Revolution—all that matters to them is staking a claim to part of New York to benefit Vermont. That, and drinking as much rum as they can and stealing anything that isn't nailed down."

Only half in jest, I answered, "Having something nailed down really doesn't stop them."

Nodding, Barnabas continued, "Obviously, I will take what I have learned back to Connecticut and to anyone else that will listen. The story of your bravery and what you have done here is remarkable. I believe these guns will make the difference in Boston. What will you do next?"

Not wanting to meet his gaze, I looked out over the water as I answered, "I could resign my commission, but I am afraid if I did so, it would leave Allen in command. That would make a bad situation worse. I think all I really can do is hunker down in the officer's quarters in the fort and wait for the arrival of the Massachusetts recruits. I have been told men are heading north. I believe that if I have a large enough group of disciplined men, Allen and his rabble will lose interest and likely move on. If I leave now, this place could easily fall into enemy hands. In the meantime, I'll do a careful inventory of what is in the fort."

Barnabas once more nodded in agreement. He then looked at me, and I could see he was hesitating to tell me something.

Having already faced so much, I girded myself and said, "Barnabas, your brother and I were friends before this war started, and our family will be friends long after this war is over. You clearly have something unpleasant to tell me—out with it. Better to lance the boil than let it fester."

Barnabas puffed out his cheeks, pushed out a long, slow breath, and said, "I'm sorry to tell you this, but your excellent efforts here are being downplayed or misconstrued. Allen has been telling people directly and through his surrogates that you played no role in the taking of the fort."

I hung my head in frustration; almost talking to myself, "We ran into the fort side by side. We took the fort together. How can men behave like Allen? How can they lie? I know he has no honor, but I am unable to comprehend that he would claim that I did nothing." Numbed by genuine shock, I looked at Barnabas for answers.

Looking down at his feet, Barnabas came to a decision and raised his head to meet my gaze. "You've made enemies, Benedict. As Silas would say, 'Sometimes Benedict forgets he's on land and not a sea captain entitled to absolute deference.' The advice I carry back to you from my brother is serenity. Less yin and more yang—if you know what that means?"

Though I felt myself becoming angry at both the message and the messenger, I checked my temper when I looked at the open expression of a good man who was only giving me what he saw as helpful counsel. "Yes, yes, I know," I replied. "But these men are bloody fools. Easton and Brown are cowards and imbeciles, devoid of honor or decency."

"I don't doubt that it's true for a minute, Benedict, but your challenge is you don't hide it well. You treat those you respect with great deference and politeness. It doesn't cost you anything to treat men you don't respect with the same courtesy."

I bristled. "I understand what you are saying, but it is dishonorable to treat such men as gentlemen when they are unworthy. It is inherently dishonest. I treat you, your brother, and others with respect because it is earned. How can I treat a scoundrel with the same courtesy?"

A look of exasperation fluttered across Barnabas's face. "I know, but that is what people do. That is what you must do. Otherwise you will leave enemies in your wake and sow the seeds of your own unhappiness."

He's asking me to play political games. I will not set aside my principles just to be liked. However, I realized that arguing with this true friend would serve no purpose, so I said with a shrug, "As you say, Barnabas. I will try. I am grateful for your counsel. In the meantime, do you think I should leave this den of vipers?"

Barnabas stood; as I did likewise, he told me, "You have asked for my advice, and I will give it. I think your instincts are right. You should stay and protect the fort. When the men from Massachusetts arrive, it will be secure. As to Allen, you should write your friends to tell the true story. Silas will help too. You have done a great service here, and I believe the word will get out, notwithstanding the actions of Allen and others." With that, we shook hands. "I'll take my leave."

Chapter 16

Fort Ticonderoga, NY - May 16, 1775

L ake Champlain is part of a series of waterways that connect New York City, Montreal, and the Atlantic. A traveler heading north from New York may cruise up the Hudson 150 miles in an oceangoing ship all the way to the port of Albany. Goods and passengers are then offloaded for a sixty-five-mile overland trip to Lake George. Once at Lake George, boats are reloaded for a thirty-two-mile trip further north. Again, portages are required to avoid a series of rapids. New boats are boarded on Lake Champlain for a hundred-mile journey down the lake to a series of rapids on the Richelieu River, where the portages require unloading at Fort St. John. A final short overland trip leads to the St. Lawrence River, Montreal, Quebec, and the open sea. This vital corridor connects New York to Montreal and, if controlled by the British, could have cut New England off from the rest of the colonies.

Fort Ticonderoga stood at a crucial chokepoint between Lake Champlain and Lake George. For most of the length of both lakes, the hills stand back, but in the areas surrounding Fort Ticonderoga, the hills rise—the fort dominates the high ground overlooking the surrounding country. The only exception is the large hill which looms over the fort, which we named Mount Defiance, which the British had named Sugar Loaf and the French called Rattlesnake Hill.

We had held the fort for only a week, but I understood the importance of dominating the lake. I was pleased to stumble upon a ship named *Katherine*, taken from a loyalist living on the lake. I renamed the ship *Liberty* and immediately affixed a four-pound cannon and carriage and six swivel guns. Having received no orders from Massachusetts, I decided to move north and invade Canada. Before we set off, I wrote another letter to Dr. Warren: "I am intending setting out in the *Liberty* directly, with a bateau and fifty men, to take possession of the sloop, the HMS *Betsey*, which we are advised this morning by the post, is at St. John, loaded with provisions, waiting a wind for this place."

The ten-gun HMS *Betsey* could control all shipping in Lake Champlain and take the fort back with little effort. While I had seized the forts on the southern end of Lake Champlain, I did not control them, because the British still held Fort St. John. With the HMS *Betsey*, the British could sail down at any time and overwhelm the two weak southern forts. Thus, to fully control the lake, the ship needed to be taken.

We set sail on the *Liberty*, along with two accompanying bateaux armed with swivel and bow guns. At Crown Point, we gathered supplies and waited for a favorable wind. On the morning of Tuesday, May 16, our small force set off for Canada, but the *Liberty* was unable to proceed because of a lack of wind. Fifteen men stayed on the ship while we rowed up toward the British fort. I selected thirty-five of the best men and put them in the two bateaux. I commanded one boat while the other was led by the dependable Captain Oswald. After rowing all night, at about 6:00 a.m. we arrived at the mouth of the Richelieu River.

The British were undoubtedly aware of our successful raid at Ticonderoga and Crown Point, yet they did not appear to fear another American attack—to our pleasant surprise, there were no sentries or patrolling ships. With our maneuverable bateaux, we were able to silently work our way up the river to within a mile of St. John, depositing our boats at the petite Rivière du Nord. We pushed the bateaux as far as we could into the undergrowth reaching out into the river and left a single guard to watch them. Most of us were thrilled to be leaving the river behind, but that was short lived, as the windless calm allowed numberless swarms of gnats and mosquitoes to attack us.

As we were securing the boats and preparing to move forward, I sent scouts to check the condition of the British and the town. The two scouts returned in twenty minutes to say the British were unprepared for our attack. I beckoned the men around me. We gathered under the heavy canopy and brush hugging the river. As the sun began to lighten, I spoke in a loud whisper, the men turned toward me like plants drawing strength from the sun. "All right, boys—I know you are tired, but we are very close. The scouts say they are not ready for us. My concern is that if we take time and rest, we could be detected by a patrol or one of the townsfolk." Seeing nods of approval, I continued. "For those of you who stormed Ticonderoga with me, help the other lads. We once again need to prime our muskets and pistols, but not cock them. An accidental firing would wake the garrison. Also, have your knives ready, as the battle may be hand-to-hand."

With that comment, I saw the look of confidence evaporate from some of the young faces. Trying to bolster them up, I continued, "I don't think that will be likely. They don't expect us, so we'll have the advantage. If we are outnumbered, remember that our goal is to go to the largest ship in the harbor, take control of it, and leave. I am not looking for a general engagement. I chose all of you because you are young, strong, and brave." With that, I saw some of the men straighten their backs with pride. "Grab your bags and kits, and take only what is necessary to fight. Try to avoid anything that is going to jangle or make noise. Any questions?"

After looking at each other, the men all indicated they were ready to go.

Turning to Oswald, I said, "You will take the rear, and I will take the point." Turning back to the group, I concluded, "Let's go, boys—we are burning daylight."

We hugged the west side of the river as we entered the outskirts of the town. The scouts, in their excitement, had forgotten to look for the HMS *Betsey* when they reconnoitered the town. We could see the tall mast of the ship through the trees. I felt a surge of relief that our trip had been worthwhile. We could see townspeople down at the wharf as we came to the edge of the woods; it was clear that we would be exposed entering the town's outskirts and moving down to the docks. The good news was that there were no signs of active patrols, guards, or fences of any kind. Unfortunately, one redcoat seemed to be loitering, perhaps avoiding duty, between us and the buildings adjacent to the docks.

All my men lay prone or crouched in the woods as I surveyed the situation. A burly Massachusetts sailor pulled his knife out of its sheath and cocked his head toward the redcoat, whose back was turned. His message was clear: he was asking me if I wanted him to sneak up and slit the man's throat. Later in the war, I would have assented without batting an eye, but the campaign was yet a bloodless "gentleman's war." I hesitated. Shaking my head, I put a finger to my lips and signaled for the men to wait.

I stepped out quickly from the woods and quietly moved a dozen paces toward the soldier. My heart raced as I approached. At the last moment, he began to turn, but he was not quick enough. Placing the muzzle of my gun firmly against his temple with one hand, with the other I covered his mouth and whispered, "Move a muscle and you die. Do you understand?" The wide-eyed, pimple-faced youth, no more than eighteen, nodded in agreement. Keeping the gun against his head, I grabbed him by the scruff of the neck and moved closer to the town, using the nearest building as cover. I signaled for my men to move, and they all joined us, their backs against two of the buildings facing the woods from which we had come.

I pocketed my gun, put a large knife in front of our prisoner's face, and whispered, "How many men?"

He croaked, "Thirteen in my squad, gov. Another two dozen in the barracks."

Looking at Oswald, I whispered, "Our numbers are approximately even—it is better than I thought."

Turning back to the young soldier, I asked one final question: "Where is your commander?"

His eyes crossed, locking onto the knife. "He is in Montreal with the rest of our men. They are planning on attackin' Fort Ti to the south, but went to get men and supplies. Please, gov. I swear on my mother's soul. Don't kill me."

Turning to the men, I ordered, "Gag him and tie him up. We will leave him here." As they began to do so, I addressed the soldier: "I am not going to have my men kill you, but if you try to make noise now or after we leave, we will make sure you die today. Do you understand?"

The boy nodded as a gag was put in his mouth.

Turning back to the group, I whispered, "Lieutenant Oswald will take ten men and head down to the wharf to take control there. I don't want you to shoot anyone unless you absolutely have to. Stealth remains our greatest asset. Guns will still remain primed but uncocked. We want everyone to surrender without a shot, so we don't alert the other half of the town to what we are doing. If we play this right, we can do this silently. The remaining men will come with me—we will go to the stone barracks and the magazine next to it." I gestured to the buildings away from the wharf. "Again, move quickly and be decisive." I repeated myself, because scared boys do not listen: "No shots without orders from Lieutenant Oswald or me. Everyone clear?"

Heads bobbed in agreement. As I surveyed the men, I was pleased no one showed the darting eyes of panic. "Good—let's go, lads. Stay quiet." With me in the front, my troop of twenty men moved between the small homes and shops that made up the village. The few townspeople who saw us scurried silently into their homes.

At the center of the village was a larger building with more-fortified walls that was obviously the barracks, magazine, and center of military operations. Fortunately, no one was immediately outside—we scurried to the door, being careful to keep below windows as we neared the entrance. Three of my men, including the sturdy Massachusetts sailor, stood ready at the magazine door.

Just as I was about to enter, a redcoat came out of the barracks, buttoning his coat. He saw me, but before he could react, I punched him hard on the side of the head with my sword handle, knocking him senseless to the ground. Waving my men with me, I burst in. None of my men initially shouted or yelled, but as they ran into each room with their guns, I heard them bark, "Hold still," "Don't move, or I'll bloody kill you!"and "You are my prisoner!"

It took about four minutes to take control of the barracks and the magazine; there was no resistance except for the corporal I had punched on my way in, who had fully recovered. One of my men had to use the butt end of his musket on an uncooperative regimental sergeant, but again the injury was not permanent. In the meantime, a messenger delivered word from Lieutenant Oswald that the docks had been secured without incident, but they had not yet rushed the ship. I took the prisoners down to the docks and had them all tied.

I met Oswald on the dock, signaling for a dozen men to follow me as we clambered on board the ship. We woke the seven crewmen in their cabins, utterly unaware of the events occurring steps away on the wharf and in the town. We added those men to the soldiers tied up on shore.

I was thrilled we had taken the ship and town without a shot, but I also knew a British force could arrive at any minute. Turning to the men, I yelled, "Strip the town of everything you can find that will be useful in a fight. Focus on gunpowder, guns, uniforms, and blankets."

Quietly, Oswald said to me, "We could use some food too, sir."

Turning back to the men, I barked, "Lieutenant Oswald is right—we also need some food. Boys, listen hard. No rum or beer. There will be plenty of that when we get home. If any man takes a drop, I am going to drown him in the lake. Understood?" I got waves and nods from the men. "Go!"

With that, my men darted in all directions. For the first time, I was able to take a good look at the HMS *Betsey*. She was a yar seventy-ton sloop with clean lines and two brass six-pound cannon. Her sails and rigging looked to be in good condition and well maintained. I promptly rechristened the ship the *Enterprise*.

We filled our prize to its gunwales, as well as loading four British bateaux with additional provisions. When I saw that everything was ready, I sent parties out to burn the smaller British boats and other supplies we could not bring with us. I gave careful instructions not to burn any homes or businesses of the townspeople.

With the boats beginning to move, our last men jumped on board. As we set sail, the sun was directly overhead, and a strong south wind pushed toward American territory. We picked up our two bateaux as we moved upriver. When the river widened back into Lake Champlain, I knew we were safe. I shouted to Oswald and all the men who could hear, "A good day's work, men! We now control the lake!" Huzzahs went up from all of the boats, and I ordered one of the swivel cannon fired in salute. I knew that with all large vessels on Lake Champlain under my command, no southern thrust by the British would be possible until they constructed a new man-of-war, which would take weeks or even months.

Approximately halfway back to Fort Ticonderoga, I was amazed to find four open boats filled with bone-weary Green Mountain Boys, led by Ethan Allen. The motley crew was within fifteen miles of the Canadian border, engaged in a vain attempt to overtake my efforts in attacking Fort St. John. I found them fatigued, starving, and suffering from exposure. The idiot Allen had failed to provide them with any food or blankets in their haste to prevent my success. My hard heart softened when I looked at his men. I provided them with food and provisions and even fired off a salute to the Green Mountain Boys from the deck of the *Enterprise*. Breaking my own rules, I pulled out rum we discovered in our hold, and we toasted each other and Congress.

Allen insisted, as he was so close to St. John, that he and his men would continue, contending that the best way to stop a British attack was to take and hold the town. I warned them that this was an "impractical scheme," as a larger British force would soon be reinforcing the British position. More importantly, I explained that controlling the major ships on the lake was the key to strategic control, not holding a mosquito-infested village. Allen was steadfast—I watched his "mad fellows" row off toward Canada as we sailed back toward Fort Ticonderoga. After a successful voyage of over a hundred miles in thirty-three hours, we dropped anchor in front of the fort with a hold full of booty. I looked north to what was now an immense *American* lake.

On May 21, Ethan Allen and his men finally rowed their boats under the guns of Fort Ticonderoga. Allen explained that, as I had predicted, the British had reinforced Fort St. John. After an initial half-hearted attempt to attack the city, Allen and his men were forced to repeat their arduous hundred-mile row back down the lake, British artillery clipping at their heels as they left the Richelieu River. I expected an attack from the British, and so informed Congress in my correspondence. I decided to omit from the correspondence a reference to the £160 I found in the cabin of the *Enterprise*'s captain, which I viewed as a spoil of war.

Chapter 17

Fort Ticonderoga, NY - June 1, 1775

Lieutenant Oswald came into the makeshift office I had comman-
deered in Fort Ticonderoga and stood at attention before my
desk. I was working on a report to Congress and had summoned him to
obtain additional information. While we were close, and I considered
him a loyal subordinate, I was not one to needlessly dispense with informality. Thus, I left him standing rather than point to a chair—I expected
this to be a short and efficient meeting. Looking up after finishing the
paragraph I was writing, I said, "Thank you for reporting so promptly.
What can you give me?"

Reaching into his jacket, he pulled out a piece of paper, referring to
it as he spoke. "I hope you will be pleased, sir. The men and I have been
hard at work. We have dug out fifty-eight heavy guns at Fort Ti, which
can be loaded onto ships or mounted onto carriages to be sent overland
to Fort George to assist in the defense of Boston. We also wrested more
than a hundred guns from Crown Point, as well as over a ton of lead and
iron cannonballs near the old ruins of Fort Frederic. I think you can
say, sir, with some satisfaction, that by the end of May, we had defeated
the British, captured ships, and recovered huge numbers of cannon and
ordinance. Men are flocking to your banner, with three to four hundred
recruits filling six new companies." Placing the paper on my desk, he
continued, "We are also making substantial progress at Crown Point.
We have increasing numbers of carpenters and wheelwrights and are
receiving wood from a nearby sawmill to build barracks. We are also
completing repairs at Fort Ticonderoga." Then, with a bit of a smile, he
added, "Ethan Allen continues to loiter, even though most of his boys
are gone."

I shook my head dismissively. "Ignore him. He is a toothless tiger at this point." As I scanned his notes, I added, "Thank you, Lieutenant. Useful indeed." Always looking for an excuse to get away from the paperwork, I stood and paced out onto the fort's ramparts. Oswald fell into step slightly behind me as we overlooked the lake.

As we strolled, I pondered our tactical situation. The enemy, I had learned, had taken to threatening the inhabitants of Montreal, indicating that if they did not support the fight against the Americans, the British would burn the city to the ground. Meanwhile, Fort St. John had been reinforced by three hundred British regulars—this meant that almost half the entire British military presence in Canada was now dug in there. If we were to attack and defeat them, it would weaken Montreal and expose all of Canada to an American invasion.

I need to understand what's happening at St. John. Stopping and turning to Oswald, I said with a smile, "It is early June—the weather is ideal. Are we ready for a reconnaissance in force?"

"Yes, sir." Oswald snapped to attention with obvious enthusiasm. "I've got 150 men ready to crew the *Liberty*, the *Enterprise*, and three armed bateaux. The only thing we have in short supply right now is gunpowder. We are limited to 150 pounds."

"Very well—if we engage the British, we will have to be economical in the use of shot and ball. Please have the men ready to go shortly before dawn, weather permitting. Dismissed."

Oswald bowed, leaving me alone to stare out over the water. The lake often shifted in character. On sunny days, when the waters were calm, it was a brilliant, inviting blue. When the clouds obscured the sun and the wind picked up, the black water boiled, looking ready to consume anyone unlucky enough to enter its troubled waters. I thought, *There are cloudy days ahead.*

We left the next morning as scheduled with a nice wind at our back. Two days after we left Fort Ti, we arrived at Pointe aux Roux on the lake's west shore, where the Richelieu narrows, just three miles south of the Canadian border. Two hours later, we dropped anchor where the river further narrowed, preventing the *Liberty* and *Enterprise* from maneuvering.

I led the squadron of three bateaux on a reconnaissance. Each bateau contained a single bow cannon and grapeshot-firing swivel guns, as well as twenty heavily armed troops to act as both oarsmen and gunners as necessary. As we came around the bend within sight of St. John, it was apparent the sleepy and unprotected town had been transformed. Hundreds of British were entrenching and building walls. Almost instantly, we were met with a hail of ineffectual long-range fire. Nevertheless, I had my boats cease their forward motion. We then returned the British salvo with equally ineffective responsive fire from our bow guns.

My goal was to stay out of range of British cannon. Within minutes, a gunboat far larger than our bateaux appeared, although not as formidable as our principal ships. This new vessel began actively firing on our positions. I told my men to put their backs to the oars in retreat. Our bateaux under oars were faster than the British ship, and we were quickly able to outdistance them. I moved our flotilla to Isle aux Noix to put some distance between our ships and the shore in the event the British decided to try to make a land-based raid in force. Meanwhile, I sent scouts ashore to continue to probe and snipe at the British outpost and regulars. Our failure to fully retreat and continue to engage the British was catching them off guard.

On the afternoon of June 8, I called all the officers to a council of war in my cabin aboard the *Enterprise*. "Gentlemen, we have already accomplished much. We have gotten a full understanding of the British position and vulnerability. We have caused them to fear our offensive power, and I deem it unlikely they will engage in serious offensive operations. This will give us more time to improve Forts Ti and Crown. Now we could return, our honor intact, and engage the enemy no further. We have suffered no casualties, but I believe we have inflicted some on the enemy." I looked around the small cabin; aggression and the desire to fight still flowed in their veins. "I also believe we have sufficient forces and, most importantly, mobile onboard artillery to inflict grievous wounds on the British and perhaps even cause them to consider abandoning St. John. What we need is a favorable wind. The river is too narrow to tack upwind, and we have had nothing but winds coming from the north for the last three days. We need to either wait for winds to blow us north or hook ropes to the *Enterprise* and *Liberty* and tow them behind our bateaux."

After a brief discussion, I gave an order summarizing the unanimous decision of the officers: "We stay and fight. Let's hope the wind comes around, but in the meantime, start making oars and rigging ropes to tow *Enterprise* and *Liberty*."

The next morning, I received further reconnaissance reports indicating the British had additional artillery and were more organized in St. John than I had thought. My concern was that we were undermanned, so I decided to take our two fastest vessels and use the favorable wind to the south to return to Crown Point and pick up additional men. I reached Crown Point at five o'clock in the morning on June 9, resolved to return, redouble our efforts, and take the fight to the enemy.

While we were ready to fight, I received utterly frustrating instructions from distant and ill-informed politicians. I was forced to send a messenger north to recall the remainder of my men and ships. The Continental Congress had apparently given theatre command to Connecticut, as New York and Massachusetts were no longer supporting the endeavor. To my dismay, the Connecticut General Assembly sent a message: "We have postponed sending further assistance to Captain Arnold."

I was infuriated—the message failed to acknowledge my colonelcy from Massachusetts and indicated that I was being reverted to my Connecticut captaincy. I later learned that one of the reasons my support in Massachusetts had evaporated was that my friend Dr. Warren had been elected president of the Continental Congress and military matters had been turned over to the unsupportive Benjamin Church.

The Continental Congress demonstrated they were unaware of our condition—and my substantial success. I saw no choice but to send my trusted aide Eleazer Oswald to Philadelphia with a detailed summary of the intelligence we had gathered that Canada was ripe for the taking.

The following day, Allen, Major Elmore, Colonel Easton, and several officers of the Green Mountain Boys attempted to pass the *Enterprise* on the lake in a bateau without showing a pass properly signed by me. I recognized this as a further attempt to undermine my authority. Captain Sloan responded by revealing the ship's guns and insisting Allen's boat come about, unless they had the proper passes. The bateau wisely returned to the fort.

Major Elmore came to my office to discuss his concern that Connecticut had sent four hundred troops to reinforce Ticonderoga—and that Ethan Allen was trying to commandeer them to lead an attack on Canada. At this point, as Elmore was explaining the situation, Easton brushed past my guard at the door and stalked into my office. Not only was this a serious breach of military discipline, but Easton, a loud-mouthed tavern keeper, was rudely barging into a private conversation between two officers. I could suffer the man no longer. Without hesitation or explanation—his behavior did not warrant either—I stood up, lifted the butt end of my sword, and brought it down on the fool's skull as he spoke.

He stood silently, holding the top of his head where I had hit him. I could smell the sweat wafting off the little man. Gesturing to the pistol on Easton's belt, I intoned, "Enough of this prattle. I am at your disposal."

When Easton mumbled a refusal, turning awkwardly to Elmore as if to ask for help, his rump was too tempting a target. I kicked him roundly, grabbed him by the lapel, and dragged him out my office door. I had achieved my goal of establishing the reputation that I was a man not to be trifled with—although some wrongfully asserted that I was out of control.

Chapter 18

Fort Ticonderoga, NY - June 17, 1775

I n response to the conflicting reports, Congress sent an investigative committee, which arrived two weeks after my successful raid on St. John. I was shocked and appalled when I was told by both Connecticut and Massachusetts representatives that I could only remain if I were subordinate to Colonel Benjamin Hinman, who was being sent to take command. Not only did he lack my experience, but his recent commission date made him my technical junior.

I recognized that if I were to accept these orders, not only would my leadership be subverted, but the seniority of all my officers and recognition of their rank would similarly be cast aside. I wrote the Massachusetts Committee that the entire matter was being conducted in a most disgraceful manner and was an insult to the men I commanded and me. I took pains to explain the great hardships that my men had suffered for nearly two months. Finally, I noted that I had received only £100 to keep our army in the field for two months, whereas I had advanced over £1,000 of my own money and borrowed money on my word to keep these men at their posts. I emphasized that "my own credit is at stake and I am reduced to the necessity of leaving the place with dishonor or wait until I can send home and discharge those debts out of my private purse, which I am determined to do."

It was not an easy decision. I never wanted to be seen abandoning my post, but I had been unfairly and discourteously supplanted. I saw only two alternatives: remain in shame or resign. I chose the latter on June 23, 1775, disbanding my regiment and resigning my commission.

My spirits were raised as I left Crown Point when the local residents came to wish me well and handed me a proclamation, expressing "their gratitude and thankfulness for the uncommon vigilance, vigor and spirit" I displayed in providing "for our preservation and safety from the threatened and much dreaded incursions of the inveterate enemy."

Chapter 19

Albany, NY - July 7, 1775

I left Ticonderoga and traveled through Albany to meet Major General Philip Schuyler, the head of the Northern Department of the Continental Army. When traveling in the Adirondacks, you always feel like you are going up or down—and while I understand it is not possible, the ups always seem longer than the downs. The only way to avoid this consternation is traveling by water, and hence Lake Champlain, the Hudson, the Richelieu, and the St. Lawrence play such a strategic role.

Unlike over the open ocean, the sky in the mountains is always close. Clouds drip down like long tendrils of white hair against the forest; large sections of exposed rock look like a giant's claw has cleaved out sections of hills. As I left the rugged mountains surrounding Lake George and Lake Champlain, the ground gave way to more gentle, rolling hills and increasingly prosperous farms. East of Albany, I arrived at the general's hilltop estate overlooking the Hudson River. From his front door, I could see in the distance the busy river that contributed to his fortune and that of a growing town. The two-story Georgian mansion was known as The Pastures. Eighty acres contained a French-style garden, barns, mills, storehouses, and a boat landing; the estate employed over one hundred people. General Schuyler could trace his lineage back to the early Dutch founding of New York—from a family of successful traders and merchants, he was at the forefront of opposing the British, yet he never adopted the radical tactics of the Sons of Liberty.

A well-appointed servant directed me into a study, where General Schuyler stood; he bowed deeply to me as I entered the room. The general was tall, with deep-set, hawk-like eyes, a billhook nose, and the small neck of a patrician never subject to hard labor. I had been told that his strength and vitality were tempered by periodic and

Philip Schuyler
Engraving by G. R. Hall of painting by John Trumball.
Courtesy of the National Archives 111-SC-94762

excruciating bouts of pain from gout and breathing problems caused by pleurisy.

The regal Schuyler recognized the importance of army discipline. He had previously openly expressed contempt for the rabble led by Ethan Allen. More than seven years my senior, Schuyler had served nobly in the Seven Years' War as a logistics officer. After the war, he had dramatically increased his family's fortune. He, and other worthy New Yorkers, were shocked by my removal from command at Fort Ti. Over five hundred men in the Hudson Valley had signed an address in appreciation of my efforts for presentation to the Continental Congress. Thus, I already viewed him as a kindred spirit as he greeted me.

Pointing to a comfortable chair in front of an open window that surveyed the beautiful surrounding hills, Schuyler said with a hint of a Dutch accent, "Colonel, please sit down. May I offer some refreshments?" As he spoke, a servant set out cool drinks and light snacks on the table between us. Schuyler could have made this a very formal meeting, with me standing before his desk, reporting on the conditions at Ticonderoga. Instead, he was taking a relaxed and collegial approach. His stately demeanor and the impressive surroundings gave him all the authority he needed to control his discussions with me, or virtually any gentleman in the colonies.

After both our glasses were filled and with a broad smile that extended to his eyes, Schuyler said, "Before we go any further, I want you to know that I believe you have been badly treated. I have told others, but I wanted you to hear it directly from me. I recognize that it is because of you, and not Ethan Allen, that we currently hold Ticonderoga and Crown Point. What is more, it is because of you that the lake is secure and cannon will be available in Boston. You have not expended the same effort singing your own praises or having your surrogates do so. As a result, you have been degraded in the eyes of some. Suffice to say I will do what I can to see that is corrected."

I found myself tongue-tied by this unexpected act of kindness. As I began to stand, I felt my face redden. "General, you are too kind."

He simultaneously waved off the compliment and directed me to sit. "Not at all, not at all. It is hard to find good men. I want you to know that I appreciate all you have done. Good leadership requires praising those who deserve it and criticizing those who act badly. Too often generals are not leaders of men, but chimney-corner politicians afraid to speak the truth. I hope you will never find that in me. Good or bad, I will give you my honest opinion."

When he paused, clearly expecting me to respond, I sputtered at first, but then relaxed. "As you may know, General, I was, for a period of time, a captain of ships at sea. Leading men fairly and honestly requires honor and truth. Whether at sea or on a battlefield, the men expect and deserve truth. I pray you will also receive nothing different from me."

Rarely in my life have I met a man whom I found so different from myself, and yet instantly respected and liked so much. Schuyler, through both the blessings of fate and hard work, had achieved great success. I wanted to emulate him. I could think of no better man with whom to establish a friendship.

He nodded in acknowledgment and raised his glass. "Well then, Colonel," he told me as I did likewise, "I am going to hold you to it. I need you to give me the complete and unvarnished truth about what has occurred up on Lake Champlain—who I can trust, who I cannot, and what is the best plan going forward."

Thrilled to have the opportunity to give my unfiltered opinion to someone I respected, I felt like a snake coiled and ready to pounce. I forced myself to appear relaxed, gripping my thighs to keep myself from bolting upright. "First, the good news. The forts are defensible and largely repaired. We possess and have armed the largest vessels on the lake. I believe we can stop, or at least substantially delay, the British progress down the lake toward New York. However, Colonel Hinman, Major Brown, and Colonel Easton are scoundrels, incapable of managing themselves, let alone men. You talked about leadership—men quickly come to recognize those who are worthy and those who are not. If and when the British come, we need to be well provisioned and well led. While many would wish otherwise, success in war often turns on providing troops with adequate ammunition, food, clothing, and structured discipline.

"But let me be clear, it is not my view that we should be on the defensive. We should take the fight to the British in Canada. They are weak, overextended, and unmotivated. There are about 370 redcoats between Fort Ticonderoga and Quebec. Two thousand properly commanded Americans could take that fortress city, and with it Canada. Time, however, is not on our side. The British will eventually send real troops from England, which even our best men and generals will be hard-pressed to stop."

Schuyler nodded in agreement. "I know you are returning home. Would you consider remaining to be my adjutant for our new Northern Department?"

I was surprised and exhilarated by the invitation. My initial instinct was to jump at the opportunity, but I felt the need to continue my journey south. "I have incurred substantial debts, and my businesses have suffered from my neglect in service of the Cause. I also need to go to Massachusetts to clear my name and address the scurrilous accusations made against me, as well as receive my entitled reimbursement."

Schuyler nodded in understanding. "I would not have you do otherwise. I would also tell you that I currently lack the troops and supplies of war to mount the invasion which you and I believe is necessary. When you have completed your tasks in Boston, would you be kind enough to contact me, so we might revisit your status in the Northern Department?"

Sensing our interview had come to an end, I stood. "Of course, General. I am tremendously honored by the opportunity, and am grateful to have spent this time with you."

Schuyler stood slowly, wincing at some unseen ailment. I tried not to notice his discomfort as he straightened to his full height and held out his hand. "Safe travels, Colonel. I hope to see you soon."

I took his hand and felt his grip, firm despite his obvious infirmity. "Thank you, General. Again, I am grateful for your assistance—it was an honor meeting you, sir."

Chapter 20

New Haven, CT - June 30, 1775

I went directly from General Schuyler to Massachusetts, but as soon as I entered the state, I was presented with a letter from my sister Hannah. My wife Margaret was dead of an unknown cause. She had only been thirty, and although we had drifted apart, I had three boys under the age of eight waiting for me in Connecticut. I saw no choice but to go home. By the time I arrived, Margaret's father had also passed away. As I would have wanted, and indeed expected, Hannah had moved into our home and was taking care of the boys.

As I stood hand in hand with Hannah and my three young sons looking down at the freshly filled grave of my wife, I felt more fatigue than emotional pain. The dead live in our imagination, whispering in our ears. My mother always said that was the true nature of ghosts. She still speaks to me from the grave. Certainly, my father's ghost dogs my every step as I attempt to escape his grasp. I cannot say I felt the same with the loss of my first wife. She was gone, and with her unhappy memories. The challenges of the war and caring for my boys directed my gaze to the future, not the past.

After remaining in Connecticut less than a month and recognizing that lingering could only lead to wallowing in self-pity, on July 26, I left Hannah in charge of my home. Within four days of my wife's death, Hannah enrolled my two older boys in a school in New Haven. I emphasized to her not to mollycoddle my boys. I wanted them to grow up strong—nothing like their weak grandfather. I also gave her instructions to proceed with business transactions she proposed and I approved—in particular, the sale of sixty thousand barrel hoops and staves to generate badly needed cash. I was once again grateful for her absolute loyalty and sound decision-making.

If I was going to return to the army, I knew I needed to face the Massachusetts Committee. Even if I had not been forced to resign, my costs should be reimbursed and my honor should remain unblemished.

Chapter 21

Cambridge, MA – August 10, 1775

General Washington was in charge of an exceedingly dirty and nasty mob comprised of the most indifferent kind of people. Seventeen thousand men lived in a shantytown without uniforms, organization, or discipline; most carried primitive weapons and lived in utterly appalling conditions. I do not mean this to be a criticism of the general—he and his officers were attempting to impose discipline at the same time as building trenches and earthworks.

I saw a few experienced men attempting to teach drill to this rabble and was pleased to witness a flogging or two instilling soldierly order. It was evident to me, and any thinking man, that what Washington lacked, above all, was experienced officers. He had at least imposed some discipline by establishing indications of rank, even without uniforms. Sergeants wore a strip of red cloth on their right shoulder, and corporals green on their left shoulder. Most officers carried a sword and pistol. Officers wore ribbons on their hats: lieutenants green, captains yellow, and majors/colonels red. Generals wore a chest sash: pink for brigadiers, purple for major generals, and light blue for Washington.

I was ordered to report to Washington on the state of affairs in the Northern Department at his headquarters, located on Brattle Street near Harvard College. I was ushered into his office by his new adjutant general, Horatio Gates. His Excellency gracefully rose from a desk covered in papers and maps. A young clerk huddled in the corner, indifferent to my entry as he continued to scratch away.

I had seen Washington briefly at the Continental Congress, but it was only at a distance, and we never spoke. At age forty-three, he was the picture of vitality. Only a hint of gray had crept into his auburn hair, tied back in a queue. His sheer size, striking eyes, and Roman nose gave him instant authority. He was simply the most impressive person I had ever seen or ever would see. He bowed deeply, and I did likewise.

"Benedict Arnold. It is indeed a pleasure to see you, sir." I noted he had deftly avoided calling me either "Captain" or "Colonel." "I am grateful for your letters updating me on your victories both at land and sea in the north. I also understand you trained a fine regiment from New Haven, which continues to serve us well." His voice was surprisingly airy and quiet for such a large man.

I bowed again. "It is an honor to meet with you, Your Excellency. I am pleased to have been of service to our country and the Cause."

Pointing to the chair across from him, he bade me sit and did likewise. "May I offer you any refreshment? I am afraid tea is in short supply..." He gave a closemouthed grin. "However, perhaps wine, ale, or cider?"

I realized that his clerk had silently stood and was now standing awaiting instructions. Nodding my head in acknowledgment of the courtesy, I answered, "No, thank you, Your Excellency. I realize you are quite busy, and I am grateful for a private audience."

Perhaps it was my intended use of *private* or some hidden signal between the two of them, but Washington's clerk bowed and left the room. When the door clicked shut, the general's pale-gray eyes locked on me with an intensity that seemed to probe my very soul. Again in a soft tone, he said, "You have demurred refreshment from me, but I require much from you."

"I am at your service," I said, accidentally interrupting him like an overly earnest schoolboy. Irritated and embarrassed, I felt my face flush.

Unperturbed, he continued, "I have heard many conflicting reports of what has occurred in the north. I would be grateful not only for your insights on what has already happened, but your thoughts on the various strategies going forward. I would also request a report on the strength of both our forces and the opposition." He gave me a broad mandate to speak. Despite all the pressures on him, he managed to appear unhurried and relaxed as he waited for me to talk.

"First, Your Excellency, the British remain at St. John, but we control

Lake Champlain. As I believe you may know, I led a raid on St. John and captured the largest gunboat on the lake; we had already secured the second-largest boat. For all practical purposes, we possess a squadron capable of keeping the enemy at bay until they build equally formidable ships to engage us. We also have bateaux in sufficient number to provide some mobile support when wind is not available. Large numbers of cannon and shot still remain on-site, beyond the munitions already en route to Boston.

"Our successes in taking the forts and the lake have caused many men to join the Cause. During my command, we strengthened as much as possible the dilapidated Forts Ticonderoga and Crown Point. The British are still relatively weak and undermanned. While they are forward fortified at St. John, I believe there are fewer than five hundred able men. While trained redcoats, I believe they could be overwhelmed and outflanked by a well-led militia of at least two thousand men."

I paused to see if the general had any questions. He nodded politely, subtly rolling his finger for me to continue.

"Unfortunately, when I left Crown Point there were nearly three hundred men without employ and having received no orders, or conflicting orders, from Congress. At Ticonderoga, there were about six hundred men in the same state. Men were building bateaux and engaging in periodic scouting parties, but again serving without clear direction. None have been employed in an active manner to reinforce their forts, provide hospitals for the sick, engineer heavy guns into place, or create drill and discipline for the purposes of creating a viable force to repel the enemy. In the meantime, I have seen St. John twice—and at close quarters. The British are fully entrenched and collecting timber to build vessels."

Never taking his eyes off me, Washington asked, "Currently constituted, can the forts withstand a British attack?"

"Yes and no, sir," I replied, unconsciously leaning toward his unblinking gaze. "We control the lake. They should not be able to come down and attack the forts any time soon. They could try an overland route, but that is a long and exposed supply line. Moreover, our ships would then be in a position to attack their rear at St. John. No, if we adequately defend the lake, the forts should not be subject to attack. However, they will eventually build ships that can engage us and attack. When they do, I do not believe the forts will hold out long, given their current state and leadership."

There it was—I had crossed into giving critiques of officers, which made me even more politically vulnerable if Washington did not agree, or if the men I criticized were his allies. I found myself suddenly hesitating.

Sensing my unease, Washington said, "My dear sir, I am grateful for your unwillingness to be critical of your fellow officers. However, you may count on two things: First, my absolute discretion. Second, I am well aware of your accomplishments in the field. I would like your honest assessment of how we should proceed and who should lead."

He then returned to the same implacable countenance, waiting for me to continue.

Nothing ventured, nothing gained. "Ethan Allen and his Green Mountain Boys are utterly disreputable and incompetent ruffians with no sense of military discipline, decorum, or even courage in a serious fight. Having them is almost worse than having no troops at all." I looked down to realize my nails were almost digging into the wood with my growing intensity.

The corner of Washington's mouth turned up slightly. "I have heard reports of Colonel Allen, despite his best efforts to tell the world otherwise. I am well acquainted with his wants and foibles."

Since criticizing Allen did not seem to offend him, I decided to give him the rest. "Colonel Hinman, who replaced me, while not a ruffian like Ethan Allen, is out of his depth. As I previously described, he is not employing the troops, the ships, or the forts in the proper manner."

Washington's head seemed to move almost imperceptibly, nodding in agreement. "So tell me—is your solution to have me return you to the forts and put you back in charge? You understand there are many who might criticize that decision."

Did he just offer me the command, or tell me I couldn't have it? It doesn't matter. Feeling my face flush again, I tried speaking calmly as my heart began pumping hard in my chest. "No, Your Excellency. I do believe that if properly led, an assault should be mounted from the south, starting at Ticonderoga through St. John, then up to Montreal. I also have the conceit to believe I could successfully perform some useful service in that operation if adequately supported. Yet that is not what I propose." Balancing on the knife-edge front of my seat, I continued, "I have no illusions about our situation. Our line is thin and brittle. It will snap when the British reinforce in the spring. I have a different plan to circumvent St. John and Montreal altogether and cut off the head of the snake. Quebec has always been the lynchpin of the British presence in Canada. If we can take Quebec, then Montreal, St. John, and all of Canada must fall. It is as true now as it was in the French and Indian War."

Washington's right eyebrow rose in interest. He shifted slightly forward in his chair and spoke for the first time in almost a normal volume. "Pray, continue."

"In 1759, I traveled to Quebec and delivered medical supplies to the British forces besieging the city. I spoke to many Indians who had traveled the land surrounding Quebec in canoes and otherwise. They convinced me that a trip from the Maine coast to Quebec was possible. Indeed, I obtained the journals of John Montresor, who described the journey along the Kennebec River of Maine, providing a virtual 'back door' to Quebec."

At that moment, there was a knock at the door, and Horatio Gates stuck in his head. "Your Excellency, your next appointment is here, and you are needed for inspection shortly."

I felt a wave of disappointment roll over me—my opportunity to propose my plan was being thwarted by the general's busy schedule. However, when I reluctantly began to stand, Washington met my eye and silently pointed down. I found myself involuntarily seated again like an obedient hound.

Turning to Gates, who was still standing at the doorway, Washington intoned, "General Gates, I require another ten minutes of Colonel Arnold's time. I would be grateful if you would adjust my schedule accordingly."

Gates could not fully hide his surprise at Washington's instructions, but nodded in acknowledgment. "Of course, sir." Turning to me, he nodded. "Colonel."

I stood and nodded in response to Gates, but sat back down as the door closed. It was not lost on me that I had now been called "Colonel" twice.

Once again locking me in his stare, Washington said, "I sincerely apologize for the interruption. I would like to hear what you are proposing."

Again, I had to fight the instinct to stand. The general had given me an incredible amount of time—I did not want to squander the opportunity. "As I was saying, Your Excellency, an overland route from Maine to Quebec is possible. I believe the people of Canada are ripe to join our Cause. In my experience as a captain and ship owner before the war, the French-Canadian merchants of Montreal and Quebec earnestly desire freedom from the British. The name of the last war says it all. The French-Canadians do not call it the French and Indian War, or the Seven Years' War, but the Guerre de la Conquête—the War of the Conquest. They have never accepted British rule, but time is not our friend. If we do not act with haste, a massive British force will arrive to quell any potential French and Indian dissent and secure a string of forts from Quebec to St. John. At best, there are six hundred regulars in all of Canada as we sit here today. These troops are spread extremely thin. If a group of Americans were to take Quebec, far to the north, the French-Canadians would likely rise up against their British oppressors. Not only would this benefit the Cause, but also open vast new tracts of land for American and Canadian expansion as part of a unified confederation of states."

"We have to win this war first, Colonel, before we start divvying up the spoils," Washington said flatly.

I've overreached. I need to pull it back and focus on strategy. "Indeed, Your Excellency. I apologize if I was getting ahead of myself. What I am proposing for your consideration is a two-pronged attack. A large force would attack Lake Champlain, seize St. John, and push on to Montreal.

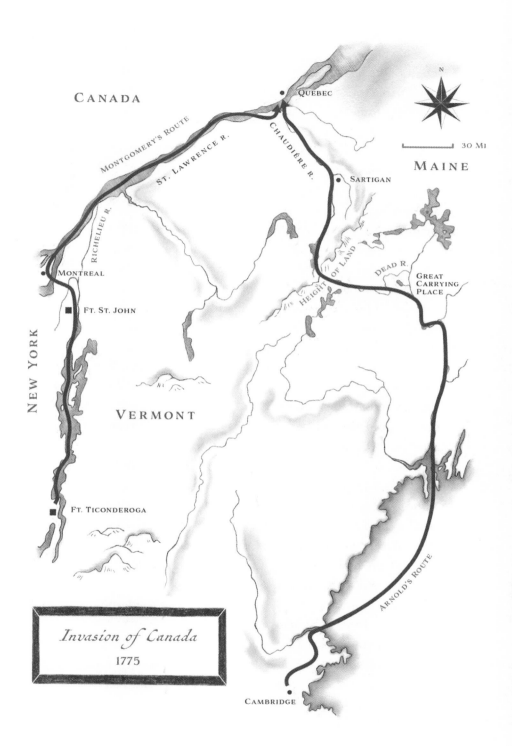

CANADA

MONTGOMERY'S ROUTE

ST. LAWRENCE R.

CHAUDIÉRE R.

QUEBEC

MAINE

N

30 MI

SARTIGAN

RICHELIEU R.

MONTREAL

FT. ST. JOHN

HEIGHT OF LAND

DEAD R.

GREAT
CARRYING
PLACE

NEW YORK

VERMONT

FT. TICONDEROGA

ARNOLD'S ROUTE

Invasion of Canada
1775

CAMBRIDGE

I recognize the challenges of putting me in command of that effort. In any event, that is not the assignment I am requesting.

"A small force of one thousand men would travel through the wilderness of Maine and take Quebec by surprise. My plan is to march through Maine's wilderness and come up over the mountains into Canada, using Indian guides and traveling in small groups." For a second, he cocked his head in what I thought was a look of doubt. Attempting to address his concerns, I continued, "I realize there is a lack of accurate maps and the route is traveled only by savages, but this is the very method that no one would expect and would secure complete surprise."

Another gentle knock at the door came, but this time the door did not open. Washington barked, "Not now!" I could feel the pressure of the army and his responsibility trying to push its way into the room; still, I could also tell that we had connected on both a personal and professional level, and he was intrigued with my plan.

A split-second of irritation fluttered across his face. Then I saw the lauded Washington self-control as he composed himself in an instant and said with all the politeness of a gentile Virginia gentleman, "I do sincerely apologize for these interruptions, my good colonel. Pray complete what you have to say. "

I nodded in acknowledgment. "Again, Your Excellency, time is of the essence. The upper reaches of Maine are already beginning to chill, and if we wait much longer, the lateness of the season will preclude the strike. By the time we could undertake the task in the spring, British reinforcements will already have arrived. Conversely, if we surmount the mountains now, the icebound city will be unable to receive reinforcements, and we can secure victory."

"Are you confident that you can make the wilderness crossing quickly and without getting lost?"

I replied so quickly, I almost interrupted him. "Absolutely, Your Excellency. With the right men and the map, I will be standing at the gates of Quebec before they even know what hit them."

Washington stood, and I immediately did so as well. "Part of your plan is already in the works. General Schuyler has sent his compliments to me on both your ability and character." I bowed with genuine gratitude. "He will lead the major expedition up Lake Champlain, taking St. John, Montreal, and Quebec. There had been no discussion, as you might imagine, regarding your alternate approach through . . . What did you call it?"

"A back door, sir."

Nodding in acknowledgment, Washington continued. "Indeed. A back door. I will need to discuss this with my staff and General Schuyler, but I am both intrigued and impressed. General Gates will be contacting you regarding my decision. Thank you and good day, sir."

He again bowed with the hint of a smile. Looking down at his desk, that smile transformed into a scowl as he surveyed the mountain of paper confronting him. The sound of a quill scratching on paper disappeared behind the heavy closed door.

I walked past officers standing in line for a few precious minutes with General Washington. General Gates, clearly exasperated by the delay in Washington's schedule, almost pushed me, albeit politely, to get out of the way as he scurried to converse with His Excellency. I was ecstatic walking back to my billet. He had given me enormous amounts of his time and seemed to agree with my strategy—and as importantly, I believed he respected me as an officer and a man.

This was precisely the sort of bold plan that Washington loved, but he did not immediately give me command. No doubt my detractors from Lake Champlain were whispering in his ear. I needed help from Silas Deane, General Schuyler, and my other friends to convince Washington that I was the leader he needed.

Chapter 22

Cambridge, MA – August 12, 1775

Barnabas Deane had dutifully reported to his brother Silas of my mistreatment during my capture of Fort Ticonderoga and successes in Canada. Silas was in Cambridge meeting with Washington, and I was thrilled to connect with my old friend. Two days after my arrival in Cambridge, we sat in the corner of a musty and overcrowded tavern on a hot Saturday night, Deane with the best glass of Madeira the tavern could provide, and me with the best ale. I never partook of whiskey or rum—those were my father's express tickets to disgrace, a journey I vowed never to take. I certainly enjoyed a fine glass of wine, and I tended to stay in control when drinking beer; this was a conversation I wanted to remember.

Silas got right to the point once we settled in. "So, Dr. Benjamin Church does not appear to be your friend. He has swallowed the libel of Easton and Brown whole and seems ready to empty the contents on you at your meeting tomorrow."

I bristled and set my mug down with controlled carefulness, then slammed down my fist, causing my beer to slosh onto the table. "By Christ! Those bastards! I'd run both Easton and Brown through if I could."

"And I'd hold your scabbard for you while you did it, but that is not the way these things work. You are going to need to set that temper aside when you deal with these"—a look of disdain marred his otherwise plump and pleasant face—"people."

"I know, I know. They are just god-damned bookkeepers, not soldiers."

Setting down his drink, Deane leaned forward and said, "Benedict, when we run our businesses, we are traders, merchants, gamblers, and yes, bookkeepers. They are trying to hold you to that same standard while you are fighting in the north."

Trying hard not to slam my hands down on the table again, I calmly spread my fingers out in an attempt to regain control. Evenly, emphasizing each word, I replied, "That is the bloody point. This is war."

Silas nodded in agreement.

I couldn't prevent myself from picking up speed with each word. "I can't be expected to be a record keeper when people are shooting at me, ships are burning, and people are getting killed!"

"Yet they will, Benedict. They will criticize you for not having records; they will criticize you for going home when your wife died; and they will criticize you for seeing General Washington before you reported to them." Raising his hands to stifle my protest, he smiled and continued, "Which was absolutely the right thing to do, but this is the sort of vermin you are dealing with. What you need to do is present your case calmly and as best you can. You are not going to 'win' before these people. They are already aligned against you. What you are doing is making a record. You must trust me, General Washington, General Schuyler, and others to see that you are treated fairly. What is the total amount you are owed?"

Reaching into my satchel, I pulled out my paperwork. "See here—it totals £1,060. They would argue that I could keep an army in the field for as little as the £100 I was given. I have ledgers for my itemized expenses, which I created both then and after the fact. I spent my money on carpenters and shipwrights, lumber, milling grain, and much more. I don't see how they can't recognize these expenses."

"Again, I want to emphasize I agree with you. But, as the devil's advocate, where are the receipts? You have ledgers showing what you paid, but you don't have any receipts from the people who received payment. You also—you will forgive me for saying so—appear to have paid very substantial amounts well above what one would expect at market."

I snapped, "This might come as a shock, but people in a war zone charge extortionary prices. I have the choice of paying it, or killing them. Frankly, I would have been fine with the latter, but my instructions were otherwise." Reaching for another pile of papers, I added, "I made sure all my expenses, even my personal ones, were proper."

Silas answered patiently, "I understand, Benedict."

Once more I slammed the table—despite regretting it the moment I did, I barked, "My victory answered the question better than any ledger could. To quote Cicero, 'In times of war the laws are silent.'"

With a broad grin, Silas said, "You never cease to amaze me, my autodidactic friend." With a poke to my chest, he continued, "Now there is a line you should use when you see them on Monday! Promise me you will control your temper, my friend. You only hurt yourself and play into their hands."

"It is just . . ."

"I beg you, Benedict. You can make a difference in the world. All you have to do is hold your tongue."

I started to speak, but he held up his hand. He looked at me with a mixture of plaintive encouragement and friendly disapproval. "Yin and yang."

Looking down, I nodded. "Yin and yang." I finally met his eyes and said, "I will try."

Raising his glass, Silas grinned and said, "That is all any of us can do."

After two and a half days of brutal, unpleasant, and difficult testimony, as bad as—or worse than—Silas had predicted, they paid me only £757, only 65 percent of the money I had demanded and spent in the name of Massachusetts. While I wanted to object to my treatment by the State of Massachusetts, I relied on Silas's advice and held my tongue. I did not issue any public complaints.

Chapter 23

Cambridge, MA - August 20, 1775

Washington summoned me to his headquarters. This time, I was greeted warmly by Gates with a friendly "Colonel Arnold, what a pleasure. His Excellency is waiting to see you." *Again, Colonel Arnold?*

I bowed in return. "Thank you, General. I am grateful for all of your kindness."

"It is a bold plan. We all wish you success." With an open palm, he gestured toward the closed door of Washington's office.

General Gates announced my arrival. His Excellency was once again hunched over his desk, but jumped to his feet with his close approximation of a smile. Politely pointing to a chair, Washington said, "Ah, my good Colonel Benedict Arnold. It is a pleasure to see you. Thank you for joining us. General Gates, will you please remain, so that you are fully aware of the plan going forward?"

There were two empty chairs—while I sat in the one indicated by Washington, Gates came around the desk and stood next to his superior. Reaching for a paper in the corner of Washington's desk, Gates slid a sheet in front of the commander. "As you may have already surmised, you will be given command of the expedition to attack through your 'back door.'" The corner of his mouth turned up with the hint of a smile. "You will be provided with formal written orders, but I have three stipulations which must be addressed before you can proceed." Reading from the sheet in front of him, he continued, "First, Canadians must be treated as fellow Americans, making common cause against the British oppressors. Second, you must complete the accounting of the amounts due and owing relating to your service at Fort Ticonderoga. Third, if your forces link up with General Schuyler, you are to immediately subordinate your independent command to him."

Unable to control myself, I jumped to attention and barked, "I respectfully and readily agree to all the terms and am honored to serve Your Excellency and the Cause. I would happily serve under General Schuyler at any time."

Washington looked back over his shoulder at Gates, who quickly stifled a growing grin. With his usual seriousness, Washington continued, "We have been calling you Colonel, as you earned that rank in service of Massachusetts, but I want to dispense with any further issues amongst the states concerning your status. As such, I will be granting you a full colonelcy in the Continental Army. I expect this to be confirmed in the next couple of days. Going forward, sir, you shall only be answerable to this command, if that is acceptable."

Once again, I had to fight my Yankee urge to interrupt his languid, gentlemanly Southern drawl. "Of course, sir. Nothing could please me more."

Looking back at Gates, then at me, Washington gave a friendly wave, pointed to the door, and said, "Off you go, gentlemen. Get Colonel Arnold's expedition ready."

A smiling Gates moved around the desk toward me and stuck out his hand. "Congratulations, Colonel."

I shook his hand a bit too rigorously, bearing a grin I could not contain. "Thank you very much, General." Turning to Washington, who stood and bowed but did not offer his hand, I said, "And thank you again, Your Excellency."

"I wish you well, Colonel. Dismissed."

As we left, General Gates and I glanced behind us to see Washington already frowning at the paper on his desk.

On September 2, I received a commission as a full colonel in the Continental Army. Four days later, Washington ordered a grand review. Six thousand soldiers stood in neat rows. They knew only that there was a secret and dangerous mission looking for men; boredom, the unpleasantness of the camp, and the desire for adventure no doubt filled the volunteers' ranks.

Colonel Benedict Arnold
Engraving by Thomas Hart. Courtesy of Yale University Art Gallery

General Washington stood in front of the group and, with a surprisingly loud voice given his demeanor in our prior meetings, proclaimed, "Gentlemen, I am grateful you are all here volunteering for this important mission. I wish I could tell you more, but that will only be for those of you selected. This mission, crucial to the Cause, will be led by Colonel Benedict Arnold. Many of you may have already heard of his successes in capturing Fort Ticonderoga and Fort Crown Point, successfully invading St. John and Canada, and capturing British ships which now serve these Colonies. Any man under him will be fortunate to serve such a leader."

Turning to me with an open palm, Washington said, "Colonel, if you would like to say a few words."

Nodding deferentially to General Washington, I took a step forward and used my booming sea captain's voice to great effect. "Thank you for being here. This is a volunteer mission involving secret orders that will include perilous service. I cannot and will not guarantee that everyone that goes with us will return. As His Excellency indicated, I can promise that it is of crucial importance and can make a decisive difference in our struggle for liberty. This again is not compulsory. There is no shame if you change your mind and decide not to continue to proceed."

I paused and looked at the group, but most seemed unfazed by the nature of the task and its danger. "This endeavor is not for everyone. I need a specific breed of soldier. I need one thousand young, brave, and tough men, ready for a challenge. I need active woodsmen and those acquainted with the bateau." What I did not say was that Green Mountain Boys need not apply.

Turning, I nodded to General Washington and took two steps back to be behind him. One of Washington's staff officers then called out, "Volunteers, advance one step!" Nearly six thousand men stepped forward.

Washington and his staff took their leave. I rode along the lines, asking men questions about how long they had lived in the woods and their ability to handle small boats. After careful questioning, I and my adjutant, Captain Christian Febiger, selected 786 rough-looking soldiers, all in their teens and twenties, and three hundred woodsmen from Virginia and Pennsylvania.

The only exception to the youth requirement was Captain Daniel Morgan, who had led a group of volunteers. Morgan's three hundred riflemen were known for killing British soldiers at 250 yards with their "Widow-Maker" long rifles. Morgan, nicknamed "the Old Wagoner," had received five hundred lashes in the French and Indian War for striking a British officer. He had a vicious battle scar where a bullet had passed through part of his neck and his jaw, knocking out teeth as it exited through his upper lip. At six feet tall, he weighed two hundred pounds with not an ounce of fat. His voice sounded like rocks scraping together, but he rarely needed to raise it. His men obeyed and never questioned his sound judgment. Wrinkles carved by a lifetime of wind and sun surrounded lively eyes. He was capable of leading his three rifle companies with merely a stern look or a slap from his powerful hands.

Morgan's men carried fifty-eight-inch rifles which were designed to kill game at a great distance—adapted to a wartime environment, they were the ideal sniper rifle. The primary drawback was a complicated and time-consuming loading procedure, wherein the fragile rifled barrels had to be skillfully handled. Each man also carried a tomahawk or axe, and a long knife—which they called a scalping knife. Dressed in homemade hunting shirts, breeches, and moccasins, they sported a distinctive hunting shirt usually made of linen and colored with blue and red hues. They wore leather capes or fringed coats, accentuating their unique appearance among the soldiers. While I preferred strict military dress, I had to admit they presented a singular and formidable group of men whose skills I admired.

Our 1,050 men pitched tents on the Cambridge commons. I broke the regiment into four divisions: "The Old Wagoner" commanded my first division and our vanguard. For second-in-command and commander of the second battalion, I chose Lieutenant Colonel Christopher Greene to lead his Rhode Island troops. As the head of the third division, I selected Major Return Jonathan Meigs of Connecticut. Lieutenant Colonel Roger Enos of Vermont led our fourth division and our rear guard.

I had five captains to serve as my immediate aides, including my most trusted aide Eleazer Oswald, Matthias Ogden, and Aaron Burr (while only nineteen, he was already an extraordinary young man). Oswald was my friend, a printer from New Haven, and a fellow member of the Foot Guard. He had resigned his commission, but graciously agreed to serve as we began our march north, acting as my private secretary and acting captain. I also appointed Captain Christian Febiger as my adjutant general. Febiger was an engineering officer in the Royal Danish Army and the son of a horse trader from the Danish Virgin Islands whom I knew well. Dr. Isaac Senter from New Hampshire joined as our company surgeon. Finally, our expedition's chaplain was a six-foot-tall captain named Samuel Spring.

Even as our troops readied themselves for the trip, we suffered shortages of weapons, blankets, equipment, and uniforms. Most of my soldiers did not have a uniform—instead, they wore sturdy, plain civilian coats or jackets made from wool. Many also had a frock, which was a simple large shirt with a button at the neck. For armaments, most carried small-caliber hunting guns known as "fowlers," whose name was derived from their use for hunting birds and other small game. Most also had a small knife or hatchet and a haversack and blanket roll slung over their shoulder, holding an extra shirt and personal articles. The men carried a cartridge box slung over their shoulder, containing ammunition, paper cartridges, and powder. The result was a ragtag group of hearty men with little uniformity in appearance, weapons, or accoutrements.

General Washington's parting instruction to my men was to be gentle in our treatment of citizens as we moved through the backcountry toward Quebec: "Consider yourselves as marching, not through an enemy's country; but that of our friends and brethren, for such inhabitants of Canada, and the Indian nations." The general further admonished that there should be strict "punishment for every attempt to plunder or insult any of the inhabitants of Canada."

I sent an order to a boat maker in Maine for two hundred bateaux. These flat-bottomed boats could haul heavy supplies and navigate shallow waters; each had four oars, two paddles, and four setting poles to propel the boat in shallow water. I chose bateaux over canoes because canoes were unstable and easily capsized in rough waters, and had far less carrying capacity than the larger bateaux.

We headed thirty miles north over dusty roads to Newburyport, Massachusetts. There, we boarded ten ships and made our way to Maine and up the Kennebec River through rainy conditions, which hid our movements from the British. When the rain finally stopped, the sun revealed a land resplendent with early autumn colors and marshes replete with yellow fern and purple aster.

At the first opportunity, I had my boat pulled to shore so I could jump on horseback and ride ahead to the shipyard of Reuben Colburn, who was building the bateaux. I was in terrific spirits to be leading this intrepid band of men. I had never felt stronger—my muscles were full and strong. I had become a superb horseman and an expert sailor, fencer, and sharpshooter. I had the endurance and skills I knew would prove invaluable as we faced the wilderness. With a light heart, I arrived at Colburn's shipyard on the eastern end of Gardinerstown. Almost two hundred bateaux were laid neatly along the river.

My good mood evaporated as I began examining the boats. As I grumbled and shook my head in disgust, a pug-faced, squat, broad-shouldered man charged down the hill toward me. He growled with a voice that sounded like rats scratching inside a barrel, "Who the blazes are you? Get the hell away from my boats!"

Turning to face him squarely, I snapped back with equal volume, "You are obviously as daft as you are a poor boatbuilder! I think my uniform should make quite clear why I am here. I have been sent by General Washington to command this expedition. I am Colonel Benedict Arnold. I can only surmise that you are Colburn. You have done an atrocious job building the required boats, and these are *not* proper bateaux."

Colburn did not slow down as he approached. I took an involuntary step forward with my left foot and moved my hand to the butt of my sword, preparing to defend myself if he continued closer than arm's length.

Like a charging bull, he stopped abruptly and snorted. "Listen, army boy, you don't know the first thing about bateaux. This is how we build them in Maine."

"Sir, I am from Connecticut and have spent more time at sea and on boats than a man like you can imagine. These boats are worthless. You built them with wet green pinewood that will shrink and bend as they dry. They are going to leak like sieves, and they already weigh too much to portage well. It will only get worse when they are put in the water. What I am trying to decide is whether you are incompetent, unscrupulous, or both."

My blood now up, I moved closer. As his face reddened, I continued, "This is one of the worst construction efforts I have ever seen. You should have used dried wood, which would have been lightweight and not likely to lead to leaks. If you didn't understand that, you are incompetent. But I don't think that is it—I think you are unscrupulous. You have built defective boats with cheap wood instead of spending the money you were given to buy dried wood for proper construction."

Ruben Colburn opened his mouth to begin to speak, but I held up my hand to silence him. "But that is not all. Not only have you built cheap and defective boats, harming the army and the Cause, but you seem incapable of building boats of the size required. I ordered the boats be constructed to a uniform length of twenty-five feet, with flared sides and a pointed bow. Many of these boats are as short as eighteen feet. They will never accommodate six large men, their guns, and their equipment as I had required."

His countenance suddenly changed, and a self-satisfied grin spread across his face. "Well, Colonel, you can certainly reach out to my *friend* George Washington and complain, but I will tell you I made extraordinary efforts under an unreasonable timeline. I don't know where in God's name you think that wood could have been found in these parts to build the boats you demanded on such short notice. You come up here in your fancy uniform complaining without any understanding. I, sir, unlike a jack-a-dandy like you, live in the real world. I defy any man in Maine to have done what I did on such short notice. In Maine, bateaux are small, heavy craft used for logging on flooded rivers. Yes, the boats require some additional work, but they are sturdy and well-built. I made them smaller to make them manageable over portages. If I had built to your dimensions, they would ride too deep and your men couldn't move them. Instead of complaining, you should be thanking me." Without another word, he spun on his heels and trundled away.

Furious, I wrote a letter to Washington: "I've found the bateaux completed," but "very badly built."

I could not remain to await his response.

Despite my misgivings, on September 27, less than three weeks after the grand review, my men boarded the heavily loaded bateaux and headed up the Kennebec River. I anticipated my fast-striking force would be able to reach Quebec in just twenty days; nevertheless, I had every man bring enough rations for forty-five days. We carried a total of sixty-five tons of equipment, supplies, ammunition, and food. Two soldiers' wives and one young Indian woman traveled with our force. Aaron Burr managed to win the favor of an Abenaki princess from Swan's Island—she was part French, but fully in love with him.

I led the vanguard of the small fleet in a birchbark canoe because it was lighter and faster, allowing me to move between the men and their boats to provide encouragement and orders. As I approached each group, the men roared, "To Quebec and victory!"

The Kennebec River was low as a result of a summer drought. Progress slowed as men were forced to use long poles to push the bateaux forward a few feet at a time. My soldiers took turns standing in the icy water in front of each boat, pulling it along with the rope tied to the bow.

I quickly realized that most of my men had overstated their experience in boating. Even skilled boatmen had a difficult time negotiating the sharp rocks and obstacles in the rushing current. To make matters worse, not only was the Kennebec shallow, but numerous whitewater rapids and waterfalls blocked our way, forcing the men to unload their laden bateaux and drag them around the obstacles. Four men at a time could carry a bateau on their shoulders, but a thousand pounds of additional supplies needed to be moved for each boat, requiring multiple trips by each man along their routes as they portaged their materials. Weary troops stumbled on slippery ground, their backs bent under barrels and heavy packs as they made their way along muddy paths. Meanwhile, the green wood continued to warp and leak. The water sloshing in the bottoms of the boats quickly ruined many of the hastily packed provisions. When men were not in the river pulling the boats along, they took turns bailing water out.

I split and staggered my intrepid band into its four divisions to avoid backlogs and bottlenecks at portages. My first division, led by Captain Daniel Morgan, would be responsible for trailblazing, while my last division would carry the bulk of the supplies through a path already prepared for them. Morgan and his riflemen hacked trees out of the way as my other men dragged the unloaded boats and equipment over the boggy terrain.

It wasn't until the evening of October 1 that the ragtag army reached Norridgewock Falls and the last English settlement. All around, mountain peaks rose like jagged fangs biting into the frozen night. Indeed, the next night temperatures plunged below freezing. Forced to sleep in wet uniforms, the men woke each morning with clothing frozen stiff. Hunger was beginning to be an issue—the food barrels were poorly made and had been penetrated by the omnipresent water, fouling meat and supplies. Much of our precious salt pork, salt cod, peas, cornmeal, and flour had to be thrown away, leaving a scant amount remaining. I endeavored to have my remaining carpenters and caulkers repair our boats and barrels to avoid the continuing damage.

On October 10, we arrived at the Great Carrying Place. Named by the Abenaki Indians, it was a thirteen-mile overland portage between the Kennebec and Dead Rivers. Heavily forested and broken only by three large ponds, the trail required a thousand-foot climb.

Cold numbed the men's exposed arms, while branches scratched and cut their skin. Nevertheless, I noted in my journal, "The men's spirit and industry seem to overcome every obstacle and they appear very cheerful." For six backbreaking days, they dragged their equipment and materials over the Great Carrying Place, this half-frozen ground that had taken on the texture of thick putty.

I agreed to build a hospital for the unwell men. Captain Enos of the Connecticut battalion was so ill from dysentery that he had to be left behind, along with a number of Morgan's Pennsylvania riflemen. I knew I needed every able-bodied man to press on to Quebec, so I left only the absolute minimum number. By the time we completed crossing the Great Carrying Place, we were down to just 950 effective men, carrying only twenty-five days' provisions.

On October 12, Lieutenant Archibald Steele returned from a three-week reconnaissance mission along the Chaudière River. Steele informed me that he had discovered no Indians and that the next eighty miles were a water journey on a river with virtually no current or rapids. This cheered my men—there would be portages, but they would be shorter, with the longest a mere four miles on firm ground. Steele also indicated there was plenty of game to fill our bellies. Morgan's men were already providing fresh moose meat and fish to fill the gap of rations lost or destroyed.

I expected to be in Quebec in two weeks. Then it began to rain and rain and rain. We soon realized that we had been caught in a late-season hurricane. The otherwise "Dead" River rose three feet in two days. By October 19, my men huddled around campfires next to the swollen water, desperately trying to sleep and stay dry. The next day, the Dead River rose another nine feet, and a surge of water overwhelmed my men, inundating our baggage and forcing us up a small hill for safety.

As a frozen sun rose on Sunday, October 22, we looked down at a wholly flooded landscape, with no indication of the location of the now submerged Dead River. Within a half mile, the current was so strong that seven boats violently smashed into upstanding tree trunks. The men were saved, but precious food was lost. After covering just a half mile, we climbed another hill my men named "Camp Disaster." We had been traveling for almost a month, and Quebec still lay far ahead.

I called a council of war to discuss our situation. The cold circled like a wolf held at bay by our meager fire. Wrapped in a cloak, I knelt sharpshooter fashion; a score of other officers crouched around me as I summarized our situation. "Gentlemen, I believe we are about halfway through our expedition. It is possible when we come out of the wilderness, the British could be lying in wait and wipe us out. While I believe that is highly unlikely, there is another enemy more certain to take a toll on the men, and that is hunger. We have lost much of our food, and we still have a great way to go. There is a saying that 'daring sometimes overcomes the odds, but wise men do not disregard nature.' Despite our men's bravery, nature is wearing us down."

These officers had earned my complete honesty. There could be no secrets between us, and there would be none if we were going to succeed. As I looked around, every officer's eyes were locked on me. Understanding the importance of our decision, I continued, "We could probably survive if we retreated, but retreat would mean failure and recriminations." I hoped they could not see that my greatest fear was not death or starvation, but humiliation. "But here is my simple view. If we are marked to die, we are enough to do our country loss, and if to live, the fewer the men, the greater the share of honor." I saw contagious grins spread across a number of the men's faces. "I have said enough. I believe in the adage 'The good Lord gave us two ears and one mouth'— officers should listen twice as much as they talk."

I believed my men knew I wanted to press on. A long silence hung in the air, broken only by the sizzle and pop of smoking wet wood. Desperate for the heat, the men stayed close, choosing to let smoke burn their eyes rather than step back and feel the bite of the cold.

In a council of war, traditionally the most junior officers give their opinions first. Daniel Morgan, never one to follow military protocol, stood to his full height, his knees cracking as he did so. "Gentlemen, I can speak for myself and my boys. We did not come this far to turn tail. Men may die in the attempt to get to Quebec, and we may die when we get there, but we are all going to die someday. I'd rather die well than be seen as quitting." He turned and looked me in the eye. "We are with you to the end, Colonel. Liberty or death." Nodding, he crouched back down close to the fire.

Major Meigs stood next. "First, it is all downhill from here, gentle-men. I earnestly believe it will be an easier trip into Quebec than it was to Camp Disaster. We'd be hard-pressed to find tougher country ahead." A smile at the grim humor spread around the fire. With that, Meigs intoned, "Liberty or death," nodded to me, and returned to the fire. One by one, all my remaining officers present voted to proceed with the exact phrase coined by Captain Morgan. While miserable, I couldn't help but be warmed with pride that I commanded such honorable men.

With the support of my officers, I ordered those too sick and weak to be sent back with four days' rations to reach Fort Halifax. After the remaining rations were distributed, we believed we had enough to last fifteen days. What was absolutely clear to me—and I said as much in correspondence to General Washington—was that Montresor's maps were useless frauds.

The next morning, recoiling from the cold, the sun made a half-hearted effort to heft itself over the horizon. I decided a small group of handpicked men, under the command of Captain Oliver Hanchet of Connecticut, would approach the nearest Canadian towns to obtain food for the starving men. I sent a letter back to Lieutenant Colonel Roger Enos, who commanded the rear of the line of march, to send forward as much food as he could spare with all "possible dispatch." By streamlining my army, returning the sick and weak, and sending ahead an expeditionary force, I hoped to reach Quebec before starvation and exposure overtook our brave band.

I later learned that when Colonel Enos finally arrived at our base camp and met with my other officers, he called for a new council of war. Without me present, he questioned my orders and discussed the possi-bility of returning to Cambridge. Colonel Greene, Captain Thayer, and my other men apparently supported following my orders, moving as many supplies and fit men forward as possible and returning only those weakest back to Cambridge with limited supplies. Enos and three of his officers voted to return home, claiming insufficient supplies. Greene, in disbelief, reminded Enos and his officers that they would be, at the very least, guilty of insubordination if they didn't follow my written orders. At worst, Enos's proposal to take nearly half my force back to Cambridge could doom our expedition.

Contrary to Enos's assertions, he had at least six days' full rations for all four hundred of his men. I had instructed him to send 150 of the weakest men back with carpenters and commissaries, carrying three days' worth of half rations. This would have allowed him to send forward the best hundred men with fifteen days of food and a sizable quantity of flour, meat, and ammunition. When word of his retreat and defection passed through the troops, my men were furious. Henry Dearborn wrote, "Our men made a general prayer that Col. Enos and all his men might die by the way, or meet with some disaster equal to the cowardly, dastardly and unfriendly spirit they discovered in returning without orders." Dearborn quipped that there was one side advantage of Enos's' treachery: "Being now almost out of provisions, we were sure to die if we attempted to return back—and we could be in no worse a situation if we proceeded on our route." It is fair to say that forty to fifty men died because of Enos's mutiny.

Much later, I was informed that Enos and his men had safely arrived in Cambridge, well fed and "abundantly satisfied" by their return. General Washington was quite rightly outraged and ordered a court-martial. However, the trial was a farce—Enos's friends rejected General Washington's charge of "quitting his commanding officer without leave." Of course, all the officers who knew of Enos's villainy had remained with me and were unable to provide testimony demonstrating his dishonor. Although he was ultimately acquitted, I am pleased to say the army recognized that he was a coward and mutineer. Eight days after the ruling, he resigned his commission and did not serve again during the Revolution.

Meanwhile, the rest of my troops under Isaac Hull had ignored my order to stay on high ground and were struggling through the swamp, completely lost, trying to locate me. The only remaining woman on the trip, Jemima Warner, ran back to find her husband, James Warner, sitting under a tree, worn out and unable to take another step. He died in her arms. Jemima stood, covered her man with leaves, and picked up his gun to follow the remnants of our army. My brave lads reeled about like drunken men, having been without provisions for five days. Sadly, they gave in and ate Henry Dearborn's beloved dog.

Cold is so much worse than heat. When it is hot, you can rest in the shade. As long as you have water, you can press on. The cold is far more lethal. It hurts until it makes you numb. It then attacks your body, but you cannot feel it. Worse, it whispers in your ear to stop, take a break, and rest. That siren song lulls and kills—too many of my soldiers simply stopped, lay down, and never woke up.

I endeavored each day to get up before my men. Moving from group to group, I would rouse them for the journey ahead. They looked so young—balling their fists in their eyes to rub the sleep off, they reminded me of my boys back home. I knew coddling them would do no good; they were desperate for a firm and encouraging hand. My morning greeting was "Up you go, lads. Food and warmth are ahead. On your feet! Don't tarry."

I have heard people say many times that the spirit is willing, but the flesh is weak. I know this to be true. My brave boys' spirits alone carried them through. I saw frozen bogs covered with an icy sheen that cut my men's legs and knees like razors, yet they slogged on. They did not stop when the frozen mud stuck to everything and drove the cold deep into their bones. Long after their flesh failed, it was their will that allowed them to push through.

We finally reached the first Canadian settlement. I paid cash for all the food supplied by the local settlers, keeping a careful account of my spending. I was able to arrange to have a cow sent back from the village toward my approaching troops. In addition to the cow, there were sheep and sacks of flour. Without bothering to cook the cow, my men jumped on the animal and ate the flesh raw, then cooked its innards and ate them as quickly. Unfortunately, despite warnings from many of us, some of my men who had not eaten for so long succumbed to gorging on food and died due to the shock to their systems.

I had left Cambridge with 1,080 troops. On November 3, I sat within striking distance of Quebec, having traveled through an impenetrable forest with 675 worn, emaciated, but most excellent men. Crucially, Hanchet's men had secured a horse for me; this permitted me to move up and down my column, which was now a broad, sad trail of soldiers spread out over twenty miles. I was grateful for the mobility, as well as the animal's heat warming my tired legs as I collected my men.

One of the dear lads in our troop, John Henry, turned seventeen on November 4. A few days later, he sat on the side of the road as I trotted by, encouraging my troops. Henry was well-liked, the "little brother" for many of the men. When I saw him, he was deathly pale and shivering, his face so cold and pale that it looked like fine linen. I dismounted and approached, knelt next to him, and held his freezing hand. "How are you, son? Let's get up and get moving. You will feel better."

His eyes fluttered with recognition, and I saw an attempt to stand, but he just could not get his body to move. He said in a whisper, "I am very sorry, sir. Perhaps you should leave me behind. I think if I just sleep for a couple of minutes, I will be able to get moving again."

Knowing that would be a death sentence, I reached down and picked him up, shocked at how little he weighed. I said as much to myself as to him: "Not today, John." Seeing a couple of stout men walking by, I shouted, "Over here, lads! Help me get young John up onto my horse."

We rode to a nearby farmhouse, and I put two silver dollars in the hands of a Frenchman to nurse the lad back to health. I am happy to say our John Henry recovered. I put over a hundred stragglers like Henry into the hands of locals; while I kept an accounting, I rarely obtained the required receipts from the illiterate peasants.

As my army straggled into the town of Sartigan, they were directed to a Catholic church called Saint Georges. The townspeople brought all manner of food, including meat and vegetables along with baked bread, to revive my emaciated men. Satisfied my troops were being reconstituted, I traveled further downriver to gain more supplies and confer with local Indians. I also wrote a letter to be forwarded to General Schuyler:

> The men having with them their greatest

fortitude and perseverance, hauled their boats up rapid streams, obliged to wade almost the whole way, near 180 miles, carried them on their shoulders near forty miles, over hills, swamps, and bogs almost impenetrable and to their knees in mire. Short of provisions, part of the detachment disheartened and gone back; famine staring us in the face; an enemy's country and uncertain ahead. Notwithstanding all these obstacles, the officers and men, inspired and fired with the love of liberty and their country, pushed on with a fortitude superior to every obstacle, and most of them had not one day's provisions for a week.

When General Washington learned of our successful operation across the wilderness, he wrote to General Schuyler praising me: "The merit of that officer is certainly great, and I heartily wish that fortune may distinguish him as one of your favorites. He will do everything which prudence and valor will suggest." However, because of Enos's cowardice, he cautioned Schuyler that "I will not be able to make a successful attack on Quebec without the cooperation of Montgomery." General Richard Montgomery was the commander placed in charge of a large army moving north to attack Montreal and then Quebec. I had heard of his reputation and was pleased with his selection.

Finally, Washington wrote a letter to me which I would not receive for many months. He complimented my "enterprising and persevering spirit—it is not in the power of any man to command success, but you have done more, you have earned it." Even members of the Continental Congress spoke kindly of my "little army" that "is thought equal to Hannibal's over the Alps." As never before or since, I enjoyed the absolute loyalty and support of my men. We shared a mutual admiration and respect that only a "band of brothers" who have lived through a crucible can understand.

Chapter 24

Château du Lauzon, Canada – November 4, 1775

I arrived at St. Marie on the Chaudière River, thirty miles east of Quebec, and selected Château du Lauzon as my headquarters. As word spread of our amazing journey through the wilderness, the inhabitants treated us with not only respect, but genuine awe. Emboldened by stories of my victory at Forts Ticonderoga and St. John, the French-Canadians shared my confidence in the upcoming battle for Quebec.

As the Indians gathered, I was keenly aware of spies—our presence would surely be known to the British at Quebec. The Indians designated Chief Natanis as their spokesman. While my men looked ragged, I wanted to give the impression of strength. My reputation had preceded me, and the Indians were pleasant and deferential. A group of leaders sat in a circle on a small grassy plain abutting the river, their expressions varying from stone-faced to curious. None evidenced any overt hostility.

I had managed to transport my formal colonel's uniform through the harrowing journey, protected in a watertight leather oilskin bag. While the others sat, I stood in my finest, faced the Indian leaders, and read my carefully written speech: "Brothers, we are children of those who have now taken up the hatchet against us. More than one hundred years ago, we were all as one family. We then differed in our religion and have come over to this great country by the consent of the king."

I had to pause because few of them spoke English—translations into French and into the local Indian dialect were required. The Indians seemed nonplussed by my opening, but I sojourned on. "We have planted the ground, and by our own labor have grown rich. Now, a new king and his wicked, great men want to take our lands and money without our consent. This we think unjust."

As the translations were shared, they nodded their heads in agreement. "The king would not hear our prayer, but sent a great army to Boston and endeavored to set our brethren against us in Canada. The king's army at Boston came out into the fields and houses and killed a great many women and children while they were peaceably at work. The Bostonians sent to their brethren in the country, and they came in unto their relief, and in six days raised an army of fifty thousand men, drove the king's troops on board their ships, and killed and wounded fifteen hundred of their men."

Though I knew these numbers were grossly inflated, I believed this misinformation would help our Cause. "Now we hear the French and Indians in Canada have sent to us that the king's troops oppress them. They press them to take up arms against the Bostonians, their brethren, who have done them no harm. By the desire of the French and Indians, our brothers, we have come to their assistance, with the intent to drive out the king's soldiers."

I opened my arms to gesture to the leaders sitting before me. After this translation, I was met with several nods and smiles. "If the Indians, our brethren, will join us, we will be very much obliged to them, and give them one Portuguese per month, two dollars' bounty, and find them their provisions, and the liberty to choose their own officers."

When I was done, the Indians all bowed, rose to walk some distance away, and held a conclave. After a few minutes, they returned to their same spots and bade me sit with them. One of my attentive aides brought a stool, for I had no desire to sit Indian style and dirty my uniform.

Natanis was slightly older than me, with skin drawn impossibly tight across his face, broken only by weathered wrinkles at the eyes. Despite being a savage, he projected both poise and intelligence. Through an interpreter, he said, "We will make a peace with you, Dark Eagle. I will provide fifty Abenaki warriors to join your attack on Quebec. You will pay them like your other soldiers. We will give you scouts and canoes. The remainder of my brothers will not fight you, but cannot yet join you."

I was simultaneously pleased and disappointed. I was getting some of the needed support, but not a full commitment. I pressed the point: "Noble Natanis, all your brothers and braves do not join our worthy fight. Why?"

Natanis nodded in understanding when he received the translation. "A wise man does not jump headfirst into a river until he knows whether the water is shallow or deep. We support you, but many chiefs will not yet jump in. Dark Eagle should know we provide these braves out of respect for you."

While frustrated by the lukewarm commitment, I knew I could press no further. Instead, I gave in to my curiosity: "Pray, Chief Natanis, why do you call me Dark Eagle?"

Holding his arms wide, he proclaimed, "The Dark Eagle comes to claim the Wilderness. The Wilderness will yield to the Dark Eagle, but the Rock will defy him. The Dark Eagle will soar aloft to the Sun. Nations will behold him and sound his praises. Yet when he soars highest, his fall is most certain. When his wings brush the sky, then the arrow will pierce his heart."

Aaron Burr, who had been translating from French to English, looked over at me with a perplexed tilt of his head. I involuntarily shrugged back. Without further explanation, the Indians lit a peace pipe, confirming our new agreement. Recognizing that discussions were over, I completed the ritual and returned to camp.

Chapter 25

St. Marie, Canada - November 5, 1775

From my base, I dispatched Morgan's riflemen to Point de Lévy, seven miles north of our troops and only one mile across the St. Lawrence from Quebec. I informed General Schuyler that "I find the English have been some time apprised of our coming of Quebec and have destroyed all the canoes." Nevertheless, I emphasized that I had already obtained replacements, and added, "I propose crossing the St. Lawrence as soon as possible." The intelligence I had received indicated there were only three hundred defenders in Quebec. Thus, I would "endeavor to cut off their communication with the country and keep them in close quarters until your arrival here."

On Guy Fawkes Day, I entered the Roman Catholic church in St. Marie to appear before the community. We had carried the manifesto from General Washington to the Canadians, translated into French, encouraging them to join the Cause. We quickly learned the French-Canadians were both illiterate and highly devoted to their Catholic faith. Thus, Washington's fine words were neither read nor appreciated. To make matters more challenging, the local priests wielded disproportionate power and were too often in the pocket of the British.

Nevertheless, we were the dominant military force in the town. When I invited all the local citizens to the church, they understood implicitly that they were required to attend. We received a tepid introduction by a priest whose wizened face was animated only by his disdain for me as he reluctantly relinquished the pulpit.

Again, Aaron Burr stood at my elbow to translate. "You are French-Canadians. Your very language and culture set you against England. Our thirteen colonies share this great new continent with you, making us all patriotic Americans. I know none of you relished the outcome of the War of the Conquest when your British overlords sought to impose their religion, their language, and their culture upon you. I speak for General Washington and the Congress when I tell you that no Canadian will ever again be forced to act against his will or conscience. Our revolution against the British is based on liberty, religious tolerance, and freedom. We invite you to join our quest and battle against the British. Any able-bodied man is welcome to join our ranks to fight and expel the redcoats from Quebec and North America."

I was met with stony silence, with few parishioners' eyes cast up toward me; I could tell asking for volunteers to stand or inviting questions was futile. I thanked them for their time, but none moved a muscle until the pudgy priest returned to the pulpit, blessed the congregation, and dismissed them. As we walked out of the church, I could feel the malevolent eyes of the priest burning a hole in my back. Turning to Burr, I murmured, "Do you think killing the priest would help the Cause?"

Knowing that I was only half joking, Burr whispered back, "I'd happily do it myself, but then we'd turn the bastard into a martyr, and they would probably make him a saint. I think the only help we are going to get from these people is the food and supplies they sell us."

I nodded in disgust.

We learned some of my letters had been intercepted by the British, ending any hope of surprise. Nevertheless, I moved our forces north the next day, the last leg of our journey, hoping that we could conquer the city before its defenses were sufficiently strengthened to repulse our attack.

I knew that I would need to coordinate with General Montgomery, who was in overall theatre command. I sent him a letter assuring him that despite the deprivations endured by my men, "most of them are in good health and high spirits."

We paraded over a three-day period to Point de Lévy, emerging a mile from the imposing city of Quebec. Looming over all the surrounding land, the city looked down on the St. Lawrence, filled with jagged

blocks of ice. We faced a citadel punctuated by church spires and tur-
reted palaces hidden behind thick granite walls atop a sheer cliff rising
three hundred feet over the river. The city's high, sharp cliffs split the
St. Lawrence and St. Charles Rivers like a mighty plow, invincible to
ice, water, and attack. My men remained enthusiastic, but crossing the
St. Lawrence River offered certain death in its current condition. As we
looked across at the British fort, we noted it was also protected by the
British sloop HMS *Hunter* and the frigate HMS *Lizard*.

On the morning of November 8, to inspire the locals and my men,
I assembled my troops for a grand review. A few officers had retained
their fine uniforms, but most men's homespun clothing had frayed to
rags stitched together with rawhide and bits of recovered cloth. Once-
stout men were now walking skeletons; long hair hung over brows and
uncut beards jutting from gaunt faces. Nevertheless, my brave lads stood
straight and proud at their accomplishment. All met me with a steady
eye. I truly loved and admired these stalwart and deserving fellows.

Later that day, a British picket boat approached Point de Lévy
intending to reach a mill owned by loyalist Colonel Henry Caldwell.
As the British longboat approached, Morgan and his men decided to
try to capture it. They opened at too great a range. When the longboat
pulled offshore in haste and under fire, it left a midshipman behind. He
tried to swim after the boat, but Morgan's men once again opened fire.
When he tried to surrender, Sabatis, brother of Chief Natanis, pulled his
knife and waded into the water with the intent of killing him. Morgan,
seeing what was happening, ran into the water and dragged the young
captive to shore—no doubt saving his life. The midshipman turned out
to be the brother of the HMS *Hunter*'s captain. As they dragged him
onto shore, the HMS *Hunter* came within range and raked the area with
grapeshot. The British now clearly knew not only that we were in the
area, but that we were directly across from the fort.

For the next five days, we sat and shivered in heavy snows. The British ships prowled the river, keeping us pinned down. The gray, overcast
skies created a monochromatic world that reflected my men's misery.

I desperately sent letters to Schuyler seeking reinforcements, and most importantly artillery to make an assault possible. Meanwhile, I received information that Quebec was further reinforced by the battle-seasoned Black Watch—130 Scottish highlanders—as well as more loyalists who'd entered the walled city. I no longer faced a handful of redcoats, but at least 1,050 defenders, including highly seasoned and experienced British fighting men.

The St. Lawrence River was not an obstacle to be taken lightly, yet I had not come this far to be stopped by mere water. I ordered Captains Thayer and Topham to find whatever watercraft they could to get us across the river. These intrepid gentlemen managed to locate twenty canoes and two dozen other craft the British had not managed to take or destroy.

The good news, if there were any, was that the intense cold prevented British ships from providing resupply to Quebec. On the coldest days, the river froze and was covered with a sheen of snow. On one particularly frigid morning, I woke up just before sunrise and walked down to the St. Lawrence. The river went quiet; I was greeted only by the sound of the wind shaking the trees and scraping the hardened snow on the ice. As the sun rose, I heard blurbs, gurgles, and pops, which gave way to rumbles and deep groans. The river seemed to be warning me that I should not consider a dash on the ice to the other shore. An unnatural tone—somewhere between a bell chime and a single note from a church organ—came from somewhere deep under the ice. Having received the message, I abandoned the idea of running across the river, yet I remained mesmerized watching the river suffer like an old man. I resolved not to hazard the ice and instead wait for our chance to cross with our small boats when the ice cleared.

As the weather continued to worsen, I was well aware that while the city was being further reinforced each day, our forces were getting no stronger. To bolster morale, I kept my men busy making ladders, reinstilling discipline and demanding improved military appearance by instituting formal reviews. A crossing, I assured them, was imminent.

While we waited, John Halstead, who operated a gristmill near the city, introduced himself to me and briefed us on Quebec's defenses. I had just six hundred men, yet I was confident that the bulk of the city's defenders were ill-trained militia and would not stand against my determined "famine-proof veterans." I explained to my men that a carefully calculated surprise assault could break the British line, and called a council of war to discuss the possibility of attack. Colonel Greene and I favored an offensive, with a majority of the other officers recommending caution. I was compelled to follow their advice, because as I noted in a letter to Washington, "My brave men were in want of everything but stout hearts, and would have gladly met the enemy though we had not ten rounds of ammunition a man, and they were double our numbers."

I later learned that if I had attacked within the first two days, before British reinforcements arrived, the city likely would have fallen. Indeed, a relief column under the hardened British Colonel MacLean slipped unseen through the gates on November 11, substantially reinforcing the garrison.

Chapter 26

Point de Lévy, Canada – November 13, 1775

A messenger informed me that General Montgomery had captured Fort St. John from the British after a forty-two-day siege. It was my earnest wish that this good news might find the British on their heels. I was pleased to see citizens fleeing Quebec as fifteen merchant ships set sail when the ice on the river began to break up. We had been waiting almost a fortnight to cross the river, and conditions finally warranted the attempt.

On the partly cloudy night of November 13, there was just enough light for us to see the HMS *Hunter* and HMS *Lizard* patrolling the mile-wide river. The moon cast a tattered lace of silver through the clouds, making the ships appear and vanish like ghosts. Undeterred by the men-of-war, my troops climbed into our boats and pushed off at about 9:00 p.m. A night crossing with the lurking warships and lethal ice was made even more dangerous by overladen canoes. Nevertheless, when I asked for volunteers to cross, every man stepped forward.

Daniel Morgan and I shoved off in the lead canoe with Halstead acting as our guide. The choppy river and current provided a challenge, but they also made it difficult for the British warships to see us. We hoped our boats would look like rotten timber and chunks of debris downstream.

We held our breath as we neared the dark shore. Rifles were cocked as we approached the woods, fearing an unseen enemy. To our relief, the only sounds we heard were the grinding of the birchbark canoes against the rocky shore and the rustle of the gentle wind moving the trees. Four silent trips across the river would be enough to shuttle my entire army. By four o'clock in the morning, the hem of night was pulling away, taking with it the stars and leaving only a lone planet to herald the rising sun. An apricot glow began to lighten the eastern sky as we completed three crossings. After about five hundred men transferred to the northern side of the river, I decided to halt night operations.

Just as we decided to stop, one overloaded canoe flipped, dumping its men and supplies into the river. The crews and some of the supplies were recovered, but Lieutenant Archibald Steele could not get back into the canoe. He clung to the stern and was dragged through the frigid water to the beach. The men attempted to rub him with snow to return his circulation, but they feared for him. To save his life, they built a small fire. Unfortunately, a small British patrol boat came to investigate. I attempted to bluff the boat away by hailing the British to come close so we might capture them. However, they refused to heave to. Rather than letting the British escape, I ordered Morgan's men to open fire and drive them off. I knew getting more men across the river would prove difficult, and the British would know we were on their shore.

Chapter 27

Plains of Abraham, Canada – November 15, 1775

The French and Indian War ended in 1759 after a yearlong siege of Quebec, when a goat path was found from the river up to the Plains of Abraham, a plateau leading to the city gates. The British managed to bring an army up that trail, enticing the French to come out and fight a battle. I led my men up that same trail; my strategy was to march up to the city gates and demand the British surrender.

Sixteen years earlier, the British and French had engaged in a stand-up battle with troops facing each other in long lines across an open field. The superior British rate of fire had won the day. I maintained no illusions about my boys' ability to stand up against an equal number of trained British redcoats. Morgan's men carried long rifles that required time and skill to load and were meant for sniping officers at distance, not participating in the carnage of a traditional European line of fire.

The majority of my men had smoothbore flintlock muskets similar or identical to the British Brown Bess, with a maximum range of one hundred yards. Maintaining continuous fire involved an intricate dance of fire and movement designed to accommodate the cumbersome reloading process. After firing the weapon, a soldier was required to draw the musket's hammer halfway back, withdraw a paper cartridge from a pouch at his side, bite off the top of the cartridge, shake the powder into the priming pan of the musket, shut the pan, and position the barrel up to receive the paper cartridge as wadding was pushed into the muzzle, along with the balance of the powder down the barrel. The soldier then removed a ball from his pouch and inserted it into the barrel, withdrawing an iron ramrod from its holder attached to the gun and inserting it down the barrel to tamp the ball and powder. The soldier then returned the ramrod to its holder, fully cocked the weapon, aimed, and fired. A well-trained soldier could repeat this evolution several times a minute. Success or failure of a military campaign often turns on the ability to bring massed fire on a specified target. Given their inaccuracy, the ideal range for these muskets was no more than fifty yards. However, the impact of a ball at that range was devastating to opposing troops.

While my men were brave and motivated, they were ill trained and underequipped. My hope was that what we lacked in martial skills would be overcome by the manly enthusiasm that was missing in the British and their tepid Quebec allies.

Large walls separated the Plains of Abraham from the city. There had been rumblings within the city among its merchants and population sympathetic to the American Cause. Unfortunately, the addition of British soldiers in early November had quashed any chance of an internal rebellion. Indeed, Colonel Allen MacLean had been placed in charge of the city's defenses and made clear that he would brook no talk of surrender.

After climbing up to the Plains of Abraham, we moved down King's Road and emerged on the snow-covered fields about a mile west of the city's walls and the St. Louis Gate. We seized the surrounding houses, and I set up my command post at the abandoned home of British Colonel Henry Caldwell. Relieved our evening's toil was over, my men fell asleep while I remained awake to determine our next steps.

After we received intelligence that MacLean was planning to attack us with six hundred men and field artillery, I decided to seize the initiative and draw him into a confrontation. I had long believed that boldness magnifies might, and I had a plan in my mind—however, as I began to sketch out the idea on a piece of paper before me, I found myself fighting to keep my eyes open. My lids fluttered up and down like a ship buffeted by the waves. Eventually, like the men around me, I slid into a fitful sleep.

As dawn broke, our men marched within a half mile of the city walls, just beyond musket range. I suspect the force still looked tiny when compared to the expanse of the Plains of Abraham. I had speculated that our torn uniforms and long, wild beards would instill fear in the refined townspeople of Quebec; most had left Boston looking like boys, but grime and fatigue now made them look like old men. As the sun touched the top of the ramparts, I saw huge crowds standing at the top of the walls. Unafraid shopkeepers, sailors, women, and children stared down at our force.

No prior moment equaled the pride I felt as my men stood behind me. Despite all the challenges and death we had faced, we were at the gates of Quebec. I felt like both the tiger and the lamb, ready to attack and ready to be slaughtered. As I walked out in front of my men, facing the wall, they roared as one with three hearty huzzahs, followed by a wild and sustained cheer. As the sound died down, we were met with a stunned and deafening silence from behind the walls.

I ordered my aide Matthias Ogden, along with a drummer carrying a white flag, to deliver my demand that Quebec surrender, citing "the unjust, cruel and tyrannical acts of a vile British Parliament." I explained that if we were compelled to attack the town, they should expect "every severity practiced on such an occasion."

As Ogden approached, a heavy cannon flashed and a twenty-four-pound ball arched toward him, followed by musket balls which narrowly missed him. In a clear breach of etiquette, MacLean was ignoring the laws of war by firing at my man under a white flag. Once again, my troops' bravery was demonstrated as they laughed and ridiculed the British, going so far as to pick up the cannonball to fire it back at the British. Regrettably, a second cannonball did serve its purpose by cutting off the leg of one of Morgan's riflemen, who died shortly thereafter.

While MacLean was dishonorable, he was also no one's fool. The French had been defeated because they had left the safety of Quebec's stout walls. Regrettably, the British were not willing to make the same mistake. I recognized my bluff had failed and pulled back out of cannon range.

On November 18, I brought up scaling ladders with the expectation that we would make a rush at the walls. Unfortunately, as I began a detailed inspection of my men's arms and ammunition, I discovered that over one hundred guns were unfit for service. We had not five good rounds for each man. Not only were we ill-equipped for offensive operations, but a concerted attack by MacLean would surely mean our defeat. Recognizing that no attack was possible, our only alternative was to withdraw, cut British communication lines from Quebec, and wait for Montgomery.

The following day, we endured yet another snowstorm as we began a twenty-mile night march to Pointe aux Trembles, leaving only a small rear guard at Quebec. As we moved along the river, we saw more crowded British warships reinforcing the city. I later learned that one of the ships we saw pass contained Governor Guy Carleton, arriving to lead the city's defense. We were disappointed by our retreat, but also heartened by the support of the local inhabitants who continued to provide us with food and lodging. I recognized that until Montgomery's reinforcements arrived, all I could do was attempt to take care of my troops.

I wrote to General Washington describing our condition: "Most of the soldiers were in constant misery as they were barefooted and the ground frozen and very uneven. We might have been tracked all the way by the blood from our shattered hooves." Thus, one of my first priorities was to use hard currency to purchase footwear, clothing, and blankets for my men out of my own personal account.

Finally, on December 1, Brigadier General Richard Montgomery arrived to take command. I was greatly heartened by the supplies he brought with him. We now had his three hundred men plus my six hundred, augmented by two hundred French-Canadians. This was still a force less than half the size of the British and loyalist forces filling Quebec, and the defenders held the better ground with more men and better supplies. Nevertheless, I believed we had a fighting chance.

I had no qualms about Montgomery's leadership; he had conquered St. John, Chambly, and most recently, Montreal. I stood at attention as he inspected my regiment. To my surprise and pleasure, Montgomery announced that every soldier was to receive a bounty of a gold Spanish dollar from the Continental Congress, a new uniform, and a heavy-lined

Richard Montgomery
Engraving by G. R. Hall of painting by Alonzo Chappel.
Courtesy of the National Archives 148-GW-135

fur coat and leggings, all captured from British transports in Montreal. Montgomery was also kind and complimentary toward me. I was aware in correspondence he had described my corps as "an exceedingly fine one. There is a style of discipline among them, much superior to what I've been used to seeing in this campaign."

A native of Ireland and a graduate of Trinity College in Dublin, Montgomery had served as a captain in the Seventeenth Foot during the French and Indian War. In 1772, he'd sold his commission and immigrated to New York. He was a relative by marriage to General Philip Schuyler. At the outbreak of the war, Montgomery joined the Cause. He was thirty-seven, bald, tall, and handsome, with a military carriage, although much marked from smallpox. An educated man with impressive credentials, I readily deferred to the experienced and courteous general.

Montgomery and I sat before an inviting hearth in a cozy tavern. When it was the two of us, he suggested we dispense with formalities and asked that I call him Richard; he called me Benedict, pronouncing each syllable of my first name with care. So often, people slurred my name, as if trying to rush through some unpleasant task. His enunciation made me sit a little straighter and drew me closer to him.

He did not wait for the fire to chase away the cold in our feet and hands as he laid out our options. Raising a finger with each alternative, he said, "We can withdraw, siege, or storm. Obviously, retreat is out of the question. A conventional siege is impossible on the frozen ground, as trenches cannot be dug. Likewise, we lack cannon capable of piercing the walls to break down their defenses. A long siege is also impracticable, as the defenders can easily last till spring, when heavy British ships will break any blockade imposed by our troops. Thus, our best course of action is to storm the city as soon as possible."

As I nodded in agreement, Montgomery continued, "I understand Carleton is in command. As you may know, he was badly wounded at the climactic battle here at Quebec when General Wolfe beat the French. When the war ended, he returned to Britain, then served in the

Bay of Biscay and in Cuba. We served in the latter together. We are both from Ireland, and we struck up a cordial acquaintance."

Montgomery turned from the fire and locked eyes with me. "We are facing an army in that city, but more importantly, we are facing a man. I will tell you that when a man is seriously wounded too many times—and in Carleton's case it has been three times—something happens inside." He tapped his chest for emphasis. "Rest assured, Carleton is no coward. But he now has a mature recognition of his mortality, and he knows that victory is not inevitable. So it begs the question: What does this mean for Carleton?"

I knew this was rhetorical and did not attempt to answer, but continued to listen, hanging on his every word.

"I think it means two things. First of all, if we can convince him that his situation is hopeless, he will not feel the need to 'fight to the death,' but might accept surrender on honorable terms. Second, and more importantly, I do not believe he will seize the initiative. He saw what happened when the French left the protection of the fort and were defeated by Wolfe. Most importantly, the fire is out of him. He was never an aggressive man to start with, but his recognition of his mortality means he will not attack."

Reaching for a piece of paper on a nearby table, he said, "I will write one more demand letter to Quebec. We will see if I can persuade him that surrender is honorable given my previous victories and our large combined force. I'm not overly optimistic, but it is worth a try. In the meantime, we need to look for the right opportunity. So often these issues seem to turn on the weather, eh, Colonel?"

I answered with a humorless smile, "We will attack the city on the next stormy night. Snow will be our ally and provide us cover as we charge the city walls."

He reached for a quill and said without looking up, "Pray for a tempest, my friend, so that we may be cast upon an unfriendly shore."

Montgomery gave his letter to an old woman who lived near the bastion. She was instructed to ensure the letter was delivered to Governor Carleton. When she presented him with the letter, Carleton gestured to a soldier, who picked up a tong next to a nearby fire, placed the unopened letter in its grasp, and dropped it directly from the woman's hands into the fire. With this news, we knew the matter would never be peaceably resolved. However, among our grounds for continued optimism were the steady stream of townspeople abandoning the city and reports of Carleton's frustration with the dependability of his local soldiers.

While Montgomery and I did our work, several officers were unenthusiastic about the prospect of rushing the ramparts. In particular, Connecticut Captain Oliver Hanchet resisted me at every turn. During our long march, I had given directions to avoid the Chaudière swamps, yet he had disregarded my instructions and almost lost his men. On the arrival of Montgomery, Hanchet befriended my enemy Major John Brown, whom I'd previously had disagreements with during the campaign at Lake Champlain. These men were malcontents, arguing against my leadership even as I planned the attack on Quebec and drew General Montgomery's praise.

Chapter 28

Quebec City, Canada - December 5, 1775

T hree weeks after our attempt to entice the British to fight us on the Plains of Abraham, a long American column approached Quebec. The city's inhabitants were ill at ease, as I had encouraged rumors that over 4,500 reinforcements had arrived from Montgomery—as far as they knew, we now outnumbered the British in the town. We knew we needed to attack, and in any event I needed to commence the assault before some of our enlisted men's terms expired on January 1.

Morgan's riflemen began to snipe at the British exposed on the walls. The New York artillery had built a five-gun mortar battery in St. Roche. They kept up a steady bombardment for two days; unfortunately, the guns were too small and the crews too inexperienced to make a difference. In response, the accurate counterfire of Royal Navy gunners forced our withdrawal. We also fired artillery from St. Foy, but these too failed to do any substantial damage. In the course of this exchange of fire, our band was saddened when a twenty-four-pound British ball sheared off the head of Jemima Warner, who had remained with us after the loss of her husband in the Chaudière swamps.

The British also responded to our gunfire by ordering a detachment of loyalist soldiers to destroy houses that were blocking the city's view of our gun emplacements. The fire started by the redcoats got out of control and burned most of the houses in the district.

We made a third attempt to resolve the matter with a letter from General Montgomery indicating that Carleton and his adjutant would be given safe conduct to England if they would strike their colors. Accompanied by a drummer, Captain John McPherson (Montgomery's aide-de-camp) and I appeared before the St. John Gate under a flag of truce. After a long delay, one of Carleton's aides shouted down from the wall that the governor would not treat with rebels. I responded, "Then let the general be answerable for all the consequences." Seeing that the loyalist soldiers were raising their guns to fire, I turned on my heel and slowly walked away, expecting at any moment that a musket ball would enter my back.

Meanwhile, one of my aides, working with General Montgomery, confirmed that he had written a highly complimentary letter to the Continental Congress recommending I be given a general officer's commission, praising my leadership and describing me as "active, intelligent, and enterprising." I found it particularly heartening that he had also been extremely critical of Ethan Allen.

I greatly admired Montgomery, his leadership, and his success. He and I both agreed that aggression was the key to success in dealing with Quebec. Indeed, I believe the two of us perfectly complemented each other. He was predisposed toward melancholia, whereas I tended to be energetic. We helped temper each other and effectively managed men under difficult circumstances.

On December 8, we almost lost the general. He was doing me the courtesy of visiting my headquarters in Menut's Tavern in St. Roche. As he walked through the door, an enemy cannonball obliterated his carriage and decapitated his horse. He paused to look back with a grimace of disappointment, then closed the door. The concussion from the shell had knocked a book from a shelf near the door; facedown, the volume blocked Montgomery's path like a wounded bird thrown from its nest. He silently, gently, almost reverently picked it up, closed it, and put it back in place before joining me as I stood before the hearth. He said almost in a whisper, "A shame, Colonel. That was a fine animal, and carriages are precious."

Amazed by his calm indifference toward what had just transpired and the continued commotion on the other side of the door, I said with genuine feeling, "Indeed, General, but I am truly grateful you are unharmed."

"My fate and yours are in God's hands, but I wish the good Lord would do us a bit of kindness with some heavy clouds and a bit of snow on a dark night. After weeks of snow, we are suddenly cursed with brilliant, clear days and bright, moon-filled nights. We can only pray for the best and make our plans."

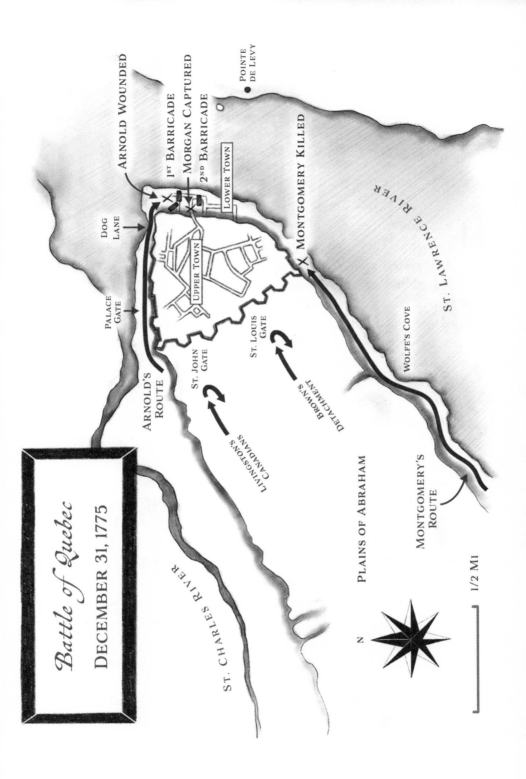

Battle of Quebec
DECEMBER 31, 1775

ARNOLD WOUNDED

1ST BARRICADE

MORGAN CAPTURED

2ND BARRICADE

POINTE DE LEVY

LOWER TOWN

DOG LANE

UPPER TOWN

MONTGOMERY KILLED

PALACE GATE

ST. LAWRENCE RIVER

WOLFE'S COVE

ARNOLD'S ROUTE

ST. JOHN GATE

ST. LOUIS GATE

BROWN'S DETACHMENT

LIVINGSTON'S CANADIANS

ST. CHARLES RIVER

PLAINS OF ABRAHAM

MONTGOMERY'S ROUTE

N

1/2 MI

123

Chapter 29

Quebec City, Canada – December 30, 1775

I was never more grateful for a cloudy afternoon. Soon flurries thickened into heavy snow, supporting our long-planned night attack. We told the men to ready themselves.

My men occupied all the surrounding houses. Each house smelled of smoke from inadequate chimneys and too many men living in confined spaces, but everyone chose to endure the fetid dust- and smoke-filled air rather than the fierce cold just outside the poorly insulated walls, windows, and ill-fitting doors.

I tried to provide words of encouragement and reassurance as I traveled from house to house. As is the way before battle, the men wrote letters home, cleaned their guns, sharpened their knives, washed their clothes, and gambled to increase their debts or pay them off. Most prayed, as was in accordance with their character. For myself, I beseeched the god of battles to steel my soldiers' hearts and give them courage.

At midnight, the men began to assemble in advance of our move toward the city's walls. Since many of my men had to wear British uniforms to stay warm, they stuck pieces of paper or sprigs of hemlock into their hats, writing "Liberty or Death" on them to distinguish themselves from the enemy and reaffirm our band's de facto motto.

As Montgomery and I looked out over our ragtag men, many were stomping their feet and blowing on their hands to fight the chill. Soldiers never look younger and more vulnerable than just before they go into battle. The general, sensing their unease, shouted to the shivering men, "We have come this far, boys, for our country. We band of brothers fight not only for each other, our wives, and our sweethearts, but for something even greater: freedom and liberty!" With the last word, he stabbed the air with his sword—even from behind their scarves and in the blowing snow, the cheer of our soldiers was a sweet sound.

We divided our thousand effective troops into four units. Our goal was to create confusion and exploit any potential weaknesses in the defense. James Livingston's Canadian volunteers were to engage at the St. John Gate and, if time permitted, also at the Palace Gate, attempting to light both on fire. Simultaneously, Major John Brown was to lead a second, diversionary party to create the illusion of a major attack at the Cape Diamond Bastion. As Brown struck, he was to ignite rockets to signal my command to proceed along a narrow pathway between the St. Charles River and the bluffs into Lower Town.

My men and I were to attack the barricades below the Sault-au-Matelot to access Lower Town from its northeast end. Meanwhile, General Montgomery and three hundred New York soldiers were to move along a treacherous narrow trail for two miles along the St. Lawrence River and attempt to penetrate two barriers blocking the route in an area known as "Près de Ville," before pushing into the southeastern side of Lower Town. If all went according to plan, General Montgomery and I would meet in Lower Town and move uphill to assault the city.

Montgomery and I were not indifferent to danger. Even with weather conditions that helped obscure our numbers and tactical goals, we knew the attack could still be viewed as rash or imprudent. However, with our troops' enlistments coming to an end and British support arriving in the spring, we had no choice. We summoned the men to Menut's Tavern at midnight.

After much delay, on the morning of December 31 at 4:00 a.m., we began our attack. The soldiers cheered as we collected our scaling ladders, artillery, and rifles and headed toward the enemy citadel. The men shared rum sprinkled with gunpowder, which was purported to provide both warmth and courage. As long as it was parceled out in small quantities, I saw no harm—besides, anything that helped men believe their own courage, regardless of its frivolity, was a useful self-fulfilling prophecy. Meanwhile, to guard against the cold and driving wind, the troops remained bundled. Their blankets were tightly wound around their flintlocks, keeping them dry and clean to prevent fouling.

The British were awake and expecting the attack. Muffled cries floated down from the city above: "Turn out! Turn out!" Every able-bodied man was on the ramparts. The basilica's bells were ringing and drums could be heard beating "To Arms," calling the city guard to their stations. I did note with some satisfaction that no one was calling the alarm in French.

Livingston's Canadians tried to set the St. John Gate ablaze at 4:30 a.m., but the wind kept putting the fire out. Meanwhile, Brown's troops began shooting at shadowy figures guarding the Cape Diamond Bastion, effectively forewarning of their attack. After a half-hearted attempt at breaching the fortified ramparts, Brown fired off the rockets, signaling Montgomery and my troops to begin our attack. In response, the British began to direct active fire against Brown's men. As you'd expect from a coward, Brown and his men immediately scurried back to their original positions, leaving behind their dead and wounded. This effectively ended Brown's participation, and permitted the British to shift units that should have been facing him against our other attacking units.

When we saw the three signal rockets light the snow-filled sky, I waved my sword, and we dashed along a narrow path, a wall looming on our right. On the northern end of Lower Town, I led my men from the front as we worked our way along the river. These moments of battle and confrontation thrilled me—the weight of responsibility to my men and my desire to show my courage in battle allowed me to lead without fear.

Twenty-five men had volunteered with me as our "forlorn hope" to act as an advance party one hundred yards ahead of the main body of the troops. I was in front of these brave lads as we shouldered on against the wind whipping along the river, progressing in single file to avoid sporadic firing from the British on the walls above. Spinning snow zephyrs climbing up into the frozen sky led our way; they would have been a spectacular sight, but for the press of battle.

Immediately behind our forlorn hope, Captain Lamb and his small crew pulled sled-mounted artillery. Even a light artillery piece weighed more than a ton and was unwieldy in any conditions, but in an ice-covered snowstorm it was especially challenging. In the middle of my line, I had placed a more mixed group of enlisted men, riflemen, Canadians, and Indians, led by captains who I trusted would keep this group under control. At their rear were Daniel Morgan and his steadfast riflemen.

The British and their Canadian lackeys infested the ramparts built upon the cliffs above. The whiteness of the storm was broken only by the muzzle flashes, giving the illusion of lightning and thunder in the midst of a harrowing snowstorm. While my men earnestly desired to return fire, I forbade such actions as fruitless and instructed them to continue to press their advance through snow and icy wind that stung our faces, but also obscured us from the redcoats.

As I passed below the Palace Gate, the previously muffled sound of the church bells in the city rang clear, drowning the sound of my men's feet as they pounded on the frozen cobblestones blown clear of snow by the relentless wind. We raced down Dog Lane, a twenty-yard-wide passage between the river and the ramparts leading into Lower Town; we then moved to the Rue St. Paul and turned onto the house-lined street of Sault-au-Matelot. Plunging fire from the upper levels and rooftops rained down on us. Caught in a maze of wharves and shops, we plowed on toward the center of Lower Town, where we planned to climb the single road providing access to the city above.

Suddenly, the British fire began to slacken as Governor Carleton shifted his forces to meet General Montgomery's attack. Breathing hard at the exertion of moving through knee-deep snow, we dashed along Sault-au-Matelot. Daniel Morgan and Captain Oswald were at my side as we reached the first barricade—Morgan should have been at the column's rear, but his temperament required him to lead from the front. I knew that British cannon loaded with grapeshot were likely embedded in their defenses. Recognizing we had only seconds to spare, I ordered Morgan and his riflemen to shove their weapons through the slits and fire point-blank at the British defenders.

Unfortunately, our cannon could not be employed because it had fallen off its sled. In battle, there is no time to dwell on disappointment. Without hesitation, I ordered my men to move over the barricade and continue their attack. Suddenly, a massive blast of musketry let loose from above, coming from houses on both sides of the street. Knowing the British would need to reload, I roared for my men to charge.

My left leg felt numb as I started to move forward—to my surprise, my knee buckled, and I fell forward into the snow. I did not yet comprehend that a bullet had ripped through my leg just below the knee. I attempted to stand and once again collapsed. As the realization that I had been shot struck me, I understood we were at a crucial point in the battle—I must not show weakness. I managed to stand on my right leg and hop forward while leaning against a wall as another volley of gunfire enveloped us. I shouted, "Go on, my boys! God damn them!" Although I was bleeding heavily and unable to put any weight on my left leg as my boot filled with blood, I roared, "Follow Morgan and take the town!"

Morgan saw that I was injured. He trotted toward me, indifferent to both the snow and lead that filled the air around us, and said in a firm but calm voice, "Are you hurt, Colonel?"

Waving off the question, I yelled over the din, "I'm fine." Pointing down to my boot, "I got nicked in the leg. I'm going to have trouble keeping up. You'll need to lead the lads."

Without a hint of hesitation, he nodded. "No problem, sir. Shame about losing our artillery." He made the pronouncement with the casual attitude of someone having just spilled a mostly empty glass of water. "No matter—I prefer rifle over cannon." The corner of his mouth rose as he finished speaking.

Trying to match his indifference to the death surrounding us, I raised my blood-soaked glove and said, "Good hunting, Mr. Morgan."

Waving my sword, I urged my men to follow him and Eleazer Oswald. As Morgan left, I slid down against the wall I was using for support and yelled, "Rush on, brave boys! Rush on!" I refused several offers to retreat and instead remained to shout encouragement. Following my orders, the men ran on with their scaling ladders towards Morgan.

My back was against the wall as I watched the last of my men moving out of sight. Glancing down, I saw blood pouring out of my boot. I found myself strangely amused and detached as I said aloud, "Steaming scarlet stains spread on the slippery snow." *I am not good at word games; those are for pretty men, cleverer than me . . .*

I could no longer hear the sounds of battle. I focused on the snow-flakes disappearing instantly as they touched the scarlet. *How sublime . . .* The world began to narrow as I tracked the individual disappearing flakes. *Maybe I should just close my eyes . . .*

At that moment, two strong hands grabbed my shoulders, and my field of vision was filled with the familiar face of Matthias Ogden. Sounds of shouts, the staccato fire of musketry, and the boom of cannon filled my ears. "Colonel! Sir, can you hear me? Stay with us!"

Over his shoulder, I saw ricochet sparks against stone walls, visible through the snow. The realization struck me like a thunderbolt: *I am bleeding to death!*

Fear brought me back. I looked at Ogden and Captain Spring, who were crouching over me, avoiding a hail of musketry. I nodded and yelled, "Yes. By Christ, I am with you!" They grabbed me by the shoulders and bravely dragged me to safety.

I was brought to the makeshift hospital a mile away in St. Foy. Dr. Isaac Senter tore away my trousers. I'll never forget the sight of steam rising in the cold from the open wound. He offered me a stiff shot of rum, which I refused. Shrugging, he told me to bite a musket ball. Proceeding in a workmanlike manner, he dug into the muscle of my leg with all the gentleness one would expect of someone gutting a deer. After what seemed like two score minutes of agony, but was probably only seconds, he pulled out a flattened lead bullet. The lead had apparently ricocheted off a rock and lodged near my Achilles tendon. Showing the ball to me, Senter said amputation would be unnecessary.

The doctor bandaged my leg and immobilized it with a splint, so that I would not put any pressure on my damaged tendon. Just as the procedure was being completed, a frost-covered soldier burst into my room. The wide-eyed youth was no more than nineteen; he searched the room without comprehension, exclaiming with a voice that was a mix between a cry and a yodel, "Where is Colonel Arnold? Where is Colonel Arnold?" As he swung his head side to side, frost and melting snow pelted the floor. One of the doctors ran up to him to try to calm him down.

Ignoring my pain, I tried to say in as calm a manner as possible, "Over here, son." He still could not hear me, so I said as loudly as I could, "Over here, soldier." That seemed to startle him to reality. The doctor reached forward to try to take his coat, but the soldier pushed him away and stomped toward me. I propped myself up in bed as he approached.

With a loose salute, he approached, still bewildered. "Colonel Arnold, sir?"

He was a part of Montgomery's soldiers brought up from Montreal, so I did not know him. Without answering his direct question, I barked in a way intended to keep him focused, "What do you have to report?"

Suddenly understanding where he was and who he was talking to, he reached up to pull the scarf from around his neck and removed his hat, holding it in front of him. "Mr. Ogden sends his compliments. He says to tell you that the Brits are pouring out of the city and a counterattack is coming. We are about a mile from the gates now, and he says you should pull back and move the wounded."

At that moment, the wounded soldier next to me, who had previously been unconscious, began to groan and thrash about. As the terrified boy stared at me, waiting for orders, from the corner of my eye I saw the doctors whispering, clearly already thinking about how to move the wounded men. I understood immediately that such an endeavor would be impractical—most men would have to be abandoned here, and captured by the British, likely with me among them.

Looking past the boy standing at the foot of my bed, I snapped at the doctor, "Where are my sword and pistols?" Uncomprehending, he stood slack-jawed and stared at me. I then shouted to the whole room, "Listen to me, every last one of you. There will be no retreat. There will be no withdrawal. Besides, we don't have the men, horses, or wagons to make it possible. If the Brits come, they will run you through on your beds. I don't know about you, but I am not going to get bayonetted without a fight."

Pointing to the surprised young messenger, I ordered, "You heard me. Go and get as many guns as you can. I want every weapon loaded, primed, and put next to each soldier who can still lift an arm and shoot. We will kill as many of the bastards as possible if they come into the room."

The attack never came, and the gunfire in the distance slowly gave way to silence. I had no idea what had happened to Morgan or Montgomery's attacking forces.

Captain Isaiah Wool arrived at the hospital later that night and told the story of General Montgomery's attack. Two miles south of the city, General Montgomery had led his New Yorkers in a pencil-thin column up the path used in the French and Indian War. Hugging the cliff, his column had stumbled into blinding snow and become strung out over several hundred yards. Great slabs of ice had been pushed by the river up onto the narrow strip of land, partially blocking Montgomery's way and forcing him and his men to proceed next to a sheer granite cliff to their left. It was already five in the morning when they found a barricade blocking their path.

Montgomery's men used a saw and cut a hole. As they crawled through the opening, they found themselves facing a two-story blockhouse and unmanned barricade about fifty yards away. Behind the structure appeared an unprotected Lower Town with no enemy in sight.

Montgomery cautiously approached. Taking out his sword, he signaled to rush this final barricade between them and Lower Town. As he led the charge, he yelled to his men, "Men of New York, you will not fear to follow where your general leads . . . come on, my brave boys, Quebec is ours!"

He and his officers had gotten within forty feet of the next barricade and blockhouse when shutters popped open and three cannon on the second story erupted with a billow of smoke and a tongue of flame, ejecting grapeshot. The cannons were essentially giant blunderbusses, striking Montgomery simultaneously in both thighs and his head. He was dead before his body hit the ground.

Most of Montgomery's staff, fourteen officers in all, were struck in this initial volley. Aaron Burr, along with Montgomery's second-in-command, Colonel Donald Campbell, scrambled back to the first barricade. Small-arms fire then erupted from troops hidden in the blockhouse and behind a barricade. I was later told that while many of the officers were dead, there were still a substantial number of men available who could have easily outflanked the blockhouse and continued the attack. Colonel Campbell, a well-known blowhard, rather than taking command, chose to consult his remaining panicky officers, and retreated, abandoning the dead and wounded where they fell, not pausing until they reached the safety of the Plains of Abraham. As a practical matter, General Montgomery's assault ended the moment the remains of his noble head touched the snow-covered ground. Here again, the retreat of Campbell allowed the British to further shift and concentrate their forces on repulsing the only other viable attack into Lower Town, led by me.

Chapter 30

Plains of Abraham, Canada – January 1, 1776

A round noon, Major Meigs came into our hospital guarded by a British soldier. Meigs informed me that those soldiers still alive under his command were now the captives of General Guy Carleton. The British had allowed Meigs to come to camp to pick up the prisoners' baggage. Meigs told me that every field officer, except for Colonel Campbell and Major Brown, had been killed, wounded, or captured. A total of 426 Americans had been taken prisoner, with 130 dead, and at least 100 had deserted from Montgomery's New Yorkers. I had to stifle my tears when the death of General Montgomery was reconfirmed. I could not help but think of General Wolfe, who had also died at the gates of Quebec, lamenting: "The paths of glory lead but to the grave."

My only solace was that it appeared Governor Carleton was treating my men very humanely. I, of course, released the baggage to Major Meigs that he might distribute it among our surviving officers. Indeed, when Montgomery's widow later asked for the general's watch, I sent a letter to Carleton, offering to pay any price for its return. Carleton gallantly secured the timepiece and returned it to me, refusing to accept any payment. I passed it on to Montgomery's bride with my deepest sympathy.

I later learned that after I was carried away, Daniel Morgan led his men to the next ten-foot-tall barricade, where he was first to climb over. Just as he got to the top of the wall, there was a tremendous blast, and he fell backward into the snow, stained with gunpowder and bleeding from the nose. Undaunted, he immediately scaled the ladders again and leaped over the wall. Three hundred Americans poured over the wall into Lower Town and reached the spot where they were supposed to rendezvous with Montgomery's force. Lower Town appeared to be Morgan's for the taking, but his fellow officers were unnerved. Fear and caution, those insidious twins that turn so many battles, raised their ugly heads. The "plan" contemplated meeting Montgomery. Unaware of his death and the cowardly retreat of Campbell, Morgan's officers counseled patience, and Morgan reluctantly acquiesced. He later claimed that hesitation cost us the ability to take the town, and I heartily agree.

The loss of momentum was confirmed when suddenly a British officer approached Morgan's group and barked, "You are all my prisoners."

Morgan's men were confused and responded, "*Your* prisoners? We think not. You are ours."

The officer, realizing that he had outrun his men in his excitement to get to the Americans, responded coolly, "No, no, my dear creatures, I vow to God you are all mine. Don't mistake yourselves."

Morgan responded, "But where are your men?"

"Oh, make yourself easy about the matter. They are all about here, and will be with you in a twinkling," he bravely answered.

Suddenly, as promised, Morgan's men were surrounded by gunfire and forced to take cover in alleys and doorways. He and his troops were pushed back into the surrounding homes and forced to fight house to house. The superior numbers told the tale, despite the accuracy of Morgan's riflemen.

One of Morgan's men later told me, "Our men were mowed down in heaps." John Lamb was shot in the left eye. Lieutenant Archibald Steele had three fingers blown off. Major Meigs was wounded, and young John Henry saw a friend take a bullet in the chest. Nevertheless, Meigs pressed on, but got lost in the snow-covered streets, twice missing the street leading to Morgan's trapped riflemen. Likewise, reinforcements under Dearborn were surrounded by five hundred of Colonel MacLean's loyalist troops. More than 150 of Morgan's men were killed or wounded, and most were out of ammunition.

By ten o'clock in the morning, the entire force had been killed, wounded, or captured—all except Daniel Morgan, who was unwilling to endure another British lashing. He stood against a wall, violently swinging his sword. Spotting a man in robes among the onlookers, he shouted, "Are you a priest?"

When the man said yes, he was, Morgan responded, "Then I give my sword to you, but no scoundrel of these cowards shall take it out of my hands." With a bow from the priest as he took the sword, the indomitable Morgan was finally captured.

Over the next several weeks, I directed the remainder of my small force to conduct a siege—although, truth be told, I understood we were outnumbered three to one, and if the British ever chose to sally out from the safety of their walls, we could be easily overwhelmed. I was down to only eight hundred men—half of whom were French-Canadian militia—yet I managed to rotate them in a manner that helped conceal my weakness to Carleton. To further hide vulnerability, I lied to the French-Canadians. I told them General Montgomery was on a long reconnaissance to the north, fearing disclosure of his death would further undermine our position.

My "army" was like a flock of sheep besieging a hungry wolf. The only thing that saved us from being gobbled up was Carleton's timidity.

Upon Montgomery's death, General David Wooster was in command of American forces in the north. Wooster was the same man I had threatened when he refused to give ammunition to my Foot Guard, eight months earlier in New Haven. Nevertheless, he reported to General Washington, "Arnold has, to his great honor, kept up the blockade with such a handful of men, that the story, when told hereafter, will be scarcely credited."

In my own letter to Washington, I said, "The repeated successes of our raw, undisciplined troops over the flower of the British army, and the many unexpected and remarkable occurrences in our favor are plain proofs of the overruling hand of Providence, and justly demands our warmest gratitude to heaven which I make no doubt will crown our virtuous efforts with success." I knew it was a hollow attempt to blockade the city. Many of my soldiers had left when their enlistments ended in January, and I did not have enough men to stop supplies from reaching the city.

While unsuccessful, the news of my harrowing overland journey, the attack, and my wounding began to reach the American colonies. General Schuyler noted, "Colonel Arnold's march does him great honor; some future historian will make it the subject of admiration to his readers."

Washington wrote, "The merit of this gentleman is certainly great, I heartily wish that fortune may distinguish him as one of her favorites." Washington promoted me to brigadier general, saying, "My thanks are due, and sincerely offered to you for your enterprising and preserving spirit."

Thanking Washington for his compliments, I wrote back, "I am greatly obliged to you for your good wishes, and the concern you express for me. I have the pleasure to inform you, my wound is entirely healed, and I am able to hobble about my room, though my leg is a little contracted and weak. I hope soon to be fit for action."

I wrote to Hannah to give her an update:

Camp before Quebec, January 6, 1776

My Dear Sister,

Before this reaches you I make no doubt that you will have heard of our misfortune of the 31st ultimo and will be anxious for my safety. I should have wrote you before, but a continual hurry of business has prevented me.

I have no thoughts of leaving this proud town until I enter it first in triumph. My wound has been exceeding painful, but is now easy, and the surgeons assure me will be well in eight weeks. I know you will be anxious for me in eight weeks. The Providence, which has carried me through so many dangers, is still my protection. I am in the way of my duty and know no fear.

Benedict

Meanwhile, as word spread of our arduous journey and my

leadership, Dr. Church, who had treated me unfairly in auditing my expenses on Lake Champlain, fell into disrepute. General Washington, along with my friend Silas Deane, wrote confirming the Continental Congress was paying the entire debt owed to me.

Weeks of a fruitless siege turned into months of cold boredom. General Wooster finally arrived in Quebec in early April. Not surprisingly, given our history, he was cool in his treatment of me. It was made clear to me that my presence at Quebec was no longer either required or desired. Thus, I asked and was granted permission by General Schuyler to travel to Montreal to recuperate. By this point, I was convinced that a continued siege against Quebec would be fruitless and that a British counterattack was far more likely.

Chapter 31

Montreal, Canada - April 27, 1776

After I assumed command of the American troops in Montreal and settled into my quarters at the Château de Ramezay, I began meeting with prominent inhabitants in an attempt to bolster our position. I realized that a retreat might be necessary, so I ordered Colonel Moses Hazen to man the forts at Chambly and St. John as well as send four battalions of soldiers from New Hampshire to guard our flanks some forty-five miles to the southwest of Montreal.

At the end of April, Major General John Thomas appeared at my château to present his compliments and take over the Canadian command. The fifty-one-year-old Thomas was a physician with military experience who'd served during the French and Indian War. Broad-shouldered and tall, he had fought bravely, using the cannon I seized at Fort Ticonderoga, to drive the British out of Boston. Despite my frustration that he had been promoted over me despite my accomplishments, I stood and bowed respectfully as he entered the château drawing room that I had been using as an office.

Without any preamble, Thomas said, "General Arnold, I am here to take command of forces in Canada. Do you acknowledge my authority?"

Somewhat surprised and offended by both his tone and question, I answered, "Of course, General." While I certainly believe in military discipline and formality, it can be used to the point of rudeness—that was evidently Thomas's intent.

He walked past me and sat down in my large chair behind the desk I had been using. "I would be grateful if you could acquaint me with the current and accurate status of our fortifications, our troops, and the disposition of the enemy."

So, this is the way it will be. Proper formality, nothing more. Moving to face him from in front of the desk, I answered coolly, "I view it as my duty, sir, to give you nothing less. Our position is weak. If we can get adequate support while the St. Lawrence is still frozen, Quebec and perhaps all of Canada could be ours. Conversely, if we are unable to defeat the British this winter, a fleet will no doubt arrive in the spring. They will then take Quebec, Montreal, and then Lake Champlain. Indeed, all New England will be vulnerable. This is our opportunity to stop the British in their tracks. We need energetic leadership and support from Congress."

As he stared back, expressionless, I continued, "I do not believe General Wooster is capable of stopping, or even materially slowing, the British advance from the north. There are several choke points between Montreal and Quebec that will permit us to inflict severe damage on the British as they move south, especially with strategic placement of artillery. Montreal itself, as I am sure you gathered on your arrival, is indefensible."

Nodding knowingly, Thomas replied, "I will do my best, and I believe a congressional commission may appear at some point. Regardless, we will do our duty and delay—and, as you say, do as much damage as we can."

I handed him a map showing both the choke points and specific locations for artillery placement. He rolled up the map and placed it under his arm; then, without warmth, he snapped, "Thank you, General Arnold. As I expected, you were well prepared and have thought about matters. Your reputation for tactical skill is warranted. I will obviously move out and inspect the fortifications and choke points all the way to Quebec as soon as possible."

As he was leaving, I said, "Quarters have been prepared for you; I trust you will find them to your satisfaction." I had earlier asked my staff to move his baggage into the nicest room in the château.

With more of a grimace than a smile, Thomas said, "I don't suspect either of us will be here much longer, but we shall do our best to place ourselves in the good Lord's hands." With that, he was out the door.

Chapter 32

Montreal, Canada – May 6, 1776

The aptly named HMS *Surprize* came into view off Quebec at six o'clock in the morning just nine days later. The British ship had raced ahead of a large convoy that had broken through the ice field in April. The convoy of fifteen ships, carrying ten thousand redcoats, was moving inland from Anticosti Island. No doubt the English were pleased to see the Union Jack still fluttering above Quebec. A large army formed on the Plains of Abraham, consisting of disembarked redcoats, local militia, and Carleton's eight hundred highlanders.

Apparently, our remaining troops saw their fate reflected in the gleaming bayonets of the immaculately presented British troops—ignoring their officers, they ran. As panicked troops moved along the St. Lawrence, the British frigates HMS *Surprize* and HMS *Martin* raked the retreating soldiers with gunfire. The troops arrived in Montreal scared, disorganized, and exhausted. Thomas had failed to follow my advice and hold the choke point at Deschambault, but the ultimate failure rested with Congress. It had dallied in providing us with resources—an army without support is like a starving tree cut from its roots.

Worst of all, Congress undercut my promises to local civilians who had risked all to support us. The hypocrites in Philadelphia left our allies to suffer at the sharp end of the bayonet as the British unleashed revenge on Canadian patriots.

Thomas and I finally reunited in a half-empty warehouse near the water in Montreal. I was shocked at his appearance—shadowlike bruises lay under his tired eyes. I knew this was more than mere fatigue. Weakened men were often vulnerable to smallpox. I asked, "Sir, have you been inoculated?"

With what energy he had, Thomas bristled. "Of course not. I

would never presume to usurp the Lord's will." Collapsing to sit on a nearby crate, he croaked, "I am glad you raised the issue, General. I understand you have been ordering men to be inoculated. That must stop immediately."

I was incredulous. "Sir, inoculations have been done for fifty years. General Washington encourages inoculations. We are going to lose our army if we don't act. Two-thirds of our men are already seriously ill."

Thomas was an inflexible puritan, which I knew too well from my days in Connecticut. There was nothing I could say or do that would soften his obstinacy. Shaking his head with what appeared to be great effort, he said, "Let me be clear, General. I have signed an order that bans inoculations. Proceeding in this manner is a capital offense. You will cease all inoculations immediately. Am I understood?"

God help us all. I don't think I hid my disapproval when I acknowledged his order. "Yes, sir."

"Good—then let's get to the business of the day. We need to stop the British ships that are attacking our troops. I understand your ship the *Peggy* is in Montreal."

"Yes, General. She was here as part of her normal routes and got caught in the melee. My captain and I discussed her status. We believe we will be able to get her out. We have some friends in Canada who might make that possible."

"I'm afraid, General, the Cause requires another sacrifice from you. I think your ship is lost in any event. The British will capture it as they move south, so I would rather see it put to good use. I propose to make the *Peggy* a fire ship and ram it into the British ships. I have spoken with several men who believe they can successfully make this happen tomorrow night. Obviously, we would need to unload your ship and load it with whatever powder we can find."

This is almost as idiotic as banning smallpox inoculations. I tried to hide my exasperation. "General Thomas. First, I want to emphasize that I have no problem making a sacrifice for the Cause. Indeed, my fortune has largely evaporated at the feet of our Revolution. Second, we have limited powder, and loading the ship with our reserves would further deplete our ability to defend against the British advance. Finally, I have never seen a fireship successfully used. Here, the British only have two ships. If there were a heavy concentration of British ships, then it might work, but given the currents of the St. Lawrence, the presence of ice, and the limited targets we will be going after, I see it as a wasteful act of futility."

As I spoke, Thomas put his head in his hands. He was so fatigued that he could barely function, and it was also clear that he was not listening to me. Without looking up, he answered, "Be that as it may, General., it is an opportunity, even if unsuccessful, to stop the British ships. I have ordered the endeavor to proceed. I would suggest that if there is anything on the vessel you want, you get it immediately."

"And the loss of my ship?" I asked, without outright demanding reimbursement for the cost.

Placing both his hands on his knees and with great effort, Thomas stood and sighed. "The fortunes of war, General." Briefly resting his hand on my shoulder, he walked past me.

I watched from the shore as Thomas and his men botched the attempt. As I predicted, British watchmen detected the *Peggy* long before she reached her targets. Accurate British artillery exploded my ship two hundred yards from the harbor entrance, doing no harm to British shipping. *"Fortunes of war"? By Christ! That ship represented years of work and more money than most people would make in their whole miserable lives! I've paid for innumerable expenses and have not been compensated, but now I'm being struck to the very core. No one gives a wit for me and all that I have sacrificed. Fortunes of god-damned war indeed. You bloody bastard!*

As to General Thomas's decision to prohibit inoculations—may the good Lord forgive me for saying this—I was not surprised to be vindicated when he died within two weeks of contracting the disease.

Meanwhile, the main British army marched and sailed along the St. Lawrence, forcing the surrender of five hundred men. I sent a message to the British commander indicating that I would hold him personally accountable if the Indians harmed any of my men who were now their prisoners; the coward replied that if we attacked the British, the Indians would slaughter the prisoners. Enraged, I was torn between the safety of my men and freeing them from captivity.

On May 26, I decided to risk an attack at La Chine. I led eighteen canoes toward the British camp. We avoided fatalities, owing to poorly aimed British grapeshot, but were forced to reluctantly retreat. I realized a more aggressive attack was required. With the death of General Thomas, I was now the senior commander. Nevertheless, I believed a council of war needed to be convened to justify a counteroffensive of the size I had planned and to rescue our soldiers being held prisoner.

Almost immediately, Colonel Moses Hazen rose in opposition, making only a cursory nod of respect to me as he addressed the group. "I believe a further attack is foolhardy. We will be sacrificing our men held in captivity, and for what? We are in retreat. General Arnold proposes to use what little resources we have in an errant mission and a reckless counterattack."

It was obvious that Hazen had spoken with many of the officers ahead of time; several nodded in agreement. I chose not to rise from my chair because, as the senior officer present, it was not my obligation. Moreover, I didn't believe this group of men warranted the respect. I responded, not bothering to hide my contempt, "First of all, we know that the British will not slaughter our men if we attack. I have already led an attack, and if that was their intent, the men would already be dead. Second, by seizing the initiative, we will slow down the British advance. Waiting for them to come to us in our current indefensible positions is folly."

Without standing—a clear insult to me—Hazen snapped, "Who will lead this expedition, General?" The last word sounded as though he were spitting on the floor.

I knew Hazen was a coward—this was an opportunity for me to call him out. "Surely not you, Hazen." I deliberately did not use his rank to return the insult. "We all know where you stand when it comes to facing the enemy. I have nothing to prove. Nevertheless, I will lead the expedition."

I could not hide my disgust when Hazen did not stand at my challenge, or even invite me to the field of honor, which any self-respecting gentleman would have done in the face of my criticism. Leaning back in his chair, he said with a self-satisfied smile, "I believe my prior actions refute your statement, General. Moreover, your rudeness and intemperate nature are what is most revealed today. Further discussions are fruitless. I call the question." As preordained by Hazen, I was outvoted.

The next day I reconvened the council of war. Without preamble, I held a paper in my hand. "Let this be a valuable lesson to all of you, gentlemen. You overestimated the enemy's resolve. Indeed, not only were our prisoners safe, but the British were ready to collapse. The British commander is offering to release our men if we will allow the British to withdraw their small force of redcoats and Indians to rejoin the main British army. Captain . . ." Pausing to read the paper, I continued, "Captain Foster says that if we do not accept the terms, he will allow his Indian allies to slaughter the prisoners. Foster requires us to promise that our men will no longer fight for the patriot cause."

The haughty Hazen quipped, "I beg to differ, General. I believe what this shows is that an attack was unnecessary, and that the British are still resolved to massacre our men if we don't comply."

I tried to take a calming breath. "My God, man. Do you understand nothing about power or how to negotiate? Only a fool, or in your case a coward, accepts the first offer." Taking up my quill, I declared, "We will delete the sentence about our boys being unable to fight. I will also send a note indicating that we will attack and slaughter the British if a single hair on one of our men is touched."

Hazen objected with a huff, "But General, we have already voted not to attack. Are you defying your own council of war?"

"I do not require a vote to correspond with the enemy. In any event, I am bluffing, but Foster will accept my terms. Mark my words."

The next day, Foster agreed to my change—the prisoners were

exchanged on May 28. I made a point of having Colonel Hazen meet the men to rub his nose in my triumph.

Recognizing that the men did not have enough supplies for the long retreat to New York, I ordered the seizure of blankets, food, and clothing from the merchants of Montreal, leaving IOUs from Congress. I sent what supplies I could to St. John and ordered Colonel Hazen to coordinate their distribution. While this action undermined my relationship with the few French-Canadians who were still our allies, I had received instructions from Congress to seize provisions since the Canadians would no longer accept our currency.

Hazen refused to sign for the goods I obtained or see they were properly stored and guarded. Instead of protecting the provisions, he left them for the retreating soldiers to grab haphazardly as they passed through. He himself abandoned his post and headed south.

No map or compass was necessary to see the way south. The detritus of our retreating army—guns, knapsacks, clothing, and the dead and dying—marked the path from Montreal to Lake Champlain. An army on the move is like any crowd of people. When well-fed and confident, it is a cacophony—talking, laughing, and even singing mixed with the sounds of horses and wagon wheels moving at a healthy clip. An army in retreat is quiet. Horses and men plod on, heads down, stumbling on rocks and ruts, shortening their strides with each passing mile. It is a parade of death engulfed by the smell of blood, bowels, and fear.

I commanded a rear guard as men boarded overloaded bateaux on the Richelieu, heading south toward Lake Champlain. We completely stripped St. John, even dismantling a British warship for parts that we loaded onto the bateaux.

On June 18, the pall of dust on the horizon heralded the approaching British army. I rode through town, ensuring that every building in St. John was set ablaze. The once attractive little village was now as hideous as an exit wound.

It was only when I heard the British drums that my aide James

Wilkinson and I galloped our exhausted mounts to the edge of the river. Jumping from my fine steed, I stood for a moment with my head against the saddle as I waited for my legs to uncramp. I dearly wished I had an apple to thank my horse and show a final act of kindness in an unfair world.

I determined that the British would get nothing of use. I pulled my saddle off, drew my pistol, and pulled the trigger against my horse's head. When I ordered Wilkinson to do likewise, he hesitated and gave me an imploring look. While I loved horses to my core, I hated the enemy far more—I said nothing.

Closing his eyes, Wilkinson pulled the trigger, and his horse, too, toppled to the ground. As bullets hit the ground and water around us, we climbed into our canoe and pushed into the river. Paddling furiously, with me at the stern, I was truly the last American out of Canada.

An hour and a half after leaving my dead horse and the British in St. John, I arrived at the most miserable location this side of Hades. A large portion of the retreating army, devastated not only by starvation and exhaustion but by smallpox and dysentery, was forced to stop at Isle aux Noix.

The smell of smallpox is unique. The corrupted skin of the "pox" gives off a distinctive sweet odor that has been described as a "hen house on a warm April morning."

The sick and wounded were assailed in the mire by swarms of blood-thirsty blackflies and mosquitoes. Fever raged, burning the life out of men, leaving only empty, pockmarked husks to mark what once had been an army. Helpless soldiers were left to the ravages of field creatures literally eating them alive. Putrefied wounds crawled with maggots. Men died in scores. While I have seen awful sights in my life, my memories of the death and agony of those men have never been surpassed.

Chapter 33

Albany, NY - June 24, 1776

With a mixture of relief and guilt, I obeyed the order to leave Isle aux Noix with my aide and meet with General Schuyler at Fort Ticonderoga. I was disoriented by the contrast between the death we had just witnessed and the sublime beauty of the stands of maple, birch, and hemlock abutting the shore, with the towering Adirondacks bathed in brilliant sunshine.

When we arrived at the fort, we were told Schuyler was at his headquarters in Albany; thus we pressed on, arriving near midnight. Despite the late hour, the general greeted us warmly. After initial pleasantries, we dismissed Wilkinson so Schuyler and I could talk freely.

Filthy and exhausted from hard riding, I felt ill at ease in Schuyler's immaculate study, standing before a man who looked to the world like a painting of a refined general. Perhaps sensing my discomfort, Schuyler let a warm smile spread across his deeply lined face. "Please, General, sit down. Don't worry about the mud on your boots. I know every mile was hard-earned." Walking over, he handed me a large glass of ale and pointed to meats, bread, and a pitcher of water at the table. "I have found that when I am tired and thirsty, I prefer ale over wine. The water is also quite good here. Please eat. I don't want you falling over while you are talking to me."

"I do not think I am that far gone yet, General, but I am grateful for your courtesies."

As he returned to his seat, his smile evaporated with the seriousness of the situation. "Please update me on recent events and the tactical situation."

I recounted the desperate retreat from Montreal and down Lake Champlain. He listened without comment until I was done, then asked,

"Given our current situation, what should be our future dispositions?" Pointing to the table, he added, "Before you answer, I insist you take a drink and at least a bite of a food."

I ate a morsel and took a drink as he waited patiently. Once finished, I said, "We should retreat down as far as Crown Point and Fort Ti, as they are more defensible positions."

Schuyler pulled over a piece of paper from his desk and began to scrawl. When he was done, he said, "I defer to your judgment on this issue, General. I have just issued an order as you recommended." He walked across the room, opened the door, and was met immediately by his aide-de-camp, who took the order without comment.

I took the moment to have another bit of refreshment. As Schuyler sat down, he said, "Pray, finish, then continue."

Wiping my mouth with a napkin, I set the food aside. I was already feeling stronger. "I regret that Generals John Sullivan and David Wooster as political appointees have neither the courage nor the military temperament to lead."

The general raised his eyes to the ceiling as if praying for deliverance. "You are correct on both fronts, Benedict, and because they are 'politicals,' there is not much I can do about it. I must set aside hope that they will stop the British advance. However, you can be assured that either you or I will be blamed for the retreat—their friends in Congress will protect them."

After a long pause, realizing that the general had nothing more to add, I continued, "The British will eventually move to recapture Forts Crown Point and Ticonderoga, and ultimately the region. They want to cut New England off from the colonies. To stop this from happening, first and foremost, we need to have adequate reserves of both supplies and troops. Second, we need to construct a fleet to repulse the vessels that the British will be building in St. John. Third, given Carleton's temperament, he will not make bold and offensive strokes, so we have some time to build our own navy."

Schuyler had been looking out the window as I was speaking; now he turned back to me, locking me in his gaze. "So what you are saying is we must act aggressively now or lose the initiative and maybe all of New England?"

I nodded.

"Within a fortnight, I will convene a meeting of the Northern Department generals. I believe you may be my man to construct our navy. What say you?"

I shrugged in agreement. I was too tired to weigh the offer in a meaningful way.

"Very well—I must now reach out and build support for what you propose. Get some rest. We will have much work to do, my young friend."

Before we parted, Schuyler told me that Congress had made Major General Horatio Gates the commander in Canada. I had previously met General Gates when he was Washington's adjutant and I was planning the attack on Quebec. We got along quite well, and I had a favorable impression of him. I knew Gates was well-liked in New England and had been born in humble beginnings in England. He had fought bravely in the French and Indian War, where he became an acquaintance of General Washington. Only fifty, he was already stooped, with a double chin and wispy gray hair; his weak eyes required spectacles that sat on the end of his nose. His disheveled appearance added to a lack of military bearing and his nickname of "Granny Gates." While I sensed some unease from General Schuyler about the appointment, nothing was said explicitly.

I stood, bowed, and left the room, guided by his aide to a small but well-appointed room. I managed to get my dirty clothes off before I collapsed into the bed and slept for ten straight hours.

Horatio Gates
Engraving by C. Tiebout of painting by G. Stuart.
Courtesy of Yale University Art Gallery

Chapter 34

Crown Point, NY – July 7, 1776

The five general officers charged with defending New York and New England and repulsing the coming British invasion met at Crown Point for a council of war. In the fields surrounding the meeting, most of the army was either sick or dying. The stench of decay filled the summer air.

We travel-weary generals, adorned in our finest uniforms, sat behind closed doors and windows in a stiflingly hot ramshackle building. Despite our fatigue, there was an air of professionalism and courtesy which I found hopeful. After initial pleasantries, General Schuyler, as the senior officer present, bade us all sit around an imposing, polished round table at odds with the rough-hewn and recently repaired officer's mess—no doubt it had been liberated from a local loyalist. A large area map was tacked on the wall behind my chair.

The most senior officers present were Major Generals Philip Schuyler and Horatio Gates. The aristocratic Schuyler and the rumpled Horatio Gates clearly disliked each other. While Gates had done an excellent job reorganizing Washington's army and demonstrated an aptitude for European-style staff work, he and Washington had also found themselves at odds. When Washington had wanted to attack Boston over the ice the preceding winter, Gates had opposed the strategy at a council of war and outvoted him, forcing His Excellency to abandon the plan.

Nor had Gates stopped there—next he had gone to Congress and criticized Schuyler's handling of the Canadian campaign, winning over John Adams. With Adams's help, Gates sought to have complete command over the Canadian campaign. Schuyler had been unaware of this intrigue and had initially cordially invited the newly promoted Major General Gates to stay with him at his manor house. By the time Gates arrived at our meeting, there was effectively no Canadian army to lead in the field, and all cordiality between the generals was over.

What was left of the Canadian army now sat on New York soil at Crown Point, under Schuyler's direction. Gates took the position that Congress intended him to relieve Schuyler of overall command. Schuyler pointed out that he had been elevated to the rank of major general a full year before Gates and thus was senior. Reluctantly, Gates agreed to subordinate himself temporarily to Schuyler while he appealed to Congress to impose "harmony."

I was ordered to report to General Gates, who in turn would be subordinate to General Schuyler. I did not see this as a problem, as I had excellent working relationships with both major generals—though at least for my part, I recognized that the regal General Schuyler should be in command and preside over the meeting. The gaunt John Sullivan sat across from me at the middle of the table. Gates was to Schuyler's immediate right, in a position of honor. To Gates's right was the stern Friedrich Wilhelm, Baron de Woedtke, appointed as a brigadier to serve on the Canadian expedition. I sat to Woedtke's right. I was the newests, and thus lowest-ranking general officer present.

As was tradition, as the most junior officer, it was my duty to provide a briefing on the current tactical situation and propose the best approach going forward. Many junior officers loathed this responsibility, as it not only required a detailed knowledge of facts but also forced them to present a plan to their superiors. These initial proposals were often subject to ridicule and "second-guessing." However, I knew more about the current tactical situation than anyone present and thus relished the opportunity to offer my views.

General Schuyler turned with an open hand, pointing simultaneously at me and the map. "General Arnold, if you may."

I had intended to essentially repeat what he and I had discussed, but I understood he wanted me to lay out the entire situation for all the generals. Standing carefully, I bowed first to General Schuyler, then to all the other generals in turn. I then moved my chair silently back into place and slid over to stand next to the map. "Generals, we face a challenging tactical situation. Light British infantry are probing through the forest as they move southward. The area immediately surrounding our fort is defended by sick, dying, and unmotivated soldiers."

I pointed to the map. "On the northern end of the lake, in addition to ten thousand British regulars, there are two thousand German mercenaries and seven hundred handpicked crewman from the Royal Navy, all ready to attack. With royal engineers, shipwrights, carpenters, and blacksmiths, the British are building at least twenty-five warships, some of which are being disassembled and carried ten miles overland to St. John to be used on Lake Champlain. Their goal is to push us off the lake, move down the Hudson, and regain control of New York City. This, as I discussed with General Schuyler, will have the effect of slicing our new nation in two, cleaving the troublesome New Englanders from the rest of the colonies." I made a point of looking at General Gates, who nodded with a wry smile at my quip.

Turning back to the map, I explained, "We have heard rumors the British light infantry is cutting a road along the eastern shore of the lake. While a land route is not likely, they may get close enough to engage in harassing attacks. We certainly do not want to leave our men so spread out that they cannot defend themselves. To that end, Fort Amhurst cannot be held, as it faces the wrong way to defend an attack from the north. It was built by the French to thwart a British invasion from the south. I do not believe the fort can be rebuilt in time—it should be abandoned."

I gestured to a poorly patched hole in the wall. "Likewise, this fort is not defensible. Its ramparts are in terrible condition. This poor excuse for a building is the best Crown Point has to offer. We should concentrate our forces at Ticonderoga. It sits on better ground, with better defenses, and is facing the optimal direction to meet the British. As importantly, we need to transport our sick soldiers away from here as soon as possible. We cannot risk having them further infect the able-bodied men that remain under our command. Moreover, if we can move them further south, they are likely to receive better care than we can offer here."

General Schuyler interjected, "I have requested as many wagons as possible be sent north for exactly that purpose."

Gates piped in, "As have I."

The tension in the room increased, as everyone was aware that both Gates and Schuyler were claiming command. I chose to focus on the positive. "That is indeed good news." I bowed to both generals; then, facing the whole group, I continued, "Those are some immediate actions we can take. But what of the enemy? What of General Carleton and his likely next steps? I discussed General Carleton extensively with General Montgomery."

At the mention of this martyr's name, all the men looked down in sadness. Out of respect, I paused briefly, then said, "He had prior experience with Carleton. His assessment matched my own during the siege of Quebec. At almost any time, Carleton could have come out and defeated our depleted forces, but he stayed within his bastion. I believe he will be cautious and does not relish a winter campaign. His delay will give us time to obtain assistance from the south. Meanwhile, we can construct new fortifications at Fort Ticonderoga to slow any assault on New York and protect New England." I chose this last phrase carefully—I knew Schuyler would want to protect New York, while Gates wanted to shield New England.

With a rare nod of approval from both generals, I grew more confident. "The British will likely take a substantial amount of time building their fleet. Moreover, recent heavy rains will make travel from Quebec to St. John extremely difficult. In the meantime, I believe we can build an American fleet that could destroy barges carrying British infantry as they come down the lake. For every ship we build, the British will be further delayed, as they must build more and bigger ships with superior firepower. This race might cost the British a season of war and give us precious time to rally, dig in, and rebuild our forts.

"You see, Generals, the British are a deepwater navy. That informs their thinking and design. They will create ships with large keels, heavy guns, and deep drafts. We don't need ships capable of surviving an ocean voyage. We need ships that can navigate and fight on Lake Champlain. We need primarily gondolas and armed galleys."

I had brought with me plans for the ships I intended to build, but I had not placed them on the table, not wanting to appear presumptuous. I also knew my ideas might be met with resistance, so I hesitated to commit. However, based upon the men's prior reactions, I took the chance, reaching down into my satchel and pulling out the large drawings. At this point, all the generals stood and began leaning over, trying to get a closer look.

Placing the larger of the two drawings on top, I explained, "The gondolas will be flat bottomed, with a single or dual square mast that can only move with the wind. They will have a large 'barn door' rudder for steering. The boat's mast will be forty to fifty feet high, about as tall as the boats are long. The vessel will be equipped with long sweep oars for rowing in the calm or going against the wind. Each will accommodate forty-five crewmen; they will be armed with a twelve-pounder in the bow, two or four nine-pounders amidships, and eight swivel guns." The officers all seemed rapt by my explanations, nodding to each other as they reviewed my detailed drawings.

Now, the blood singing in my ears with excitement, I placed the other drawing on top. "The larger two-masted row galleys, some seventy or eighty feet in length, will use guns salvaged from Forts Crown Point and Ticonderoga. They will be fitted with lateen sails, making them maneuverable in any direction. The row galleys, as you can see in the drawings, will have quarterdecks and cabins and space for eighty crew. They will have a curved hull and a keel like a sloop or schooner. Armament will consist of a single twelve- or eighteen-pound cannon in the bow; three or four six-pounders on each side, which will project through holes in the rail, well above the water line; there will be two nine-pounders in the stern; as well as up to sixteen swivel guns. With shallow drafts, they will be perfect for rivers and coves, and could be propelled by their crews by hauling eighteen deep oars.

"Finally, we need to build at least one 'ship of the line' to meet the larger British ships. Here I am looking for a schooner of approximately

120 tons, carrying at least a half dozen twelve-pound cannon. It will have full oceangoing sails and at least an eighty-man crew. This should allow us to go toe-to-toe with any British ship.

"I believe my designs, specifically adapted to the conditions, will give us a tremendous advantage against the enemy. Ideally, our fleet should consist of one large ship of the line, eight to ten row galleys, and eight gondolas—twenty ships in all to face a British force and slow their invasion."

As they continued to look at the plans, I plunged on. "I will need a thousand workmen and five hundred experienced shipwrights and carpenters, and as many axemen as possible to fell timbers. Most of all, I will need nine hundred experienced seamen to sail our fleet."

As the generals moved back into their chairs and faced me, I concluded, "Generals, I believe this can be done. It requires a fierce commitment of both time and money. The alternative, the splitting of the Colonies, is unimaginable." With that, I smartly bowed and returned to my seat.

Broad smiles and nods came from all around the table. Turning to the other men, General Schuyler said, "Does anyone have an alternate plan than that proposed by General Arnold?" Silence filled the room as the generals looked at each other. "Does anyone have a criticism of the plan formulated by our aggressive young general?"

Recognizing that I had forgotten to say something, I stood. "One additional matter. Normally, sailors expect to receive 'reprisals'—that is, taking prizes of enemy ships, whether warships or commercial vessels. It creates an incentive and attracts sailors. Here, there is no possibility of reprisals, so we must offer generous bonuses to attract experienced sailors."

A look of concern passed over Schuyler's normally impassive countenance. I was fully aware that the army's coffers were empty and I was asking for money that did not currently exist; however, Schuyler regained control in an instant and glanced over at Gates.

Gates responded without standing. "General Schuyler and I have already discussed many of these issues. We will do our best to obtain the financial wherewithal for you request. Forts Amhurst and Crown Point are not defensible and should be abandoned. I recognize that abandoning Crown Point will not be popular in New England, but I must agree this post is no longer tenable."

At this, he looked over at Schuyler, who tilted his head in agreement, as did the other two generals present. Gates continued, "While I am not a naval man as you are, General Arnold, I do know something about logistics and resources when it comes to this army. Your designs for gondolas and armed galley are . . ." He paused as if searching for a word, then grinned and said, ". . . brilliant. However, I believe your desire to build a large ship of the line is not practical. We simply do not have the time, money, or experience."

Schuyler spoke up, almost interrupting Gates and forestalling my objection. "I am afraid, General Arnold, that I must agree with General Gates. I think the focus needs to be on the more nimble ships. Fighting the British toe-to-toe with a ship of the line would only doom that vessel."

The irritation on Gates's face gave way to relief. Nodding to him, Schuyler added, "Thank you, General Gates, for your comments. Does anyone else have any further insight?" The two remaining officers stayed silent. "I propose that we proceed with the abandonment of the forts and the reinforcement of Ticonderoga. Additionally, General Arnold shall be placed in charge of the shipbuilding and be given broad discretion to engage in such activity as he deems appropriate, subject to the limitations we have now imposed on the types of ships. It will be our task to provide him material and men to meet his needs."

Courteously turning to me, Schuyler inquired, "General Arnold, is this acceptable to you?"

I was disappointed not to be building a ship of the line, but I relished the opportunity and deeply appreciated Schuyler's generosity— as my superior, he had not owed me the question. Standing, I bowed and replied, "Very much so. Thank you, General."

Turning to the group, Schuyler said, "All those in favor?" Unanimous ayes came from the table. He stood, signifying the meeting was over. "Farewell, gentlemen—we have much work to do and little time."

With the formal conclusion of the meeting, all walked around to congratulate me on my excellent plan and presentation.

After the meeting, Gates wrote to Congress, "General Arnold, who is perfectly skilled in naval affairs, has most nobly undertaken to command our fleet upon the lake. With infinite satisfaction, I have committed the whole of that department to his care."

Schuyler similarly wrote, "I am extremely happy that General Arnold has undertaken to command the fleet. It has relieved me from great anxiety."

I left with the powers of a commodore and the unanimous backing of my generals to construct a fleet. General Washington endorsed my plan as well, writing to Gates, "I trust neither courage nor activity will be wanting in those whom the business is committed. If the fleet is assigned to General Arnold, none will doubt his exertions." Once I arrived, General Gates encouraged me to "give life in spirit to our dockyard."

I had my work cut out for me. The men were lethargic and idle, and boat construction was haphazard; it cried out for relentless organization and discipline. However, there was a bright spot: I had an excellent location to build our ships. Skenesborough is at the narrowing of the river at the extreme southern end of the lake; it permitted placement of artillery on high nearby hills, presenting the ideal position to strike any British ships coming up the lake. Before the British could reach my shipyards, they would need to run a forty-mile gauntlet of deadly crossfire to reach our base, hidden behind an island at the elbow where Wood Creek and Lake Champlain merge. Here, a natural harbor was flanked by a protective high hill and guarded by blockhouses. At the same time, the river was also deep enough to accommodate all the boats I intended to build, and there were large sections of flat land immediately next to the river, ideal for boat building. With my men well protected, I divided crews into day and night shifts to keep things moving twenty-four hours a day.

As my men began working on new ships at Skenesborough, a messenger arrived with a copy of the Declaration of Independence. I ordered work stopped for a reading—the men listened, cheered, and immediately went back to work. In a sweltering July heat, I had teams chopping trees, sawing planks, and hammering boards together in makeshift boatyards all around the lake. The region offered abundant oak and white pine, ideal for building ships. The town had two sawmills, an iron forge, blacksmith facilities, and an expansive, gentle shoreline. We colored the ships red with the local paint used for barns.

I still needed more carpenters, more ammunition, more cannon, more nails, more rope, more blocks, more hourglasses, more spyglasses, more pots, more bowls, more cutlasses, more anchors, more of everything. Despite my protests, I was especially burdened with "landlubbers." I was desperate for men capable of rigging the sails and ropes and securing the guns. General Schuyler's aide, Captain Varick, spared no effort in procuring material for my little navy and moving it to the shipyard for construction. Unfortunately, he failed to find experienced sailors. I could hardly blame my fellow American mariners—with the lucrative opportunities available elsewhere, sailors were hard to find. Being a privateer was a great opportunity for seamen and ship owners, and indeed I could have made a fortune if I had put my ships in service of the country as privateers. Privateers obtained from the American government letters of marque and reprisal permitting privately owned ships to be heavily armed and engage in activities that would otherwise be considered piracy. Specifically, they could capture an enemy ship and keep it as a prize. The Continental Congress in March of 1776 passed uniform rules of conduct and required the posting of bonds to ensure regulations were followed.

In contrast, I received a steady stream of misfits or reluctant soldiers who were sent to me after losing when drawing lots. I did not flinch in the face of malcontents, slackers, or troublemakers—I did my best, imposing iron discipline, flogging when necessary, and also explaining the importance of our mission to the men as they arrived. My brave boys from Quebec spread the word of my worthy leadership and our noble

Cause. I was both pleased and surprised to see, as time progressed, a new élan develop.

I pressed Gates and Schuyler for help: "If you want breeches, they give you a vest. As for sailors, they give you tavern waiters." Frustrated at the inadequate support, I also wrote letters to friends in Boston and Congress demanding more supplies. At the time, my sole purpose in doing so was to obtain the necessary support to serve the mission. I later learned that these actions annoyed both Generals Schuyler and Gates.

Chapter 35

Fort Ticonderoga, NY - July 26, 1776

While I was busy begging for supplies and men and building a fleet to serve the Cause, my "real" enemies continued their assault. Colonel Moses Hazen and his fellow conspirators Easton and Brown infested Philadelphia, spreading rumors that I had robbed shopkeepers in Montreal.

I had ordered a court-martial against Hazen for his failure to do his duty in Canada. While the court-martial was based upon my charges for his malfeasance in Montreal, he quickly convinced his friends presiding over the affair to turn the tables on me. Hazen directly accused me of thievery, and I responded in kind. My aide Wilkinson spoke in my defense that he always found me to be an "intrepid, generous, friendly, upright, honest man."

The court-martial quickly digressed into chaos. I confess, I was both belligerent and at times ungentlemanly. The smug Hazen had the advantage of a court stacked with his cronies. I proclaimed with lethal courtesy to the biased judges, "As your very nice and delicate honor, in your apprehension, is injured, you may depend, as soon as this disagreeable hearing is at an end, which God grant may soon be the case, I will by no means withhold from any gentleman of the court the satisfaction his nice honor may require."

I understood that I was not going to be treated fairly; thus, my best approach was to move aggressively by challenging the entire panel of judges to a duel. To my disgust, but not surprise, on August 2, the court-martial exonerated Hazen. They then sought to impanel a court-martial of me and order my arrest.

When Gates was informed of my reaction to the farcical court-martial, he wrote, "The warmth of General Arnold's temper might possibly lead him a little further than is marked by precise line of decorum to be observed before and towards a court-martial. Seeing and knowing all the circumstances, I am convinced there was a fault on one side, there was too much controversy on the other." Nevertheless, the massing of the British fleet and the impending battle prevented Gates from allowing anything to interfere with my command. General Gates concluded, "I was obliged to act dictatorially, and dissolve the court-martial the instant they demanded General Arnold to be put under arrest. The United States must not be deprived of that excellent officer's service at this important moment."

With irony that would be humorous if it were not so painful to recall, and at the very time I was serving my country on Lake Champlain and being accused of improperly enriching myself, I received correspondence from my sister proclaiming, "If you live to return, you will find yourself a broken merchant."

Chapter 36

Skenesborough, NY – August 24, 1776

B y the time my court-martial was completed, we had built ten new ships in just five weeks. The heavily armed galleys were in the process of being rigged and armed. Our existing double-masted schooners were battle ready. They had both square and lateen sails, with port and starboard heavy-gun ports. By the end of August, our armada was growing weekly, although we were still in need of experienced sailors and gunners.

We continued to hear steady reports of British raiding parties moving as far south as Crown Point. I knew that the safest place for our fleet was out on the lake, where it could not be trapped by British infantry. I decided to send some ships out while others continued to be built. General Carleton was cautious, but even he would eventually become courageous enough to probe our weaknesses. I saw no choice. We needed to take the initiative and attack.

I led my half-completed fleet north, our newly made sails fluttering in the summer breeze. The few remaining soldiers at Crown Point cheered as our small fleet passed. After weeks of sweat, disease, and biting insects, my men and I were thrilled to be heading north and escaping the heat and smells of too many men crowded together.

My flagship, the *Royal Savage*, was a twelve-gun, seventy-ton schooner, followed by the schooner *Revenge*, mounting twelve cannon and ten swivel guns; the eight-gun schooner *Liberty*; and the ten-gun sloop *Enterprise*. These four larger ships protected the six gondolas named the *New Haven, Providence, Boston, Spitfire, Connecticut,* and *Philadelphia*. These fifty-nine-foot boats each carried forty-five men with a single large square sail. All the row galleys were still under construction in Skenesborough.

Winds at this time of year can be vicious and unpredictable, rising from a light breeze to fifty-mile-per-hour gusts in a matter of minutes. As a result, I carefully moved our squadron, keeping in mind the inexperienced seamen manning our vessels. As fate would have it, a beautiful southern breeze gave way to darkening clouds, shifting winds, and a fierce northerly gale coming up the lake. The hiss and thrum of large, stinging cold droplets began pounding the deck. The lake churned, and thunder rumbled in the distance, more felt than heard.

At sea, storms cause great swells. In a lake, a storm results in high, chopping waves that violently shake the boat and make control difficult. As the storm got closer, the flashes of lightning now nearly connected with the twin booms of thunder. I knew I had to get to the safety of a bay before the two merged.

Twenty-five-year-old Philip Ulmer was struggling with the *Spitfire* as it drifted toward the rocky shore. I grabbed my bullhorn and tried to shout instructions to him, but the wind and rain drowned my voice. I ordered a small skiff lowered from the *Royal Savage*, and four reluctant sailors joined me as we plowed through the tumult to the floundering *Spitfire*. When we got close enough, I again used the trumpet horn to instruct Ulmer to drop anchor and stop trying to keep up with the remaining ships. I was pleased to see him follow my order and drop sail to ride out the storm. When I got back to the *Royal Savage*, I was met with smiles and rare slaps on the back from my men. As a rule, the men never touch an officer, especially a commander, but we were all thrilled that we had saved the *Spitfire*. To celebrate our success, I ordered rum for my four brave rowers.

The storm raged for a full day and night. The mast of the *Connecticut* snapped, but the sailors of the *Revenge* tossed them a rope and towed the disabled ship to safety. The schooner *Liberty* went aground, but the other vessels were able to pull her into water. When the skies began to clear, my sailors all cheered when they saw the *Spitfire* come around a point to join us. We had weathered the storm without the loss of a single man or ship, and my sailors had gained invaluable experience and confidence that they would sorely need in the days ahead.

Notwithstanding these challenges, I was determined to obtain more information concerning British shipbuilding activities and troop deployments; thus, we worked our way north up the entire length of the lake. On September 6, we approached the mouth of the Richelieu River and dropped anchor near Isle La Motte. I dispatched teams of scouts ashore. I am happy to report that when the British loyalists saw our fleet, they promptly retreated to avoid engaging us. I, therefore, advanced my ships further to probe the enemy's weaknesses and display our growing strength.

The British ultimately attempted to trick the *Liberty* into coming too close to shore to meet a French-Canadian envoy. Three or four hundred British and Canadians opened up on the boat from the surrounding woods. She returned fire from her swivel guns, and I brought the *Royal Savage* within range, firing several broadsides of grapeshot and dispersing the enemy.

My scouts ashore learned from a deserter that two British schooners had been taken apart piece by piece and brought to St. John. The British were also building four or five sloops, a large number of gondolas, and several large floating batteries. One of the batteries would apparently hold eighteen-pounders in addition to mortars. The raid, on the whole, was successful. We had obtained further intelligence, and more importantly, my "bluff" delayed the enemy's advance by almost a month.

Almost a month later, I was further informed by a reliable scout that the British had designed and built a three-masted ship in St. John, to be named the HMS *Inflexible*, mounting twenty guns, both nine- and twelve-pounders. This boat would be nearly twice as large as any vessel under my command and was the sort of dominant warship I had proposed to be built during our July 7 council of war. The British now had precisely the significant tactical advantage I wanted and could not match.

I remained at Skenesborough to supervise and encourage construction, but I was preoccupied by another pressing matter. Walking away from the men and the incessant hammering and sawing, I unconsciously strolled north toward the lake as my thoughts turned to the battle to come. *There is no need for a council of war. I do not need to consult the major generals. They have placed this squarely in my hands, and none know the first thing about naval battles. This all rests upon me.* The weight of the responsibility had slowed my pace, but my mind continued to race. *Carleton is timid, but he will come, especially when the Inflexible is completed. God damn it! Stop focusing on that ship. What is the current tactical situation, and what are your potential advantages?*

I have fifteen ships at my disposal, but the Brits are more likely to have superior maneuverability, firepower, and experienced crew. Coming to a dead stop, I stared unseeing at the empty river. *On both land and sea, topography matters. It is the high ground on land. At sea, it is the water depth and wind, and who sees the enemy first. Carleton must come down the lake to meet me, but where do I meet him?*

He will expect me near either Crown Point or Fort Ti, adding their guns to my ships. I could even deploy cannon in the woods near Fort Ti to augment the fort's firepower, but he is going to expect that. He is going to land men ashore before he gets here and will probably turn the cannon against me.

Kicking the ground in frustration, I continued to walk north, indifferent to the dust that boiled up from each step on the sun-scorched road.

I had spent days looking at a map and detailed soundings on the depth of the many inlets and bays that lined the enormous lake. *Where? He expects me in the south, so I should hit him in the north. At the Richelieu River? My galleys and gondolas could outmaneuver their large ships, and they certainly would not expect it.*

I shook my head. *No. I would be too far from any supply lines, and they could easily reinforce from St. John. My galleys and gondolas are slow, and if the wind is blowing the wrong way, the entire force would be totally exposed . . . so the question is: Where?*

It is about wind and water depth. They will have ships that are suited for deep water. I need to limit the water depth and cut off the wind. The predominant winds are west to east. North and south vary, but the further we get into fall, the more likely it is a north wind, allowing them to quickly move up the lake. But that could also benefit my retreat . . .

My mind traveled up and down the lake, searching the map that I had reviewed so many times, and then it hit me. *Valcour Isle. Yes! It is a little too far north, but the channel between the isle and the west bank of the lake is narrow enough that my ships could block it, especially in shallows, where the British couldn't go. Our soundings on the north side of the isle mean that the heavy British ships could never make it through without running aground. The isle and mountains will kill the wind, and the shallows will keep them back.*

It is my opportunity to catch the British at a disadvantage while maximizing our strengths. The isle is nestled against the side of the lake, covered in white spruce trees, with gray cliffs on its southern shore. Almost two miles long and covered by a thousand acres of thick woods, it will provide an ideal shield as the British move down the lake. I imagined the British ships coming around the point and struggling against the wind to reach us. Like a wolf whose leg was caught in a trap, they would be vulnerable to our cannon fire, with no ability to escape or maneuver without the wind.

With the finality of steel hitting flint, my mind locked into place. Looking up, I realized I had walked almost two miles from the shipyard, but now I had a purpose. I strode back with a plan that was fully formed by the time I reached my men. It was late September, and we needed to be in position before the British came south.

Chapter 37

Valcour Isle, NY – September 26, 1776

We arrived at Valcour Isle after a slow but uneventful trip north. Near the New York shore, I had my ships drop anchor. My small fleet was deployed in a three-quarter-mile arc across the narrow channel between Valcour Isle and New York, a half mile north of the southern tip of the isle. The waterway was too shallow to permit the British ships to come from the north; the hills deflected the wind, making maneuvering difficult. We anchored bow-to-stern across the channel, our broadside guns facing south, anticipating the British arrival.

I covered the bulwarks with spruce trees and had sharpened points placed to disguise our presence and repel boarders. I noted with approval that hanging on the back of some of the ships was the new American flag, with the coiled black-and-yellow rattlesnake and the statement "Don't Tread on Me."

I had chosen the location. I had limited the British advantages. We were safely hidden behind the isle from any British force moving south up the lake. I was betting that surprise, water depth, and wind would defeat the enemy's maneuverability, firepower, and experienced crews. It was now up to the British to decide the time of battle.

We waited for over two weeks in the growing cold for the British to come up the lake. People on land do not understand that temperatures that would be comfortable ashore are bone-chilling on a ship. The men huddled, transforming decks into villages of wood and canvas. On many of the boats, there was no ability to go below decks to escape the moisture and the pitiless wind. The cruel frost ruled the dark, but the morning glow promised the warmth my sailors so badly craved.

Food and water were also an issue. Fresh water is always a precious commodity at sea; not so on a lake. Yet at sea, the water is always moving.

As we waited at anchor, human waste presented a particular problem, fouling the water near the ships and rendering it undrinkable. Every day, the men had to go out on skiffs to recover fresh water. Rations consisted of meat and dried biscuits; while we sent some men out to hunt on shore, they always risked running into British and Indian patrols. On rare occasions, fresh meat, potatoes, or vegetables were brought by newly arriving ships. Each ship had its own small brick-lined cooking fireplace to warm stew.

The men under my command were inexperienced in naval engagements. Nevertheless, I found most to be loyal and hardworking. The best of them were my "brothers," who had trekked with me through hell and back to Quebec; I knew I could depend on them to lead in the upcoming battle.

The inactivity not only tried my men's patience, but also presented real challenges to continuing as a viable fighting force. The ingredients of gunpowder—ash, saltpeter, charcoal, and sulfur—tend to separate over time, the heavier saltpeter sinking to the bottom. If left unattended in barrels, the mixture is rendered useless. Powder barrels need to be carefully overturned at least once a week. Ubiquitous moisture ruins gunpowder—bags of charcoal are suspended above the barrels to absorb water, and the barrels themselves are carefully sealed and tended to every day. In the event of rain, they are covered with canvas tarps and double-checked.

In ships of the line, gunpowder is stored deep below decks, with young boys called "powder monkeys" bringing the dangerous mixture to the guns to minimize the chance of an "unlucky hit" setting off the magazine. Our smaller ships did not have that luxury. A large barrel of powder was stored in the middle of the deck; during battle, the men would have to shuttle back and forth from their guns to the powder and pray that the ship remained in Neptune's good favor.

Each gun had next to it the items necessary for firing. I had my gunners practice the loading and firing procedures for cannon over and over again. I knew that in the heat of battle mistakes were made, sometimes with catastrophic consequences.

The first step, even if the gun had not been recently fired, was to mop out the interior of the barrel to extinguish any ember, preventing a premature firing of the powder. Gunpowder loaded before a cannon had been swabbed out could kill an entire crew in an instant.

Next, a long ladle was used to scoop out exactly the right amount of gunpowder—usually approximately the same weight of powder as the ball being shot, although experienced men sometimes adjusted the powder depending on the range of the target. The powder was put inside a cloth bag, which would later be pierced through the touchhole. Cloth wadding was then rammed down the barrel with a long pole, followed by the ball.

Another section of wadding was placed in front of the ball, and again packed into place with a poled rammer. The men then would "run out" the gun into position against the ship's bulwark with block and tackle, with the barrel protruding outside the ship. A wheel on the carriage allowed the gunners to adjust elevation. Large crowbars known as handspikes allowed the gun carriage to be adjusted to the right and left; although the guns often weighed more than two tons, their balance allowed easy aiming through the use of pivots, or trunnions.

While some more modern guns had a gunlock, which was a flintlock mechanism wherein a lanyard could be pulled to ignite the gun from a safe distance, our cannon came from the forts and were of older designs, so we were required to use a linstock—a pin pushed through the touchhole to pierce the powder bag inside the barrel, leaving a trail of powder to be lit. A pole with a lit rope on the end was extended to ignite the powder on the touchhole and fire the cannon. The gun would then recoil violently against the thick ropes attached to the ship's gunwale or hull.

Standing next to a cannon when it fires overloads your senses. You do not so much hear the explosion as feel the compression of air that shakes your innards, causing instant pain in your ears, even if wadding has been wisely stuffed in as closely as possible. As the ball leaves the ship, the water ripples, reflecting the violence of the shot escaping the gun. Once the firing has occurred, the process needs to be carefully repeated. In ideal circumstances, each step of the loading process would be performed by a different man to avoid confusion and accidental firing. However, we lacked both the trained personnel and manpower to follow the strict rules adopted by the Royal Navy.

After two long weeks waiting next to the Isle, I was pleased to welcome the *Congress* and her sister ship the *Washington*. Upon the arrival of the *Congress*, I gladly transferred my flag from the large but cumbersome *Royal Savage*. The *Congress* was smaller but better armed, with a larger crew. I put my loyal friend from Connecticut, Captain David Hawley, in command of the *Royal Savage*. However, because of limited space and time, I left much of my personal belongings aboard that ship.

I stood on the deck of my new flagship, covered in a broad cloak obscuring my blue-and-buff regimental coat, as I tried to control the shiver that cut through me. Even in the protected channel, the wind was brisk, kicking up a light chop. The cold hit my unprotected legs, making me keenly aware that we could not dither much longer. If the British did not kill us, the cold surely would. The sun was low in the sky to the west, casting the Adirondack Mountains in shadow, while on the far shore the crisp fall light highlighted red maples and yellow birches. I knew that as the days wore on, the leaves would lose their color and begin to brown and drop, matching my men's spirit if we continued to wait on the cold lake. The late-afternoon shadows swallowed the valley. I whispered a silent prayer—first, that the enemy would come soon, and second, that the winds of war would blow in my favor.

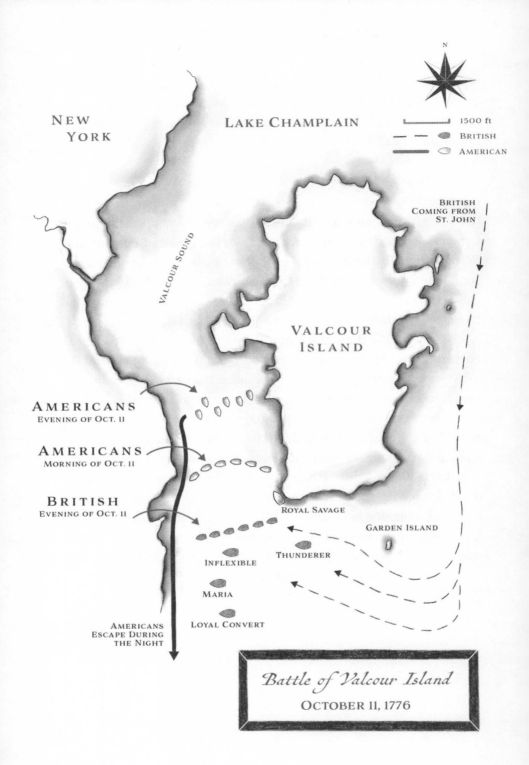

NEW YORK

LAKE CHAMPLAIN

N

1500 ft

BRITISH
AMERICAN

VALCOUR SOUND

BRITISH
COMING FROM
ST. JOHN

VALCOUR
ISLAND

AMERICANS
EVENING OF OCT. 11

AMERICANS
MORNING OF OCT. 11

BRITISH
EVENING OF OCT. 11

ROYAL SAVAGE

GARDEN ISLAND

THUNDERER

INFLEXIBLE

MARIA

LOYAL CONVERT

AMERICANS
ESCAPE DURING
THE NIGHT

Battle of Valcour Island
OCTOBER 11, 1776

Chapter 38

Valcour Isle, NY – October 11, 1776

T he clouds kissed the mountain peaks as the frosty dawn broke clear. A fifteen-knot wind blew from the north, raising three-foot waves and numerous whitecaps on the open sections of the lake. The water remained relatively calm in the sheltered channel between Valcour Isle and the New York shore.

All concerns about staying warm evaporated when I heard the unmistakable report of the guard boat I had kept north of the isle to detect any British movements. I immediately sent a scouting party to the north end of the isle to determine whether the enemy would pass on the east side of the isle (as I hoped) or swing through the channel and come in behind us. After what felt like an eternity, I received a report: the British were indeed heading down the east side of the isle.

I had a small white pennant raised along the stays of the *Congress*, calling my captains over to the ship. Small boats and skiffs quickly rowed to my flagship, and all my captains and many other senior officers, dressed in their best uniforms, crowded into the small cabin on the *Congress*. I faced the prospect of battle with more excitement than trepidation. I am told other men dread that ultimate martial test, yet it always represented for me the supreme moment of self-confidence and validation.

With everyone assembled, only the gently rocking boat broke the absolute silence as the men stared at me, awaiting my orders. Even the crew was quiet with so many captains on board. I wore a blue coat, a sash suspending a sword, an epaulet on my shoulder, and a gold-rimmed tricorn hat, which I tucked under my arm. "Gentlemen, thank you for joining me. At least in this cramped room, we can all be warm." Smiles spread across their wind-burned faces.

"I believe we will face an enemy with a comparable number of sailors and soldiers, but the British will have more guns, including the HMS *Thunderer* with her twenty-four-pounders. But to remind you, I chose this spot deliberately." With that, I gestured to the map on the table, showing Valcour Isle and the surrounding area. "Given the British ships' limited ability to maneuver, they will need to travel downwind. They will most likely sail past Valcour Isle before they see us. The hilly terrain of the isle and the steep New York shore will hide our ships as the British sail past. For many of their ships, tacking upwind will be impossible, and for all, it will be difficult. They will be forced to come before our guns on a piecemeal basis. Our ships' broadsides will fire in concert, while the British must act as individuals. You have all taught your men how to use their spring cables and further refine your ships' positions to optimize our shots on the enemy."

Pointing to the north side of the isle, I continued, "I know some of you have some concern about the channel to the north, but the water is shoaled, blocked by sunken rocks, and nowhere more than five feet deep. In the unlikely event a few small British ships slip through, a couple of our galleons could weigh anchor and row north to meet them. If they try to hug the isle too close, there is a hidden underwater ledge three hundred yards long. This channel will either destroy the British ships or severely impact their ability to maneuver."

General David Waterbury, one of my more skittish commanders, addressed the group rather than facing me as the commander. "Gentlemen, we are restricted in this bay. The British can simply blockade us, and it will become a deathtrap. They will send bateaux to the north of the isle and come down the channel while their capital ships pummel us from the south and savages attack us from the isle and mainland. We will be pulverized in a vice of our own design. With all due respect to General Arnold, his plan requires the British to attack us without stopping to think about the strategic situation. Moreover, if they come to face us from the south and the wind changes, we will be at their mercy. No, gentlemen—before the British fleet gets here, I believe we should meet the enemy in open water, not lie where we can be surrounded."

I was able to hide my irritation because most of the men either looked noncommittal or shared my frustration with this last-minute cowardice. Facing the room with my head up and my shoulders back, I said, "We have discussed this strategy before. Even if we had a head start, our slower ships would not outrun the enemy. The Brits will take us down piecemeal. Moreover, as General Waterbury well knows, a fighting retreat is difficult, even for the most experienced mariners. Pitting our brave yet inexperienced lads against crack sailors and gunners of the Royal Navy would guarantee our annihilation. We would have no hope of protecting the gondolas. I am not about to sign their death sentence so that some of us in larger ships may retreat."

This was a clear shot at Waterbury, whose larger ship would most likely be able to outrun the British, whereas many of the captains in other ships could not. I could feel the room shifting to my way of thinking as I continued, "We have set up an ideal situation to catch the British in a crossfire when they come around the point. They will become becalmed heading into the wind, and we will have our broadsides facing them. Never forget—we are all that stands between the British hell-bent on splitting the Colonies in two. We will stay and face the enemy. If we are marked to die, then the greater the honor." What I did not add was that a retreat to Fort Ticonderoga would be futile. We did not have enough gunpowder there to repel a concerted British attack.

I turned to Waterbury, who shrugged and gave a half-hearted bow with his hands open at his side. "I have given my opinion, General."

This was not a council of war—I had no need to call for a vote, and I knew we had no time for further discussion. "Thank you, General." As I looked around the room, all nodded in grim determination. I concluded, "Godspeed, gentlemen—you have your orders." I knew the plan made sense. As long as the wind continued to blow from the north, we had a chance of victory.

After all this waiting, I was finally able to order the fleet ready for action. Awnings that had been providing minimal shelter over the decks were removed; cartridges were passed, linstocks were lit, and sawdust was spread on the decks to absorb the blood of the dead and wounded.

Buckets of water were distributed to fight fires. All sails were tightly furled and secured.

Our flotilla pitched and strained against its anchor lines as the activity on board rocked the ships. Gunports were opened, and the wooden wheels screeched under the weight as guns were rolled back and loaded, only to be pushed back into their firing positions. On the hospital ship *Enterprise*, Dr. McCrea readied the tables, knives, saws, probes, and retractors that were necessary for the battle to come.

A surge of confidence spread throughout the fleet as men readied for the coming fight. My line of battle was placing the *Trumbull* at the extreme left (east) side of our crescent, closest to the isle, under Colonel Wigglesworth, but just out of musket range of tall trees. Next in line, staggering slightly to the north, were the gondolas *Boston, Providence, Connecticut, Jersey,* and *New York*. Then, next in the curved line, back toward the New York shore, was the schooner *Revenge* with her four four-pounders and four two-pounders; my flagship, the *Congress,* was in the center; next to the gondola *Philadelphia*; and the row galley *Washington* to our right (west) under Waterbury was carefully stationed closest to the New York shore to fire across the entire arc of the channel and down the lake at any approaching British men-of-war. I placed our hospital ship, the *Enterprise,* to the rear and near the New York shore.

As I had planned, the British arrogantly sailed past Valcour Isle without scout ships. Shortly after ten o'clock, a young midshipman on one of Carleton's longboats saw the *Royal Savage* at full sail, along with the *Trumbull, Congress,* and *Washington,* coming out to meet Carleton's armada. My goal was *not* to permit the British to sail by my force unseen—indeed, that would be a disaster, because the southern half of the lake would be exposed. I sent the ships to entice the overconfident British to step into my trap. Once the ships were seen, they were instructed to come about and return to their positions in our anchored line.

I began to deliberately pace about the deck, showing confidence to the men. Hoping they would not see the truth, I kept moving to outrun any remaining fears. I knew that all would be lost if the wind shifted and started coming from the south, or if the British decided to ignore us and proceed to the south. I moved from man to man, putting my hands on their shoulders and wishing them well.

Going into battle, every man's pocket is a reliquary. Each appeared to be fondling an amulet to ward off death. I had spent enough time at sea to know better than to mock the superstitions of the men. More often than not, those who believed they would live fulfilled their destiny—as did those who believed they would die.

I let out an enormous sigh of relief when a British longboat fired a signal cannon, alerting General Carleton to our presence. I tried not to smile when the British ships began to come about to accept my thrown gauntlet. They moved to attack the three-masted *Royal Savage*. The British had no choice but to turn into the wind and fight without a battle plan.

As we had practiced a dozen times, our galleys returned to our crescent line of defense, pivoted, and dropped anchor to join the other ships ready to ambush the British. The *Royal Savage*, meanwhile, veered toward Valcour Isle's southern tip, where Captain Hawley knew from my soundings that there was a ledge only three feet below the surface. He hoped to lure larger British warships close to the tip and run them aground. Unfortunately, the expertly sailed British man-of-war HMS *Inflexible* managed to both overtake the *Royal Savage* and avoid the trap on the tip of the isle.

The British cannon barked with a puff of smoke, its report arriving after we saw the devastation. The more experienced British gunners used twelve-pounder cannon with chain shot to bring down the *Royal Savage*'s rigging, ropes, and tackle like hands through a spiderweb. The second volley was even more lethal, smashing through railings and showering the decks with deadly splinters flying through the air like stilettos searching for exposed flesh. One of the volleys broke and shattered the mainmast, causing the *Royal Savage* to heel over.

Meanwhile, British gunboats under oars were able to chase the stricken *Royal Savage* as it drifted toward shore. The *Royal Savage* was now heading directly for the underwater ledge at the tip of Valcour Isle;

with her mast pitched forward, she jammed hard aground, settling on one side with her guns pointed skyward on the port side and straight into the water on her starboard. The men all abandoned ship. My most impressive warship was out of the battle. Captain Hawley tried to use the ship's longboat to tow the *Royal Savage* off the ledge, but Hessian gunners took deadly aim at the small boat and quickly sunk her, forcing the crew to swim to the isle. The British scampered on board, and our men counterattacked.

I am proud to say my men remained undeterred in the face of this setback. As the first British ships came within range, my flotilla fired almost simultaneously, covering the bay with a massive plume of smoke crisscrossed by sheets of flame. The deck of the *Congress* seemed to raise my feet into the air as the pressure of cannon fire rippled across the deck. For an instant, the horizon disappeared in a cloud of impenetrable smoke.

Whenever the British gunboats came within 350 yards of our defenses, they were decimated under withering fire and compelled to drop leeward. As I had planned, the enemy were unable to direct significant fire toward our crescent-shaped line. One British boat after another came around the tip of Valcour Isle and was suddenly exposed to our overwhelming crossfire. Their sheets shivered helplessly, caught "in irons" as they faced the headwind, leaving them unable to maneuver or aim their guns. In contrast, we were anchored in place. Holding our positions, we hammered the enemy hour after hour.

At times, the British gunboats would approach under oars. They would recklessly come straight at us, alone or in small groups, facing our coordinated and increasingly lethal fire (as my gunners learned and improved with repetition in the heat of battle). Whenever the British came within seven hundred yards, we raked their decks with grapeshot with very useful effect. My men continued to fight as the engagement became general, and very warm. Iron fists slammed into our hulls, throwing lethal shards of wood splinters in the air while grapeshot clattered like hail around us. Screaming at the top of my lungs, I encouraged my men to return fire.

As noon passed, the British were still struggling to get into position, but all my boats were engaged in the battle. The British fired heated cannonballs with the goal of starting my ships ablaze. My men extinguished the fires, but many burned themselves in the process. Strips of skin hanging like birch bark paid testament to their bravery and determination.

Fighting against the wind, the HMS *Maria* finally worked its way north into gun range. Our boys directed an eighteen-pound ball at General Carleton as he stood clearly visible on the rear gunner deck, badly wounding his brother only feet away. Indeed, this and a few other carefully placed shots forced the most powerful British warship to sail away from our line. The sight of the HMS *Maria* retreating cheered my men and obviously dispirited the British.

Salvo after salvo filled the sky with lead. Not a single man on any ship had a chance to admire the spectacle—all were too focused on killing, or in many cases avoiding being killed. By one o'clock, the British ships HMS *Thunderer* and HMS *Inflexible* were still out of sight, but Hessian artillery boats repeatedly attempted to maneuver against the wind. These square-rigged vessels faced multiple problems: They lacked the required lateen sail for tacking upwind, and the large, flat-bottomed HMS *Thunderer* did not have a deep enough keel to prevent the ship from slipping sideways when tacking upwind. Finally, the narrow confines of the Valcour channel prevented the British ships from building momentum and jibing through the wind to reset their sails. Each time they attempted to do so, the ship would be caught in the wind and slide further backward.

Casualties continued to mount for both sides. At least one British ship blew up when our cannon shot hit its magazine. We also suffered a serious loss aboard the *New York* when a cannon misfired, killing many of its crew.

One additional fear continued to gnaw at me, something I never shared with my officers. At any time, the British could simply drop anchor and wait us out. Eventually, a breeze could give them a tactical advantage. Fortunately, the bit was in their teeth, and Carleton continued to actively engage.

As the battle raged, blinding cannon smoke filled the air, burning everyone's eyes and often choking sailors. Men gagged, vomited, and immediately returned to their posts without their comrades noticing. Meanwhile, each thundering report of cannon and squeal of wood gun trucks overloaded the men's ears, replacing the din of battle with a deafening ring. This pandemonium was periodically interrupted as iron balls crashed through the ships' sides and rigging, throwing deadly shards of wood into unprotected men.

More often than not, a sailor would realize his mate had been wounded or killed only when he turned and saw some or all of his friend's remains on the deck next to him. I saw young boys look death in the eye, stay at their posts, and never blink. I saw brutes scream in fear, cower, and beg for their mothers. It drove home my belief that death awaits us all; it is only honor that endures.

A successful ship captain in battle does not stand next to the wheel with his hands behind his back. I slipped on the bloody deck as I moved from one end of the ship to another, giving firing instructions as I shifted from gun to gun. I barked orders to be relayed to my flotilla. For hours I never stopped moving, encouraging my men and wreaking havoc on the enemy. Everywhere I went, I heard the sweet whoosh of balls shooting wide and the terrible smack of those hitting their target. A cannonball struck a man near me, covering me with blood and gore. I tried to wipe it off. The salty taste of another man's blood always finds its way into your mouth.

There are rare pauses in a battle, like the calm in a hurricane—moments when all shooting and cannonade stops. Everyone is either taking a breath or reloading. In those fleeting moments, I shouted myself hoarse through a speaking-horn trumpet to instruct nearby ships, although my words were quickly drowned out by the renewal of cannon fire by both sides.

It was clear the British were concentrating their fire on me and my ship. I knew I stood out in my uniform, but it provided courage to my men. I saw a cannonball gouge our mainmast and crack our cantilevered yardarm. Our location in the center of our arc of ships gave us some protection and advantage. In any event, my ship and crew held up under the pounding.

While the wind was calm in the channel, the maelstrom of misdirected cannon and musket balls churned the water as fierce as any storm. The ships strained at their moorings like horses ready to bolt from danger. Pumps spurted as men working below deck struggled to keep ships afloat. Everywhere, the flotsam of battle bobbed amongst the waves.

Rowboats shuttled to the hospital ship *Enterprise* to deposit the wounded and dying in that vessel filled with pain. Dr. Stephen McCrea and his assistants performed valiant service. We all witnessed their gruesome handiwork as arms, legs, and bodies thrown over the side without ceremony floated amongst our ships.

The British also landed their Indian allies on the isle and the western shore of the channel. Death enveloped us as the red devils poured musket fire and arrows onto our ships. I had anticipated this possibility by stationing our ships as far from shore as possible, and also by protecting the vessels from enemy fire by building aboard five-foot-tall fences called a fascines (essentially thick bundles of sticks tied together). I also ordered our best marksmen to the tops of our masts to provide counterfire.

With our initial success and the retreat of the HMS *Maria*, we were able to concentrate our fire on the HMS *Carleton*. Indeed, I had the pleasure of tutoring the gunners on the *Congress*, as well as aiming a couple of shots with my own hand that struck the HMS *Carleton* amidships. The twelve-gun, sixty-six-foot British schooner received constant raking fire from our half-moon formation. My plan of engaging one man-of-war at a time seemed to be working. The HMS *Carleton* unsuccessfully attempted to drop anchor because its chain was severed by one of our cannon shots; we were able to fill her with cannonballs to the point that she began to list. My men, eager for a prize, boarded rowboats and began to approach the HMS *Carleton* to take her. Unfortunately, a gust of wind allowed her to get underway with her surviving skeleton crew. I recall with admiration the sight of a young British midshipman—he single-handedly ran out on the bowsprit, exposing himself to a hail of fire, and released the anchor cable, allowing the ship to drift out of our reach.

At the same time, the British tried again to secure the listing *Royal Savage*. Regretfully, we had to turn our fire on our abandoned vessel, raking the British and irreparably disabling our ship by setting it ablaze.

One of the truths for soldiers and sailors is that they rarely go by their given names—almost immediately they adopt some friendly or teasing moniker. So it was for Putt. The name struck me because it seemed like a nickname one would give to an old man. Putt was barely twenty, yet he embraced it. I generally called men by their last names or ranks, but on rare occasions, I fell into using their nicknames—as I did with the affable Putt. I looked across the deck of the *Congress* as he dutifully manned a cannon, ready to swab out the barrel after firing. At that moment, he was struck by a chain shot aimed at our mast.

Modern war is so fierce. It is no longer the wound of axe, sword, or arrow. You hear people say a man was "cut down in battle." It sounds like a scythe neatly ending a life. The truth is more like trying to cut a piece of meat with a sledgehammer. Parts disappear, and what is left are mangled chunks of flesh. So it was for Putt. In an instant, his top half disappeared in a spray of blood and bone. What was left crumpled and spilled its contents onto the deck. Nothing in my life had prepared me for such carnage, but I also had no time to dwell on it.

The *Liberty, Lee,* and *Washington* were near the New York shore and taking heavy casualties from sniper fire. Likewise, numerous deaths occurred in attempting to repel bateaux and canoe boarding parties. Enemy gunners had found their range, and twenty-four-pound projectiles were arcing toward our ships from nearly a half mile away. The *New Jersey*, the *Philadelphia*, and the *Congress* each had over twenty holes in them. Repeated hits from British cannonballs had chewed away large portions of their hulls. Fortunately, most were above the waterline. The *Trumbull* received a twelve-pound round in the stern and twenty or thirty other hits—they were almost out of twelve- and eighteen-pound shot, but her gun crews defiantly continued to fire their remaining ammunition at the enemy.

I had anticipated a short engagement, but hour after hour the guns screamed their hate. Ball, chain, grapeshot, and acrid gray smoke from cannon fire filled the air. Dead and dying lay on the decks of all ships, made slick with blood. Bodies floated around the lake, having been tossed overboard to make room for the remaining fighting crew. Sailors on both sides now embraced each other in death as they never could in life, as rival brothers eternally bonded in a shared violent end. The smell of battle filled our nostrils. Vomit, the contents of men's bowels, and their innards lay strewn across the decks, mixing with the unforgettable stench of burnt flesh, burning wood, and gunpowder. So much blood was flowing off the decks that it looked like the ships themselves were bleeding.

As it passed five o'clock, the battle had been raging for over seven hours. By removing the HMS *Carleton*, the British had opened the line of approach for their most powerful ships to engage my men. The HMS *Inflexible* had been forced to hang back all afternoon because of the HMS *Carleton*'s positioning. Now the two-hundred-ton man-of-war with her twelve-pound cannon pummeled our line for almost an hour, inflicting heavy casualties.

By sunset, the superior British gunnery and firepower began to tell the tale. It was only the coming of darkness that allowed our line to hold. However, the enemy dropped anchor, blocking off escape with their own crescent-moon formation at anchor to our south. I had our ships pull back an additional three hundred yards to give us some space from the enemy and tighten up our lines.

Chapter 39

Valcour Isle, NY – October 11, 1776

The day's battle ended with the moans of our wounded, taken below decks, and the roar of the *Royal Savage*'s powder magazine replaced the sounds of musket and cannon fire. Around seven o'clock, I ordered a pendant raised and word sent that a captains' meeting was convening on the *Congress*. I knew I would receive a report on the condition of my fleet, but I was more interested in the British dispositions. Anchored just outside cannon range, the enemy showed no sign of pressing the attack into the night. Cannon and musket smoke dissipated as the night crept in. The haze from burning wood and canvas still filled the air, despite attempts to douse the remaining fires.

All the British capital ships, including the HMS *Maria*, HMS *Inflexible*, and HMS *Thunderer*, were present. Even the HMS *Carleton* had been dragged into line and was clearly under active repair. The vessels were arranged so that the east flank of the British line was up against the southern tip of Valcour Isle. However, to my surprise, there was a large gap between the west side of the British line and the western shore of the lake. In no small part, this seemed to be caused by the fact that the HMS *Maria* and the HMS *Inflexible* were not truly in line with the other ships, but over a half mile or more back.

As skiffs and launches approached with the captains from our flotilla, I decided to take a few minutes to move around my ship, provide comfort to the wounded, and compliment my men for their bravery. Most of the able-bodied men were making repairs or tending to the wounded. As I looked over the gunwale at the British ships, I began to ponder a potential opportunity as my bedraggled, blood-covered, and exhausted captains saluted and climbed aboard. With twenty holes in the *Congress*, she was no worse off than most. All vessels were leaking badly, not only from battle damage, but from the recoil of their massive guns tearing apart the ships.

Earlier in that impossibly long day, the captains had met in my tight but orderly cabin. Now it was a blood-soaked operating room, too jammed with the wounded to accommodate another meeting. Instead, we stood in a circle on the fetid open deck. Once everyone had arrived, I made sure my back was straight and my head held high as I said, "Before we say anything else, well done, gentlemen. Each of you and your men fought with tremendous bravery, and we have severely wounded the Royal Navy. We have bludgeoned the enemy, sunk several ships, and caused massive damage to many others. I could not have hoped for more. I have some thoughts about next steps, but before we proceed, I would be grateful if you could indicate the current status of your ships and sailors."

Each captain then tallied the butcher's bill and the conditions of his ship in a professional and forthright manner. Every vessel had suffered major damage, with at least sixty men killed and many more wounded. The gondola *Philadelphia* had so many holes in her that, as we all turned, we saw her slide under the water. Every officer on the *Lee* had been killed. The *Providence*'s mainmast was so weakened that she could not accept any wind. The row galley *Washington*'s foremast was shot through, and her hull was leaking badly, with all her officers dead or wounded. There were heavy casualties on the *Congress*. The *Royal Savage* was lost. Three-quarters of the ammunition was gone. All knew the British would wipe us out in the morning with a combination of artillery fire and infantry attacking in bateaux and canoes.

As I looked out at the soot- and gore-covered captains or their surviving alternates, I could not help but feel admiration for their performance. Glancing down at my boots, I took a deep breath to collect myself. I spoke with a throat scratched raw from shouting. "I will not keep you long, gentleman." My eyes swept the circle of men anxious to return to their ships. "However, we have an important decision to make. I see four options."

Raising a finger, I said "First, we can stay and fight." Seeing several of the men glance uncomfortably at each other, I cut off discussion and said, "Obviously, that is untenable." Raising a second finger, I said, "We could simply surrender." Several men shook their heads, but at least a few seemed resigned. Again, foreclosing any further discussion, I intoned, "That is also unacceptable."

"Third, we could attempt to sail the remaining fleet in a line through the gap between the British ships and the shore. As you know, we took careful soundings while we waited here at Valcour Isle, and the water remains very deep right up to the shoreline." I pointed to the western shore, where well-lit British ships were silhouetted against the dark woods. A number of the men looked where I was pointing and appeared to notice the gap for the first time.

Continuing and raising a fourth finger: "We could turn the ships and head north, circling around the north side of the isle, through a narrow pass and across rocky shoals. I have made a careful sounding, and I believe there is just enough deep water for our ships to pass along the shore before looping around the tip of the isle and heading south, but I have two concerns with this approach. The wind is dying and certainly not pushing north. I am not sure how we could manage to go north undetected, because we would have to tow the ships under oars. More importantly, even if we got around the northern tip of the isle, the British ships are in the perfect position to cut us off as we try to head south. They can both outsail us and shoot us in open waters." There were murmurs of agreement around the group at this conclusion.

"So, gentlemen, I see only one viable alternative. That is to use the light southern breeze to silently escape between the British ships and the shore." Most men were nodding in approval. I knew they would follow my instructions, but I thought it better to confirm the plan. Knowing I already had majority approval, I said to the group, "What say you?"

Each officer, with varied enthusiasm, agreed to the approach—except for Waterbury, who, while not directly saying he favored surrender, made his inclination clear. Nevertheless, having received overwhelming support, I pronounced, "Gentlemen, we have a plan."

It was a moonless night. Each captain lit a low-flamed lantern on the back and front of his ship so that only those in line would see the lights. Men wrapped shirts around their ships' oars to muffle the sound and gently rowed along the lake's edge. Led by Colonel Edward Wigglesworth, our flotilla glided silently past British vessels filled with the sounds of repairs, hammering, and the groans of injured sailors. Our long single line of ships was swathed in a blessed fog.

The flames of the burning *Royal Savage* to the east both drew the attention of the British soldiers and likely diminished their night vision as our ships began to move. The *Trumbull* was in the lead, followed closely by the *Enterprise*, the *Revenge*, the *Lee* and the *Washington*, and the gondolas *Providence, Boston, Spitfire, New Haven, Connecticut, New York*, and *Jersey*. My ship, the galley *Congress*, was the last in the line. Some oars hit battle debris, and a couple of ships scraped bottom, but all blessedly made it past the British lines.

I wish I could have seen the shock on General Carleton's face when the sun rose, the fog lifted, and he realized my fleet had slipped away. He must have initially assumed that we had headed north to outflank him and attack St. John—thus, he mistakenly headed out of the bay and moved north, to our great relief and happiness. Unfortunately, someone must have seen our sails in the distance, for the British reversed themselves. Regardless, precious time had been gained due to General Carleton's mistake. With an eight-mile head start, it was a race toward Crown Point, thirty-five miles to the south. From there, I would have the protection of the fort's guns.

Our men frantically repaired masts and sails, bailed water, and pulled on oars to maintain our lead. With the British armada in pursuit, we had no choice but to toss valuable cannon overboard to lighten the load and improve the buoyancy of ships rapidly taking on water. Whitecaps slammed against our hulls, with many gunwales barely clearing the waterline. Already-frozen men were inundated with cold spray, but the stalwarts struggled without complaint.

Examining the gondolas *Providence* and *Jersey*, we determined they were too severely damaged and ordered them stripped and scuttled. The *Spitfire* also slipped under the waves, even after putting her guns overboard to lighten her load. We sent the *Enterprise* ahead with the wounded to alert Crown Point and provide General Gates an update on the battle. We knew it would be a chase south, but at the end of the first day, our hopes soared.

On the second day, October 13, our luck changed as we were met by rain squalls and shifting winds. Although weary and hungry, my men rowed against a strong wind blowing to the north, pushing us toward the approaching British force. We only covered twelve miles by nightfall.

The following morning as the fog lifted with the sun, the British were now close enough that we were easily spotted by their lookouts. I wanted to make it to Split Rock and form a line of defense in the narrows of the lake, where we could not be outflanked. As the day went on, it became apparent that we would not be able to make it. The *Washington* was taking on water; its sails had split, and the ship was falling behind. Meanwhile, I ordered the *Trumball* and four other less damaged galleys to row on ahead to Crown Point as fast as possible while the *Congress* and *Washington* acted as a rear guard along with four gondolas.

On board the *Washington*, General Waterbury saw the HMS *Inflexible* approaching. Waterbury signaled, asking permission to strike his colors, but I refused and ordered him to fight on to buy time for our remaining ships to escape. Nonetheless, as the HMS *Inflexible*'s twelve-pound cannon opened fire with a single salvo, Waterbury struck his colors without firing a single gun. He would later claim that the entire engagement was an overly aggressive folly and that I had "sacrificed" the fleet unnecessarily to gain personal fame. Such statements, of course, resonated with my enemies Brown, Easton, and Hazen, who did not hesitate to spread this unfair claim to Congress, where I had no friends.

In battle, I did not have the luxury of dwelling on my disgust with Waterbury's cowardice; instead, I turned to the matter at hand. The HMS *Inflexible*, HMS_Maria, and HMS_Carleton had all caught up with my ship and four gondolas near Split Rock around noon. While the surrounding ships opened fire with five times the firepower we possessed, we fought for two more hours, blasting away with our eighteen-pounders and buying invaluable time for the remainder of our fleet to escape to the south. Even though our sails, rigging, and hull were in tatters, I ordered my rowers to pull with all their might as we turned sharply between two of the enemy ships and headed for shore; our gondolas *Boston, Providence, New Haven,* and *Connecticut* closely followed. Caught off guard by our hairpin turn and unable to turn into the wind, the British could not initially follow. They were close enough that I doffed my hat and bowed as we slipped away from them yet again. I laughed aloud, along with my crew, as the enemy shook angry fists in the air.

I recognized we were doomed if we continued to fight. We needed to find a spot where we could disengage from the British in shallow water. With twenty-seven of my seventy officers and crew dead or seriously wounded, and almost out of ammunition, we had held out for five turns of the sandglass—over two hours—buying crucial time for the remainder of my fleet to reach safety.

I slipped the *Congress* and our gondolas into Ferris Bay, a three-hundred-foot cup-like opening on the Vermont shore. The bay presented a challenging angle for the larger British ships and gave us an opportunity to reach the shore while not under heavy fire. Running our ships ashore, we managed to unload our wounded and burn our vessels so they could not be captured. The *Congress*, despite her condition, was the last to touch ground, and I was the last man to set foot on dry land. One of my sailors asked if we should remove the colors. I yelled, "By God, no! Leave them up and burn the ship. No man shall say we struck our colors!"

Musket balls chewed at the foliage as I moved in the woods. While the flames engulfed our ships, I looked back with pride to see thirteen stripes with the Union Jack still in the upper left canton begin to catch fire. That was the last time I saw the Union Jack still a part of the American standard. I ordered my men back into the woods and high bluffs to provide covering fire to repel British longboats attempting to put boarding parties on the *Congress* and salvage her before fire got to her depleted magazine.

Peter Ferris and his patriot family were located near where we ran aground. He bravely guided us south and helped us avoid rampaging Indians. We made a nine-mile march, then ferried across to the New York side of the lake on October 14. Dog-tired, wounded, and at wit's end, my men and I collapsed into Fort Ti. I wrote to General Schuyler that I was "exceedingly fatigued and unwell having been without sleep or refreshment for nearly three days."

Chapter 40

Fort Ticonderoga, NY – November 2, 1776

My men mixed and shared stories with the rested and well-fed troops guarding Fort Ticonderoga. We all believed the British were on our heels and about to attack. If I had commanded the British, I certainly would not have sat on my laurels—I would have finished us off. The fort, while manned, was woefully undersupplied with ammunition.

To my shock and relief, the impending attack did not come. Almost two weeks after our arrival, we finally spotted British ships probing our defenses. General Carleton apparently concluded that his supply lines were too long and the fort was too well defended; when it began to snow on November 2, he turned his ships back toward Canada. Two-thirds of my fleet had been destroyed, eighty men were dead, and 120 further were prisoners, but my little navy had protected America and our Revolution for another year; that year of delay arguably saved the Cause.

General Gates praised me immediately following the battle: "It has pleased Providence to preserve General Arnold. Very few men ever met with so many hair-breadth escapes in so short a space of time. It would have been happy for the United States had the gallant behavior and steady good conduct of this excellent officer been supported by a fleet in any degree equal to the enemy. Such magnanimous behavior will establish the fame of the American army throughout the globe." In fact, the popular *Annual Register* in England described me as a versatile warrior who "not only acted the part of a brave soldier, but aptly filled that of an able naval commander."

Up until that point, General Gates and I had nothing but the closest personal and professional relationship. However, while he was generous and kind to me, our appearances and personalities could not have been more different. Where I favored aggressive risk-taking, he was cautious. Where I paid careful attention to my appearance and attire, General Gates, a decade older than me, wore spectacles, dressed in a slovenly manner, and allowed his thinning gray hair to be disheveled. I sometimes tended to be taciturn in groups of gentlemen, and my lack of formal education made me ill at ease. In contrast, General Gates was lettered, and could amuse officers and politicians with stories and anecdotes. He loved political argument almost as much as I loathed it.

Years later, I learned that despite his public praise, Gates was apparently jealous of my success—in private he had begun to support a whispering campaign against me, although I had (at that time) nothing but respect and trust for my superior. Meanwhile, I was appalled to learn that Congressman Richard Henry Lee of Virginia was openly denouncing me: "This officer, fiery, hot and impetuous, but without discretion, never thought of informing himself how the enemy went on, and had no idea of retiring when he saw them coming though so much superior to his force."

These unfair and ill-formed criticisms perpetuated by scoundrels like Waterbury, Moses Hazen, and James Easton, coupled with the Continental Congress's repeated promotion of officers junior to me in both rank and seniority—and with far less actual combat experience—were a bitter pill indeed.

Chapter 41

McConkey's Ferry, PA - December 16, 1776

I left Fort Ticonderoga when it became clear the British were with-drawing for the winter. I had not seen my family in over eighteen months. On my way back, I decided to meet General Schuyler in Albany—in so doing, I learned more details about Easton's and Brown's attacks on my good name while I had been fighting the British. A year and a half earlier, I had defeated their claims against me relating to the retreat from Quebec; now I learned from Schuyler that they were renewing their slander against me in Congress. While I was preparing to fight the British on Lake Champlain, Brown had managed to rehabil-itate himself and get reinstated as a colonel.

I decided that I had no choice but to put off going home, and instead determined to speak with General Washington. If necessary, I would go to Congress to petition for reinforcements, as well as reassert the righ-teousness of my behavior. I finally met Washington in Pennsylvania on the shore of the Delaware River, near McConkey's Ferry. It was our first opportunity to meet since I had led the march north to Kennebec to attack Quebec.

I arrived at a sturdy stone farmhouse that had been converted into his temporary headquarters. After minimal waiting, I was ushered into a dining room strewn with documents and maps. As the door opened, I realized that the front door was open too. A gust of air came in, sending papers into the air like a flock of birds. Washington's aides, who only moments before had been utterly motionless, sprang into action to catch their escaping charges. An amused Washington, who had been facing the window, turned and said, "The world does indeed swirl around you, my fine General Arnold."

Lacking a clever retort, I forced myself to smile and bow in response.

With a rare toothy smile, he bowed deeply and said, "We are thrilled to have you here." I snapped to attention, but he waved off the formality. "My dear sir, you have traveled very far. Please sit down. I want to hear everything about your latest naval battle and the disposition of Ticonderoga and the British." As he spoke, tea was brought in and placed before me and His Excellency. Several other officers entered the room and sat at the table, intent on listening but not participating in the conversation.

I briefed him on the battle at Valcour Isle and the bravery of our men, concluding, "I believe that Carleton will stay in the north through the balance of the winter. He will rebuild his forces and wait until spring, when the next round of British ships traverses the St. Lawrence. Unless Ticonderoga is substantially reinforced with able leadership and substantial men, I do not believe the fort will hold."

Washington nodded, then suddenly stood. A man of action, the sedentary life of an administrative general was clearly contrary to his nature. In response, I too rose, but was surprised to see the other men in the general's military family did not do likewise. A couple of hands rose to shoo me back down into my chair as an officer whispered, "He does that. It is fine. Remain seated."

With his hands behind his back, Washington stared at the floor for several minutes; he took a couple of steps, pivoted, and took a couple more, clearly lost in thought. Then, like a curtain opening to the sun, he locked his gaze onto me, and I once again involuntarily stood.

"You bought us a year, General. I know that price was paid in blood, but you purchased it as cheaply as possible." With approval, he declared, "You got the most out of your little navy."

Looking down and nodding to himself, he pivoted toward the window, again lost in thought. After several minutes of silence, he turned toward me. I was once more transfixed by his unblinking gray eyes. "I wish I could send you back, General. I need active generals who can lead men. That is a commodity rarer than gunpowder." His eyes flicked to his staff, and they inclined their heads in agreement.

Sighing, Washington continued, "No. You have done enough, my friend. We must put you to good use somewhere else. I need a leader in New England. Seven thousand British troops have landed in Rhode Island, detached from General Clinton's main army in New York. They have seized Newport to squeeze our New England privateers. The Royal Navy has over fifty ships and seem content to blockade New England without invading the surrounding country. I need your help in Providence to contain the British, so they don't move inland.

"Let me be clear—I don't want you to act offensively here unless you are sure you can secure victory. I need a general who knows the difference between victory and defeat, when to attack and when to retreat. You, sir, have consistently indicated you understand the strategic reality of a situation. Aggression tempered by sound judgment—that, sir, is what I want and expect."

Still standing, I bowed and said, "Of course, Your Excellency, I am glad to serve wherever I can be of use." After a moment's hesitation, I added, "I was planning on going to Congress to address some financial issues which remain outstanding, and criticisms that have been unfairly made of me."

Smiling, Washington quipped, "If you would be willing to follow my advice, you should stay as far away from Congress as you can. There is a reason I am in the field and not amongst the politicians." He paused to look at the men around the room. "I can assure you, General, you are in good stead with those who matter."

I again bowed in acknowledgment. "As you say, Your Excellency. I was also hoping to briefly return home."

"A capital idea, General Arnold. See your family—then return to New England and protect it from a British incursion."

With Congress avoided and Washington's blessing bestowed, I let a relieved smile escape. "I would be glad to return home and avoid congressional entanglements. Of course I will follow your advice."

Honor bound, I felt compelled to change the subject. "As you may be aware, Your Excellency, Captain John Lamb commanded the artillery assault at Quebec and was severely wounded and taken prisoner. I would be grateful if you could use your good offices to see if he could be exchanged. He has suffered much in service of the Cause."

Washington, maintaining his positive countenance, glanced at his aide as he responded. "We will look into it, General. We will do our very best for the noble Captain Lamb." The aide scribbled down the general's instructions. Washington then paused and nodded, as if reaching some internal agreement. Gesturing to the set of plans spread out on the desk before him, he said, "I wonder if I could impose upon you and seek your advice. I would be grateful for your insight on a plan I am formulating. You have proven yourself to be a master tactician."

I could feel myself blushing as I answered, "You are too kind. Of course, I am honored to help in any way."

Washington looked to his staff and gestured to the maps on the table, which were promptly rearranged and placed before me. I saw the area immediately surrounding his current headquarters across from the city of Trenton, New Jersey. From the other side of the table, His Excellency gestured at the map and explained, "My men's enlistments are coming up. We have been on our heels for too long. There are about fifteen hundred Hessians encamped in Trenton. While General Gates has counseled against this, I believe we should attack the British garrison before Christmas."

Pointing to the highlighted markings, he said, "My preliminary plan is to execute three crossings to attack the town. I will remain with the largest group, along with General Sullivan, looping in from the north. I shall put a second column under General Cadwalader, who will cross at Dunk's Ferry, and a third column under General Ewing, who will cross at the Trenton Ferry and hold the bridge." He then pointed at a spot on the map. "Here, at the bridge across Assunpink Creek, just south of Trenton. My goal is a pincer movement, coming at them from all sides. Once Trenton is secure, we could move on to Princeton, or even New Brunswick. I am even thinking about having General Putnam further surround the British force."

I could feel everyone's eyes upon me. The plan of attack was too complex, but the strategy was correct. "You will forgive me, General— there is much to absorb—but the principle of attack I believe to be not only sound, but bold and likely to meet with success. The British are rarely aggressive and indeed are overconfident and complacent. An attack on or before Christmas would catch them especially unprepared. No doubt the Hessians have gone into winter quarters with minimal security. As to the order of battle and the division of forces . . ." I struggled to find the right words. "Water crossings are challenging. As you know, I experienced difficulties at Ticonderoga, Quebec, and Lake Champlain moving men over water. Coordinating their activities and getting everyone to arrive at the same time, I respectfully suggest, will be your greatest difficulty."

"I've got a regiment of men from Marblehead, Massachusetts, and seamen from Philadelphia who tell me they can get us across," Washington replied. "Colonel Knox managed to drag the cannon you captured at Ticonderoga all the way to Boston. I'm confident he can get us across the Delaware."

I certainly didn't want to argue with him. The plan looked like it had too many moving parts—I would have simply crossed in force and then surrounded the town once we got close—but I didn't want to be contradictory. I agreed with Washington's approach in principle, and under no circumstances did I want to publicly question or embarrass him. Thus, I concluded, "I believe it is a very good plan. I have no doubt that you and your staff will continue to refine it. Your bold actions in the face of British arrogance will lead to victory. As importantly, defeating the Hessians will have a particularly salutary effect, as they are loathed by the people."

One of the generals intoned, "England must hire mercenaries to cut our children's throats." Murmurs of agreement filled the room.

Pleased with my response, Washington clapped his large hands together and began rubbing them. "Well, that is enough business for now, General. Would you be kind enough to join us for supper before you begin your sojourn home?"

I could feel everyone in the room relax as I answered with a grin, "It would be my distinct pleasure, Your Excellency."

My trip back home to New Haven was one of the most enjoyable and rewarding journeys of my life. Everyone seemed aware of my reputation for bravery in the face of overwhelming odds. My successes, especially in light of the Continental Army's recent failures in New York and New Jersey, only enhanced my reputation with the public. Everywhere I went, crowds came out to meet me.

As I passed through Hartford and Middleton, cannon announced my arrival, and veterans of the march to Quebec were present to greet me. Many of them I was meeting for the first time since we'd stormed the walls. I was often overcome meeting men who'd been wounded or, in the case of Eleazer Oswald, had lost their youth in prison. We wept and embraced as tested brothers in arms.

The greatest welcome of all came upon my arrival in New Haven. Crowds lined the streets leading to the green, where my Foot Guard turned out to salute me. Everyone was waving flags and cheering as I got down from my carriage. Standing in front of me were my dependable sister Hannah and my three boys, now eight, seven, and four. I spent wonderful hours with family, friends, and neighbors discussing my battles and adventures.

Everywhere I went in New Haven, people who had previously snubbed me because of my family's reversal of fortune now greeted me and congratulated me on my victory. In the Revolution, I saw the opportunity to remove the shackles of my family's disgrace and enter a new world where an "aristocracy of talent" would determine status. I reveled in the accolades of my friends and neighbors, yet I still pined to return to the sharp points of the world where action gives life meaning. After several wonderful months at home, as spring gave way to summer, I received orders from Washington to proceed to Rhode Island.

Chapter 42

Providence, RI - January 12, 1777

When I arrived in Providence, I was disappointed to see that Major General Joseph Spencer and his four-thousand-strong Rhode Island force were too ill equipped and unmotivated to challenge the large British force occupying Newport. While I was interested in attacking, General Washington's orders were quite clear. I was proud of my reputation for being an "aggressive" leader, but I was never reckless—I believed in taking calculated risks. The strategic situation in Rhode Island made going on the attack foolhardy—and I was no fool. Indeed, I wrote General Washington, "I believe your Excellency will not think it prudent for us to make a general attack."

We were also desperately short of supplies and troops. I traveled to Boston with the goal of not only seeking recruits, but also meeting the best of New England society and enjoying the city's many fine distractions. Anticipating my promotion to major general, I contacted Paul Revere, requesting his assistance in securing a sword knot, a sash, one dozen silk hose, and two superb epaulets.

At the center of society was Mrs. Henry Knox, wife of the head of Continental artillery. General Knox was the antithesis of a soldier—soft, obese, and a former bookseller—yet a skilled tactician and leader whom I respected. His highly educated wife saw no contradiction in hosting loyalists at parties in her home while absolutely supporting independence.

For my part, I was delighted to meet beautiful ladies of any political persuasion. In my best formal attire, I was introduced to the lovely sixteen-year-old Elizabeth DeBlois, the "Belle of Boston." I flirted with Ms. DeBlois, despite her mother's disapproval. Elizabeth was, in every way, the opposite of my late wife—loquacious where Margaret had been taciturn, polished where my wife was shabby. I admit I freely over-looked that her parents were Tories and that her mother was the worst sort of snob. I had seen so much death and endured so much loss. I was enthralled by Elizabeth's youth and vitality—I felt myself pulled to her like a moth to a flame. I thus bought her expensive gifts and imposed on General Knox's wife, Lucy, to act as an intermediary. While Elizabeth did not rebuff me, neither did she give me manifest hope of success. I viewed my time with her as an island of joyful anticipation amidst a sea of struggles.

I had worked dutifully to maintain good relations with both of my superior officers. I wrote to Generals Schuyler and Gates about one of the problems afflicting not only myself, but most of my troops: the lack of any financial ability to support oneself and one's family. The year 1777 was known as "the year of the hangman," because the three sevens, "777," resembled a tiny row of gallows. For the officers of the Continental Army, the hangman was appropriate, because we found ourselves in dire financial circumstances. My substantial personal fortune had been sacrificed for the Cause. I proposed to my commanding generals, given my performance on Lake Champlain, that I resign from the army and return to the sea as a privateer. This request was ignored.

Chapter 43

Boston, MA - February 19, 1777

I n early 1777, I read Thomas Paine's remarkable pamphlet *The Crisis*, which proclaimed, "These are the times that try men's souls. The summer soldier and sunshine patriot will, in this crisis, shrink from the service of their country; but he that stands by it now, deserves the love and thanks of man and woman. Tyranny, like hell, is not easily conquered; yet we have this consolation with us, that the harder the conflict, the more glorious the triumph." It spoke directly to me. I had seen so many unworthy men profit themselves at my expense and that of the Revolution. Additionally, the great mass of people was indifferent to the sufferings of the soldiers. As Paine rightly noted, too few men had "laid their shoulders to the wheel." Many felt the Revolution was on the brink of collapse—not for want of bravery or sacrifice of the army, but for lack of public support.

On February 19, 1777, Congress promoted five brigadier generals to major generals over my head. All the officers promoted were inferior to me, not only in seniority, but also in experience and ability. In fact, only one of the new major generals, William Alexander, had served with any distinction, and in his case had achieved far less than I.

General Washington's enthusiastic recommendation provided me no solace, nor did that fact that he fumed, "Surely a more active, a more spirited, and sensible officer fills no department in your Army." Washington anticipated that I would view getting passed over as a major general as a personal insult. On March 3, he wrote me, "I am at a loss whether you have a proceeding appointment or whether you have been omitted through some mistake. Should the latter be the case, I beg you not to take any hasty steps in consequence of it; but allow time for recollection, which, I flatter myself, will remedy any error that may been made. My endeavors to that end shall not be wanting."

As I looked out the window and contemplated my mistreatment, I beheld a false spring. Unseasonably warm weather was causing flowers and trees to blossom early, no doubt only to be betrayed by the inevitable return of the cold. I felt betrayed by Congress as much as the budding flowers.

My triumphant return from the northern campaign now burnt like mock praise. I sat alone staring at a blank page, trying to decide what to do next. *How can I possibly return home to these same people when Congress obviously holds me in such contempt? If the politicians want me to simply resign, they should ask me to do so. Why must I endure the twin tests of both battle and humiliation? So many unworthy men have been elevated over me without facing combat. Their skill was licking the boots of congressmen; mine is winning battles. Let those men fight on their knees; I will resign.* Resolved, I wrote to General Washington:

My commission was conferred unsolicited and received with pleasure only as means of serving my country. With equal pleasure I resign it, when I can no longer serve my country with honor. The person who, void of nice feelings of honor, will tamely condescend to give up his right, and retain a commission at the expense of his reputation, I hold as a disgrace to the Army and unworthy of the glorious cause in which we are engaged. When I entered the service of my country my character was not impeached. I have sacrificed my interest, ease, and happiness in her cause. It is rather a misfortune than a fault that my exertions have not been crowned with success. I am conscious of the rectitude of my intentions. In justice, therefore, to my own character and for the satisfaction of my friends, I must request a court of inquiry into my conduct. And though I sensibly feel the ingratitude of my countrymen; yet every personal injury shall be buried in my zeal for the safety and happiness of my country, in whose cause I have repeatedly fought and bled, and am ready at all times to risk my life.

On April 3, 1777, Washington responded that the oversight had not been merely a mistake, but the result of political considerations and rivalries in Congress:

It is needless for me to say much upon a subject, which must undoubtedly give you a good deal of uneasiness. I confess I was surprised when I did not see your name in the list of Major Generals, and was so fully of the opinion that there was some mistake in the matter. As you may recollect, I desired you not to take any hasty step before the intention of Congress was fully known. The point does not now admit of a doubt, and is of so delicate a nature that I will not undertake to advise. Your own feelings must be your guide. As no particular charge is alleged against you, I do not see upon what ground you can demand a court of inquiry. Besides, public bodies are not amenable for their actions. They place and displace at pleasure; and all the satisfaction that an individual can obtain when he is overlooked is, if innocent, a consciousness that he has not deserved such treatment for his honest exertions. Your determination not to quit your present command while any danger to the public might ensue from your leaving it, deserves my thanks, and justly entitles you to the thanks of your Country.

General Greene, who has lately been at Philadelphia, took occasion to inquire upon what principle the Congress proceeded in their late promotion of General officers. He was informed that the members of each state seemed to insist on having a proportion of general officers adequate to the number of men, which they furnish, and that as Connecticut has already two major generals, it was their full share. I confess this is a strange mode of reasoning, but it may serve to show you, that the promotion, which was due to your seniority, was not overlooked for want of merit in you.

Writing to Horatio Gates, whom I erroneously considered a close friend and confidant, I said, "I cannot . . . help thinking it extremely cruel to be judged and condemned without an opportunity of being heard, or even knowing my crime or accuser. I am conscious of committing no crime since in the public service that merits disgrace."

Both rejected and mortified, I returned home to New Haven. My stalwart sister met me at the door with a wry smile—my boys charged past her and into my arms. After we'd had dinner and put my excited sons to bed, I sat across from Hannah before a welcoming fire. She knitted quietly and spoke without looking up. "Haven't you done enough, Benedict? You have fought, bled, and been humiliated. To what end? Can't you be done and stay home?"

All I could do was nod in mute agreement. I felt the first cracks starting behind my eyes, a portent of the headache to come. Hannah had endured much and been steadfast in supporting me, my boys, and my business. At some level, I knew she was right. "It is not in battle or in the struggle in the field where the light of my patriotism dims. No, in that crucible it burns brightest. The self-interested little men that douse the lamp of liberty and replace it with the darkest wrongs are what make me lose heart."

Her eyes still downcast, the corner of her mouth turned up as she said, "That's a lot of fancy talk, Benedict." Though quiet, her words held an edge. "I am not an educated woman, but it seems to me you are not fighting for your family. You are fighting for people who don't appreciate you."

The silence stretched, with only a pop or crack from the fire and the continuous clicking of her knitting needles. "I joined this fight," I told her, "because I thought men would be judged based on their merit rather than their lineage."

She inclined her head. We both knew I was referring to our father's disgrace.

I continued, "I am beginning to wonder whether we have simply replaced one form of tyranny with another. This is not the meritocracy we had hoped for. Instead, it is a system where politics and favoritism replace inherited position. I fear I have traded unworthy aristocrats for unworthy politicians." I shifted uncomfortably in response to the gout torturing my leg wounded in Quebec.

She glanced up at me for a second in response to my discomfort. "I know you don't believe this, but you are a hero now. Whether you are a general or a major general, you are respected and have bled for the Cause. Isn't it time to focus on your family and business and meet a good woman?" Hannah focused on the word *good*. She knew that Elizabeth DeBlois had refused my advances and returned my gifts while announcing her intention to marry an apothecary's apprentice. As was her way, Hannah had struck at the heart of the matter, drawing a neat line between my public humiliation and my private rebuke from DeBlois.

The house and I groaned in unison as I stood. We both faced implacable foes: politicians and the wind.

Bowing an acknowledgment, I wished Hannah a good night's sleep. Dejected, I shuffled off to bed.

Chapter 44

New Haven, CT - April 26, 1777

Everything changed in an instant when my eyes snapped open at three o'clock in the morning. Three frantic, dirt-covered young men in colonial uniforms were pounding at my front door. The light of my lantern revealed lathered horses over their shoulders, giving testament to a night of hard riding.

The soldier closest to the door removed his hat and touched his forelock, as did the man to his left. The speaker then looked to the man to his right and elbowed him hard in the ribs. In an instant he'd also removed his hat, which he held to his chest like a little boy caught misbehaving. "General Arnold, sir. I mean, you are General Arnold, sir, correct?"

I could tell by their demeanor that I had nothing to fear, so I merely nodded as the frantic young man continued, "We have been sent to get you, sir."

With a mix of amusement and irritation, I responded, "Perhaps, son, you should tell me why."

"The British are here, sir."

"Indeed?" I felt my eyebrow raise at these bumbling fellows—there were clearly no British in New Haven.

"Begging your pardon, General. There are three dozen ships spotted off Norwalk and two thousand redcoats landed at Cedar Point. It looks like they are burning their way toward Danbury."

A wave passed through me, washing away my pain and filling me with energy. I barked a single word in response: "Wait." As I turned, my lamp's light revealed Hannah at the top of the stairs, her hands tightly squeezing her shawl to hold back her tongue more than the chill. Her shadowed face screamed disapproval. I bolted up the stairs.

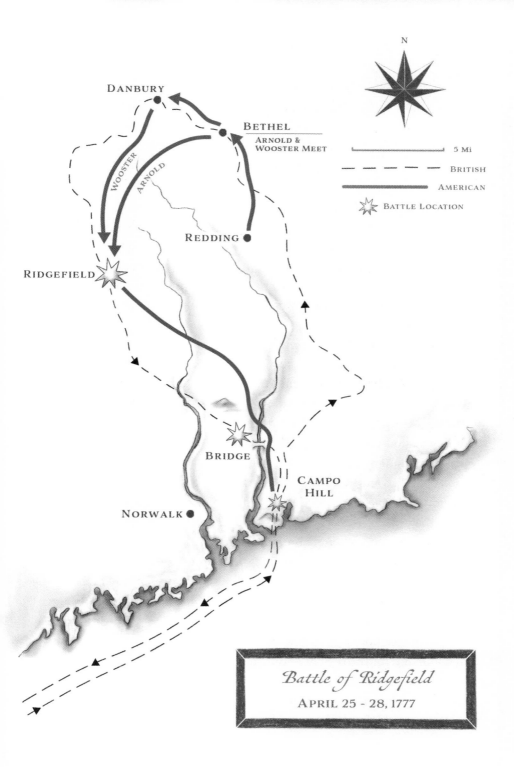

N

DANBURY

BETHEL
ARNOLD &
WOOSTER MEET

5 Mi

WOOSTER

ARNOLD

REDDING

BRITISH

AMERICAN

BATTLE LOCATION

RIDGEFIELD

BRIDGE

CAMPO
HILL

NORWALK

Battle of Ridgefield
APRIL 25 - 28, 1777

She only reluctantly moved aside as I murmured, "It's Connecticut. It needs me." She remained quiet as she watched me get ready; rarely have I ever felt a more effective verbal lashing than her silence.

Almost out of earshot, she finally said, "I will tell your boys you said goodbye." I felt a pang of guilt, but shook it off and moved out the door to the waiting men.

Once outside, I leaped on my horse and raced toward the American supply base at Danbury in a driving rain. It felt like the heavens themselves were ripping open, dropping weeks of rain in a single night. My horse's hooves plunged deeply into the mud-covered roads; at times it felt more like running rapids, as the horses slid and stumbled on the slick surface. The red of burning towns lit our way as we raced thirty brutal miles.

I could hear the crowing of cocks and the barking of dogs as we moved through the countryside, but these animal greetings were all we received. Not a single farmer or townsperson came out to provide support—even though everyone was aware the British were nearby. The enemy had marched twenty-three miles inland, unopposed by any militia to slow their progress. The "Spirit of '76" was now replaced with pervasive indifference.

As fate would have it, the general in charge in Connecticut was David Wooster—the same David Wooster whose supplies I had taken from the armory in New Haven. We'd later had a disagreeable, albeit polite, interaction when he took over the Northern Campaign in Canada. After his pathetic performance there, he had been relegated to homeland defense; in response, he had resigned his Continental commission, and was now a militia general. As I was a general in the Continental Army and he was now a militia general, there was some issue concerning seniority. I resolved to put aside our differences and issues of command for the benefit of our state.

I approached with my escorts in tow. An exhausted Wooster stood inside an open barn, his son at his side. Removing my hat, I bowed and said, "General Wooster."

He also removed his hat and bowed to me. "Ah, General Arnold. Thank you for coming. As you know, I have no authority to order you—"

I held up my hand. "I beg to interrupt, sir. I am here to help. You have a better lay of the land than I. What needs to be done?"

With a sigh of relief, his shoulders gave way to fatigue and tension. "Thank you, General Arnold. Today is not about the nicety of command. Here is our situation. We were unable to reach Danbury before the British burned seventeen hundred tents, five thousand pairs of shoes, sixty hogsheads of rum, twenty hogsheads of wine, four thousand barrels of beef, and five thousand barrels of flour, as well as more than forty houses. We are just two miles from the British. They are burning a path toward us as they return to the sea and their ships." Pausing to make sure no one could hear him, he said in a lower voice, "We are outnumbered, outgunned, and outclassed. We cannot stop such a large force or hope to defeat it."

Given my reputation for aggression, I could tell he was concerned I would disagree, but I motioned for him to continue. "I'll be damned if they are going to come into our state and burn our towns without a scratch." *Strong language from a hardline puritan.* "My plan is to divide our force. I propose to lead six hundred militia to attack the British rear and flanks, while you take five hundred men and build a barrier near Ridgefield. I've got a man here from the area who knows a good choke point where you could build a defensive line. We will both have independent commands and make the British pay a dear price for coming to our home."

It was a simple plan, but when dealing with militia, the most direct route is usually the best. I stood straight and said formally, "An excellent plan, General. I have no changes or suggestions."

Glancing over at his son, the corner of his mouth turned up slightly. "Very good. We will take you to your troops, and we'll both get on our way."

I eventually maneuvered my force in front of the British when they were a mere five miles from their ships at Long Island Sound. General Wooster and his militia attacked the British rear two miles out of

Ridgefield. The enemy's expert use of artillery and the judicious use of grapeshot not only broke Wooster's men, but mortally wounded the general with a shot to the groin. His son fought by his father's side, refusing to surrender. Both were run through with a British bayonet.

As Wooster's soldiers attacked the British rear to slow and distract them, my men worked all night on our defenses to block the redcoats' path to the sea and safety. I chose a defensible position at a narrow point in the road, flanked on one side by a rocky ledge and on the other by a massive farmhouse near the town of Ridgefield. This allowed our troops to build a large barricade consisting of logs, wagons, chairs, and anything else we could get our hands on to block the road and protect our flank. After an exhausting night working in the rain, my mud-covered men and I were pleased to see a clear dawn. The morning revealed a sky rinsed clean to a brilliant cobalt blue. It raised our spirits and hopes for the day to come.

We smelled the British before we saw them. We were downwind, and smoke from their abuse of the countryside heralded their arrival. What is smoke but bits of the world now forced into the air—a barn, a part of a fence, gunpowder, trees, grass, horseflesh, and death? Smoke does not carry the smell of fear; that came off the men in great waves as we waited for the British. What I dreaded was not the smell of fear, but the stench of panic. For now, my men held.

Speed, discipline, and focused violence win the day in battle. I knew that I had none of these advantages. I prayed that fighting for their nearby homes and families would give the men the motivation to act with the aggression and violence necessary to overcome a superior enemy.

I put about two hundred men behind the barrier and three hundred men on the sides to protect our flanks. About three in the afternoon, three columns of British approached. With terrifying precision, they lined up in two columns outside our musket range, their brilliant red uniforms shining in the sun. I beckoned my officers to me. "Gentlemen, tell your boys: when the drums start, the redcoats are going to march within musket range and fire two volleys, one from each row. They will then fix bayonets and charge. Our lads need to keep their heads down until the second volley. I don't want a single man looking up. This is why we built the barricade and worked all night." I looked around and saw nods of agreement and understanding. "Wait for my signal, but when they are within three rods, we will unload our first volley. Every man should have two guns. They should wait for the smoke to clear or until they have a target to fire their second volley. If we are lucky, the British will falter on the first volley."

Just as I finished, we heard the drums announce the British advance. My officers darted to their men, relaying my instructions as they ran. My boys loaded "buck and ball," a large lead ball with two or three buckshot known as "Yankee peas." I was relieved that our men followed my instructions. Even though we were outnumbered at least four to one, we were very effective at pinning the British down with plunging fire from the ledge above. For a crowded hour, we managed to repulse three British charges at heavy losses on both sides. Our barricade withstood repeated grapeshot from enemy cannon. I stood directing the battle next to a brave lad, no older than seventeen. He was hit by grapeshot. His chest tore open like a freshly plowed field, blood spreading on the already wet ground. I saw the life go out of his eyes as he looked at me in shock and surprise.

After the third wave, I could sense fear stood poised, ready to pounce. Our men fought their base desire to simply run and keep running. Homegrown courage, and that of their officers, had kept them in line. While outnumbered, we had killed at least seventy British.

Despite our best efforts, the Brits managed to outflank us. Black shapes came scuttling out of the woods, resolving into redcoats preparing to line up for a charge. The impact of a British bayonet charge should never be underestimated. The Brown Bess was a clumsy musket, and even in the hands of a skilled British soldier, it is difficult to load and accurately fire. What sets the Brown Bess apart is a bayonet that can be added when a charge is ordered. The sight of the British fixing bayonets strikes fear in the hearts of even the best-trained soldiers—and Lord knows my militia was far from elite. I signaled for the men that it was time to withdraw and was pleased to see they moved back in good order.

I wheeled in my horse and looked up to see a British platoon coming down on me from the rocks above. I turned to fire at them with my pistol—but before I could shoot, eight bullets hit my horse simultaneously. My foot, caught in the stirrup, pulled me under the falling animal, leaving me alone to face the coming British charge. As we hit the ground, I managed to avoid getting crushed. I felt my boot catch on the stirrup as I hit the ground and the air was knocked out of me. Thankfully, the horse had not landed on my leg, but I was caught.

As I lay on my side, I looked toward the British with dread. I saw a redcoat's head snap in my direction. Still forty yards away, he began barreling toward me with his bayonet down. I violently kicked to get out of the stirrup, desperately looking for my gun and catching sight of it just out of reach of my left hand. As precious seconds went by, the lone redcoat charged toward me. With all my might, I clawed at the dirt. The weapon was just inches beyond my grasp. Willing my fingers to be longer, I heard the redcoat bellow, "Surrender! You are my prisoner!"

With one mighty lunge, my finger caught the trigger guard. I flipped it up into my hand and in a smooth motion cocked and fired, roaring, "Not yet!"

The look of shock was permanently fixed on the brute's face as the bullet entered his forehead. He collapsed next to my horse—the point of his bayonet cutting a furrow in the ground less than a foot from my head. With him dispatched, I was able to reach down, extricate my boot, and get moving.

I vaulted a fence and escaped through a swamp, the distinctive sounds of bullets whizzing all around me. The tug on my hat as one grazed my head gave me a further incentive to pick up my pace as I ran toward safety.

While we were dislodged from our defenses, we also prevented the British from reaching their ships, requiring them to stop for the night. I put my exhausted men to work digging new trenches and building new barricades to yet again block the British march to the safety of their ships.

When the sun rose, it revealed my men strewn across the open land immediately behind the barricade they had built, as if a hand had magically passed over them and put them all to sleep.

With the help of my friend John Lamb and his artillery regiment, we hoped to catch the British at a crossroads two miles from Ridgefield, where our artillery could be used to great effect. Lamb had been grievously wounded in our attack against Quebec; Washington had acted upon my request and had him exchanged and returned home. Notwithstanding his severe wounds, Lamb still bravely stood ready to defend against this British invasion. Unfortunately, the British column was alerted by a local Tory and managed to bypass our roadblock.

Undaunted by this disappointing news, I woke my troops. We slammed into the fleeing British late in the afternoon as they reached the relative safety of Compo Hill, where their fleet could provide artillery support. Galloping ahead, I raised my sword, my eyes blazing with the thrill of battle. Suddenly the air was filled with the crackle of musketry. I looked to either side and realized that I had been galloping alone. I heard the sounds of balls pinging off trees and nearby rocks. Under British fire, the militia had faltered. A bullet tore through my coat, and my horse staggered as it was struck by a round. I reluctantly spun the animal around and returned to the safety of our lines, frustrated, exhilarated, and truly alive.

The British then mounted a counterattack, seeking to take our precious artillery. Quebec veterans Oswald and Lamb were completing a makeshift battery for their three six-pound cannon to fire at the enemy when the British commander led four hundred regulars to quickly overrun their position. The men fought bravely, but the indomitable Lamb, who had already lost an eye in the assault on Quebec, was hit squarely by a round shot. Forced to retreat, Lamb's men dragged him to the rear. Once again, he survived what would have been a mortal wound for most men.

I rode up to our line, ignoring the enemy's grapeshot and demanding we continue to engage the British, until yet another horse was shot out from under me and a musket ball creased my collar. Having captured the guns, the British retreated to the protection of their ship batteries. We too backed off, having honorably protected our homeland.

When news of my bravery reached Congress, they apparently reconsidered their prior actions—at last, I was promptly promoted to the rank of major general. Regular army soldiers were saying that I "fought like Julius Caesar," and even the British said I was a "devilish fighting fellow." John Adams, who had previously played a central role in denying my promotion as a major general, endorsed my elevation because of my "vigilance, activity, and bravery in the late affair at Connecticut."

Nevertheless, five recently appointed major generals would still have seniority over me. I was somewhat gratified by the appointment, but the sting of disrespect was still keenly felt. I was also deeply disappointed by the behavior of the citizenry of Connecticut. My own state had failed to mobilize in large numbers to repel the British. While my men were dying, the public seemed increasingly indifferent to supporting the Revolution.

Chapter 45

Philadelphia, PA - May 19, 1777

O n the same day I was lauded by Congress for my bravery, John Brown, my old enemy from the Fort Ticonderoga campaign, circulated a pamphlet accusing me of having "character not worth a sixpence," claiming that "money is this man's god, and to get enough of it, he would sacrifice his country." Outraged by the pamphlet, I openly declared, "Whenever I have the opportunity to see him, he shall no longer have reason to complain for want of satisfaction."

Washington, as promised, gave me a letter to take to Congress to address my seniority concerns. In the letter to President of Congress John Hancock, Washington wrote, "It is needless to say anything of this gentleman's military character. It is universally known that he has always distinguished himself as a judicious, brave officer, of great activity, enterprise and perseverance." When I finished reading the letter, I was deeply disappointed. While he praised my gallantry in battle, he never backed me up as a man. He made no effort to refute the slanderous allegations of Brown or seek to overturn my inferiority to other recently appointed major generals.

On May 19, I arrived in Philadelphia with the goal of meeting Brown's accusations with the same intensity with which I'd rushed the British guns. Both Generals Washington and Schuyler, who were present in Philadelphia, counseled patience and recommended I should use a light touch in dealing with Congress. At that time, I still naively believed that Congress would appreciate my forthright manner and honesty in meeting Brown head on.

I wrote to Congress on May 20, "I am exceedingly unhappy to find that after having made every sacrifice of fortune, ease and domestic happiness to serve my country, I am publicly impeached in particular by Lt.

Colonel Brown of a catalogue of crimes, which, if true, ought to subject me to disgrace, infamy, and to just resentment of my countrymen. Conscious of the rectitude of my intentions, however, I have erred in judgment. I must request the favor of Congress to point out some mode by which my conduct, and that of my accusers, may be inquired into, and justice done to the innocent and injured."

I did not understand that I had stepped into a larger political battle. John Adams and others who opposed the power held by General Washington and his generals worried that the popularity of myself and General Washington would make Congress irrelevant. My manifest success on both the battlefield and in business prior to the war intimidated these little men, and caused them to ignore the merits of my claims to seniority and the unfairness of Brown's claims. My demand came at the exact moment when Washington was in a power struggle with Congress—I was the pawn in a greater political chess match.

My only solace was that while my seniority was being ignored, the merits of my claims against Brown were not. John Adams, who had been vociferously attacking me on the issue of seniority, came to my defense when examining Brown's defamatory assertions.

As the Board of War met to evaluate Brown's claims against me, Congress chose to make a public statement of faith in my bravery and leadership by passing a resolution: "That the Quartermaster General be directed to procure a horse and present the same, properly caparisoned to Major General Arnold, in the name of this Congress, as a token of their approbation of his gallant conduct in the action against the enemy in the late enterprise to Danbury, and which General Arnold had one horse killed under him and another wounded."

On May 21, 1777, Congress and several generals sat down to examine my records relating to the Canadian campaign and respond to Brown's claims of misappropriation. Fortunately, Charles Carroll corroborated my rendition of the chaos in Montreal and my attempts to stem a smallpox epidemic, defend the city, and feed a starving army. Nevertheless, I was still required to testify as to all my financial dealings from the time I left for Quebec to the end of the battle at Valcour Isle.

I reminded the panel that I had begged Congress repeatedly to appoint a paymaster to keep track of the multiple accounts, but they had failed to do so. Likewise, I was never provided with either a commissary quartermaster or a paymaster to address any of the various accounts while I was battling the British. I kept the best records I could, but many were lost when the *Royal Savage* was burned. While I had claims for $66,671, I could not produce receipts for $55,000 of those amounts. I testified, quite simply, "I am not a clerk. I was too busy fighting to bother with receipts and accounts."

On May 23, the Board of War reported to the full Congress its "entire satisfaction concerning the generals' character and conduct, so cruelly and groundlessly aspersed by John Brown's publication." Even John Adams wrote that I "had been basely slandered and libeled." They also ordered their report published so that I would be free from any taint of Brown's unfair assertions. At the same time, they did not make any conclusions about monies that were owed or indicate that a decision would be forthcoming anytime soon.

After weeks of attempting to bully, cajole, or appease members of Congress, the battle was lost. My name was cleared, but seniority was not to be restored, and I was reimbursed nothing. I met with men who said they believed I had been wronged, while praising my bravery, but then whispered against me behind my back. No one stepped forward as my champion. I had thought the British were my enemies; my real foes were far more vicious and dishonorable.

On July 11, in submitting my letter of resignation, I said, "My feelings are deeply wounded. It is not in my power to serve my country in the present rank I hold. Honour is a sacrifice no man ought to make; as I received, so I wish to transmit it inviolate to posterity."

Chapter 46

Hudson Valley, NY - July 19, 1777

The "politics" also extended to Generals Schuyler and Gates. Schuyler had retained command of the Northern Army, to the irritation of the New Englanders who backed General Gates. Moreover, Schuyler was seen by the radicals as in sympathy with the anti-democratic forces within the military.

As I enjoyed good relations with both generals, I was claimed by neither side and thus received no protection from any party. Meanwhile, General Washington had begun to formulate his "Fabian strategy" (in reference to Fabius Maximus, a Roman leader who famously defeated Hannibal by fighting a defensive war). It became Washington's primary strategy to fight a defensive campaign, preserving his army and defeating the British through a war of attrition. Such a defensive strategy ran contrary to my aggressive temperament and overall strategic view.

On the same day I resigned, a British force began moving down from Canada. They were seeking to complete their plan of effectively cutting New England off from the rest of the Colonies. Under General "Gentleman Johnny" Burgoyne, nearly eight thousand redcoats, Hessians, Canadian loyalists, and Indians were sweeping down the shores of Lake Champlain with 138 pieces of artillery destined for Fort Ticonderoga. Washington knew the Revolution hung in the balance. As I was delivering my letter to Congress, he was writing to them, seeking to have me play the lead role in the upcoming battle:

> There is now an absolute necessity for their turning out to check Burgoyne's progress or the most disagreeable consequence may be apprehended. Upon this occasion, I would take the liberty to suggest to Congress that the propriety of sending

an active, spirited officer to conduct and lead them on. If General Arnold has settled his affairs and can be spared from Philadelphia, I would recommend him for the business and that he should immediately be set out for the northern department. He is active, judicious and brave, and an officer in whom the militia will repose the greatest confidence. Besides this, he is well acquainted with that country and with the routes and most important passes and defiles in it. I do not think he can render more signal services, or be more usefully employed at this time, than in this way. I am persuaded his presence and activity will animate the militia greatly and spur them on to a becoming conduct. I could wish him to be engaged in a more agreeable service, to be with better troops, but circumstances call for his exertions in this way, and I have no doubt if he is adding much to the honor he has already acquired.

Congress, as a practical matter, chose to ignore my resignation and instead ordered me to the north. Questions of my seniority were simply not addressed. Like a beaten but loyal dog, I followed the commands of my abusive masters and reported to Washington's headquarters on the Hudson. His Excellency did me the honor of leaving his tent and greeting me warmly as I alighted from my horse.

After I cleaned up, I was escorted back into his tent for a private meeting and a light supper. Washington sat quietly, comfortable with the silence, as the food was placed on the table. Unable to sit in silence any longer, I started to open my mouth, but the general held up both his hands. "My dear General Arnold. You have been badly mistreated. I am doing everything I can to restore your seniority. John Hancock has promised the issue will be addressed. You are my finest general in the field, and there is no more worthy leader I can send north to confront General Burgoyne."

I had been leaning forward like a ship tilted toward a gale, but Washington's words took the wind out of my sails. I sat back as he continued, "It is your efforts at Valcour Isle and elsewhere that kept the British on their heels and bought us a year. Burgoyne has taken Ticonderoga and is now cutting his way through the forest from Lake Champlain to the Hudson River Valley. If he succeeds . . ."

"New England is cut off, and we are lost." I found myself speaking despite my resolution to remain silent.

"Indeed, my able friend." Despite his great size, Washington rose from the table quickly and, with the grace of a dancer, glided over to a large map. "I obviously need to keep my main army here near New York to prevent the British from taking Philadelphia, but I need you to stop Burgoyne at Albany." He punctuated his sentence by pointing so hard at the map that it gave a pop.

Gesturing to the areas between Lake Champlain and Albany, I could not hide my enthusiasm. "I know this country well, General. There are roads, but they go through extremely dense forests with innumerable streams and gullies. We could destroy bridges, cut down trees, and divert streams. I am told Burgoyne's army is enormous, with a huge supply train." Washington looked from the map to me without expression as I continued, "I know many would support attacking the British, but they are too strong right now. A frontal assault would be futile. No, a death by a thousand cuts is the way to go. I know you have experience in these challenging situations, and it is better to hit them in the sides or from behind than head-on." I thought carefully before making this comment. I was referring to his brave actions during the defeat of General Braddock in the French and Indian War. While a loss for the army, it had been a personal victory for the then-young Colonel Washington.

Nodding in recognition to the reference, Washington answered, "Indeed. Times may have changed, but the mentality of the British Army has not. They are not well equipped for bush fighting, and we will have the advantage of cover. I've already exchanged some correspondence with General Schuyler, and he has reached a similar conclusion. I understand he has recruited woodsmen from New York and Massachusetts to bedevil Burgoyne's progress while our troops snipe and skirmish."

Nodding in agreement, I decided to ask for a favor. "There is a group of men who I believe would be especially well suited for this sort of fighting."

A rare smile, albeit closemouthed, spread across Washington's face. "Morgan?"

I grinned in response. "Yes, Your Excellency. Daniel Morgan and I are well matched, and I believe he is one of the army's best commanders in a fight."

"You shall have him, but I need to ask a favor from you. We have not yet settled your seniority; you may be required to take orders from men who are senior to you in rank, but inferior in skill and accomplishment. For the good of the Cause, are you willing to do that, General Arnold? Again, I will do what I can to have your proper seniority restored, but in the meantime, I need you to honor the chain of command . . . such as it is."

I stiffened to attention and said formally, "Yes, Your Excellency."

Nodding in acknowledgment, Washington snapped, "Very well, General. Thank you."

The general's head involuntarily turned back toward the stack of papers on his desk in the corner. Understanding I was dismissed, I bowed and left the tent.

Chapter 47

Albany, NY - August 12, 1777

A few weeks later, I sat at a council of war with General Schuyler and a group of officers I did not know well. The sour smell of fear filled the air.

Schuyler signaled for a junior officer to describe our current situation. Pointing to a map, the pimple-faced youth of no more than twenty croaked, "We have about six thousand soldiers, half of whom are sick. Meanwhile, Burgoyne's eight thousand soldiers are slowly but steadily advancing. A second force, under British Lieutenant Colonel Barry St. Leger, is working its way from the west with about 750 regulars and 1,000 Mohawk Indians, with their goal to take Fort Stanwix." Stanwix was a small American fort located at the headwaters of the Mohawk River. The square structure, two hundred feet on each side and constructed of wood and sod, was crucial in protecting Albany, New York. "If it fails, our remaining army will be caught in a pincer between St. Leger and Burgoyne."

General Schuyler had become a man wrung out by stress and time. The color of his skin was bleached, leaving behind gray hair and a sallow complexion. With a force of will overcoming fatigue, he turned to each of his officers and asked them whether he should keep his army together, or divide it and send some of his men to ensure Fort Stanwix did not fall. Every man voted to keep the troops together and leave Fort Stanwix to its fate. Then they turned to me.

I stood slowly and faced the room full of defeated men. "The answer is obvious. We must divide the army. Fort Stanwix must not fall."

A silence spread. Schuyler rose and began to pace on the opposite side of the room, biting down so hard on the stem of his clay pipe that it broke in two. He took the pieces and violently tossed them in the corner, his face turning to a deep shade of red as he spun toward the group and announced, "Gentlemen, I will take the responsibility upon myself. General Arnold is right—Fort Stanwix and the Mohawk Valley must be saved." He fixed the group with his steel-blue gaze. He was old; his eyes were not. "Where is a general who will command the relief?"

Everyone looked at me.

A wry smile spread across my face as I answered, "Give me nine hundred men, and you will hear of my victory, or no more."

As is the nature of fate and war, a horrible incident turned out to be a boon for American militia recruitment. A loyalist, Jane McCrea, was scalped by one of Burgoyne's Canadian Indians, who sought to collect a bounty, equivalent to a barrel of rum, which Burgoyne was offering for each scalp. What this incident made clear was that nobody, neither loyalist nor patriot, man nor woman, was free from Burgoyne's murderous Indians. Making the most of this unfortunate event, I stretched the truth, writing that Miss McCrea and her friend Sarah McNeil were "shot, scalped, stripped, and butchered in the most shocking manner." Galvanized by this atrocity, the New Englanders flocked to our banner.

American troops continued harassing attacks as Burgoyne's army became bogged down heading south, and his Indian allies abandoned him in the face of a flood of angry Americans seeking vengeance. Weakened, and now largely blinded without Indian scouts, Burgoyne found himself caught in a hostile land, surrounded by a populace up in arms as a result of his allies' acts of cruelty. Worst of all for Burgoyne, British General Howe would not be providing relief, and General Clinton remained in New York with no ability to assist. Nevertheless, Burgoyne still had some reason for hope. If St. Leger could take Fort Stanwix, he would then be within striking distance of Albany, freeing Burgoyne from the trap closing around him.

At the same time I was mobilizing to defend Albany, a motion was made in Congress to reinstate me to seniority equal with the other five major generals, backdated to February 19, "on account of his extraordinary merit and former rank in the army." Once again the men from Massachusetts, led by John Adams, voted against my seniority. To make matters worse, I heard that some from the Massachusetts delegation said that I had resigned because my "self-love was injured in a fanciful right which is incompatible with the general interest of the union."

There were some who had words of kindness, including Henry Laurens from South Carolina, who said that I had been turned down "not because he is deficient in merit, or that his demand was not well founded, but because he asked for it." Congress's behavior toward "good old servant, General Arnold," he said, "will probably deprive us of that officer and may be attended by further ill effects in the army." The salt of this insult was being driven deeper into the wound by nineteen-year-old French aristocrat the Marquis de Lafayette's promotion to major general, the same rank as me, despite his complete absence of military experience.

I tried hard to set it aside, but every snicker on the edge of earshot, every sideways smirk, made me keenly aware that I was the butt of many jokes. While I was cleared of wrongdoing, and despite my unquestioned bravery and success in the field, the "leaders" of the Revolution seemed to revel in my destruction. Even men like John Adams, who had defended me when slandered, opposed the restoration of my rank, based on some bizarre pretext that preventing my elevation constituted some mythical victory of republican principles. Such metaphysical and philosophical justifications for insults to my honor are as lost on me now as they were then.

Chapter 48

Fort Stanwix, NY – August 21, 1777

C olonel Peter Gansevoort stood over six feet tall, was twenty-eight years old, and had distinguished himself for bravery in 1776. In May 1777, he was given command of the crumbling fort that dated back to the French and Indian War. Gansevoort and his men struggled to rebuild the fortress's fifteen-foot-thick walls and two-foot casemates, as well as the pear-shaped bastions that jutted from each corner. Seven hundred and fifty men were crowded into the small fort which stood thirty miles upriver from Albany.

On August 7, Gansevoort received a letter from British commander, Lieutenant Colonel St. Leger stating that unless the Americans immediately surrendered, St. Leger's Indians would "kill every man in the garrison." St. Leger made the strategic blunder of insisting on capturing the fort when he could have simply bypassed and raided down the valley toward Albany. He unwisely attempted to intimidate Gansevoort's men by parading the British before the defenders and firing six-pound cannon to reduce the walls of the fort.

His demonstrations had the opposite effect on the Americans. Gansevoort responded, "It is my determined resolution to defend this fort and garrison to the last extremity, on behalf of the United American States, who have placed me here to defend it against all their enemies."

I approached the fort with my nine-hundred-man expeditionary force. When it finally came into view, the flag at its center hung limply on its pole. Suddenly, as if called to action by our approach, a gust of wind pulled open the flag, and I saw the new design that was the subject of much discussion. A blue square sat in the upper left corner, containing a circle of thirteen white stars; beyond it were thirteen red and white horizontal stripes. It followed the same color scheme as the Union Jack.

I liked its continuity and symbolism; however, I was somewhat concerned that its color scheme might cause confusion on the battlefield.

Scouts confirmed St. Leger had nearly twice our men. He was an experienced commander who had fought in the French and Indian War and gained a reputation as an excellent frontier fighter. While I wanted to immediately attack, my officers desired otherwise; I reluctantly agreed to their counsel. I was frustrated that I was unable to attack, but only a fool proceeds without the support of his men.

While I know my reputation was for being extremely aggressive, I never went off half-cocked. Sometimes a plan springs out of the ether fully formed in my mind; sometimes I must brood and ponder before it coalesces; and sometimes it knocks at the door. The latter was the case as I paced in the small cabin I was using as my headquarters outside the British encampment surrounding Fort Stanwix.

A sturdy woman burst into the cabin. In her forties, with a mixture of gray and blonde hair in a bun, she pushed away my guards and threw herself at my feet. In English, but with a discernable Dutch accent, she held my ankles in a vice grip and said, "General. I beg you, do not kill my son. He is a goed boy. He means no harm. He is not right in the mind."

Looking toward my officers, who'd poured into the room in response to the commotion, I shrugged. I had no idea what she was talking about.

A frustrated and breathless captain rushed in. "I am very sorry, General. This woman's son, Hon Yost, has been caught recruiting loyalist soldiers to join the British. He has been tried, found guilty, and condemned to death."

Understanding the situation, I reached down and removed her hands from my ankles as the captain pulled her to her feet. I said matter-of-factly, "Madam. I am sorry to say your son is a traitor, and he will be executed as scheduled."

She persisted, "No, my lord, you do not understand. He is not bright. He doesn't understand what he is doing. Would you kill a boy that does not know right from wrong?"

I don't know if it was the look in her eyes or some little voice deep inside me, but I agreed to meet with her son before the execution was carried out.

A few minutes later, a large, sloppily dressed young man in chains was dragged into my cabin. Looking him up and down, I said, "Your mother begs for your life, but I am told you were a traitor recruiting loyalist soldiers. What do you have to say for yourself?"

"I have a goed moeder."

"Indeed, your good mother says you are addle-minded and do not know right from wrong."

At that moment, a sly and knowing grin made me believe he was not as dumb as his mother claimed. "Some say so," he said.

"What do the Indians say?" I asked.

With a knowing nod of his head, he indicated, "Many would agree."

I understood that many Indian tribes gave special deference to those unfortunate individuals who are weak of mind. They believed they held special powers to communicate with their heathen gods. A plan began to form on how to use this lad to my advantage. Leaning forward, I said, conspiratorially, "See here, boy. Do you want to live?"

A smile spread across his face, and he nodded vigorously.

"I am going to hold your mother and younger brother hostage to ensure you do what I want. If this goes well, you, your mother, and your brother shall be set free, and the British will leave the fort. If not, you, your mother, and your brother shall all die." I would never have killed his mother or his brother, but the boy didn't know that—he nodded in agreement as I explained my plan.

I had his coat removed and several shots put through it. After the coat was given back to him, he was allowed to escape into the woods heading toward the British. The next morning, as he stumbled into St. Leger's camp, he was caught by a group of Mohawks. Hysterical, Hon Yost explained that he had barely escaped from the Americans and that I was attacking with an enormous army to support the fort. When interrogated, he indicated that the Americans had as many soldiers as leaves on the trees. Dragged in front of St. Leger, Yost said that I had over two thousand troops and would be arriving within twenty-four hours.

Because of his perceived mental deficiencies, his story was given added credence by the Indians.

The Mohawks were aware of my reputation from the Abenakis, where I was known as "Dark Eagle." I had spread rumors through Indian scouts that I would punish the British and the loyalists, but not Indians who did not oppose me. The Mohawks, hearing this, jumped on the excuse to leave and ran out of the camp. Many of St. Leger's soldiers also panicked and took off into the woods. St. Leger had no choice but to retreat to Lake Ontario, seventy miles away.

On August 24, I entered Fort Stanwix without firing a shot—my strategy had worked. I freed Yost and his brother; I had never held his mother in custody. We had forced the British withdrawal despite our inadequate reinforcements, Indian support, food, horses, or men. St. Leger's retreat permitted all American forces to be redirected against General Burgoyne. With Fort Stanwix reinforced and safe, I returned to the American headquarters near Albany.

Having secured a bloodless victory in the face of a superior force, I thought I would be greeted as a hero when I returned to headquarters. Instead, I learned that when Congress had debated whether I should be elevated in rank because of my repeated military success, seven states had actively opposed my elevation. More upsetting, I was told Horatio Gates had not spoken to any delegates on my behalf, even when asked for his opinion. He had even sent a notice to Congress claiming that it was he who had engineered St. Leger's withdrawal, saying that he had achieved a "brilliant victory that gives the brightest luster to American arms, and covers the enemies of the United States with infamy and shame." While praising several other officers, he failed to mention me by name.

I had been once again overlooked for promotion. This time, I was undermined by someone I considered a brother-in-arms. Gates had not only betrayed our friendship, but was willing to steal my victory for his own.

Chapter 49

Confluence of Mohawk and Hudson Rivers, NY –
August 30, 1777

I reported to the headquarters of the Northern Army. Despite this failure to restore my seniority, I felt great confidence that the upcoming
battle would provide the final impetus to confirm my rightful position
in the army once and for all. Meanwhile, Generals Schuyler and Gates
battled each other more than the British. Ultimately, Gates won because
Congress chose to blame Schuyler for the loss of Fort Ticonderoga.
Moreover, Gates was the favorite of the powerful New Englanders.
Infuriated, Schuyler turned over command to him, saying, "The palm
of victory is denied to me, and it is left to you, General, to reap the fruits
of my labors."

Ten days after my victory at Fort Stanwix, I arrived at the American
encampment at Stillwater, about fifteen miles above Albany. General
Gates assigned me divisional command of the left wing.

I was pleased when Daniel Morgan and his riflemen rode into
camp to provide reinforcements. I always chose to focus on abilities,
rather than politics; thus, I appointed Henry Brockholst Livingston and
Richard Varick to my staff. These worthy gentlemen had strong ties to
General Schuyler and thus were soon to be attacked by Gates and his
cronies. He was upset I had not vetted my proposed staff with him prior
to appointment. I wanted to surround myself with the best men possible
for the upcoming battle. In contrast, General Gates appointed my old
nemesis Enoch Poor as a brigade commander. Poor had served as one
of Hazen's supporters during his court-martial; nevertheless, I resolved
to attempt to work with him and honor my promise to Washington.

At a more fundamental level, Gates and I had differing tactical styles. I believed in attack, whereas Gates believed in defense. While I wanted to rush at the British, Gates wanted to force the redcoats to crash into the American defenses. He was convinced that the British would impale themselves with a direct assault on our well-defended lines. I felt equally confident that the British Army's unparalleled siege work could drive us out of defenses or outflank us. I still felt compelled to meet with Gates to prevent a strategic disaster.

There was a time when Gates would have asked me to sit down by the fire, a drink in his hand, and seek my counsel. Now, in addition to the increasingly tense political situation, the presence of Wilkinson, my former aide and Gates's sycophant, replaced relaxed courtesy with tense formality. When I walked into Gates's office at Stillwater, "Wilky" did not rise as was proper in the presence of a superior officer, instead slouching further in the upholstered chair placed to the right of the general's large desk. Trying to hide my displeasure, I directed my gaze at Gates, who looked up at me over the glasses on the edge of his shark-fin nose. His eyes were bright and intelligent, but also cruel and cold.

He croaked, "General Arnold, why are you still here? You should be with your men."

I could feel my face flush. His lack of foresight in choosing Stillwater needed to be addressed. I gambled he would listen, given his obsession with fortified defenses. "I met with my senior officers, General. They have their orders. In the meantime, I am concerned about the vulnerability of this location." I pointed to the map on the table. "We are in a low area with wide fields and easy river access. The British could come on us quickly by land or river, and we would be totally exposed without any ability to defend. The militia would be on their heels at the first glint of a British bayonet."

Gates's face contorted as if he had just bit into a lemon. With an edge of hostility, he asked, "And your point?"

Keeping a measured tone, I answered, "My point, General, is that we need to scout a better position to engage the enemy. Colonel Tadeusz Kościuszko and I have seen a spot three miles from here with high ground where we would hold the advantage." As a general rule, I did not want to fight the British in open fields, preferring my men snipe from the woods to create chaos and attack if there was an opening. I also disfavored excessive reliance upon militiamen, whose brief terms of enlistment made them unreliable—Gates, on the other hand, constantly lauded militiamen as "my Yankees."

I knew he wanted to fight from behind impenetrable defenses, so I played to that desire. "Artillery placed on top of the bluff's high, steep hillside will prevent the British from getting around us from the west or getting past us along the Hudson. Almost three hundred feet above the Hudson River, this spot called Bemis Heights presents an ideal vantage point to shell any incoming Burgoyne troops and prevents them from using the only road to Albany."

Gates removed his glasses and set them on the table, clearly listening to me for the first time.

I continued, "Burgoyne will be pushed back from the river, up into the hills, and into the teeth of our defenses. The thick woods and hilly forest will prevent the British from outflanking us and using their artillery to their advantage. Indeed, their open-field tactics will be useless. The terrain will present an ideal venue for our men, where the British can be beaten piecemeal. Dearborn's light infantry and Morgan's rifles should be placed on the far left of our American line to stop any British flanking attempt. In the center, you can take personal command. I recommend you put the best of the battle-hardened New Englanders in a heavily fortified right flank overlooking the river, to be protected with artillery."

Gates glanced over at Wilkinson, a man without any military acumen or moral compass. He didn't know how to respond to my plan, so he merely made a neutral shrug at Gates's unspoken question. The general leaned back in his chair and looked up at the ceiling, either thinking or praying to heaven for some guidance, as he also lacked any strategic sense. Falling back on his instincts for defense, I could see him reach a decision as he sat forward again in his chair. With reluctance, he said in a measured and neutral voice, "Very well, General Arnold. Proceed as you recommend."

I did not dally. Instead, I pivoted on my heels and raced out to meet Colonel Kościuszko, who was waiting outside the headquarters.

For a solid week, seven thousand of our boys dug earthworks and redoubts for more than a mile across a narrow, flat area of ridges. By the time the British arrived, our defensive position was virtually impregnable, and we (for a change) had them outnumbered with fresh and well-fed troops. Gates's acceptance of my defensive plan, while not the high point of our relationship—that had occurred long earlier—was the last time he took my advice or treated me with even a modicum of respect. Afterward, with the urging of Wilkinson, the general invited Lieutenant Colonel John Brown to staff meetings to irritate me.

Once I had completed construction of the defenses at Bemis Heights, Gates and I disagreed on virtually every strategic and tactical issue during staff meetings. As a result, he excluded me from meetings and barred me from making further suggestions concerning the upcoming battle. Meetings were held among a cadre of Wilkinson's and Gates's favorites, while I and other members of the "New York Gang" were not invited. I felt compelled to formally protest this failure to include me in strategy meetings.

On the morning of September 18, I was granted permission to lead a foray toward General Burgoyne's encamped troops. Moving a column through a dense patch of woods was like ants caught in a hairbrush. My men thrashed blindly toward the enemy.

Suddenly, we came out of the thicket and ran into British soldiers foraging for food. My men immediately opened fire, killing and wounding fourteen and taking a prisoner. I followed Gates's standing orders and pulled our men back to Bemis Heights, informing him that I believed the enemy would likely attack within forty-eight hours and engage in a flanking maneuver. Gates merely shrugged off my report and ordered the troops to further entrench, rather than seize the initiative and prepare to meet the attack.

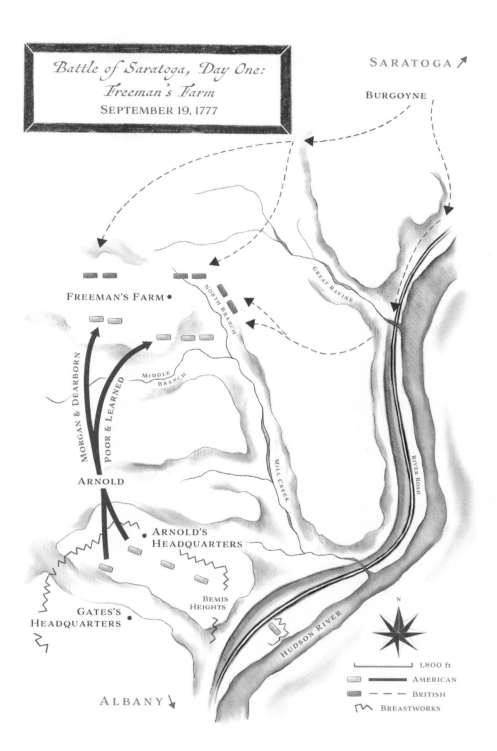

Battle of Saratoga, Day One:
Freeman's Farm
SEPTEMBER 19, 1777

SARATOGA ↗

BURGOYNE

GREAT RAVINE

FREEMAN'S FARM •

NORTH BRANCH

MIDDLE BRANCH

MORGAN & DEARBORN

POOR & LEARNED

MILL CREEK

RIVER ROAD

ARNOLD

ARNOLD'S
HEADQUARTERS

BEMIS
HEIGHTS

GATES'S
HEADQUARTERS •

N

HUDSON RIVER

1,800 ft

AMERICAN
BRITISH
BREASTWORKS

ALBANY ↓

Chapter 50

Freeman's Farm, NY - September 19, 1777

The next morning, the sounds of the lark, the crowing cock, and the protests of an unmilked cow all ceased with the beat of British drums—each cadence reflecting different orders for the troops. I looked out over the thick forest to the valley below the little cabin I called my headquarters. Above, a hawk balanced on a column of air. *What do you see, my feathered friend? What is Gentlemen Johnny doing?* He responded by sliding out of reach and moving to quieter hunting grounds, as indifferent to my query as he was to the carnage about to unfold below. The hoarfrost whitening the ground quickly disappeared under the clear skies as I waited for battle.

The British moved into the woods and fields in front of our positions. Their armies extended from the banks of the river westward up to our troops holding Bemis Heights. While we were aware of their movements by drums and signal guns, they were largely obscured—spotters would occasionally catch glimpses of the flash of metal, bright scarlet uniforms, or large battle flags peeking through the trees.

At 10:00 a.m., British guns coughed, announcing the forward movement of three columns. While we outnumbered the British, Burgoyne still had more than six thousand crack redcoats with their backs up against a wall. The enemy needed to either win this fight at Bemis Heights or face the prospect of a protracted and bloody retreat back to Canada.

I immediately understood what was going on when I heard a snicker of musketry at our center. Burgoyne had divided his army and was attempting to outflank our defenses. He commanded the center; meanwhile, he sent 2,200 troops to our left to get around our long lines while his Hessians protected his other flank. I knew his bold attack at the center must be a diversion and that the flanking attack was his real objective. If not opposed, the attack on the front would act as the perfect diversion to allow British artillery to be well-placed on our left flank, forcing us to maneuver from the heights and lose our advantage. I was appalled to see that besides men readying themselves in the trenches, there was no activity whatsoever, not even an attempt to go forward and probe the British advance.

Shortly after noon, the British center reached a three-hundred-yard clearing broken by a half dozen ramshackle buildings known as "Freeman's Farm." Meanwhile, the balance of enemy forces continued to move on our flank. Knowing Gates's indecision would lead to disaster, I strode to the small house that was acting as his headquarters. Before I opened the door, I took a second to compose myself and vowed not to raise my voice.

With the battle occurring just two miles away, I expected to see a group of officers standing around a map, assessing the situation and preparing to give orders. Instead, Gates sat in a comfortable folding chair, chatting amicably with his staff, appearing to all the world at his ease on a lovely fall afternoon. Neither he nor any of his staff bothered to stand at my entry, although everyone (excepting of course the general) was junior to me. Gates looked up with irritation, and I noted sideways glances and smirks exchanged among his staff.

Standing erect, I said in my most measured tone, "Good day, General. As I predicted yesterday, General Burgoyne is moving forward both directly below us and on our left flank."

Without looking at me, Gates gave a confident and dismissive toss of the hand, replying, "Yes, yes, indeed, General. I have seen to our defenses this morning. The British will move forward and impale themselves as they did in Boston." He then turned his glance from me to his fellow officers and said, "A day of patience to be followed by celebration, eh?" He was met by universal nods of approval. Acknowledging the approbations, he chortled, "Quite so," signifying the discussion had come to an end.

I realized for the first time that his smile was an affectation—it started at his mouth, but did not reach his eyes.

Damn his eyes! I involuntarily took a step forward, now looking down on the general. I could feel my intensity pushing his staff to uncomfortable silence. I whispered in a way that projected like a shout, "Burgoyne comes not merely at our front, but more importantly at our flank. We have received reports of artillery being moved. If he is not aggressively met, the artillery *will* be expertly placed, we *will* be bombarded, and we *will* be forced to give up defensive positions, including where you sit right now . . ." After a pause, I said with all the respect I could muster, "Sir."

The stench of overconfidence began to slip from the room; for the first time, Gates moved uncomfortably in his chair. I knew I would not get permission to attack through intimidating him, so I tried another tactic he did not expect. "I am begging you, General. Let me take a force forward and meet them." It was time to compliment this self-satisfied horse's arse. "You will be here in command to make sure we remain solid within our fortifications, but if I am simply given Colonel Morgan's and Captain Dearborn's men, we can keep the British from turning our flank and secure *your* victory."

His grant of permission was like a parent making a concession to an unruly teenager. "Very well. Proceed with the men you propose, but let me be clear—I do not intend to abandon these works. It is precisely what Gentleman Johnny wants me to do. He wants to pull us out into the open, where their superior training will give them an advantage. No, General, it is these works that tip the odds in our favor." For a moment, he paused as if to reconsider; then he snapped, "Don't be coming back to me, sir, for any additional reinforcements."

I bowed in agreement.

At that point, any decent and courteous officer would have stood. Gates merely reached for a drink and toasted with it. "You have your orders, General Arnold. Dismissed."

I'd long ago learned that when you receive what you want, do not stay and gild the lily. I was out the door in a flash and on my horse, galloping to where I knew Morgan's men were encamped and yelling orders to Dearborn to get his men ready to move. Within fifteen minutes, the men were outfitted and their officers ready. We stood just inside our breastworks. I shouted in full voice so that I could be heard by officers and the men alike, "Here it is, boys. If we don't stop the British, they are going to outflank us and force us off these heights. Don't fool yourself—the British 'attack' is an act of desperation. If we stop the bastards, they will have nowhere to go. If we do nothing, they will push us back with artillery."

Turning toward one of my favorite officers from Quebec, I said, "Captain Dearborn, your men and I are going to go toward the sounds of the guns. The British won't expect us. We will have the element of surprise. Meanwhile, Colonel Morgan, get your men up in the trees and go to work. Have them aim for the officers' gorgets. If we are lucky, the British advance will falter for lack of leadership."

Morgan accepted the order with an approving nod, moving away with a predator's efficiency. He always carried his gun at the ready, his left hand balancing his weapon so that it pointed in front of him like the nose of a good hound, sniffing for any danger. His right hand rested on the hammer, ready to pull back and fire in an instant. He and his men were my finest shots and never hesitated when a target presented itself.

Shooting officers was not popular among "gentlemen" of either side of the war. However, once started, battle was no place for gentlemen. War was, and will always be, a vicious arena where aggression and ruthlessness wins the day. I proceeded using all the weapons at my disposal. To that end, nothing made Morgan's riflemen happier than my orders to shoot aristocratic British officers.

When the scent of smoke reached my horse's nostrils, it became white eyed and harder to control. I gave it a hard jerk on the reins, causing it to rear up slightly. I took the moment to brandish my sword and bellow, "Come on, boys! Follow me, and let's kill some damn redcoats!" As my agitated horse vaulted the trench and headed down the hill, I could hear my men cheer. The lads raced across open fields toward the enemy.

Dearborn and I crashed out of the woods into the leading British elements in the vicinity of loyalist John Freeman's farm. Outnumbered two to one, we managed to overwhelm the unprepared British line. With the effective fire from Morgan's snipers and our initial surprise attack, we pushed the British back into the woods at the end of the far farm.

Every single officer in the British regiment facing Morgan was either wounded or killed. Once they were in the cover of the trees, more British were brought up; they counterattacked, pushing my men back and forcing our troops to hide behind stumps, trees, and buildings, and returning fire from the opposite edge of the farm. The brave Dearborn led from the front, screaming, "Aim low, boys! Shoot 'em in the bread-basket! Start with the god-damned officers!"

Morgan's riflemen had been scattered in the counterattack. Placing four fingers in his large mouth, he let loose a deafening, shrill whistle, known to his men as the "turkey call," that allowed them to find him, reorient, and quickly reengage the enemy with a newfound fury.

As we fought at close quarters, sometimes hand to hand, there was too much chaos to focus. The mind cannot fully process a melee at its peak, when men grapple with death. They screamed an incomprehensible language understood only by those locked in a savage embrace. The red-stained grass was rolled flat by writhing men. Teeth bare, they attacked like feral animals, their humanity long forgotten.

Our skilled enemy once again pivoted, putting themselves on higher ground, overcoming our numbers with their superior training. I saw a gap between two British columns—we charged, but did not break through.

During long battles, time both compresses and drags. Hours can go by in an instant, and an instant can seem like hours. For three hours, a half dozen charges and counterattacks moved across the open field and into the woods surrounding the Freeman's farm. Cannon filled with grapeshot fired at point-blank range, disintegrating men in a flash, followed by a plume of smoke covering the carnage. Immersed in grime and gore, both sides battled beyond exhaustion.

I have often heard people talk about the fog of war, but it is more appropriately called the smoke of battle. The continuous fire of muskets and cannon obscures what is happening even a short distance away. Then, a breeze pushes aside the gray smoke, revealing both the battlefield and its aftermath. Torn paper cartridges cover the field as both sides bite open small bags of powder to load their muskets. The paper creates the odd illusion of snow or flower petals covering the dead and dying.

There is one piece of equipment that dominates the battlefield: it is the Brown Bess. You never forget the flat boom of the sturdy musket, followed by a tongue of flame and a belch of smoke heralding a half-inch lead ball moving at a thousand feet per second. It always gets your attention, even if often inaccurate.

I had over three thousand men under my command. Riding my formidable black stallion Warren in front of my men and the enemy, pointing my sword upward, I yelled at the top of my lungs, "The bastards are just over the hill! One good push and they will be on their heels, running for their mothers!" Rearing my horse, I looked back at my men. "Are you with me, boys?"

As one, they roared and broke into a run. We slammed into the British like a hammer breaking glass. Both men and bits of trees fell, caught in the halo of bullets surrounding me. I knew pondering my mortality could weaken my resolve, so I chose to put the danger out of my mind and focused on the battle at hand.

Our bold counterattacks worked—we nearly overran the British, but for heavy reinforcements from a platoon of Hessians. Late in the afternoon, I found myself choking on the smoke as the wind shifted and swirled around me. When I looked up, it gave me a new view of the battlefield.

As I paused to decide what to do next, my men scurried desperately for water. Nothing gives a man a greater thirst than a fight. I looked up to see a riderless horse gone mad with fear bolting through the mayhem and crashing into a fence, screaming in an explosion of dirt, splintered wood, and flesh. I registered only relief that no men had been trampled underfoot.

With a good look at the field in front of us, I determined the British could not withstand another supported assault. I sent a message back to Gates calling for reinforcements to break the British line.

As we began to weaken the British, Burgoyne sent five hundred Hessians through a supposedly impassable ravine known as Mill Creek to attack our undermanned right flank. Our men were enduring lacerating small-arms fire. Getting no responses from messengers, I spurred my stallion up the hill to speak to Gates, dismounted feet from the entrance, and flew into his headquarters. My composure of our prior encounter was lost in the day's battle; my once-immaculate uniform was covered with soot, dirt, sweat, and the blood of my men and the enemy.

In a rare concession, Gates stood from his chair when I entered, as much in response to my blazing eyes as any sense of decorum. He still tried to maintain his nonchalance, examining his fingernails as he spoke: "Ah, Arnold, I see you are back. What do you have to report?"

It took every ounce of my being not to throttle the man. While my words betrayed nothing, my demeanor had every man in the room on a fearful edge. With a voice hoarse from shouting orders, I answered, "I have to report, as my messengers no doubt told you, we are in earnest. The British are attempting another counterattack to outflank us, yet simultaneously exposing their own weakness. If you will release four thousand more men to me, I can turn their flank, and win this battle . . ." Again it stuck in my craw to acknowledge his rank. ". . . General."

Sitting back down, Gates pointed to an empty chair, which I ignored. He responded in a slow and patient tone, "Did you not hear me this morning, General Arnold? I told you that our army would remain in these works, where we could realize our tactical advantage. I am fully aware of the Hessians moving, and have released another brigade who will address the issue and protect our flank. Your blood is up. I know your reputation is to be aggressive at all costs, but I do not believe it is either warranted or appropriate here."

Gates was timid. He spoke with the perverse satisfaction of a pessimist, pleased when his predictions of stalemate were proven true. I could take it no longer. My voice began to rise as I said, "You're goddamned right my blood is up! Soldiers have been fighting and dying all day, while you sit here and drink tea with these *men*." My look made clear that I considered his group of officers anything but. "Battles are, by their very nature, dynamic and fluid. The plan made in the morning can be both moot and irrelevant by the afternoon. If you give me the men I asked for, I can give the army victory."

At this, the languid Gates stiffened in his chair. When he wanted to be, he was as sharp as a harpoon and just as barbed. I surmised that the prospect of me securing a "victory" for the army was the last thing he wanted. For the first time, Gates raised his voice in response. "General Arnold. Let us be absolutely clear. Your request for additional troops is both refused and unwise. I have addressed your concerns about Hessians on our flank. You will not engage any further troops. You will remain here pending further instructions."

Once again, I saw smirks exchanged among the officers as the general leaned back in his chair. I decided I could not stay in the house anymore and began to walk out. Gates raised his voice: "General Arnold. While you have not asked my leave to exit the room, you may do so. However, you may not return to the engagement, as your services there are no longer required."

I left without saying another word. Since I was permitted to do nothing, I stood outside, fuming. Within fifteen minutes, a messenger arrived. After I followed him into the tent, he reported that the American brigade Gates had sent to engage the Hessians had become hopelessly lost. In response, I proclaimed, "By God, I will soon put an end to it!"

Hearing no objection, I turned on my heels and headed outside. As I mounted, my horse snorted, chafing at the bit, feeling my excitement for the battle to come. I did not need the spurs to gallop to the front.

It was my intent to break the stalemate. However, it was not to be. Concerned that I would succeed and thus be able to claim a victory, Gates sent his sniveling adjutant Wilkinson to order me back to headquarters. I honored the order and returned, seething; I knew that annihilation of the British force was at hand, but for Gates's nonexistent leadership.

Our men pulled back to our fortifications, and Burgoyne was left in control of the field. The sun retreated over the hills, leaving the sky the color of bruises and blood. Burgoyne had lost twice as many men as we, with 620 dead or wounded British to the three hundred American casualties. Gates went to bed that night the beneficiary of my efforts and those of my men. Morgan's men had decimated the officer corps, but the British remained in the field.

Sleep did not come for me. I lay awake, listening to the sounds of wolves feeding on the dead and dying. I was sure that in the morning, the British would be forced to either attack or face a long and arduous retreat to Canada. Most of all, I seethed at the lost opportunity and the lives sacrificed on the altar of Gates's weak-kneed leadership. As the hours rolled by, the screams and cries gave way to the silence of death, interrupted only by men calling out the watchword as they moved about the camp. *You can say what you want about the bastard, but Gates knows how to maintain security behind his defenses, even as his men die out of reach.*

The next day, we received intelligence from a deserter that Burgoyne's "whole army was under arms, and orders had been given for an attack on our lines." While our defensive positions were generally secure, our left wing was extremely vulnerable because of a lack of ammunition. If Burgoyne had chosen to attack, he most certainly would have turned our flank. Nevertheless, on that fateful day, he had received a notice from General Clinton in New York that he did not have enough men to attack Albany; he would make a push up the Hudson as far as Fort Montgomery. Burgoyne hoped this would distract our troops and provide him some needed relief. Gates couldn't be distracted, because he wasn't going anywhere. What ensued was a "digging in" by both sides.

Chapter 51

Bemis Heights, NY - September 22, 1777

I bit my tongue when Gates continued to rebuff my plans and suggestions at staff meetings. I partially managed to control my fury when he refused to attack at the height of the battle and deliver the coup de grâce. I even remained silent when he ignored my bravery in his official report to Congress—written by Wilkinson, who lied when he said, "General Arnold was not out of camp through the whole action." However, when Gates published orders without consulting me and removed Morgan's riflemen from my command, I lost all control. This decision made no sense to me. Colonel Morgan and I had repeatedly demonstrated an excellent working relationship and success in the field. I surmised that Gates's only reason was to prevent me from winning the battle to come.

My rage was rising to the surface like a river overflowing its banks, ready to give way in a flood. I felt the dam break as I stormed into Gates's headquarters—when one of his omnipresent minions tried to bar my way, I fairly shoved him aside. Gates rose to his feet in open-mouthed surprise as I barged in.

A red veil of anger blurred my vision as I spoke through clenched teeth. "You stand here today only because of other men. Everyone knows that General Schuyler prepared the means of victory and coordinated a defense. He had the courage to let me secure victory at Fort Stanwix. I constructed the defenses with Colonel Kościuszko. You failed to acknowledge those efforts, or anyone else's, in order to aggrandize yourself. Why? Because you do nothing!"

Taking a menacing step forward, I continued, "By Christ's body, General, I am done with your repeated indignities. You choose not to mention me in the battle reports. Your dishonorable backside barely ever left the chair. I believe this is the first time I have seen you standing in days." Cocking my head toward Wilkinson: "You dare to mention this peacock in dispatches? You lead from neither the front nor the rear. You steal other men's thunder and elevate the most pathetic among us."

In my peripheral vision, I saw Wilkinson creep closer, and I put my hand on the hilt of my sword. *As God is my witness, if you take one step closer, I will part you from your miserable life in a single stroke.* As if reading my mind, he immediately retreated.

Gates sputtered, "Damn you, man. Everything they say about you is true. You are a lout and a horse's arse. You are welcome neither in this room nor in this army. Be off with you before I have you arrested! As to leadership, you would have lost the entire battle by overcommitting the army and leaving the defenses. You would have played directly into Burgoyne's hands, you blinkered idiot. All you know is attack. I have no use for you. You may view yourself as relieved—I will have a new commander of my left wing."

I closed the gap. We now stood only a foot apart. With a face like thunder, I roared, "What? It is not surprising the men call you Granny Gates! You horse jockey! You know nothing about battle, and certainly nothing about what transpired here. You let victory slip through your hands because you'd rather see us lose than allow me to succeed on the battlefield."

"Enough!" It was the loudest voice I'd yet to hear from the cowardly little man.

Two of his officers, who had yet been silent, moved as if in response to the general's order. Shaking my head, I now fully grabbed my sword's hilt without pulling the blade. *I've killed better men than you with this sword.* They instantly halted their advance.

Growling in disgust, Gates continued, "Your status here was only the result of my generosity. You submitted your resignation to Congress before coming to the Northern Army. I always doubted your viability as a major general. I have ordered General Benjamin Lincoln to relieve you. He is a gentleman who understands strategy. Let me say it plainly: there is no reason for you to be here."

I am here because General Washington requested it. Now, this son of a bitch is using my very loyalty to the army against me. He certainly had no problem acknowledging my authority when it served his needs, but now he wants to take all credit for my victories, and cast me off.

I snapped, "I can brook no such usage. To leave the service of some-one of your disreputable character brings me great joy." Without asking permission, I turned and left the house.

Furious, back in my tent, I wrote a letter to Gates itemizing the insults I had endured since my arrival.

> From reason, I know not, as I am conscious of no offense or neglect of duty, but I have lately observed little attention paid to any proposals I have thought it my duty to make for the public service and when a measure I have proposed has been agreed to it has been immediately contradicted. I have been received with the greatest coolness in headquarters and often treated in such a manner as may mortify a person with less pride than I have and in my station in the Army.

Gates, always the politician and a liar, responded, "I do not know what you mean by insult or indignity." As he'd planned, I replied by ask-ing for a pass to join General Washington.

When word of my dispute with General Gates and my intent to leave the army spread, a petition was circulated among the army's officers in camp (except for Gates's family). All signed a petition "requesting Gen-eral Arnold not quit the service at this critical moment." This took some of the wind out of the general's sails. I was told informally that Gates was willing to create some sort of peace between us, if I would only jettison my aide Henry Livingston. Livingston was a protégé of Philip Schuyler, and thus by implication an enemy of Horatio Gates. When told of this symbolic offering, I was outraged. I insisted that Livingston would remain at my side and that I would not sacrifice my loyalty to soothe another's ego.

On October 1, Gates officially stripped me of command. He took control of the left wing and placed General Lincoln in divisional command. Gates made clear that I could leave Bemis Heights or stay in my cabin, but in any event, I would have no further control of the troops.

I wanted to leave, but the men begged me to stay wherever I went around the camp. I knew we were on the cusp of victory, and to head south would allow Gates to reap the fruits of my labors. So, I stayed—a general without a command, but also surrounded by an army that loved me.

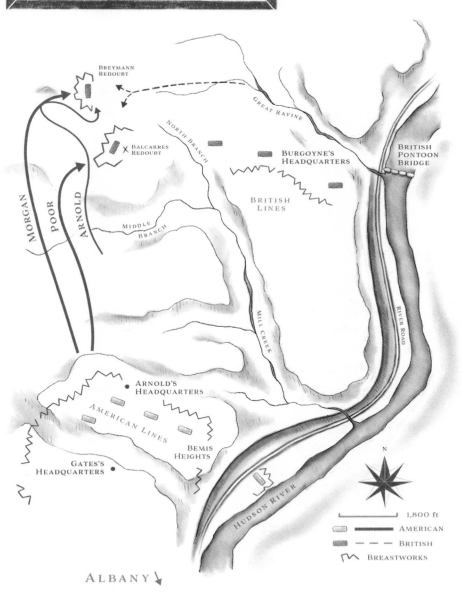

Battle of Saratoga, Day Two:
Bemis Heights
OCTOBER 7, 1777

SARATOGA ↗

BREYMANN REDOUBT

GREAT RAVINE

BRITISH PONTOON BRIDGE

NORTH BRANCH

BALCARRES REDOUBT

BURGOYNE'S HEADQUARTERS

MORGAN

POOR

ARNOLD

MIDDLE BRANCH

BRITISH LINES

MILL CREEK

RIVER ROAD

ARNOLD'S HEADQUARTERS

AMERICAN LINES

BEMIS HEIGHTS

GATES'S HEADQUARTERS

HUDSON RIVER

N

1,800 ft

AMERICAN

BRITISH

BREASTWORKS

ALBANY ↓

247

Chapter 52

Bemis Heights, NY – October 7, 1777

I n the intervening weeks, our army continued to grow. The addition of four thousand new soldiers, many of them militiamen from New England, raised our total number to almost thirteen thousand men, close to double that of the British. At night, the tents covering the hills looked like cobwebs, their occupants ready to scuttle out in the morning, thirsting for British blood.

Burgoyne had not been idle. His men built several redoubts and breastworks extending two and a half miles. Each redoubt was a deep scar cut into the rolling hills—a series of trenches, piled logs, and spikes sticking out of the ground, punctuated by angry gashes holding cannon that dared the brave or foolhardy to approach. Despite these formidable defenses, the British were completely surrounded, cut off from supplies. Trapped and under the constant attention of our excellent snipers, Burgoyne's camp must have been a very unsettling place.

Meanwhile, the seasons were changing. The first battle had been fought in verdant woods. The highlands were now transformed into a mixture of orange, red, and yellow. If our troops didn't dislodge the British, winter eventually would.

Thus, it was not surprising when the British once again went on the move. Rather than decamping at daybreak, Burgoyne waited until 1:00 p.m., when he fired two signal guns. Two miles away, fifteen hundred slow-marching regulars and six hundred Canadian loyalists ventured out from behind British fortifications. Understanding that General Henry Clinton would not be coming from New York to save him, Gentleman Johnny decided to make one last attempt to turn our left and escape the tightening noose around him. The British lined up for a pitched battle, but our troops remained behind defenses.

While I had been excluded from staff meetings, by necessity I partook in the officer's mess. We rose from the table at the sounds; I turned to General Gates and said, "Shall I go out and see what is the matter?"

We both knew I meant to reconnoiter in force.

Gates initially made no reply. I attempted to look relaxed, keeping my hands behind my back, but involuntarily rose onto my toes and rocked back onto my heels. With some hesitation, the general said, "I am afraid to trust you, Arnold."

In the intervening weeks, the fire between us had cooled. My aides, Richard Varick and Henry Livingston, had decamped to Albany, and with them some of the animosity and drama had left. While Gates and I were far from friendly, professional courtesy had replaced red-hot anger. Thus, I took a conciliatory and deferential tone when I said, "Pray, let me go. I will be careful, and if our advance does not need support, I will promise not to commit you."

He replied evenly, "Fine, but you shall be accompanied by Lincoln." After another pause, he emphasized, "He is in command."

I nodded in acknowledgment, and was gone before he could change his mind.

Lincoln and I rode in great haste to the enemy line, where we could see through a spyglass Burgoyne and his officers standing on the roof of a cabin, surrounded by over a thousand men. The British occupied a nearby farm and were amid a field of uncut wheat. It was apparent to both General Lincoln and myself that they were preparing to attack our left flank.

We promptly returned to headquarters. I bit my tongue and allowed General Lincoln to take the lead as he announced, "General Gates, the firing on the river is merely a feint—their object is your left. A strong force of fifteen hundred men are marching circuitously to plant themselves on yonder heights." He gestured to the large wall map. "The point must be defended, or your camp is in danger."

Looking out the doorway with his hands behind his back, Gates replied with a soft voice that still grated on me like the sound of a ship's hull against jagged rocks. "Well, then, order Morgan to begin the game."

The game? You pompous windbag. It is not a bloody game!

Appalled by this timid response to the British advance, I spoke with perhaps more force than I should have. "Morgan alone? That is worthless. You must send a strong force."

Spinning on his heels, Gates glared. "General Arnold, I have nothing for you to do. You have no business here." He pointed to the exit, staring at me with undisguised loathing—and just a hint of fear.

Lincoln, clearly uncomfortable, interjected, "It might be helpful, General, if we also sent regiments from Learned and Nixon's brigade."

Gates answered without taking his eye off me, pointing to the door. "Very well."

I left his presence and returned to the small red cabin I was occupying on the northwest corner of Bemis Heights, fuming as the battle raged in the fields and forests below me. Heavy artillery bellowed, sounding like great peals of thunder, assisted by the echoes of the woods and surrounding hills.

Finally, unable to stand the confinement any longer, I left the cabin. Looking down at the battlefield below, in the distance, I saw Daniel Morgan and Henry Dearborn with their men heading toward the fight. These were *my* men.

Gates had not barred me from the battlefield; rather, he had dismissed me from his headquarters. I saw a courier heading to report to Gates and flagged him to me. I learned that the British were advancing deep into the wheat field.

I could take it no longer. I was not "technically" disobeying an order. There are times in life when it is better to rely on the letter of the law than its spirit. Here was such a moment. I knew if I led my men to victory, all would be forgiven; or, if I died in the attempt, it would not matter. With this in mind, I spurred the chestnut horse I had borrowed from a friend and raced to the sounds of the guns.

Approaching, I could see Morgan's marksmen trading fire on the left with the British light infantry. As I arrived at a full gallop, the men recognized my blue-and-buff Continental general's uniform and hailed me, shaking their guns in the air in salute. Reining in my horse in front of a group of soldiers, I asked, "Whose regiment is this?"

The men responded, "Colonel Latimer's." He was one of the Connecticut men I knew I could depend upon and would accept my orders.

I rejoiced, "Ah, my old Norwich and New London friend! God bless you! I am glad to see you. Now come on, boys—if the day is long enough, we'll have them in hell before night!"

I realigned the soldiers for an attack. Burgoyne had formed a line of battle more than a half mile long with forward-deployed artillery pieces. Our men crashed into this line in a flurry of bullets and steel. Both sides eventually fought desperately hand to hand—men swung muskets like clubs, the sickening sound of gun stocks connecting with skulls repeating like popping corn. The clang of metal on metal mixed with shouts, and the barks of muskets filled the air. Underneath it all, the screams of injured and dying horses added to the symphony of death.

I had cannon dragged through the woods and fields, employing canister at short range from behind trees and bushes. I was everywhere at once—cajoling my men, swinging my sword, and encouraging the troops to be aggressive. My bellowed orders were only partially heard, the sentences blotted out by the surrounding gunfire. At one point, I was so animated waving my boys forward that I accidentally hit one of them in the head with the flat side of my sword. I apologized profusely, but the hardened lad shook it off with a friendly grin.

The violence of battle and exhaustion were beginning to take their toll. As we fought a group of loyalists across an open cornfield, I saw that a cut on a soldier's forehead was bleeding so profusely that it had fouled his flint. In frustration and incomprehension, blood covering his hands and gun, he continued to cock the gun back and refire to no effect. I knew there was no time to stop and help him, but such sights stay with you long after the battle.

A mounted loyalist brigadier was urging his men forward and threatening our line. I galloped to Morgan and yelled, "That man on the gray horse is a host in himself and must be disposed of!" The first shot from Morgan's best sharpshooter, Timothy Murphy, staggered the man's horse as the bullet hit his saddle; the second cut the horse's mane, and the third struck home. The officer collapsed forward, grabbing his stomach and slumping off his horse. Without their commander, the British began to pull back as we advanced.

The surest way to kill a snake is to cut off its head. It is not pretty, nor pleasant, but neither is war. I gave no quarter to my British counterparts. War is about killing—plain and simple.

The British, meanwhile, were using their cannon to great effect. At longer range, cannonballs are ideal for shooting into troop concentrations—a cannonball can bounce along the ground multiple times, digging into men, horses, and structures with equal gusto. I knew that if we didn't take the British redoubts, they would continue to dominate us with their superior gunnery.

From a strategic standpoint, the British Army was anchored by two key forts, the Balcarres Redoubt and the Breymann Redoubt—named for their commanding officers. A more timid general might have seen the setting sun, coupled with the fact that enemy had been driven from the field, as a chance to withdraw and declare victory. Not I—if we could take one of these two forts, we could outflank the enemy and attack their rear. If I was going to defeat the British, I would need to act now.

Some have said I "ignored" Gates's orders. Again, this is not correct. He was not there—I was. I seized the opportunity and led the charge at the Balcarres Redoubt, hurling myself and my men into a storm of British musket fire and grapeshot.

Men went down all around me. A few even grappled with the British hand to hand, yet we were forced again to withdraw. As we regrouped, I looked across a group of trees at the other redoubt. I realized that the Breymann Redoubt was weaker and more vulnerable to attack. Rather than take time to safely ride around the fighting, I rode directly between the two lines for over 120 yards as the British (and some Americans) fired at me with abandon. In a full gallop, I focused only on the ride, avoiding bodies, equipment, and uneven terrain, oblivious to the whistle of bullets missing both me and my steed.

I dismounted at the bottom of a small hill, where I hoped my horse would be safe for the moment, then ran up the hill and flopped next to Morgan. At that moment, a shell screamed overhead, followed by an impossibly loud thump and a rain of pebbles. Morgan casually brushed the dirt off his shoulder. "You do know how to make an entrance, General."

As we crouched behind some fallen trees facing Breymann's Redoubt, death hissed inches above us. I was breathing too hard to reply with a clever retort; instead, I focused on the matter at hand. Endeavoring to be heard over the din, I shouted, "Get Learned's men to advance immediately and displace the enemy from those two log huts in the gap between the two redoubts. That should cut any communication between them." A lieutenant, crouching next to Morgan, nodded and was off at a sprint. "Daniel, we can take this weaker redoubt. I will take two hundred men around the rear and assault the sally port, while you use two dozen riflemen to keep the bastards pinned down!"

Morgan growled, "My boys will make them think they are facing a brigade."

As we spoke, men crawled around like crabs, keeping as low as possible as they collected cartridges or muskets no longer in use by their fallen comrades. Those who weren't on the move were drinking precious water from their canteens, as much for the fluids as to take the bitter taste of powder from their mouths.

Slapping Morgan on the back in approval, I said, "Give me fifteen minutes to get my men around to the rear. We will make our charge when we hear your boys open up." He nodded, already giving orders to his men as I ran for my horse. I was relieved to see my mount was unharmed, although stomping the ground and snorting nervously as the world exploded around him. The dead were strewn about, frozen in the moment of death, their hands clasping wounds, their innards exposed, and their bowels relieved. On the edge of the battlefield, horses milled about, some covered in blood and riderless, while others carried their lifeless charges. They watched with uncomprehending eyes as death spread its pitiless wings over the battlefield.

I steadied my horse and rode to my remaining troops. I positioned them to attack the back side of the redoubt. To be in a saddle was to be a target; I knew the wiser approach was to dismount and lead on foot, but my presence on a horse allowed the men to see me.

I saw a gap where the British lines had opened up. It was a critical weakness in their defenses. Waving my sword in the air, I charged when we heard the increased rifle shots from Morgan around the front of the redoubt. Heading straight for the gap in the British line, my men let loose a savage cry of rage and fear. About halfway there, some well-placed British artillery took out a swath of my troops. The carnage spread across the grass in chunks of flesh and crimson-stained grass, punctuated by dead or dying soldiers dragging themselves to the rear. Facing such losses, my men staggered. I knew we were losing the initiative, and saw some men begin to retreat. I rode back, screaming and swinging my sword. "This is our opportunity, boys! Give them steel before they reload the cannon!"

Most of my men turned with me to charge. I rode in front of our troops into the teeth of the defenses. Our goal was a sally port in the Breymann Redoubt. If we could get through that opening with a quick frontal attack, the entire fortification would collapse.

Henry Dearborn raised his sword, his men cheering as we pressed our assault. In the melee, I spurred my horse through the sally port and turned sideways to the redoubt's defenders. When I yelled for the defenders to surrender, one of the Hessians raised his musket and shot me at point-blank range in my left leg.

From the moment my horse whinnied and reared up, I knew he was going to fall. I desperately tried to kick my feet out of the stirrups, but I was caught. As my mount toppled over, time slowed. This must be what it is like for a man falling off a cliff, knowing the end is nigh, but powerless to stop it. I remember thinking as the beast began to tip over, pulling me with it, *No, this can't be happening.* But it was.

As we struck the ground, I felt my upper leg shatter. Not break. Not crack. It was like a walnut getting hit with a hammer. White-hot pain filled my world for a few unimaginably long seconds. Then, sound returned and I was trapped, helpless and in agony. Still I screamed,

"Rush on, my brave boys, rush on!" I saw them take the redoubt and break the British line.

I was lifted from beneath the horse and pulled to a nearby tree, where a tourniquet was quickly put on my leg to stanch the bleeding. Henry Dearborn ran over to check on me, concern showing through his soot-covered face. "Where are you hit?"

I gasped, "The same leg as Quebec. I wish the ball passed through my heart."

A makeshift stretcher was made from blankets and poles. Just as my men were about to pick me up, the man who'd shot me was dragged forward. The anger in the eyes of my soldiers made clear he was about to be dispatched. I looked at the terrified German mercenary and mumbled, "Don't hurt him, boys. He's a fine fellow. He only did his duty." With that, I collapsed in pain back onto my stretcher. As I was being carried from the field, a messenger informed me that Gates wanted me to return to the camp before doing "some rash thing."

Not only had the Hessian bullet shattered my left femur, but I suffered a compound fracture when my horse crushed my leg. I knew I had won the day, but I had paid the dearest price. *Rash indeed.*

I endured a thirty-mile carriage ride to Albany. Every bump caused more agony as the fractured bone dug into my flesh. When I finally reached a military hospital four days later, my doctors told me that the leg would have to come off. They feared putrefaction or gangrene. Through gritted teeth, I insisted this was "damned nonsense." Disagreeing with me, the doctors nevertheless followed my instructions and did the best they could by immobilizing my leg in a wooden frame known as a "fracture box," telling me that I would have to lie on my back for several months and pray for the best.

The next two weeks are lost in delirium. The walls flexed in and out. I shut my eyes to stop the floor from moving, and then the world began to spin. Down to the right, then up to the left, the descending path to perdition. Fighting to regain control, I would hold onto the edge of my bed with a death grip.

When the spinning stopped, the true suffering began. I was a caged animal. I raged at my misfortune. I was trapped in the midst of a thousand other sick and dying men. Each night the room was transformed into a house of horrors. Men moaned, while grotesque shadows cast by the flickering candles on the dirty walls revealed wraiths circling to feed on the dying.

My fevered dreams were filled with color and confusion. One moment there was victory, the next defeat. I would see Washington lauding me in Congress, and a second later a headless Montgomery explaining what it is like to be dead in the matter-of-fact way old men discuss the weather. In the worst moments, I would be back home—people reveling in my father's humiliation as I collected him at the wharf, his honor and our good name lost. Then I would startle awake, relieved to be met with the sharp pang of my leg and escape from my mind's torture.

As I lay waiting in misery, stories came in from the front. I learned that after the British defeat, Burgoyne had attempted to retreat to Canada. Outnumbered three to one and out of food, on October 17, 1777, British soldiers and their allies surrendered to the Americans. Gates received the honor of Burgoyne; the latter removed his hat, bowed, and said, "The fortunes of war, General, have made me your prisoner."

Gates responded with equal eloquence, "I shall always be glad to testify that it was through no fault of Your Excellency." Burgoyne then withdrew his sword and handed it over. After carefully examining the weapon for a few seconds, Gates handed the sword back and directed Burgoyne into his cabin, where the men enjoyed dinner.

I read these reports in the newspaper with trembling fury, telling everyone I could that Gates was "the greatest poltroon in the world." Gates was lauded as the hero of Saratoga, and a special gold medal was struck by Congress in his honor. It was a bitter pill to swallow, realizing that Gates had never set foot on the bloody battlefield.

Gates also heaped praise on his aide, Wilkinson, who had undermined me at every turn, describing the young man as a "military genius" and securing his elevation from lieutenant colonel to brigadier general. The only passing reference to my efforts was to incorrectly imply that I fought side by side with General Benjamin Lincoln. Meanwhile, not a single note came from Gates or anyone else complimenting my bravery in the battle.

I wanted them all to remember the taking of Ticonderoga; my capturing ships and supplies at St. John; my trek over the mountains to Quebec; my attack on Quebec in the blizzard with Montgomery; the naval battle at Valcour Isle; my defense of Connecticut; my saving of Fort Stanwix; and my bravery on both days at Saratoga. Every day I looked out the window at an apple tree in full fall bloom, carrying the fruit of life, yet out of reach—an apt reflection of my suffering in this unfair war.

Chapter 53

Albany, NY - December 5, 1777

A lmost two months after the battle, my leg became grossly puru-
lent, exuding large quantities of pus. Meanwhile, I endured the
indignities of bedpans and bedsores. While I lay suffering, Congress
decided to restore my seniority, making me superior to the five generals
who had been promoted ahead of me ten months earlier. They made no
mention of my actions at the victory at Saratoga and no acknowledgment in my restoration of rank that any wrong had been done to me in
the first place—in fact, they said my elevation in rank was nothing more
than a "legal correction."

My rank was restored in mid-December, but General Washington
did not deign to inform me of this news while I lay alone and abandoned in a miserable Albany hospital. Once I had been a flame leading the Revolution; now I was a flickering candle left in the darkness to
sputter out and die at the hands of the doctors.

*Doctors indeed! Butchers and ignorant pretenders! They know nothing
and care not a whit for me. I am a piece of meat. I admit I was short with
them, but they are fools.*

I tried hard to fight the horror. *My life as I know it is over. I was always
the strongest, the man with boundless energy. I will never run again. I will
never vault a fence again. I will never dance and spin with a woman in my
arms. It is almost impossible to get my head around it . . . NEVER.* With
that brute realization, a wave of despair pressed down on me, squeezing
out all joy and hope.

*Regardless of what anyone says—and by the way, no one says any-
thing—I will be a lesser man. Most likely, I will be looked on with pity.
The young and the strong will be irritated as they press to pass me while I
hobble along.*

Who am I fooling? I will be grateful to hobble. Right now, I lie in this bed day after day, week after week, "giving my body a chance to heal." God, how I wish I had died in battle or on the surgeon's table! All I face now is a life of unrelenting, persistent, and endless pain.

I thought I understood pain. The shot in the leg in Quebec was "temporary pain." Mind you, it hurt, but I knew it would heal. In truth, the wound itself was a badge of honor. This life now—and worse, what is to come—is totally different. It is the agony of knowing that today, and every waking moment for the rest of my life, will be filled with a sharp stabbing into my flesh. It is the first thing I feel when I wake and the last thing I perceive when I fall asleep. Even in slumber it gnaws, preventing real sleep.

Pain is my adversary. I fight "pain," but he pokes, prods, and tortures me, delighting in my suffering.

What do the doctors say? "Rest." There is no rest. There is no sleep. There is only pain. Potions to ease the pain are useless.

Worst is to know that any joy or happiness will be tempered by the presence of pain, ensuring that I never forget it is there, whispering in my ear, "You are lesser and weak." Waiting. Pushing me to give into despair. Nudging the bottle across the table. Offering me a taste of freedom in the form of liquid oblivion. A seducing solution my father embraced to wash away his failure. Then I think of him, covered in his own filth . . . no, by God! I will replace despair with resolve. I will battle pain with iced anger. I damn the pain. I will fight.

In early January 1778, Washington finally wrote a personal note: "May I venture to ask whether you are upon your legs again? If you are not, may I flatter myself that you will be soon? There is none who wishes more sincerely for this event than I do, or who would receive the information with more pleasure. As soon as your situation will permit, I request you will repair to this army, it being my earnest wish to have your services in the ensuing campaign and a command which I trust will be agreeable to yourself and of great advantage to the public." Trapped and in agony, I could not accept this tardy request.

When I mustered the energy to respond to the general's letter, I indicated that it would be at least another five or six months until I was fully healed. I concluded, "It is my most ardent wish to render every assistance in my power, that your Excellency will be enabled to finish the arduous task, and you have with so much honor to yourself and advantage to your country, been engaged in, and have the pleasure of seeing peace and happiness restored to your country on the most permanent basis."

When I reread my letter before it was sent, I realized for the first time that I had described the Colonies as "your country" when writing Washington. Somewhere in the course of betrayal, disgust, politics, and grievous injury, it had become no longer "our country," but a country that belonged to others. I considered rewriting the letter to correct the unconscious admission. I decided to leave it, as neither Washington nor anyone else really cared about me anyway—the letter was as likely as not to be simply left unread.

Chapter 54

Albany, NY - March 7, 1778

The femur is the strongest bone in the body. When my femur was fractured by the horse and a musket ball at close range, the bone shattered into hundreds of splinters—these did far more damage than the bullet itself, piercing muscle and tendons throughout my upper thigh. The physicians in Albany used cinchona bark to stave off gangrene. While I kept my leg, it had actually shrunk a full two inches as a result of atrophy and muscle damage caused by the wound. I was coming to understand and accept that splinters of bone would continue to pierce my muscles with every step for the rest of my life, and I would have a profound limp.

I was fortunate that my hearty constitution staved off infection, which overwhelms so many wounded soldiers. I sat up for the first time in January, three months after the battle. The result of my effort was to tear my wound open and renew the agony. It would be two months before I would try again.

After five months in the Albany hospital, I was loaded onto a wagon for the long journey home. Forced to ride in a springless carriage, I felt every bump as I lay supine on the cart. I repeatedly suffered the indignity of being carried into inns on a stretcher while onlookers viewed me with a mixture of curiosity and pity.

I was given a grand reception in Middletown, Connecticut, where my sons attended school. After the event, I decided to remove a previously undetected bone splinter which was continuing to impede my recovery. Writing Washington on March 12, I said, "My surgeon assures me in perhaps two and possibly five or six months I will be able to serve again. As soon as my wounds will permit, I will immediately repair to headquarters."

While I continued to brood on Gates and Congress, hope had arisen at the back of my mind. Betsy DeBlois had broken her engagement with the apothecary's apprentice, leaving an opening for me. Writing her as I traveled, I told her, "Twenty times I have taken up my pen to write you, and as often as my trembling hand refused to obey the dictates of my heart . . . neither time, absence, misfortunes, nor your cruel indifference have been able to efface the deep impressions your charms have made." She wrote back requesting I cease all correspondence. I wrote a final note terminating the relationship: "Forget there is so unhappy a wretch, for let me perish if I would give you one moment's pain."

To my joy and surprise, I was greeted with a hero's welcome upon my May 4 arrival in New Haven. Crowds lined the streets, fife and drum played, and a thirteen-cannon salute was fired in my honor. Even the governor attended, welcoming me home as a local hero. The people paraded me all the way to my house on Water Street.

Meanwhile, Gates tended to grudges like a dutiful gardener. He steadfastly refused to acknowledge my success at Saratoga, even as the word spread that I had made the decisive difference in the battle. I later came to learn that even General Burgoyne was publicly giving me credit for the victory.

Chapter 55

Valley Forge, PA - May 21, 1778

I arrived at Valley Forge wanting to reenter the fight and serve the Cause, but with a caveat. As a true patriot, I had placed the Revolution above my happiness and prosperity. After spending six months lying in a hospital bed without any recognition of my accomplishments and sacrifice, I resolved my needs would be my new top priority.

General Washington was using a sturdy Pennsylvania stone house as his headquarters. As I arrived, I was met by a large group of men, many of whom I had fought beside at Saratoga. I was given a heartfelt welcome and huzzahs as my carriage came to a stop.

His Excellency surprised me by dispensing with his usual formality, bounding down the steps and warmly embracing me as I exited my carriage. I had never seen Washington touch another human being, let alone embrace someone—I was both embarrassed and moved by the gesture. It ultimately took four men to help me inside while Washington gave careful instructions to minimize my discomfort. When we were settled into the study, he insisted that I sit with my leg propped up on a stool as we spoke.

We were joined by my former aides Matthew Clarkson and Aaron Burr. Washington had invited them into his official family on my recommendation. Both men were profuse in their praise of my bravery and strategy—over a drink of Madeira, we laughed at Gates's timid leadership.

Turning to the conditions at Valley Forge, I asked, "Your Excellency, I passed through the camp . . ." Hesitating to find the right words, I finally managed, "How do they fare?"

A wave of darkness passed over Washington's face. "Not well. Spring has helped, but we endured the hardest of winters. Nearly two thousand men died of malnutrition, the flux, and smallpox. I tried to inoculate as many men as we could, but if men are weak it is unwise."

All nodded in agreement. Unable to contain his exasperation, Washington suddenly stood with his hands behind his back. Out of habit and respect, I began to stand, struggling from my chair.

The general's face changed from frustration to horror when he saw me beginning to rise. "No, no, my dear General! Please be seated. I apologize. I certainly did not expect you to stand." In two quick strides, he was over me, guiding me back into the chair. "Indulge me. Sometimes I get so vexed, I simply find myself unable to sit. I have written Congress more times than I can count, begging, pleading, imploring . . . I have given up all sense of propriety and dignity in service to my men, and yet the politicians leave us here to starve and freeze." Burr and Clarkson nodded in agreement, but remained silent.

Then, in a demonstration of his famous self-control, Washington carefully straightened his uniform, took a deep breath, and returned to his chair. In an even voice, devoid of the anger that had surfaced just seconds before, he said with forced optimism, "We can only control that which is in our hands. We must do each day the best we can. I see reasons for hope. Mr. Franklin has secured an alliance with France as a result of your victory at Saratoga." I felt myself sit a little straighter at the acknowledgment that Saratoga was *my* victory. "But, General, this army needs you more than ever. I know it will be a while until you can ride a horse, but you are a superb leader of men. I have no general more respected than you. I need a strong hand whom I can trust. I have been told the British will be leaving Philadelphia. I need a trusted military governor should the enemy return."

Washington paused, looking for a reaction, but I tried to remain impassive. He continued, "This will be a difficult assignment. You will need to balance the sensitivities of the local authorities and Congress while treating loyalists honorably. Many patriots were persecuted under British occupation and will be looking for revenge. While I believe most loyalists will flee the city, there were many who attempted to remain neutral. These individuals are likely to be targets for patriots looking for revenge. It is not a combat assignment, but there will be challenges worthy of a man of your stature. The benefit is that you will be in the city, in comfortable surroundings, and presented with a chance to heal before you are recalled to the field of honor, where your proven skills can again be brought to bear." With the formality of a general and a gentleman, he looked at me with his characteristic unblinking gaze. "So, General Arnold, will you accept the position of military governor of Philadelphia when it becomes available?"

Once again, I involuntarily began to stand, which he waved down. Sitting as straight as I could in my chair, I replied, "Of course, General. I serve you and the Cause wherever I can."

Following his habit, he clapped his hands together and rubbed them vigorously. He looked over at his aides with a closemouthed smile. "That is enough business for today. Milady and Mrs. Knox have prepared the best meal possible, given our meager provisions."

"I am grateful for their and your company, Your Excellency," I replied with a seated bow.

With that, the general took his leave. His aides assisted me into the dining room for a lovely and relaxing meal. Over the next couple of days, I met with Washington and his staff about the current strategic situation and engaged in extended discussions regarding my upcoming assignment in Philadelphia.

Before I left, I was informed that Congress had mandated all officers take a formal oath of allegiance. On May 30, Henry Knox gave me the gift of a pair of new epaulets and a sword, "as testimony of my sincere regard and approbation of your conduct." He then asked me to place my hand on the Bible. I swore to "support, maintain, and defend the United States against King George the Third," and to "serve said United States in the office which I now hold, with fidelity, according to the best of my skill and understanding."

Chapter 56

Philadelphia, PA - June 18, 1778

I accepted the position in Philadelphia with an entirely different attitude. I had achieved the rank and seniority to which I was rightly entitled. I had been severely injured fighting bravely in battle, and while inadequately acknowledged by Congress, I knew the great majority of the "people" understood my heroism.

I recognized that attempting to ingratiate myself to the "politicians" in Congress would never serve me. Thus, I would no longer defer to Congress or seek to secure political advantage. I would do my job as instructed by Washington and start taking care of myself. I had sacrificed both my health and my fortune for a cause led by unworthy men.

Neither Washington nor I fully appreciated that I was stepping into a political nightmare, with factions set to tear to shreds anyone who came between them. There was the new radical revolutionary government in Pennsylvania. The streets were filled with an anti-Washington faction, an anti-Schuyler faction, an anti-army faction, and a faction that supported Washington—all of whom despised each other. Additionally, there were still some loyalists and Quakers (who tried to be neutral) to further complicate the situation.

Recognizing the fall of Philadelphia was imminent, I began assembling my staff. I appointed Major David Franks as my aide. He was a dashing, quick-witted and bright young man whom I trusted, the son of a wealthy Jewish merchant and supporter of Quebec Governor Carleton, which made him suspect to the radical revolutionaries. I realized that Franks had taken great risks in the Revolution, broken with his father, and provided financial and political support to those brave Canadians who fought in favor of the Cause. For his courage and bravery, I saw him as a natural choice as my aide-de-camp. Many denounced him as a coxcomb and an excessively coiffed soldier. That might be true, but it didn't change the fact that he was a brave and honorable man.

With Washington's endorsement, I added Matthew Clarkson, who I recognized as a loyal soldier who had been forced out of service unfairly by General Gates because of his loyalty to General Schuyler. I once again appointed him as my other aide-de-camp. It did not concern me that some of those in the anti-Schuyler faction would view this with suspicion.

The last British soldiers and desperate loyalists took everything of value from Philadelphia that they could find, loading it onto British ships headed for New York. The British, as they were leaving, did all they could to harm the city and the American army. Cannon were broken and thrown off the wharf. Thousands of muskets were shattered, a large number of barrels of pork and beef were thrown into the harbor, and four thousand blankets were pulled out of the hospital and burned. Half the ships, along with building materials in the shipyard, were set ablaze, which grew to encompass the entire shipyard and many of the homes of some of Philadelphia's poor.

When the last British ship pulled out of the harbor, filled to the brim with soldiers and supplies, they looked back on a city in flames and covered in garbage. Homes of citizens had holes cut into their floors and were turned into privies, their basements filled with excrement. Flies and filth ruled a city stripped bare.

On June 18, thousands of Philadelphians filled the streets to cheer the American army's arrival, led by me as its new commander. I wore a new uniform with elaborate gold trim given to me by Washington. Waving from my carriage with my leg comfortably propped up, I reveled in the adulation and warm reception. I had suffered much personally with the separation from my family, professionally with the loss of my fortune, and physically with the loss of my health. As I rode into the city, I saw Philadelphia as an opportunity to receive overdue recognition and finally regain some of the wealth lost in service of my country.

Emaciated and drawn citizens came out to greet me, but behind them I saw a city that had been badly abused. Whole neighborhoods of houses on the northwest and southern parts of the city had been dismantled for firewood. Over six hundred homes had been destroyed. Presbyterian cemeteries had been overturned by the British, who used the space to exercise their horses. Public buildings had been left with broken windows, and even important buildings had been stripped of their furniture. Mud and debris covered everything. Mass graves of American prisoners of war were located at the very center of the city. The statehouse had been used as a prison—its immaculate floors were now piled with human waste.

In contrast to the devastation, the excellent condition of loyalist homes made me furious. Upon arrival, I was given a list of five hundred individuals the radical Americans wanted charged with treason and hanged. I remembered General Washington's admonition that all parties should be treated fairly, so I tempered my wrath, tabling their petition for later consideration.

My staff quickly identified the spectacular Penn mansion as my new headquarters. Also known as the "slate roof house," it was the same building previously occupied by General Howe. Posting well-uniformed guards, they quickly furnished the house in a manner consistent with a commanding general. After more than three years of active service and having been wounded twice, I felt I was entitled to some reasonable comfort; however, I later learned this display irritated a city stripped clean. Unfortunately, shortly after arriving, either deliberately or inadvertently (I now suspect the former), I was served something quite disagreeable to my bowels, leaving me much fatigued and ill-tempered as I faced a myriad of problems taking over the unruly city.

I quickly realized that command of Philadelphia was not a good fit for me. I knew that an active command in the field was virtually impossible, given my wounds. However, my past naval experience presented a potential opportunity to the benefit of the Cause, and to escape the intrigue of Philadelphia. A day after my arrival in the city, I wrote to General Washington, suggesting I take command of the navy, or potentially lead a naval expedition to Barbados and Bermuda, freeing the island slaves and enlisting them as privateers against the enemy. In my letter, I wrote, "I must beg leave to request your Excellency's sentiments respecting a command in the navy." Neither General Washington nor Congress had an appetite for this bold venture, and my request was denied.

After a couple of weeks in the city, it was clear that I would be remaining. I sent for my sister Hannah and my seven-year-old son, Harry, to come and join me in Philadelphia; I would have Hannah coordinate my household and act as the hostess for events in my new residence.

Chapter 57

Philadelphia, PA - June 28, 1778

My initial charge from Congress was to determine what supplies remained in the city to assess what might be useful to the army. More importantly, I learned from spies that Tory merchants had hidden their goods and would try to sell them at far higher prices to the Continental Army when the British exited. As a result, I was forced to suspend all business in the city and embargo all trade until a joint committee of Congress and the Supreme Executive Council of Pennsylvania could "determine whether any or what part thereof may belong to the king of Great Britain or to any of his subjects."

Shortly after I arrived, Joseph Reed appeared at my door, claiming to represent the citizenry of Philadelphia, and was escorted into my presence. Lank, severe, and dressed in all black, he had predator's eyes that framed a narrow beaked nose; they stared at me with all the compassion of a bird of prey surveying its quarry. Without any preamble, or even half-hearted attempted at courtesy, he barked, "The mob is raiding our shops and looting whatever food they can lay their hands on. What do you intend to do about it?"

I was well aware of the problem, and had already had my aides draft off the appropriate document. Reaching into my pocket, I held out the declaration to this repugnant little man. "I am about to declare martial law, and I also intend to suspend all trade until such time as civil order shall be restored. You may take the proclamation and post the order."

For a moment, Reed stared at me, dumbfounded, his jaw opened in surprise to expose his yellow teeth. He blinked; his jaw snapped shut with an audible click. Then, nodding noncommittally, he spun on his heels and walked out without a further word.

In many ways, he was my enemy before I even met him—he had

Joseph Reed
Engraving by B. L. Provost of painting by Du Simitière.
Courtesy of the Library of Congress #2001699816

signed a petition to acquit the deserting Enos during my march to Quebec. The son of a wealthy merchant, Reed had been educated at the finest schools in America and later became a lawyer at London's Middle Temple. He married a puritanical English wife. Outspoken, he had the habit of antagonizing both friend and foe alike.

In 1776, Reed had been a trusted aide of General Washington. While Reed was away from headquarters, a letter had arrived from Washington's rival, Major General Charles Lee. Assuming the letter related to official business, Washington had promptly opened the letter and discovered that Reed had been criticizing him behind his back. This letter revealed a man without honor and possessing an elastic conscience. The resulting rift between Washington and Reed was never mended, and Reed eventually left the army, returning to Philadelphia.

After his betrayal of Washington, he persecuted twenty-three sus-pected loyalists for treason. He focused his wrath on those in Philadel-phia's upper classes, who had been unfriendly to him and his wife. He had become the ultimate Revolutionary radical. Anyone who was not a radical was a subhuman Tory; any reasonable behavior in dealing with the British or having acted in a gentlemanly manner was viewed, in his skewed perception, as treason. Because I sought a balanced approach, I was an immediate enemy.

Reed's elevation to the state's supreme executive council made him one of the most powerful men in Pennsylvania and gave him a platform to purge any attempts at reconciliation. Indeed, he was so warped that he saw both the Continental Congress and the Continental Army as akin to loyalists. He always placed the needs of Pennsylvania above the com-mon national government. In a final act of hypocrisy, Reed purchased the mansion of Joseph Galloway, a loyalist who had fled Philadelphia, and had the state militia evict Galloway's wife, Grace, by carrying her out in a chair so that he could occupy the mansion prior to the Conti-nental Army entering the city.

Put simply, Reed genuinely loathed me (which put me in good company) as a leader of the Continental Army. What I did not fully appreciate at the time was that he also hated me as part of a struggle between the states and Congress on one side and the army and General Washington on the other.

I underestimated Reed as a petty, little, cowardly politician. His complaints fell on my deaf ears. To my later harm and detriment, I ini-tially relished his unhappiness and criticisms.

As promised, for one week I kept the city closed. I forbade radicals from carrying out arrests, and prevented any property being sold without it first being cataloged by the staff. My failure to abuse the loyalists was quickly misinterpreted by the radicals as sympathy on my part. Nothing could be further from the truth; when General Washington overturned the protection of the loyalists, I promptly permitted the roundup and seizure of their homes and businesses, for which I was criticized as attempting to "steal" their goods for my own benefit.

My orders and actions were completely consistent with my directions from Washington, yet I was assailed from all sides. It seemed virtually every petitioner in the city was lined up outside my door. One day, as I sat in my office rubbing my throbbing leg, I was told that James Mease wished to see me. Irritated by the interruption, I nevertheless nodded and allowed him to enter. Mease waddled in looking more like a corpulent butcher than the army's clothier general. Leaning back in my chair, I asked curtly, "What can I do for you, sir?"

Mease attempted to stand at attention in front of my desk. Turning nervously toward Major Franks, he whispered, although it was obvious that Franks could hear him, "It is of a confidential nature, General."

Simultaneously intrigued and further irritated, I nodded my head toward the door. Franks bowed and left. "Very well, you have my attention."

"An opportunity, General. A rare opportunity, as a result of unique circumstances which could prove profitable to both you and me, if handled wisely and discreetly."

I had not been paid for the better part of three years and had expended my fortune at the feet of the Revolution. An opportunity to make up some of those losses certainly intrigued me. "As I said, you have my attention."

Mease flushed, looked at his hands, and then pressed on. "You see, General, at your orders, we have done a census of all of the buildings and inventory in the city." Pausing uncomfortably, he continued, "That is, we know the property of those who suffered under British tyranny, and their property is being returned to them. We are also endeavoring to prevent price gouging and are providing for a fair distribution of goods."

Rolling my hand, I said, "Pray, Mr. Mease, get to the point. I am aware of my orders." I'll admit that I had little patience for clerks in soldiers' uniforms. This sweaty little man, who would not last a moment on the battlefield, was catching me in a particularly foul mood.

"The thing is, General, that a large portion of property that was owned by loyalists, and is subject to confiscation, is essentially owned by no one. You see, the property was that of 'disaffected persons.' So nobody is in a position to claim it." A hint of a smile pushed up his moist upper lip as he finished speaking.

The veil lifted, and I saw the opportunity. "What are you proposing?" I asked flatly, hiding my growing interest.

"What I am asking, sir, is that I be permitted to use the public credit to buy these unclaimed goods. We could sell them to the army and to the public. We could then return any monies borrowed from the public coffers, and the profit would be divided. You would not be required to do anything, General, other than provide some orders and permission for me to proceed. I would then provide you with an accounting and twenty-five percent of the profit associated with the transaction."

I tried hard to look bored and disinterested. My prior petulant attitude had the beneficial effect of keeping Mease off-balance. "I appreciate your discretion. However, I think we both need to understand that what you are proposing is not illegal," I said with a firmness that made clear I was controlling the discussion.

In truth, I did not know whether or not it was illegal. There were certainly parts of the public, no doubt led by Reed, who would criticize such actions. At the same time, I did not want Mease to later argue that I knew I was doing something outside the law. In any event, I was never going to settle for a quarter of the profit with this little man. "Your project," I told him, "will require my cooperation. Indeed, without me, I cannot conceive how you could move forward. Thus, obviously the only acceptable division would be for us to split the profits. To the extent you are required to compensate other individuals, that will need to come out of your profit. I'll require, as you indicated, a detailed accounting. I want to be clear that I am not paying for anything more than the cost of the goods. All other costs will be borne by you."

I had been negotiating on behalf of the Lathrops since I was a teenager. They had taught me that all discussions of this type were about power. I knew if I took too much, then he would not be incentivized and would be resentful. "Subject to these caveats, profit will be split equally."

I watched his beady eyes dart back and forth as he weighed his response. Finally, he nodded in agreement. "As you say, General."

Leaning forward in my chair, now fully in command, "I don't want there to be any disagreement or argument between us. This will be a private agreement, but memorialized in a writing you will create and bring to me for review."

Holding out my hand, I reached across the desk and said, "Thank you, Mr. Mease." I could not bring myself to mention his rank.

Taking my hand, he chortled, "Yes, thank you, General. Thank you very much indeed."

As he went to let go of my hand, I squeezed his soft fingers harder and pulled him over the desk toward me so that our faces were close. I looked him hard in the eyes and growled, "Don't let me down."

The smile evaporated and the color went out of his face as he looked down and nodded, murmuring, "Of course, General, of course. Thank you, sir."

I continued to squeeze his hand for several more seconds as his face showed the discomfort of my viselike grip. When I felt I had made my point, I abruptly released him. "That will be all."

Returning my gaze to the papers on my desk, I saw Mease bow and leave the room in my peripheral vision. Once he was out the door, I leaned back in my chair with a wide smile. It was about time I began to make some money again.

Chapter 58

City Tavern, Philadelphia, PA - July 4, 1778

T he radicals' behavior and animosity toward anyone who disagreed with them extended to the absurd. They viewed any woman who wore her hair in a high headdress or any man who wore a high hat (as opposed to a tricorn) as a "Tory." Indeed, even a silver toe buckle or powdered wig could be viewed as an indication of Tory sympathies. I viewed such trivialities for what they were: the ruminations of small-minded men who focused on form over substance. Our goal was to defeat the British in battle, not defeat ourselves. If we were going to win this war, we would have to do so as one country.

Reed and his radicals also failed to acknowledge the necessity and adjustments required to accommodate the severe wound to my leg. Reed seemed oblivious or indifferent to the fact that my mangled leg required a springed transport to minimize my discomfort. It was only practical for me to use a high-quality carriage of the type ridden by the British during the occupation. Nevertheless, the radicals attacked me both in public and private for my "Tory" displays of excess.

The radicals' last straw was my attendance at balls and theatre productions. Reed viewed such events as a frivolous distraction from the war effort. I ordered that a July 4 celebration be held throughout the city, hoping that the activities would momentarily unite a divided metropolis. At ten o'clock, after the fireworks displays had ended, carriages began arriving at the corners of Second and Walnut Streets, where I held a reception for the new French minister. In a large ballroom at the City Tavern, glittering chandeliers lit elegant ladies and gentlemen dancing the minuet as eight musicians performed on an elevated platform. Servants moved about the crowd, offering imported wines.

I sat at the edge of the dance floor, my leg propped up on a satin pillow, and encouraged my dutiful aides Majors Clarkson and Franks to leave my side and join the dancers. While no longer able to dance myself, I still enjoyed the music, the atmosphere, and most of all, flirting with the ladies. I spent a good deal of time with my friend Silas Deane, who had recently returned as the minister from France. I was greeted by some of the wealthiest men of the city, including Robert Morris, who had personally raised over £20,000 to help the American troops in a summer campaign. I was particularly pleased that Joseph Reed had boycotted the ball as an unnecessarily ostentatious display.

As I scanned the crowd, my eyes moved to a quiet, pretty, and shy-looking blonde. Major Franks, who happened to be at my side, seemed to understand my interest; in a moment, the young lady appeared on his arm before me. Major Franks bowed and said with a theatrical flourish, "Major General Arnold, may I present Miss Margaret Shippen."

Momentarily forgetting my infirmity, I began to stand, both moving my chair and knocking over the stool on which my leg rested. The normal shot of pain was overcome by my excitement to meet this apparition. Franks's look of happiness at the introduction immediately turned to concern as I tried to rise, and he shifted the stool back in place. The only person who seemed comfortable and unfazed was the young Miss Shippen. Sliding closer to me, she offered her hand while dipping into a curtsy so deep that our faces were at the same level. With her eyes downcast and her delicate hand perfectly placed in front of my face, she said in a gentle voice, "General Arnold, what a pleasure. We are so grateful to have a true hero in Philadelphia."

As I reached out to kiss her hand, she looked up, and I beheld her soft blue-gray eyes. I felt Cupid's arrow pierce my heart. A twenty-year-old fair-skinned beauty with a yielding chin and lovely smile made me forget everyone and everything around me. I stared, dumbfounded.

She continued in a soft but lovely voice that carried to my ringing ears, "It is so nice to see you again, General." I cocked my head in confusion. If it is possible for a smile to become even more radiant and an eye

Margaret Shippen
Sketch by John André. Courtesy of Yale University Art Gallery

to twinkle even more, hers did. "It was when you came to the Continental Congress. You met my father, my sister, and me."

My mind scrolled back to meeting the famous Judge Shippen and being presented with his two lovely daughters, the younger of whom was still awkward and gangly. Apparently my eyes widened in recognition—she laughed, and so did I. I felt like a tongue-tied buffoon as I tried to search for the perfect gallant comment. Stumbling, all I managed was, "Well . . . well . . . you have certainly grown up."

We both laughed again, and she sat down in the open chair next to me. "You have brought light and happiness back to our city, General."

Slightly more relaxed, I risked a rare moment of salon eloquence: "My dear, as long as you are in Philadelphia, it will never want for light or happiness."

She looked down at her lap at my compliment, but I prayed it had struck home.

People continued to greet and thank me. Miss Shippen stayed longer than politeness required. When she eventually took her leave, I fought every instinct to keep an eye on her no matter where she went in the room. I was thrilled that whenever I looked at her, she always seemed to be sneaking glances at me too.

The morning after the dance, I sent "Peggy," as she'd insisted I call her, a lavish bouquet of flowers; her father received nice bottles of wine. Soon thereafter, I began to make regular visits to the Shippen mansion, located on the northwest corner of Fourth and Prune Streets. Four stories tall, forty-two feet wide, and nearly as deep, the handsome red-and-black Flemish-bond brick façade was divided symmetrically by a heavy doorframe fluted to resemble Greek columns, supported by a pyramid stone pediment.

I came to learn that Peggy, born on June 11, 1760, was preceded in the world by a brother and three sisters. The Shippens were one of the colony's leading families. Edward Shippen, the first to immigrate to America, came to Boston in 1688 with a £10,000 fortune and married a Quaker. They were granted sanctuary by the then-governor of Rhode Island, my great-grandfather and namesake, Governor Benedict Arnold. They'd ultimately resettled in Philadelphia and continued to prosper. The family was known not only for its success, but also for its integrity and willingness to speak the truth, even if it had adverse political consequences.

Peggy's father had inherited wealth but lacked the entrepreneurialism that drove his father and grandfather. A far more bookish and timid man, he focused more on preserving the family estates than on growing them. Trained as a lawyer in London, he'd married well and accumulated wealth as part of the city's elite. He served in several important offices, including admiralty judge, prothonotary, and recorder. His positions put him clearly on the side of the British government at the time of the Revolution, though he tried to maintain a "neutral" position as the tension grew between the Colony and the Crown and as Peggy came of age.

When Peggy was ten, her father's position as admiralty court judge was abolished, but Governor Penn appointed him to the upper house of the provincial legislature. This made him unequivocally a member of the British ruling elite and a target for unhappy revolutionaries. Nevertheless, he maintained a stance of strict neutrality and measured "fairness" to both sides, keeping his ultimate opinion on the Revolution private.

By the summer of 1776, Peggy's father was regularly accused of being a "traitor." He was required to renounce his oath of allegiance to the king or be charged with treason. While I did not learn this till much later, Peggy told me that her father was firmly opposed to the Revolution and believed that separation from Mother England would lead to disaster. Nevertheless, he shared his true feelings with only his closest friends and relatives.

The Shippen family was directly impacted by the war. Peggy's oldest sister Elizabeth's fiancé, Neddy Burd, was missing and presumed killed in the rout of the Americans at Long Island. Word came a week later than Burd was alive but a prisoner of war on a British ship in New York. In December 1776, Peggy's only brother, eighteen-year-old Edward, had joined the British Army, along with several of their cousins. He chose the worst possible place to join the Hessians in the Christmas celebration in Trenton, New Jersey. Captured by Washington in his brave and daring attack, Edward was personally freed by the general because of his prior contact with the Shippen family. Judge Shippen was furious at foolish Edward's breaking the family's vow of neutrality and jeopardizing their standing; he stripped the lad of any family duties and threatened him into silence. From that day, Judge Shippen began to refer to the American Continental Army as "our army" due to the magnanimous gesture by George Washington.

If I was going to begin courting a vibrant young woman, I needed to do so in style. Peggy and I drove around the city in a handsome new carriage, drawn by a matched pair of bays and liveried attendants.

A wizened-faced maid of Peggy's mother joined us as a chaperone when I took Peggy to John Bartram's famous gardens in Eastwick, southwest of the city. As we moved through the park, I found myself transfixed by her beauty. Comfortable with my staring, she nevertheless jarred me from my revelry as she cast an elegant hand towards the gardens. "The world is so lovely. The sun is gentle but bright. The flowers and grass fill my eyes and heart with color while the birds proclaim the joy of nature's bounty. It is hard to believe that war and death can happen in this Eden. That men will face and kill each other—it all seems so senseless in the sublime world that surrounds us. Yet, it is here—even in this lovely space—the snake is slithering down from the tree. It is the humid stillness in the afternoon before the storm clouds roll in."

I marveled at her insight, but also hoped that she would never fully understand the horror of war. Grasping her hands, I said in earnest, "All the more reason, my dear, that we should savor this moment." I ignored the chaperone's disapproving scowl.

I ordered the carriage stopped, and we moved toward an open section of grass near the river. Peggy had brought a lovely picnic with china, silver, and rare delicacies. With the chaperone out of earshot preparing our lunch, her countenance changed. Gone was the young woman poetically commenting on beauty and war; instead, I was met with searching eyes with probing intelligence. "I want to know everything about you. I have lived a sheltered life, but you have seen and done so much. Tell me about where you grew up, tell me about your parents, tell me about your sons, tell me about life at sea, tell me about *you*."

Well, that was unexpected. Again, more than meets the eye. Either she is either genuinely interested, or I am being vetted. Either way, I can't begin by lying to this remarkable woman. I need to tell her the truth.

I gestured to a well-placed bench, and we sat down to my relief. "I am afraid my lineage is not much to speak about. I am the fifth of my name, but in many ways, I am the first. My ancestors rose to prominence in Rhode Island and Connecticut, but by the time of my father—I regret to say he had lost his way." I continued without meeting her eye. "He squandered positions in the community and lost his fortune." *I cannot tell you, my sweet, the full depth of his depravity.*

Taking a deep breath and finally meeting her gaze, I said with a tentative grin, "My sons are strong and healthy. My sister Hannah is a great help in both my businesses and with raising my sons. But we cannot claim an august family name like the Shippens. The fortune I have made has been my own doing." I spoke with growing confidence, "I believe there is more to come."

"My dear General. I find you all the more noble. My father is a very fine man, but he stands on the shoulders of all the Shippens. He could not climb much higher and did not risk falling. He is wise, and I love and respect him, but he is tame. You, General . . . you are a phoenix. You rise from the ashes. You are not limited in how high you will fly. You make your own destiny: an apothecary, a merchant, a sea captain, a pirate, a shipowner, a smuggler, a duelist, a war hero, and now a great general."

She has done research. I blushed and said, "Well, you are too kind, but I should tell you, it is not all true."

She laughed, not with the chortle of a salon or a polite giggle, but with an open-mouthed, joyous laugh suited for the company of good friends. "Very well, then; I retract the pirate comment. How about that?"

I roared with a joy I had not felt in years. It was as if she had pulled away a dark veil that was preventing me from being truly happy. I gave an exaggerated seated bow. "As you say, milady." *She is like no woman I have ever met. I am always working, thinking ahead of the other women. She is so bright. She is ahead of me.*

Still in control of our conversation, she bombarded me with questions: "So, what makes you happy? What makes you sad? What do you read? What is your greatest accomplishment? What are your goals in life?"

This is unusual. She asks nothing about the war.

I answered her as best I could, and asked her questions in return. I learned of the Shippen mansion's extensive library, which had allowed Peggy to absorb not only the classics, but also the latest newspapers from London and America. My Peggy received the finest possible education available to a young woman of her station. I learned she was not one to waste time on the frivolous issues of vacuous women. Instead, she devoted herself to her father's business and political efforts in supporting her family. Her father, recognizing her exceptionalism—as I immediately had—relied far more heavily on her for counsel and support than he did her older brother Edward. In turn, he provided her with beautiful gowns and accoutrements at a level which strained even his considerable resources.

My first wife had been a bundle of twigs held together by sinew and dry skin, animated only by cold disapproval. In contrast, Peggy projected warmth and was well-rounded and soft in the way a good woman should be. But it was her smile, and her radiant flash of adoration, that was the greatest distinction from my straight-mouthed and unloving first wife.

In my entire life, I had never met someone so interested in me—not General Arnold, Captain Arnold, or Dr. Arnold, but *me*. I was utterly amazed and overjoyed that such an exquisite person was interested not merely in what I was, but in *who* I was.

We had planned a relatively short visit to the gardens, but after three hours had flown by, our impatient chaperone could finally be delayed no longer. When I showed my disappointment at having to leave, Peggy grasped my hand and said, "This is only the beginning, Benny, not the end."

Somewhere in the course of that magical afternoon, I had become her "Benny"—a name no one had ever used. But even more so, my heart almost burst with joy because she was "my Peggy."

When we returned to the city, I resolved that I wanted to win this remarkable woman's love. I needed to stop hobbling around on crutches. Thus, I hired the best cobbler I could find to build a special high-heeled left shoe that allowed me to walk with a gentleman's cane. I was finally able to stroll the streets with a limp, tapping my gold-headed cane on the cobblestone.

Chapter 59

Philadelphia, PA - July 17, 1778

B y this stage of the war, virtually every officer had been forced to either resign because of lost income or pursue economic opportunities to take care of his family and make ends meet. Indeed, General Washington, in a letter to Congress, summarized the plight of officers after three years of war. He noted that gentlemen entered the service believing it would be temporary, "but finding its duration to be much longer than they had first suspected, and that instead of deriving any advantage from the hardships and dangers, to which they were exposed, they on the contrary were losers falling far short of even a competency to supply their want, they have gradually abated in their ardor; and with many, an entire disinclination to the service under the present circumstances has taken place." My financial resources had reached their breaking point.

While in Valley Forge meeting with General Washington and his staff, I was approached by a merchant and vessel owner named Robert Skewell. He and his partners James Seagrove and William Constable had a reputation for "flexible" loyalties where business opportunities were concerned. They had straddled the American and British lines in New York and Philadelphia, and Skewell had been ejected from the American camp as a Tory sympathizer and a profiteer.

Major Franks knew that I was looking for business opportunities to regain my fortune, and when he heard that Skewell was looking for a patron, he directed him to me. Skewell was nothing like the awkward, timid, and obsequious Mease. Well-dressed, but not excessively so, Skewell projected the aura of a highly sophisticated businessman and merchant cut from the same cloth as me. He was a direct and polished negotiator.

After initial introductions, he got to the point: "General, we are gravely concerned about our cargo currently held in Philadelphia in the *Charming Nancy*. We need to set sail as soon as possible. American privateers are gathering in Delaware Bay and waiting to pounce. We need permission to leave, and more importantly, a pass of safe conduct to present to any privateer. The Philadelphia authorities and General Washington's staff are unwilling to help us."

I simply stared back at him, knowing that some offer of remuneration would be forthcoming. Silence can be a very effective negotiating tool.

Flustered by my implacability, Skewell continued in a honeyed tone, "Of course, we would want to ensure that you are not ignored for the kindness you are extending to us." Again, I stared back impassively. "Much of the cargo is spoken for, but we will gladly split with you our profits on the vast majority of the ship's contents." Sensing I was still unsatisfied, he continued, "We have a privateer under contract. I don't know if you know, but it has been named the *Benedict Arnold*." With that, I could not stop a closemouthed smile from escaping. "We would be pleased to give you a one-share interest in that vessel."

Nodding my head in agreement, I grinned broadly. "I would be happy to give you the pass to get your ship out of Philadelphia, and safe conduct through the privateers. Please see Major Franks to draw up the appropriate papers." While it was not explicit, the quid pro quo was clear. I would sign the passes when I received the interest in the privateer. I also knew that Skewell was wise enough to keep this matter confidential, so no warnings were required.

I was upset to learn that while the *Charming Nancy* had successfully left Philadelphia, it was immediately accosted by the Pennsylvanian privateer the *Santippe* and forced into the port of Chestnut Neck, New Jersey. The *Charming Nancy* was ruled a prize by Bowes Reed, cousin of Joseph Reed.

Major Franks discreetly brought Skewell into my study in Philadelphia. Much of his ease of manner and impeccable appearance of our first meeting was gone in the face of hard riding. After Franks closed the door, Skewell began, without preamble, "I assume you've heard, General." He kept talking without waiting for an answer. "First the bastards ignore your pass and rule us an American prize, and now there is a British naval force about to attack Chestnut Neck and seize the ship as *their* prize! We will lose everything, including your share of the ship."

Unable to hide my irritation with the man who had promised me a profit, I barked, "What do you want?"

Skewell started to take a step closer, but then stepped back and took a breath to calm down. "What we need are wagons, sir. A dozen should do it. If we could get wagons from you, and a pass, we could remove our goods before they are taken. We both know Reed's order to treat the ship as a prize is ridiculous. Using wagons will avoid that entire issue. The ship might be lost to the British, but we would at least get its cargo."

Without further discussion, I reached out and issued an order requisitioning twelve government wagons and provided written orders and instructions to "remove property which was in imminent danger of falling into enemy hands." The wagons, which belonged to the State of Pennsylvania, were only supposed to be used for government purposes. I didn't see any harm in recovering cargo that would otherwise go to the British.

As planned, the wagons returned loaded with linens, glass, sugar, tea, nails, and more, which were sold, the profit split between my partners and me. While the goods were being retrieved, I made secret agreements with merchants in Philadelphia to store them in the basement of the Penn Mansion and redistribute them to merchants for sale. I retained Stephen Collins on Second Street in Philadelphia to oversee their sale. Between November 4 and December 8 of 1778, I received £7,500.

I was head-over-heels in love with Peggy. What captivated me most about her was her intelligence and quick wit. While she knew how to dress like a fine English lady, there was nothing in her conduct that was frivolous or vain. She was the perfect balance of beauty and intelligence.

I am not a poet. Thus, in a September 1778 letter, I borrowed much of the same language that I'd used in my unsuccessful courting of Betsy DeBlois:

Dear Madam: —

Twenty times I have taken up my pen to write you, and as often as my trembling hand refused to obey the dictates of my heart—a heart which, though calm and serene amidst the clashing of arms and all the din and horrors of war, trembles with diffidence and the fear of giving offense when attempts to address you on a subject so important to its happiness. Dear Madame, your charms have lighted up a flame in my bosom which can never be extinguished; your heavenly image is too deeply impressed ever to be effaced.

My Passion is not founded on personal charms only; the sweetness of disposition and goodness of heart, that sentiment and sensibility which so strongly mark the character of the lovely P. Shippen, renders her amicable beyond expression, and will ever retain the heart she has once captivated.

Suffer me to hope for your approbation. Consider before you doom me to misery, which I have not deserved but by loving too extravagantly. Consult your own happiness, and if incompatible, forget there is so unhappy a wretch; for I may perish if I do not give one moment's inquietude to purchase the greatest possible felicity to myself. Whatever my fate may be, my most ardent wish is for your happiness, and my latest breath will be to implore the blessings of heaven on the idol and only wish of my soul.

Adieu, my dear Madame, and believe me unalterably, your sincere admirer and devoted humble servant.

B. Arnold

While I was infirm as a result of my wounds, I remained optimistic that Peggy would take me. At thirty-six, I was still a young man with proven self-made success both on and off the battlefield. I believed I had demonstrated my honor and generosity on many occasions. Most notably at this time, I had undertaken to donate five hundred dollars to support and educate three of the children of my mentor, Dr. Joseph Warren, who had been killed at Bunker Hill. I berated politicians who dragged their feet in providing a pension for his dependents.

I hoped my demonstrated goodwill in the face of congressional indifference would have a salutary effect on Peggy's father's view of me. Judge Shippen viewed me as nouveau riche and somewhat uncouth. I was guilty on both fronts; at the same time, I was also hardworking, successful, and deeply devoted to his daughter. Attempting to further bolster my position as a prosperous member of the community, I purchased Mount Pleasant, a mansion overlooking the Schuylkill River. This ninety-nine-acre country estate's centerpiece was a Georgian manner house with richly paneled and corniced drawing and dining rooms, large casement windows, and manicured gardens with stunning views of Philadelphia.

While the purchase had the desired effect on Judge Shippen, it had the opposite effect on Joseph Reed. On December 1, he became president of the Pennsylvania Council. He publicly speculated about where I had received the money to purchase Mount Pleasant, and implied the worst.

Chapter 60

Morristown, NY - February 6, 1779

I was being vilified both publicly and privately at every turn. After seven months of constant attacks, I desperately wanted to leave Philadelphia. Philip Schuyler and John Jay encouraged me to return to northern New York, where my bravery at Fort Ti, Valcour Isle, Fort Stanwix, and Saratoga had ensured I continued to be held in high regard. These gentlemen believed that I had sacrificed enough and should resign my commission to return to northern New York as a respected landowner. In fact, I was offered two large manors confiscated from loyalists, at either Skenesborough, near the foot of Lake Champlain, or Johnson Hall, on the Mohawk. I preferred the forty-thousand-acre plot in Skenesborough. Relying on their generous offer, I planned to head north to see the land. This was an estate where I could have ruled while being respected by my tenants and neighbors—a true opportunity to live like a country gentleman.

At the same time, virtually every issue of the *Pennsylvania Packet* contained taunts and attacks on me. As Reed rose in power, he removed all moderate elements from Pennsylvania and concentrated his attack on the most visible symbol of a strong central government: the military governor of the city of Philadelphia—me. "When I meet your carriage in the streets, and think of the splendor in which you live and revel. It is impossible to avoid the question, 'From whence have these riches flowed, if you did not plunder Montreal?'"

I responded publicly, "I shall only say, that I am at all times ready to answer my public conduct to Congress or General Washington, to whom alone I am accountable." Offended by the response, Reed wrote to Congress of the "indignity offered us."

It was clear to everyone in Congress, as well as General Washington, that I had been dragged into a political quagmire. I rode to meet Washington in New Jersey to discuss the situation. Before I reached the headquarters, my aide Matthew Clarkson approached me with the *Pennsylvania Packet* in his saddlebag. Included in the packet was a list of eight charges brought against me by the Pennsylvania Executive Council, accusing me of:

1. Granting an unauthorized pass to the *Charming Nancy*

2. Taking possession in the city of closed shops and stores for my own benefit

3. Imposing menial offices on militia

4. Disputing the capture of the *Active*

5. Using wagons of the State of Pennsylvania to transport the contents of the *Charming Nancy*

6. Granting unworthy persons passes through enemy lines

7. Refusing to provide explanations to the Council of Pennsylvania regarding the use of wagons (referenced in charge 5 above) and responding in an indecent and disrespectful manner

8. Engaging in a cold and neglectful treatment of patriot authorities while treating adherence to the king with an entire line of conduct

I was obviously extremely alarmed by the charges, which the Pennsylvanians had viciously released to all the congressional delegations and the public in an attempt to besmirch my reputation. I continued to Washington's camp at Middlebrook, New Jersey, where I intended to show him the charges. Caught in a snowstorm, we pressed on, only to have our carriage slide off the road. A cripple, I could no longer get out to push the carriage, or even mount a horse to proceed. Instead, like an old woman or baggage, I was forced to watch while others extricated our carriage. Pathetic and helpless, after much delay, I arrived at camp boiling with frustration.

By the time I was brought into Washington's presence, he was already aware of the charges. Gone were the warm embraces and informality that had characterized our prior meetings. As I was helped into the room, he stood and bowed formally, as did his aide-de-camp. Pointing to a chair he said politely but without warmth, "General Arnold."

I knew I should have waited for him to set the tone of the conversation, but I was too agitated. I felt like a wolf caught in a trap. "I gather you have seen these?" I growled, gesturing for the aide to hand the charges to Washington.

Looking down, he nodded and made a face like someone swallowing a bitter pill. Again, I should have waited for him to speak, but I couldn't help myself. "Reed and his mob are out to get me, General! These charges are absurd. We need to convene a court-martial to address them as soon as possible. I told you it was a nest of vipers. I want to transfer my flag to New York, or join the navy, or even resign. I can barely walk into this god-damned room with all I've bled for my country, and they accuse me of being in service of the king!"

I regretted the profanity immediately. Poorly hiding his irritation, Washington spoke as someone using all his powers of self-control. "I share your frustration. Reed, as you know, is no friend of mine or the army's. However, I do not believe you can simply resign at this point. It would be tantamount to acknowledging the validity of the charges." I shrugged in acknowledgment as he continued, "I know you wish earnestly to visit General Schuyler and move to New York, but again, I do not believe you can be seen as running from the charges. I am sure you agree."

Downcast and unable to meet his eyes, I felt my anger giving way to a profound fatigue and sadness.

With a voice that cut like blades of ice, it was clear he was giving an order. "I am afraid you must return to Philadelphia and meet these charges head-on. I have no doubt you will succeed."

Seizing on his professed confidence, I asked with hope and trust to my mentor and friend, "Perhaps, Your Excellency, you could give me a letter of support, reaffirming my character, my service to the Cause, and your belief in the baselessness of the charges?"

Washington involuntarily looked over at his aide, then back at me. "I am sorry, but I cannot do that. I cannot be seen as taking sides. There are factions within Congress influenced by the Pennsylvanians and others who would seek to undermine the army's position if I were seen as participating in a political dispute. I am sure you understand."

My disappointment was so visceral, I winced as though I had been lashed. I wanted to scream. *I don't understand! You appointed me to this god-damned position. Now you are sacrificing me and my honor in the name of your political agenda. We both know that if you stood beside me, this matter would be resolved. You simply do not care about me. I am political cannon fodder.*

After a long silence, as if Washington could sense what I was thinking, he said with a finality constituting a dismissal, "I appreciate you coming to see me, General. Please keep me apprised of your defense." With that his aide was at my elbow, guiding me to the door.

In shock, I shuffled toward the exit, barely holding back the scream, *You lying, two-faced bastard!* I could feel the panic of being abandoned. I understood that every painful step I took for the rest of my life would be a reminder of what I had suffered for my country, yet I received no support from *anyone*.

Despondent about my situation as well as the conditions in Philadelphia, I picked up my pen and wrote Peggy:

My Dearest Life,

Never did I so ardently long to see or hear from you as at this instant. Six days' absence, without hearing from my Dear Peggy, is intolerable. Heavens! I am heartily tired with my journey and almost so with human nature. I daily discover so much baseness and ingratitude among mankind that I almost blush at being of the same species, and could quit the stage without regret was it not for some few gentle, generous souls like my Dear Peggy. You alone, heard, felt, and seen, possess my every thought, fill every sense.

From time to time, British newspapers were smuggled through the lines. In New York, a friend gave me a copy of the *Royal Gazette*, in which British General Clinton praised me for my valor and perseverance and noted that "General Arnold heretofore has been styled another Hanni-bal, but losing a leg in service of Congress, the latter considering him unfit for any further exercise of his military talents, permitted him thus to fall into the unmerciful fangs of the Executive Council of Pennsyl-vania." It struck me that the British appreciated me and had a better understanding of my challenges than either Congress or my supposed benefactor, General Washington.

When I arrived home, I was relieved that Peggy's love for me was undiminished by the accusations. She helped rally friends to my defense. For the first time in my life, I had found someone, other than my sister Hannah, who unconditionally loved and supported me.

The week after my return to Philadelphia, we met at her home at a time when we knew most would be otherwise occupied. In the front parlor, we did not require a chaperone and thus had blessed time alone. With all the chaos around me, I found myself simultaneously grate-ful to be enveloped in her love and profoundly nervous that I would be rejected. As we sat before a roaring fire, frost covering the nearby window, I hesitated. Peggy, sensing something was wrong, moved to sit next to me on the settee and took my hand in her own. "Benny, what is the matter? You can tell me anything. Is it Reed? Has he done something else?"

Raising her hands to my lips, I replied, "No. This is not about him."

The elegant engagement ring I had purchased now felt like it weighed two stone in my pocket. I had practiced the next few min-utes—rising from the settee, I pivoted, bending my right leg and trying to keep my left leg as straight as possible behind me. I could not get all the way down to my knees, of course, but I wanted Peggy to have a proper proposal. I tried not to wince at the sharp stab as I maneuvered. "You are my only one true love. I speak to thee as a plain soldier. If thou canst love me, take me. Take me, take a soldier, and we shall be happy and want for nothing."

Her look of concern as I had maneuvered onto my knee gave way to a glowing smile with the recognition of the reason for my nervousness. I could see she also appreciated my literary allusion. She did not wait or play games; looking at the ring I was holding in my hand, she took it and said, "With all my heart, Benny. Yes, a thousand times yes. Now pray, sit. I am the one who should kneel, because to be your wife would make me the happiest woman in the world. I have loved you from the first moment I saw you, when you came here to visit my father."

My mind went blank after so much tension and anticipation, only for my rapture to be replaced with a wave of pain at my decision to partially kneel. Peggy guided me back next to her, and then gently kissed me. Her kiss had more eloquence in its sweet touch than anything she could ever have said.

As was her way, she was already thinking ahead. "Of course, we can tell no one of this, Benny. You must get my father's permission—which will not be easy. You have not spoken with him, correct?"

I looked down. I had been carrying the ring around for a while and had intended to speak to her father first, but Washington's betrayal had made me hesitant. In truth, I feared that, as with Betsy DeBlois, I might be rejected again. I didn't want the embarrassment of having asked and been rejected by both Peggy and her father. In front of everyone else, I was the brave and renowned Major General Benedict Arnold, yet when I stood before Peggy's father, my confidence fluttered like a candle in the breeze. I was reduced to an ill-educated upstart from a disreputable family, unworthy of his daughter. In response to her question, I simply mumbled, "No."

She fully understood my faux pas, but ignored it, taking a positive tone. "Excellent. This will give us both an opportunity to work on him together and build him toward acceptance. I expect he will refuse at first, but I always get my way with him." A devilish grin spread across her lovely face. "This must remain our secret until we have his permission." She continued looking me hard in the eyes. "You will be my lord and master. I know you are used to being in command, but in this campaign, you must allow me to be the general to win my father's approval. It will not be easy, and will require careful strategy."

With a surge of relief, I reached and pulled her to me, and we kissed again. My relief and joy began to get the better of me, but she gently pushed me back. "Not yet, Benny—we don't want to be interrupted, and we must be careful."

Not releasing her, I replied, "But my dear, we are the makers of manners."

As she smiled and pushed me back, she said, "A worthy try, my noble soldier."

I retreated with perhaps the greatest joy of my entire life.

Chapter 61

Philadelphia, PA - February 22, 1779

S ilas Deane and I sat in the sumptuous study in the Penn Mansion. Since his return from France, he had been staying as my guest. He too was under attack from enemies in Congress. Rather than being thanked for the extraordinary work he had performed in service of our country in Europe, he was being wrongly criticized for alleged financial improprieties.

We had always been kindred spirits, but our shared persecution had drawn us even closer together. Holding the *Pennsylvania Packet* in his hand as we sat in front of a warm fire, he said, "You know, before I joined you here as your guest, Reed warned me not to stay with you. He said that you were a Tory. Apparently Tories are everywhere. But take heart—you are in good company, my friend. Reed believes both John Ross and James Wilson are also Tories. Wilson signed the Declaration of Independence, but that now means nothing. Oh, and by and by, if you ask the Adamses or the Lees, I am a Tory too."

I shook my head in disgust. "It is all so absurd, Silas. The majority of the arms used in our army at Saratoga were obtained through your efforts. I have fought, killed, and almost died for my country, and Ross and Wilson were among the first to the Cause."

Holding the paper up, Silas said, "Not everyone is against you. General Cadwalader sang your praises in the *Packet*: 'The charges are absurd. They may serve the designs of certain factions, but they can never injure the character of a man to whom the country is so much indebted.' Even Charles Lee wrote, 'Arnold has been attacked by a banditti of ignorant and mercenary clowns.' Mind you, I loathe Lee, but he does have a way with words."

"You are very kind, Silas, but I still must defend against these claims, and I am under almost constant attack. I know I am not alone suffering under their tyranny. They have passed a new anti-loyalist law that says anyone who has fled the state for more than thirty days must reappear and surrender to a charge of treason, or all their property will be forfeit to the state, and if captured, they will be hung. Reports of disloyalty, even on hearsay, are accepted by these farcical courts, and many 'neutral parties' or honorable loyalists have been unfairly prosecuted without any due process of law. Any thinking man who challenges this abomination of justice is labeled a Tory sympathizer. Everyone is now facing tyranny and injustice far worse than anything the king or his ministers imposed before the Revolution."

Silas nodded in acknowledgment. "In light of all this, I laud you, my friend, for defending the Quakers."

"We must do what is right and speak against evil," I said, looking into the flames in the hearth between us. "Reed and his cadre denounced Roberts on such unfair grounds that I was forced to oppose them."

John Roberts was a sixty-year-old miller with Tory leanings who had fled into Philadelphia when the British took over. There, he supported himself by providing the British with provisions. General Howe privately warned Roberts to remain with the British to avoid reprisals; Roberts, a devout Quaker, believed there would be peace with all his neighbors. On May 8, 1778, in response to the new anti-loyalist law, he had surrendered himself, affirming his allegiance to the United States and ready to stand trial.

Ten of twelve jurors acquitted him. The jury noted that Roberts's many acts of humanity, charity, and benevolence had saved many American lives. Nevertheless, Reed and the radicals proceeded with plans for execution. Roberts's wife and ten children appealed on their knees to Congress for mercy, and more than a thousand civic leaders wrote a petition for clemency, yet Roberts was ordered hanged, his reprieve denied by Reed.

On November 4, as Roberts was led through the streets with a noose about his neck, four thousand Quakers demonstrated against the action. My soldiers stood at attention and played the "Rogue's March" as a sign of defiance as Roberts died with dignity, his wife and ten children looking on. The night before the execution, I had demonstrated my loyalty to Roberts's cause by holding a public reception at City Tavern and inviting leading Quakers and loyalists. I knew this would antagonize Reed, but I could not ignore such evil.

Grabbing my elbow, Silas whispered, "No good deed goes unpunished, Benedict. I often thought you failed to see the nuance of politics, but I now understand I was mistaken. You see through the fog with a clarity, discerning the good from the bad, the right from the wrong. Unlike most men, you do not compromise, you do not equivocate—you speak to truth." Patting my shoulder as he rose from his chair, "Sleep well with a clear conscience, my most honorable friend."

Congress was to decide Pennsylvania's case against me. The charge of illegal trading was the most problematic—the trading business is not for the faint of heart. But what I had done was legal, and in any event, I had been careful not to leave any trail of incriminating evidence.

While many in Congress were inclined to dismiss the case, they were also afraid of upsetting Joseph Reed and the Pennsylvania Council. Congress ultimately dismissed six of the eight most serious charges. Then, to my shock and surprise, they tabled the acquittal as a result of Reed's pressure. The entire matter was referred to George Washington, to be tried before a military court-martial. While I had reason to hope General Washington would treat me fairly, his recent demeanor gave me pause. Moreover, it was hard to ignore the fact that even when I won a victory, Reed's cadre seemed able to raise the same issues over and over again, despite prior vindications of my conduct.

I responded by writing Washington and Congress, asking for a speedy trial:

> I consider myself bound to make my appeal to that honorable body in whose service I have the honor to be; and whilst my conduct and the charges against me are under their Congress's

consideration, I think it is my duty to wait the issue, without noticing the many abusive misrepresentations and slanderous reports, which are daily circulated by a set of wretches beneath the notice of a gentleman and a man of honor; yet permit me to say that these slanderers, employed and supported by persons in power and reputable stations, whilst my cause remains undetermined before Congress, considered themselves secure, and industriously spread their insinuations and false assertions through these United States, to poison the minds of my virtuous countrymen and fellow-citizens and to prejudice them against a man whose life has been devoted to their service and who looks on their good opinion and esteem, as the greatest reward and honor he can receive. This the circumstance, I cannot be charged with undue impatience for soliciting an immediate decision on the charges brought against me.

Two days later, I decided to write Washington again and remind him of my abilities in the field: "As soon as my wounds will permit, I shall be happy to take a command in the line of the Army and at all times of rendering my country every service in my power."

Reed objected to an immediate trial. He said that if he were not given adequate time to prepare, Pennsylvania might be less helpful in the war effort. In fact, Reed threatened Washington, telling him that Pennsylvania's support of the army hung in the balance in my court-martial. In a letter to Washington, he wrote, "Such is the dependence on the Army upon the transportation of this state, that should the court martial treat it as a light and trivial matter, we fear it will not be practicable to draw further wagons in the future, be the emergency what it may, and it will have very bad consequences." Reed then demanded an indefinite postponement to gather evidence and witnesses.

Washington wrote to me, "Dear Sir, I find myself under the necessity of postponing your trial to a later period. In a future letter, I shall communicate my reasons and inform you of the time which shall be finally appointed."

Philadelphia, PA - February 22, 1779

I was shaken by Washington's letter more than any correspondence I had previously received in my life. I considered the general my friend, and yet he was explicitly casting me aside while others destroyed my reputation. Up until this point, I could rationalize his behavior or make excuses for him, but now there could be no doubt. An ungrateful country, Congress, and now my mentor and commanding general were all abandoning me. Hurt, scared, and angry, I wrote Washington:

> If your Excellency thinks me a criminal, for Heaven's sake let me be immediately tried, and if found guilty, executed. I want no favor; I ask only justice. If this be denied me by your Excellency, I have nowhere to seek it but from the candid public, before whom I shall be under the necessity of laying out the whole matter. Let me beg of you, Sir, to consider that a set of artful, unprincipled men in office may represent the most innocent actions and, by raising the public clamor against your Excellency, place you in the same situation as I am in. Having made every sacrifice of fortune and blood and become a cripple in the service of my country, I little expected to meet the ungrateful returns I have received from my countrymen; but as Congress has stamped ingratitude as a current coin, I must take it. I wish your Excellency, for your long and eminent services, may not be paid in the same coin. I have nothing left but the little reputation I have gained in the Army. Delay in the present case is worse than death.

After all my military successes, the blood and treasure I had sacrificed for my country, my "reward" was three denials of promotion, two court-martials, and now abandonment by the man whom I had admired above all else. The only person in my life in whom I could ultimately repose trust and love was my dear Peggy. Everyone else had either abused or betrayed me.

Chapter 62

Philadelphia, PA - April 8, 1779

M y battles with the radicals and my court-martial made the timid Judge Shippen ill at ease. He initially rejected my marriage proposal. I was undaunted, for I knew I had won Peggy's heart and merely needed to convince her father of my worthiness. His objections focused upon my infirmity, but he was also displeased that I was not from an established, moneyed family. Finally, marriage to me would remove his last vestige of neutrality. The Shippen family would, once and for all, be aligned with the rebel camp.

Following Peggy's wise advice, and contrary to my nature, I practiced patience in a determined yet respectful campaign to obtain Judge Shippen's consent. It was her insistent and sometimes even hysterical demands to her father that ultimately caused him to relent and allowed us to proceed with our happy union.

Every lamp in the Shippen mansion shone out into the dark on the night of April 8. Bishop William White officiated in a house full of family and friends. In the library, Peggy stood in a beautiful gown, next to me in my major general's uniform. Unable to stand comfortably without a cane, I leaned on the arm of my aide David Franks. After a brief ceremony, we climbed into my carriage to begin our married life. Unfortunately, because of my diminished financial condition, I could not take Peggy to the new mansion I had purchased—the home that I intended for her was being leased to the Spanish ambassador until my finances improved. Instead, we went to a small house owned by her father called Master's House.

Dare I describe our wedding night? And yet, I must—for it gives the full measure of my sacrifice to my ungrateful country.

When we finally arrived in our bedchamber, I pulled her to me and felt her tremble with pleasure, yet I was aware that even brushing against my leg could push a sharp, broken bone into my flesh. Thus, though I shared a bed with my sweet Peggy, there was no respite from my suffering. My old enemy pain was there with us, taking away the unrestrained joy of marital bliss. The coupling itself was a heartbreaking act of pleasure and pain. Each necessary movement was met with a jab which I must ignore, trying to focus on the rapture of being with my Peggy.

Gone forever is the carefree joy of being with the woman I love. Instead, I must always remain careful, tempering my actions to minimize my pain. To lose "control" is to feel ecstasy overcome by agony.

What of my poor Peggy? She must endure life with a broken man, constantly worried about her master, whose suffering is relieved only by moments of half pleasure. Oh, by the heavens! Would she have known me when I was a complete man, vigorous and strong.

Yet I resolved, *I cannot give in to despair like my father. I do my best— for "my Peggy" and myself.*

PART III

Audentis Fortuna Iuvat

Chapter 63

Penn Mansion, Philadelphia, PA - April 27, 1779

N ewlywed happiness did not forestall my battles with Reed and his surrogates. Within weeks of my wedding, the charges against me were front-page news all over the country. I was alternately lauded or vilified, depending on the respective camps in this political trial. More and more Americans were becoming hostile toward the Continental Army, viewing its officers as Hessian mercenaries who could turn on their masters, leading an antidemocratic revolution and imposing new monarchy.

After a long day, Peggy and I sat alone in the parlor, the servants dismissed for the evening. Peggy moved from her customary location to sit next to me as I rested my aching leg on a cushion. As she handed me a glass of Madeira, she murmured, "Many of my dearest friends, Benny, have been complaining that life under the British occupation was preferable to the mob that currently rules Philadelphia." She saw me begin to stiffen at the implicit criticism of my leadership, and immediately laid a comforting hand on my arm. "No, dearest, everyone knows you are all that stands between decent, honest people and radical anarchy.

"Is this why you have given up so much for our country, Benny? You have lost your fortune, and you live in pain every day for these people." Her lovely face contorted at the mention of the "people," but relaxed as she continued, "Haven't the Colonies made their point? Surely the king would now take us back and treat us as Englishmen. If we continue down this path, we will be overtaken by the mob or cast into the arms of the French." As she spoke, she reached out and placed my hand on the thigh peeking out from the folds of her nightdress. Her silk-like skin and the spell of her perfume relaxed, aroused, and distracted me.

It had been a hard day, and my Peggy's words rang too true. There were times, when our faces were only inches apart and I looked into her large sparkling eyes, that I loved her so much it ached. I thought, *How is it possible one so lovely could care for me? I would give you my soul to make you happy.*

Apparently, I had been silent, lost in my revelry. Peggy said with concern, "Are you all right, dearest?"

I snapped back to the conversation. "You are right, of course. I have been abused more than anyone I know at the hands of these so-called 'revolutionaries' and unsavory chimney-corner politicians . . ." I struggled to both control my emotions and find the right words. Shaking my head, I sighed, "I have been cast aside by those who I considered my friends." I saw the images of Gates, Wilkenson, and worst of all, Washington in my mind's eye. Even to Peggy, it was too awful to say his name, explicitly acknowledging the most ghastly betrayal.

Peggy moved down from her chair and onto her knees, sitting next to my wounded leg as it rested on a stool. She kissed the top of my hand and placed her head upon my arm; without looking up, she said quietly, "You have always been a fighter. I don't think you should stop now, but maybe it is time to fight against your real enemies: Reed and his mongrels. I have told you about Captain André, who I met during the occupation. He is a British gentleman and would never behave like the people that infest the city now."

I reached across with my other arm to raise her face. As she looked up, she started to stand and inadvertently knocked her leg into mine, transforming our quiet tête-à-tête into a roaring chorus of pain. I instantly forgot our conversation. I forced myself to fight the irritation caused by her innocent mistake; instead, I silently hobbled to bed, frustrated that yet again even the most mundane acts of domestic tranquility were vulnerable to searing interruption.

Unfortunately, rest did not come as the pain eased. As it so often did these days, my mind again and again returned to the reality that I was running out of money. Congress had not paid me in over three years of faithful service. My ships were gone, my store closed, and my fortune squandered. My lifestyle in Philadelphia, including the purchase of my new home, was wiping me out.

I wanted to sell my house in New Haven, but failed to receive any offers. I was becoming delinquent on the mortgage on Mount Pleasant. I continued to spend lavishly on Peggy and me, as well as paying Hannah's expenses and school costs for my three sons. My position required me to hold large parties in my official capacity as military governor. At the same time, Congress irregularly paid my major general's salary of $332 per month in worthless Continental currency. Indeed, a nice pair of pants went for $1,000 in Philadelphia. I was going broke just trying to keep my household afloat and do my duty to my ungrateful country. My pain and poverty left me with a bitterness that congealed into a settled malice for all those who had caused my suffering.

Chapter 64

Bartram's Garden, PA - May 5, 1779

Peggy and I returned to Bartram's Garden, outside the city, less than a month after our wedding. She spread out a large blanket on a rock overlooking the river; as the water gently flowed below us, we shared a basket lunch and a bottle of wine. Peggy turned to me and smiled with a radiance that lit my darkened soul. I knew there had always been an emptiness inside me; I hoped she would be there forever to fill it and make me a whole man again.

After refreshment, I pulled her close and kissed her on the neck, eliciting a warm purr. She reciprocated my affections, but as I held her close, she returned to the topic that filled all our private time together. "It is not merely how they treated you, Benny. Look at the Revolution itself. It's failing. It is collapsing in on itself. I hear that fifty thousand loyalists stand ready to serve the British and need only strong leadership. An army of that size would be more than double Washington's entire force. The British are also making peace overtures—if the war ended now, status quo ante would be reestablished back to the period before 1763, when the Crown and the Colonies were able to maintain a productive relationship."

I released her, accepting that she wanted to have a meaningful discussion, but could not meet her gaze as she continued, "You've told me there were mass desertions in Massachusetts. Men are starving in the Hudson Highlands and New Jersey. Inflation is so rampant that no one will accept Continental currency, and British sterling remains the only coin of the realm. Even your own Connecticut regiments were in mutiny, correct?"

I mumbled in response, "Those weren't my boys . . . They weren't from New Haven." *As if that made a difference.*

"I know, sweetheart, but without you, there have been no victories in the field. America has been bled dry. We both know the French have not met their obligations. I think they are just using us as cannon fodder to weaken the British so they can succeed elsewhere. The Revolution is doomed. They have disregarded and mistreated good men like you and elevated scum like Reed."

She shifted closer, gently raising my chin so I would look at her as she continued. "You are the man who can bring the Colonies back into the fold and end this madness. I know you have given so much, but your country needs you. This is our chance to serve both ourselves and the greater good. Certainly nothing is accomplished when men like Reed, Hazen, Brown, and worst of all, Gates are allowed to succeed while you suffer in every way." She rested her head on my shoulder and murmured, "My dearest love."

With both sadness and resignation, I whispered, almost praying she would not have an answer, "But how would I even contact the British?"

Her head popped off my shoulder in an instant, her eyes flaring with excitement. At some level my heart sank—she already had everything figured out. "We can contact Captain André. I have reason to believe he is now an aide-de-camp to General Clinton and would allow us to deal at the very highest level of the British military establishment."

With some exasperation, I pressed, "Fine. But that doesn't answer my question. You may know this Mr. André, but how do we actually communicate? Who could be a trusted intermediary?"

Again, Peggy had thought this through—without hesitation, she answered, "Why, Mr. Stansbury, of course."

I understood communicating with the British was taking a titanic risk, but I had always been a gambler. Whether it was starting a new apothecary in Connecticut, being a ship's captain, or dueling when necessary, I had understood long before the Revolution that the only way to rehabilitate my family's reputation was by taking risks that other men dared not face. Turning the tables on my enemies and bringing peace to the Colonies presented both the greatest risk and the greatest opportunity of my life.

As if reading my mind, Peggy concluded, "This is our chance, Benny. The ship is floundering and taking on water. The sails are in tatters. A mutiny is at hand. You are the admiral who can return the vessel to safer and more profitable waters. The king and the *good* people in the Colonies will be grateful and reward us for your role in ending this unhappy struggle."

Some men might have hesitated at such a momentous decision, but that was not in my nature. In any event, the long train of insults, indignities, and pain had pushed me onto this new path. I nodded in agreement, resolved to risk all yet again.

"Please contact him, my dear." I knew this was the only way to save my country, my reputation, and my fortune.

Chapter 65

Penn Mansion, Philadelphia, PA - May 8, 1779

J oseph Stansbury was a thirty-three-year-old amateur poet and lover of fine clothes. He owned a glass shop in Black Horse Alley, by the Delaware River waterfront. Peggy was not certain that Stansbury was a spy, but she knew he had loyalist tendencies and could convey messages behind enemy lines.

Peggy wisely gave the servants the afternoon off. Even though it was a warm day, she closed the windows to ensure that our conversation was entirely private. She met Stansbury at the door and brought him to me in the parlor.

He was exquisitely dressed—while he did not don a wig, as it would likely attract abuse from the radicals, his hair was still carefully coiffed, lightly powdered, and tied in a queue. Again, while frowned upon in Philadelphia, he wore subtle facial makeup, accentuating his dark blue eyes and adding a slight rose to his lips. He carried himself like a French courtier with the perfect posture and elocution of a fine English gentleman.

After polite inquiries as to the health of each other's families, Peggy got to the point. "As I have explained to my husband, our family holds you in very high regard and has been grateful for the kindness and service you have been able to provide over the years."

Stansbury bowed his head in acknowledgment. "It has been my honor and privilege, madam."

Up to this time, I had been silent, but I realized it was my turn to speak, as both Peggy and Stansbury stared at me in anticipation. I stammered, "These have been indeed challenging times, Mr. Stansbury. I know many merchants who did nothing more than ply their trade and yet have been falsely accused of treachery by those now in positions of power." Stansbury's eyes involuntarily darted between Peggy and me. I now clearly had his full attention. "Even the way one dresses or goes about the street subjects one to ridicule. As one who has fought and bled for his country"—I involuntarily looked down at my foot, resting on a cushion—"I must wonder if we did all this to have less freedom?"

Stansbury looked at Peggy, who almost imperceptibly inclined her head in agreement with my comments. I continued, "Have you been fairly treated? Persecuted for being a just and reasonable businessman? I ask you, sir, have I been falsely accused by these same gentlemen, if I deign to call them that, who attack me only to aggrandize themselves?"

Stansbury's eyes widened and his face flushed, but he did not take his eyes off me. "Indeed, indeed, General."

I paused, recognizing that what I said next would be stepping over a line from which retreat would be difficult. As the silence grew, Peggy interjected, "I am sure you remember our good friend Captain John André?"

Stansbury looked over to her and realized the question was directed to him. With a start, he smiled and returned to his normal solicitous demeanor. "Oh yes, quite well. The captain visited my store regularly and is a fine gentleman."

Peggy continued, leaning forward in her chair, "I understand the captain is now in New York?"

Here again, she had wisely taken control of the conversation. She was asking Stansbury to admit that he regularly crossed the lines or communicated with André in New York. Such communication would be a technical violation of the law—however, given my prior statements and his relationship with the Shippen family, he said after a moment's hesitation, "Indeed." Then, in almost a whisper, he added, "I have seen him in New York on several occasions."

I sensed it was now time to reinject myself into the conversation. "See here, Stansbury—those men like Reed and others are dividing this country. I cannot fully express my abhorrence of the ruinous conflict that is destroying the Colonies. I would like to communicate with General Clinton and this Captain André about healing the rift between us."

Peggy and I had decided I would couch my message as part of an overall political solution, rather than focusing on my personal goals. Placing the discussion in a political context would give me cover if the communication were later discovered.

"Indeed, indeed." I tried to hide a smile at what was evidently Stansbury's favorite phrase when he was playing for time. After a pregnant pause, it was apparent that an internal dialogue had been concluded— Stansbury sat even straighter and said, "I would be honored to carry a message to Captain André and General Clinton."

Peggy again spoke up. "You understand, Joseph, this is of the most confidential nature. We rely on your complete discretion, to share this with no one, excepting the three of us, Captain André, and General Clinton." I noted her wise decision to use his first name, emphasizing the close relationship we were establishing with him.

"Indeed, indeed, I understand."

"Initially, I do not even want Clinton's office to know my husband's identity. I merely ask that you say that you represent a high-ranking general who is interested in bringing this conflict to an end. Please tell them that my husband's code name will be Monk. We are also in earnest to know the British remain committed to fighting until victory."

Stansbury nodded in agreement. "You may rely on me."

I nodded to Peggy, who stood; Stanbury and I did likewise. "It has been so good to see you, Joseph. I know the general and I can rely upon you." And with that, she guided him to the door.

John André was the logical person for us to approach. Peggy told me that he frequently visited the Shippen home, reciting poetry and engaging in pleasant conversation. He had also done several sketches of her and her friends.

During the British occupation, Peggy had quite rightly attended balls that included British officers and men of good breeding. Like many of her class, she could not help but recognize the professionalism and efficiency of the British Army when compared to the ill-clad and raucous colonial troops. I was assured that she never became excessively close to any man, although she had developed a strong friendship with John André.

Let us be clear on this subject. I have since heard scurrilous accusations about the relationship between André and my beloved Peggy. If I believed an affair had ever occurred, I would never have married her, let alone proceeded with my later negotiations with André. Indeed, if, as some have suggested, he had deflowered my lovely wife, I would have crushed his skull at our first meeting.

When General Howe was recalled to England and General Clinton took over as supreme commander in America, most of Howe's favorites fell into disfavor. Clinton despised Howe—a reserved man by nature, he liked solitude, a dependable mistress, and physical exercise, eschewing the public displays typical of highborn British officers. Of all Howe's old aides, only André had managed to attach himself to Clinton and survive the transition.

André was added to Clinton's military family and given a desk at his headquarters in the Archibald Kennedy mansion at One Broadway. In short order, he became a constant companion of the general. When we reached out to him, we did not know that he had been promoted to chief of the British secret service—a position for which he had no training, expertise, or field experience.

I sat at my desk, ignoring my aching leg and doing paperwork. Washington's latest letter to me only confirmed the fact that I was being sacrificed and abandoned: "I have received your favor of the May 5th instant, and I read it with no small concern. I feel my situation truly delicate and embarrassing. I am sure that you wish me to avoid even the semblance of partiality. I cautiously suspend my judgement till the result of a full and fair trial shall determine the merits of the prosecution."

I was beginning to understand the true nature of Washington. *Can he not judge me based upon my actions? Does he now know what kind of man I am? He was a "friend" during victories, but now, when I am truly in need, he equivocates and plays politics! No one can be trusted, especially this two-faced liar.*

Reading the letter, I saw myself as a shark moving through the current of events. When the British had imperiled my trading business and my liberty, I had flowed with the current of history and fought for independence. The tide had turned, and liberty had been hijacked. I needed to redirect my attack toward those who would submerge the rights of all free men. Congress and Reed were far worse than the Crown—I needed to turn my fangs on those who drove me to the shore. I would ride the tide of history to its righteous conclusion.

Chapter 66

Penn Mansion, Philadelphia, PA - May 24, 1779

We received a notice from Stansbury that he was in town and would like to meet us. It had been two weeks, and we knew he had gone to New York. We were quite anxious to know what he had learned and communicated.

We scheduled a meeting for when we knew the servants would not be in the house. After Peggy had escorted him into the parlor, she dispensed with the preliminaries and asked, "Did you meet with Captain André?"

A flushed Stansbury lacked his normal deportment. Instead, he fairly babbled, "Indeed, indeed. I met him directly. I did not get to see General Clinton, but I can tell you they are tremendously excited to learn of that General Arnold was interested in bringing the matter to a close."

I looked over at Peggy, shocked and appalled that he had violated my explicit instructions and revealed my identity. When I was about to lose my temper, Peggy gently placed her hand on my good leg in warning. "Obviously, Joseph, the general did not want to disclose his identity." Stansbury reddened and attempted to explain, but Peggy spoke before he could answer. "What's done is done. What specifically did Captain André say?"

He spoke quickly, poised on the edge of his chair. "They were extremely interested. Oh, yes—by and by, it is *Major* André now. A promotion, you see. In any event, he asked I repeat this to you word for word: 'Should the abilities and zeal of that able and enterprising gentleman amount to the seizing of an obnoxious band of men, to delivering into our power or enabling us to attack to advantage and by judicious assistance completely defeat a numerous body, then will the generosity of the nation exceed even his most sanguine hopes.'" He paused and looked at me expectantly.

I understood that the "obnoxious band of men" could only mean the scoundrels in Congress who were hell-bent on ruining me and reveling in my humiliation. Nodding in acknowledgment, I rolled my hand for Stansbury to continue.

Stansbury clearly was no longer repeating verbatim. "They also wanted me to assure you that they are fully committed to the war effort, and indeed more decisive steps to end the conflict are in the works. With your assistance and coordination, they believe a profitable result can be reached." Then, with a smile of appreciation, he added, "They also liked your choice of 'Monk' as your code name and hope you will be as well rewarded."

I had selected the name "Monk" in honor of George Monk, who had been one of Cromwell's generals in the English Civil War. When Monk saw the revolution had devolved into chaos, he conspired to restore the monarchy. He was recognized as a national hero for his actions and given a dukedom and pension by the king. The message I was sending to Clinton was that I expected nothing less here.

Less animated as he calmed down, Stansbury continued, "At the conclusion of our conversation, André asked for some specific evidence to establish your sincerity. He also suggested that a correspondence could begin between Mrs. Arnold and Major André, using Peggy Chew."

Chew had been a friend of both André and my wife, and was the ideal dupe in our process. "André said they could communicate on some meaningless topic, while the real message would be encoded in invisible ink between the lines, made from onion juice. To create an even further layer of protection, the major also proposes we use a code where each word of the coded message is made up of three numbers: a page number from Blackstone's *Commentary on the Laws of England*, a line number, and a word number. I was told writing and decoding is slow and tedious, but it is a solid code, impossible to crack without knowing what book the correspondents are using."

I decided it was time to take control of the discussion. "That is fine, but we are not going to use Blackstone. The commentaries are too unwieldy. We should use the twenty-first edition of Bailey's *Universal Etymological English Dictionary*."

Stansbury merely blinked back without comment and looked at Peggy. Recognizing he had communicated everything, she stood and took him to the door—thanking him a bit too profusely, she promised we would be getting back to him about a response.

Once we were alone in our home, Peggy and I spent a great deal of time formulating a carefully written letter following the code relayed by Major André: "Sir Henry may depend on my exertion and intelligence. I will cooperate with others when an opportunity offers, and as life and everything is at stake, I shall expect some certainty, my property here secure and a revenue equivalent to the risk and service done. I cannot promise success: I will deserve it. Inform me what I may expect. Could I know Sir Henry Clinton's intentions, he should never be at a loss for intelligence. I shall expect a particular answer through our friend, Stansbury." I added a postscript at Peggy's suggestion to make it clear to Major André that she was fully aware of my actions: "Madam Arnold presents her particular compliments."

I was still intensely torn by my decision. I could break off the negotiations and later claim that I had engaged in espionage in an attempt to befuddle the British with misleading information. Before I crossed the Rubicon, I was determined to make a final attempt to reconcile with General Washington and determine if the army would defend me from Reed's relentless attacks. Thus, I wrote him, asking to rejoin the army. I saw two benefits from this approach. If I were genuinely allowed back into the army and decently treated, I might forgo my British foray. Conversely, if I continued to be ill-treated, I would then be in a better position to serve my new masters in a more advantageous position. In either event, Peggy and I agreed that reaching out to His Excellency made sense.

I explained to Washington that I wished to "render my country every service in my power at this critical time; for, though I have been ungratefully treated, I do not consider it as from my countrymen in general, but from a set of men who, void of principle, are governed entirely by the private interest. The interest I have in the welfare and happiness of my country, which I have made ever evinced when in my power, will I hope, always overcome my personal resentment for any injury I can possibly receive from individuals."

Washington unsympathetically wrote in response, "Though the delay in your situation may be irksome, I am persuaded you will be of opinion with me it is best on every principle to submit to it, rather than there should be the least the appearance of precipitancy in the affair." Once again, his indifference to my suffering was manifest—I resolved, once and for all, to move forward with my contacts with General Clinton.

When I showed the letter to Peggy, she nodded knowingly. "It was Congress, and now it is Washington, my love. What is worse—to be ruled by one tyrant three thousand miles away, or three thousand tyrants one mile away?" She took the letter from my hand and raised my palm to her cheek. "At least with the king, you will be dealing with gentlemen, not the rabble."

I had done everything I could and more. The "Revolution" was unworthy.

Chapter 67

Middlebrook, NY - June 1, 1779

As this correspondence was going on, Washington finally set a date for the court-martial. The proceedings were to begin on June 1, 1779, at his New Jersey headquarters. Travel was a study in agony. I could not walk on my wounded left leg, while my right experienced my worst attack of gout in years. Being bounced about in a carriage on rough roads was not only painful but deeply humiliating, as I was required to be lifted from my carriage at each stop and carried into General Washington's headquarters.

When I finally arrived, I was brought to His Excellency. My frustration boiling over, I began cursing both Congress and Joseph Reed. Washington raised his voice to cut me off, apparently fearing the conversation would be overheard and he would be accused of "favoritism." I was dismissed from his presence and escorted out of his headquarters, both shocked and mortified by his rudeness.

I knew that not everyone in America viewed me with contempt, like Reed, or indifference, like General Washington. A rare exception was my friend Silas Deane, who gave me a letter to present at my trial:

Great God! Is it possible that, after the bold and perilous enterprises which this man has undertaken for the service and defense of his country, the loss of his fortune and the cruel lingering pains he has suffered from the wound received fighting their battles, there can be found among us men so abandoned to the base and infernal passions of envy and malice as to persecute him with the most unrelenting fury, and wish to destroy what alone he had the prospect of saving out of the dreadful wreck of his health, fortune, and life: his character?

Just as my trial was about to begin, the movement of the British Army required Washington to leave camp, further delaying my day in court. Injured and discouraged, I returned to Philadelphia.

In contrast, André promptly responded on behalf of General Clinton: "Can concur with you in almost any plan you can advise and in which you will cordially cooperate." He then pressed for me to identify a spot where I could make a "substantive difference in the war." General Clinton "begs you that you proposed your assistance for the delivery of your country. You must know where the present power is vulnerable, and the conspicuous commands with which you might be vested may enable us in one shining stroke, from which both riches and honor would be derived. To accelerate the ruin to which the usurped authority is verging and put a speedy end to the miseries to our fellow creatures."

André continued with suggestions of what I could do: "Join the army, accept a command, be surprised, and be cut off; these things may happen in the course of maneuver, nor you be censured or suspected. A complete service of this nature involving a corps of five or six thousand men would be rewarded with twice as many thousand guineas."

Concerned that I would not be rewarded if detected, I instructed Stansbury to say, "Monk expects to have your promise that he shall be indemnified for any loss he may sustain in the case of detection that 10,000 pounds shall be engaged to him for his services." To demonstrate my bona fides with this offer, I provided Clinton with the latest troop strengths and expected turnout of the militia; the location of supply depots and cannon bound for Detroit; Gates's location and the strength of his force in Rhode Island; Lincoln's troop strengths and weaknesses; the state of the navy and the locations of its ships; and the latest news on the movement of the French fleet.

The amount I was requesting, at first blush, may seem large. In truth, it did not begin to compensate me for all I would lose if I returned to the service of the king. By my calculations, Congress owed me at least £12,000, not taking into account all the homes, contents, and other valuable property I would likely lose if I forfeited my position. Fundamentally, my decision was not financial; rather, it was a reflection of years of mistreatment I had endured serving unworthy people in a lost cause. Congress and the Pennsylvania Council were far more dangerous than the king or his ministers. As importantly, the Revolution was no longer supported by the people. In 1775, there had been 27,500 Continental soldiers; now just 3,000 still carried the banner of a failed rebellion. The best solution would be to rejoin England with guaranteed liberties and representation in Parliament.

André now pressed for a face-to-face meeting: "Would you assume a command and enable me to see you. I am convinced a conversation of a few minutes would satisfy you entirely and I trust would give us equal cause to be pleased."

I stood on the precipice. I needed to get a major command in the army to give myself credibility with the British, but I couldn't do anything until my court-martial was completed—and I didn't even know when it would start. The subtext of André's communication was clear—Clinton did not trust me. They were concerned that this entire exercise could be a ruse by the Americans to provide false information. In any event, in my current situation, I was not a sufficiently well-placed officer to merit my demands.

Peggy and I decided to break off the negotiations because the British were unwilling to provide me with any promised payment until I secured a position. I had Stansbury transmit one last oral message: "However sincerely General Arnold wished to serve his country in accelerating the settlement of this unhappy conflict, it is unfair for the General to hazard his all when he has received no guarantees from the British."

Chapter 68

Philadelphia, PA - October 4, 1779

As summer gave way to fall, French ships arrived in Philadelphia. One might think this would improve our situation—in actuality, it made conditions worse in the city. The French paid for grain in gold, and their sailors needed to be fed; thus, what little grain existed in America was being stored in Philadelphia's warehouses and sold to the French.

Americans had long since spent all their gold, and Continental paper was virtually worthless. Reed and his radicals were once again blaming merchants, accusing them of limiting grain sales in the city's markets. Through the summer of 1779, radicals formed armed committees determined to force merchants to sell their grain and roll back prices. Any merchant who defied their will was called a Tory and subject to attack.

The radicals' horrific solution to this crisis was to deport women and children of loyalists to New York City to ease food shortages in Philadelphia. Over time, their aims broadened to include driving out all Republicans (nonradicals) or anyone else who would stand in opposition to Reed and his thugs.

Not satisfied with abusing the vulnerable, the radicals became increasingly violent. I received messages from two different couriers almost simultaneously—Republicans had gotten wind of the radicals' plan to start attacking people in their homes. Those under siege gathered in a stout three-story brick mansion owned by James Wilson, which they dubbed "Fort Wilson."

When I arrived at Wilson's home, George Clymer—a signer of the Declaration of Independence—exclaimed, "Thank God you are here, General. Are your troops coming?"

As I gingerly exited the carriage and hobbled to him with the assistance of a cane, I shook my head. "No, sir. My orders are quite clear. I cannot use Continental troops to quell domestic disturbances."

With a knowing nod and look of disgust, Clymer spat the words, "The bastard Reed."

I clasped his hand in my own. "Exactly."

A barricade of bricks, hay bales, and wood had been built around the front door, and all the downstairs windows had been boarded and shuttered. Nevertheless, the front door cracked open and James Wilson waved his hand, encouraging us to get inside.

As we entered the vestibule, the signs of preparation for war were everywhere. Muskets lay near boarded windows with firing holes cut. Powder, ball, and cartridges were well-placed. The sounds of women and children could be heard in the cellar, and the footsteps of many men upstairs drummed continuously. Looking at the two of us, Wilson intoned, "General Arnold. We have been told two hundred of Reed's radicals are gathering in the commons, and they even have field artillery."

At that moment, a lad of no more than thirteen rushed to Wilson's side and said, "They are moving down Second Street, Father. They are grabbing anyone they think is an enemy and parading them in front of the mob while they play the, Rogue's March,"

As the boy spoke, the men around froze and looked at me. In a loud but firm voice, I declared, "The Continentals cannot help us, but I am here to fight with you, come what may. This is a mob. I know that sounds bad, but it is actually good news. Most men in a mob are cowards and do not know how to fight. We will try to avoid a fight, but if it starts, we must act decisively and with extreme violence." Turning to Wilson again, I asked, "How many men do we have, and what is our status of ammunition and water?"

Wilson answered immediately, "We have close to forty armed men ready to fight to protect their families. We have plenty of ammunition and much water and food in the cellar. We could hold out for days."

"Can we get the women and children out of here? With a mob coming, I would rather not have them with us."

Wilson looked down at his shoes as he answered. "My wife and children are here, General. A few other men brought their families as well and did not want to leave them behind. I think it is too late now to try to slip them out."

I gave him what I hoped was a reassuring nod. "I understand. They must remain in the cellar." I didn't say that what I feared most was not enemy ball or shot, but fire. If they attempted to burn us out, the women and children could find themselves in the worst possible situation.

Again shouting an order to the entire room, I said, "Make sure every window in the house is covered and every door is nailed shut. They will likely come to the front door, but will fire from all sides. The walls are stone and brick and should provide good protection, but everyone needs to keep their heads down. Do not fire until they start shooting. Then aim for those who are the leaders. Don't shoot randomly. Kill the men in front, and those in the back will run. Does everyone understand?" I saw nods all around. "Make sure everyone upstairs understands, and do not fire until you hear my order." A couple of the men scurried upstairs to relay my instructions.

Turning back to Wilson, I said, "The mob will want you to come out and be humiliated or worse. There is a chance they will attack right away, but usually they like to bluster before they act." The irony was not lost on me that I had done something similar years earlier in New Haven, when I wanted ammunition to go to Boston.

As I predicted, the radicals arrived and began throwing rocks and bottles at the house. A particularly loudmouthed ruffian stood in front of the house and demanded everyone vacate Fort Wilson and "account for their crimes in service of the king."

Wilson yelled back through a slit in the front door, "I am no Tory. I advise you I am well armed and ready to defend my home!"

When he looked back at me, I whispered, "We have done what we can at this point. I will go upstairs and lead from there. Colonel Chambers will be here with you." Both men gave me a grim-faced look of acknowledgment before I struggled up the stairs.

Seconds later, shots rang out as muskets began to pelt the home from all sides. The second floor appeared to be well manned. Despite the pain, I hobbled up the narrow stairway to the third floor in time to see George Campbell, a captain in the Pennsylvania militia, open a shuttered dormer window to look out. At that instant, a bullet took off the top of his head, spraying the ceiling as he toppled backward. A cheer went up from outside in response.

Rage overwhelming better judgment, I stepped over the fallen captain, pulled my brace of loaded pistols, pointed them down into the crowd, and fired. I heard yells of my name as I slammed the shutters, which were impacted with bullets the instant they were closed.

At the top of my lungs, I yelled, "Fire!" and the thunder of musket fire and smoke filled the house. I picked up Campbell's musket, which I sighted through a hole in the dormer window and fired at some of those most animated ruffians in the front rows. A man stood behind me, ready to take my place—handing him the spent musket, I shuffled downstairs to direct the firing from the second floor. As I looked out through a crack in the shutters in Wilson's study overlooking the front door, I was horrified to see a militia cannon being rolled up to the front door. I looked for a musket to shoot the gun crew, but did not see one. I screamed over the din, "They've got cannon! Shoot the gun crew! Shoot the god-damned gun crew!"

My words were drowned out by the sounds of shots, both inside and outside the house. I limped over to the men shooting from loopholes in other second-floor windows as I heard the roar of cannon, the sound of splintering wood, and screams from downstairs as the front door was blown open. Again, a cheer went up.

I yelled to everyone I could to meet me on the stairs—we grabbed furniture and built a blockade at the top of the landing looking down at the front door. Following the cannon shot, Colonel Chambers entered the vestibule to fill the breach, carrying a brace of pistols and a blunderbuss. As the first of the mob attempted to enter through the hole that had once been the front door, he fired the blunderbuss. It enveloped the mangled doorway with smoke and flame. The approaching men screamed—some fell dead as others retreated.

Following my orders, men upstairs were now focusing their shots on the cannon. Every time a gun crew tried to load, they were inundated with a deadly barrage from above. Meanwhile, at the front door, Chambers bravely held his ground. Wilson and others built barricades out of furniture in the dining and drawing rooms, hemming in the vestibule from every side.

Another group of rioters tried to come into the front door and were met with Chambers's pistols, one in each hand. Again, there was a satisfying flash and screams as men dropped. However, Chambers was out of guns and went for his sword. We could not support him, as he blocked our view of the hole that had once been the doorway. Four brutes came in shoulder to shoulder and swinging clubs—they knocked Chambers to the ground, dragged him by his hair, and ran him through. As they did so, I opened up from the stairway, as did Wilson and others from both sides. Chambers's murderers now lay on top of him in a permanent embrace of death.

The doorway was now effectively blocked by a pile of bloody bodies. What once was a lovely home had been turned into a charnel house in a matter of minutes.

The front door was secure for the moment, so I hobbled back upstairs to direct fire into the mob. I looked out through one of the cracks in the shutters and saw that Reed had arrived. Quickly opening the shutter, I yelled down to the crowd, "Your president has raised a mob, and now he cannot quell it."

At that point, I was relieved to see Baylor's Virginia Regiment gallop up Chestnut Street on horseback, slashing at the rioters. The crowd was forced to give way. Reed, as the highest-ranking member of the Pennsylvania Assembly and Executive Council, took control and ordered everyone, both inside and outside the house, arrested. I, for my part, was of course exempt from arrest. Wilson's people posted bail and were immediately released. Afterward, Reed, the most biased man I had ever met, sought and received the release of all of the radicals from the Pennsylvania Assembly, saying the bloodshed was merely an "overflowing of liberty."

Peggy's nerves completely snapped during this episode. I could not dissuade her from her reasonable fear that the next mob might come to our home. She alternately cried and cowered in the corner, later throwing crockery, furiously demanding that I solve this intractable problem. Out of earshot of servants, she demanded I abandon the Cause once and for all, rather than be subject to the violence from the very people I was charged to lead and protect.

I wrote to the Board of War and told Congress of my need to fortify our residence. I armed my servants and barricaded my wife and family inside the Penn Mansion. Wherever I went, the radicals threw stones and jeered me. I wrote to Congress,

> There is no protection to be expected from the authority of the state for an honest man, I am under necessity of requesting Congress to order me a guard of Continental troops. This request I presume will not be denied to a man, who has so often fought and bled in defense of his country.

However, Congress once again refused, claiming this was an issue for the State of Pennsylvania and not themselves. I was placed at Reed's mercy. The "State of Pennsylvania, in whose disposition to protect every honest citizen Congress has full confidence."

I stood alone in the midst of a dangerous mob, with no chance of protection or acknowledgment of my service. A group of ruffians attacked me on the street, and it was only my brace of loaded pistols and my willingness to use them that caused them to back down. Night after night, I slept with every gun in my home primed and ready to fire, resolved that no one, including those who I once trusted and admired, would raise a finger to protect me or my family. Unwilling to continue the insanity, I allowed Peggy to reach out to Major André to restart negotiations.

Chapter 69

Norris Tavern, Morristown, NJ - December 23, 1779

T he bad roads and a rough carriage ride again took their toll as I
rode from Philadelphia to Morristown, New Jersey. Nevertheless,
I resolved that I would stand as much as possible at the trial—I did not
want to project weakness.

When I was able to sit and relax, the ache in my leg was constant but
manageable. However, when placed under physical or mental stress, my
leg muscles contracted, pressing against the broken bones that dug into
the muscle and nerves, causing sharp and grinding pain. It felt like there
were tiny glass tubes in my leg, cracking and cutting with every step. If
I remained perfectly still like an invalid, the pain would subside. I chose
to keep moving; to do otherwise would let the bastard win.

I believed I was ready for my court-martial. I tried to marshal my
arguments like armies; I find it easier to win with blood and steel than
with wit and guile. Nevertheless, the more I considered the charges
against me, the more resolute I became in the righteousness of my
position. I had been horribly mistreated by the Pennsylvanians, Congress, and bureaucrats in the military. My vindication at the court-martial would justify contacting the British. By the same token, if the
court-martial failed to exonerate me, it would only hit home that I had
been entirely abandoned.

Two days before Christmas, dressed in my best pale-blue-and-buff
major general's uniform with gold epaulets of honor, I stood before a
panel of generals and colonels chaired by Major General Robert Howe.
A wealthy Southern planter, Howe had lost everything to British raiders.
He was a man who, like me, valued honor; he had engaged in duels and
had been court-martialed on similar unfair charges, only to be acquitted. The panel also included Henry Knox, with whom I had established

a prior pleasant acquaintance; I had confidence that he would treat me fairly, and had heard encouraging descriptions of Brigadier Mordecai Gist of Maryland.

However, to my fear and disgust, Moses Hazen, who had first accused me of looting in Montreal, now also sat on the panel. I immediately challenged Hazen's inclusion, given his demonstrated bias. Howe agreed with my objection and removed him from the court; he was replaced by William "Scotch Willie" Maxwell of New Jersey. At the time, I was ignorant of the fact that Maxwell had previously criticized me. I had hoped, as an ally of General Schuyler, he would be sympathetic.

The twelve officers sat at a long table. Only the sound of a split log burning in the fireplace to keep out the winter cold broke the silence. At a nod from General Howe, I rose with difficulty—I wanted to emphasize both the extent of my wounds and my strength of will to stand before the panel. I spoke with a voice strong and filled with indignation:

"Mr. President and gentlemen of this honorable court, I appear before you to answer charges brought before me by the late Supreme Executive Council of the Commonwealth of Pennsylvania. It is disagreeable to be accused, but when an accusation is made, I feel that it is a great source of consolation to have the opportunity of being tried by gentlemen. Of whose delicate and refined sensations of honor will lead them to entertain similar sentiments concerning those who accuse unjustly—and those who are unjustly accused.

"When one is charged with practices which his soul abhors and which conscious innocence tells him he has never committed, an honest indignation will draw from him expressions in his own favor.

"When the present necessary war against Great Britain commenced, I was in easy circumstances and enjoyed a fair prospect of improving them. I was happy in domestic connections and blessed with a rising family who claimed my care and attention. The liberties of my country were in danger. The voice of my country called upon her faithful sons to join in her defense. With cheerfulness I obeyed the call.

"I sacrificed domestic ease and happiness to the service of my country, and in her service have also sacrificed a great part of a handsome fortune. I was one of the first that appeared in the field, and from that time to the present hour, I have not abandoned her service. The part which I have acted in the American Cause, has been acknowledged by our friends and by our enemies to have been far from an indifferent one. My time, my fortune, and my person have been devoted to my country in this war."

I then presented letters of thanks from Washington and Congress sent to me over the years. "Is it probable after having acquired some little reputation, and after having gained the favorable opinion of those whose favorable opinion it is an honor to gain, I should all at once sink into a course of conduct equally unworthy of a patriot and a soldier? Every method that men ingeniously wicked could invent has been practiced to blast and destroy my character. Such a vile prostitution of power, and such instances of glaring tyranny and injustices, I believe are unprecedented in the annals of any free people. Indeed, I have suffered in seeing the fair fabric of reputation, which I have been with so much danger and toil raising since the present war, undermined by those whose posterity (as well as themselves) will feel the blessed effects of my efforts."

I rejected any assertion that I had mistreated the militia or showed bias. "My ambition is to deserve the good opinion of the militia of these states, not only because I respect their character and their exertions, but because their confidence in me may prove beneficial to the general cause of America; but having no local politics to bias my voice or my conduct, I leave it to others to wriggle themselves into a temporary popularity by assassinating the reputation of innocent persons, and endeavoring to render odious a principal, the maintenance of which essential to the good discipline of the militia, and consequently the safety of these states. The time is not far off when, by the glorious establishment of our independence, I shall again return into the mass of citizens. 'Tis a period I look forward to with anxiety. I shall then cheerfully submit, as a citizen, to be governed by the same principle of subordination which has been tortured by Pennsylvania's charge into a wanton exertion of arbitrary power."

After going through all of the charges against me and refuting them in great detail, I concluded, "I have ever obeyed the calls of my country, and stepped forth in her defense in every hour of danger." Then, after apologizing for taking so much of the court's time, I indicated that I looked forward "with pleasing anxiety" to the court's decision where "I shall, doubt not, stand honorably acquitted of all of the charges brought against me."

Chapter 68

Philadelphia, PA - October 4, 1779

A s summer gave way to fall, French ships arrived in Philadelphia. One might think this would improve our situation—in actuality, it made conditions worse in the city. The French paid for grain in gold, and their sailors needed to be fed; thus, what little grain existed in America was being stored in Philadelphia's warehouses and sold to the French.

Americans had long since spent all their gold, and Continental paper was virtually worthless. Reed and his radicals were once again blaming merchants, accusing them of limiting grain sales in the city's markets. Through the summer of 1779, radicals formed armed committees determined to force merchants to sell their grain and roll back prices. Any merchant who defied their will was called a Tory and subject to attack.

The radicals' horrific solution to this crisis was to deport women and children of loyalists to New York City to ease food shortages in Philadelphia. Over time, their aims broadened to include driving out all Republicans (nonradicals) or anyone else who would stand in opposition to Reed and his thugs.

Not satisfied with abusing the vulnerable, the radicals became increasingly violent. I received messages from two different couriers almost simultaneously—Republicans had gotten wind of the radicals' plan to start attacking people in their homes. Those under siege gathered in a stout three-story brick mansion owned by James Wilson, which they dubbed "Fort Wilson."

When I arrived at Wilson's home, George Clymer—a signer of the Declaration of Independence—exclaimed, "Thank God you are here, General. Are your troops coming?"

As I gingerly exited the carriage and hobbled to him with the assistance of a cane, I shook my head. "No, sir. My orders are quite clear. I cannot use Continental troops to quell domestic disturbances."

With a knowing nod and look of disgust, Clymer spat the words, "The bastard Reed."

I clasped his hand in my own. "Exactly."

A barricade of bricks, hay bales, and wood had been built around the front door, and all the downstairs windows had been boarded and shuttered. Nevertheless, the front door cracked open and James Wilson waved his hand, encouraging us to get inside.

As we entered the vestibule, the signs of preparation for war were everywhere. Muskets lay near boarded windows with firing holes cut. Powder, ball, and cartridges were well-placed. The sounds of women and children could be heard in the cellar, and the footsteps of many men upstairs drummed continuously. Looking at the two of us, Wilson intoned, "General Arnold. We have been told two hundred of Reed's radicals are gathering in the commons, and they even have field artillery."

At that moment, a lad of no more than thirteen rushed to Wilson's side and said, "They are moving down Second Street, Father. They are grabbing anyone they think is an enemy and parading them in front of the mob while they play the, Rogue's March,"

As the boy spoke, the men around froze and looked at me. In a loud but firm voice, I declared, "The Continentals cannot help us, but I am here to fight with you, come what may. This is a mob. I know that sounds bad, but it is actually good news. Most men in a mob are cowards and do not know how to fight. We will try to avoid a fight, but if it starts, we must act decisively and with extreme violence." Turning to Wilson again, I asked, "How many men do we have, and what is our status of ammunition and water?"

Wilson answered immediately, "We have close to forty armed men ready to fight to protect their families. We have plenty of ammunition and much water and food in the cellar. We could hold out for days."

"Can we get the women and children out of here? With a mob coming, I would rather not have them with us."

Chapter 70

Norris Tavern, Morristown, NJ - January 26, 1780

A month later, as I returned to the court-martial to hear its decision, the pain in my leg had lessened substantially, and while I would never again be light on my feet, I strode with confidence that I would be exonerated. I stood ramrod straight as the panel issued its decision. They found me innocent of mistreating the militia and buying goods when stores were being sequestered—however, they did find me guilty on two lesser counts. They ruled I had violated the catchall provisions of the articles of war, which forbade acts that prejudice good order and military discipline.

While absolving me of any fraudulent acts of using government wagons, the most troubling portion of the order read,

> Respecting the fourth charge, it appears to the court that General Arnold made application to the deputy quartermaster general to supply him with wagons to remove property then in imminent danger from the enemy; that wagons were supplied to him by the deputy quartermaster general on this application which had been drawn from the state of Pennsylvania for the public service; and it appears that General Arnold intended this application as a private request and that he had no design of employing the wagons otherwise than at his private expense, nor of defrauding the public, nor of injuring or impeding the public service; but considering the delicacy attending the high station to which the General acted, and that request from him might operate as commands, they are of the opinion that the crest was imprudent and improper and that, therefore, it ought not to have been made.

They acquitted me of all intentional wrongdoing regarding my speculation and investments. The court specifically found that I had no design to defraud or injure the public. Almost as an afterthought, they concluded, "The court sentences him to receive a reprimand from His Excellency the commander-in-chief."

At first, I considered myself vindicated by the decision and viewed the reprimand from General Washington to be a mere formality which would likely never occur. Indeed, I initially arranged for the entire 178-page court record to be published and circulated, demonstrating my innocence.

To my surprise, the Pennsylvania Supreme Executive Council, the very entity that had been my tormentor, wrote to Congress after the decision that they did not want to "impose a mark of reprehension on General Arnold . . . We find his sufferings for, and services to, his country so deeply impressed upon our minds as to obliterate every opposing sentiment." It begged Congress to dispense with any "public censure that might affect the feelings of a brave and gallant officer." Even Reed seemed chagrinned by having gone too far in attacking me. I was confident that Washington felt likewise.

With the hope that I could put these matters behind me, including my possible actions supporting the British, I wrote General Washington and the Board of Admiralty suggesting I lead a naval expedition with three or four hundred marines to strike at the enemy. General Washington not only ignored my request, but informed the admiralty that no soldiers could be spared. Without marines, I knew my plans for an expedition were dashed.

On March 19, 1780, Peggy gave birth to our son Edward. In May, unable to afford the Penn Mansion any longer, we were forced to move into one of Peggy's father's houses. I sought a loan from the new French ambassador the Chevalier de la Luzerne, explaining to him that I was in want of cash because of my services to the Revolution—a French loan would allow me to continue to serve common cause benefitting both countries. Rather than looking me in the eye, his gaze lingered on my short leg. He then stood and paced about the room without deigning to look at me directly.

Disdain dripping from his voice, he purred, "Monsieur Arnold, we in France do not sell our loyalty or demand payment from others. As a virtuous public servant, you should not be at my door seeking loans and implying that if such are not forthcoming you may no longer be able to serve your country. I will tell you that I too bear financial hardship being here serving France, but to do so is my honor. France expects nothing less from me, and I suspect your countrymen should expect nothing less from you. Good day, sir." And with that, he held out an open hand, pointing to the door, and walked out without waiting for me to leave, rise, or even respond.

I could feel my face burn as I endured yet another humiliation. If I had been a whole man, I would have bounded after him and dashed his brains against the wall. Instead, I struggled to my feet. My fury propelled me from the room and forever set in stone my loathing of the French.

Chapter 71

Philadelphia, PA - April 6, 1780

Washington took two full months before writing a short letter which was published in the general orders for the day, distributed throughout the army, and picked up by the newspapers:

> The Commander-in-Chief would have been much happier in an occasion of bestowing commendations on an officer who had rendered such distinguished services to his country as Major General Arnold; but in the present case, a sense of duty and regard to candor oblige him to declare that he considers conduct in the instance of the permit to the *Charming Nancy* as peculiarly reprehensible, in both a civil and military view, and in the affair of the wagons as imprudent and improper.

I had no forewarning that this letter would come. I felt the eyes of everyone on me as I moved through town. My joy at exoneration was crushed by the mortifying impact of Washington's very public letter. I wrote to my friend Silas Deane,

> I believe you will be equally surprised with me when you found the court martial have fully acquitted me of the charge of employing public wagons, of defrauding the public or injuring or impeding the public service, and in the next sentence say "as requests from him might operate as commands," ought to receive a reprimand: for what? Not for doing wrong, because I might have done wrong, or rather, because there was a possibility that evil might have followed the good I did.

Almost simultaneous with his public reprimand, Washington wrote me a half-hearted letter to soften the blow. I have little respect for a man who is willing to dishonor a "friend" in public, but provides encouragement behind the scenes. It seemed the ultimate act of cowardice. If Washington loved and respected me, then he should have said so publicly. This was a political act from a man who had forfeited his honor in exchange for his need to toady to Reed and Congress:

Our profession is the chastest of all. Even the shadow of fault tarnishes the lustre of our finest achievements. The least inadvertence may rob us of the public favor, so hard to be acquired. I reprimand you for having forgotten that, in proportion as you have rendered yourself formidable to our enemies, you should have been guarded and temperate in your deportment toward your fellow citizens. Exhibit anew those noble qualities that have placed you on the list of our most valued commanders. I will myself furnish you, as far as it may be in my power, with opportunities of regaining the esteem of your country.

As I read the words over again, I felt my blood boil. "Regaining the esteem of your country." *REGAINING THE ESTEEM OF YOUR COUNTRY! I have lost my fortune, my health, and now my honor in service of my country. What more can they take from me that I have not already given? And yet Washington proclaims I must give more?*

After this insult came further injury. The Treasury Board of Congress issued a lengthy report on April 22 finding that I was indebted to the United States for $70,000. I provided proof that I had expended all but $3,333. I insisted that this missing amount had been given to John Halsted, the commissary of provisions in Canada, but Halsted denied receiving the funds. The board refused to credit me for the payment unless I could produce a voucher. I had deposited a voucher with the board that I believe someone deliberately destroyed.

Neither the Treasury Board nor Congress was willing to take into account the chaotic conditions that occurred during the Canadian winter campaign and our retreat. The board also ignored the substantial expenditures of my own funds to feed the troops. Likewise, the board refused to issue to me four years' back pay as a Continental officer and refused to reimburse me for over $8,000 I had expended as a military governor performing official functions. In the end, it was concluded that I owed the astounding sum of $9,164. I now found myself not only publicly humiliated by Washington's rebuke, but destitute as a result of my service. I quite simply could not afford to serve the Cause as it heaped one abuse after another upon me.

In the two years since I had arrived in Philadelphia, I had come to realize that the Revolution had lost its way. Many of my dear friends, including Silas Deane, Daniel Morgan, and Eleazer Oswald, had been mistreated by Congress or forced out of the army. Indeed, Silas Deane had been rendered penniless by petty bureaucrats serving Congress. In hope of locating proof of his many expenditures and obtaining reim-bursement, he begged travel on a friend's ship; he left America a broken man, never to return.

Hot resentment turned my stomach bubbling and sour. I was com-ing to the realization that the best possible solution to these troubled times was a return to status quo ante, a period when I was a wealthy and content man in Connecticut. For myself and my country, I had to act.

Chapter 72

Philadelphia, PA - May 12, 1780

A s I pondered my situation a month after Washington's reprimand, I saw the utility of obtaining a position commanding West Point. This would be exactly the sort of position General Clinton and Major André had requested I secure. West Point presented a significant advantage if I chose to defect. If I were in the field, Peggy and I would inevitably be separated; in a fort, we could escape together.

West Point was at a strategic choke point on the Hudson River, fifty miles north of New York City. Often called the "key to America," the fort prevented British ships from controlling the Hudson River and cutting off New England from the rest of the country. To that end, Clinton had worked north, capturing the American forts between New York and just south of West Point.

West Point is surrounded by peaks looming up to twelve hundred feet above the Hudson. The two-hundred-foot channel narrows and bends nearly ninety degrees, then immediately bends another ninety degrees in the other direction, squeezed between two high cliffs on the west bank and the rocky shores of Constitution Island on the east. If properly fortified, no British man-of-war could run this S-shaped gauntlet when facing American cannon. The ring of six forts create a virtual amphitheater, protecting each other and exposing the river to devastating crossfire. Between the two forts at the shore, the Americans laid a five-hundred-yard-long chain across the river, composed of twelve hundred linked iron bars two and a quarter inches thick. The chain weighed almost sixty-five tons and was supported by a series of rafts.

West Point effectively prevented Sir Henry Clinton from moving north and connecting with British forces in Canada, but despite its extensive defenses, it was only as secure as its defending garrison.

Controlling the fort would provide precisely the sort of leverage I needed when negotiating with the British.

In restarting my communications with Major André, I made clear that I required certain indemnifications for the losses of myself and my family, including the loss of my private fortune (£5,000 sterling) and what would be lost public opportunities (an additional £5,000 sterling). I also emphasized that I required the rank of brigadier general in the British Army with an independant command of a new loyalist battalion. I made clear that were it not for my family, I would break with the rebel army immediately—I demanded this paltry sum to minimize hardship on those I loved.

In response, André provided a "trifle" of £200, along with a "token" in the form of a ring which was to have an identical pair carried by any emissary sent by the British. This would avoid the possibility of being entrapped by an American agent. As a sign of my good faith, I provided information concerning the secret Franco-American invasion of Canada headed by the Marquis de Lafayette, who was to sail up the Connecticut River and march across Vermont to attack St. John while the French fleet, with eight thousand men, attacked Quebec. After Washington shared this information with me, I had the dispatch coded and sent to the British. Also at that time, I told André that I had hopes that I would have command of West Point offered to me shortly.

On Washington's orders, in mid-June, I went on an inspection tour that included West Point. General Robert Howe, who had presided over my court-martial, had allowed the works and garrison to fall into extreme disrepair. I sent my assessment to General Clinton that the works were "wretchedly planned" and that the key fort at the top of the highest hill, Rocky Point, was formidable, facing the river but "defenseless" in the rear. An English force could land three miles below and take the fort from behind. Likewise, the enormous chain blocking the channel could be removed by a single large ship. I encoded a blueprint for a potential British attack on West Point and sent it off by courier.

After I returned from West Point, I visited Hartford, Connecticut, where the assembly added my name to officers in the Continental

Army who would be paid the difference between their salary and what had been lost by the depreciation of Continental currency. I remained desperate to make up for the shortfall caused by the unfair imposition by the Treasury Department, and also sought to collect debts and sell property. Wherever possible, I demanded payment in sterling, which I deposited in New York banks to be transferred to London.

The winter of 1779–1780 had been the harshest thus far. Virtually all soldiers were on starvation rations. When I visited the American camp in Morristown in June 1780, I saw poorly fed, ill-clad, and miserable men whose situation had been caused by a lack of leadership and support. Soldiers and officers either remained unpaid or were given worthless Continental scrip.

The opportunity to lead a loyalist brigade and put an end to this senseless war once and for all was obvious wherever I looked. While the army starved, Congress bickered. Meanwhile, the rest of the country was prospering on a war-related boom. In the spring, two Connecticut regiments mutinied, reflecting the suffering of the men and indifference of the people at large. Finally, at this crucial time, the army was put further on its heels when General Lincoln suffered a brutal defeat in Charleston, including the capture of almost his entire army of 5,500 soldiers along with priceless cannon and supplies.

Peggy and I discussed these issues at length. All pointed to the same thing: America was a dying man. Only my leadership at this crucial time could make the difference in a swift, fair, and reasonably negotiated peace, saving the country from further loss of blood as well as the continued civil war perpetrated by radicals like Reed.

By the middle of July 1780, I still had received no promise of indemnity or guarantees from the British, despite new and useful intelligence I was providing to them to demonstrate my bona fides. I told Clinton that unless definite progress was made, I would break off all negotiations and cease assisting him.

General Schuyler, who longed to see me back in New York and who had similarly suffered at the hands of the radicals, wrote me of his efforts to get me appointed head of West Point:

I believe you will either take charge of an important post with an honorable command, West Point, or your station in the field. Your reputation, my dear sir, so established, your honorable scars put it decidedly in your power to take either. The state of New York which has full confidence in you will wish to see its banner entrusted to you. If the command at West Point is offered, it will be honorable; if a division in the field, you must judge whether you can support the fatigues, circumstances as you are.

Under a molten sun, I finally met General Washington as his men crossed the Hudson. This was the first time I had seen Washington since his unfair reprimand of me. My anger at the maltreatment was mollified by my realization that securing West Point would allow me to wreak my revenge. The man I had once admired above all others, I now loathed as a political opportunist. At least Reed had never pretended to be my friend; Washington, without a second thought, had cast me aside and thrown my wife and children to the wolves.

I had only recently returned to horseback. I found a gentle mare and a comfortable saddle; while trotting was impossible, I was able to walk the horse without too much pain. I approached Washington, who sat straight as an arrow atop his large white charger. The normally taciturn Washington broke into a rare broad grin. "My dear General Arnold, you look hale and healthy. How fare your lovely bride and new son?"

My wife would be happier if you had not publicly humiliated me, you pox-ridden swine. The first thing out of your fetid mouth should be an apology.

More than anything, I wanted to draw my sword and run him through. Instead, I pulled my horse to a slow stop. Removing my hat and bowing in the saddle, I forced myself to respond in the same friendly tone, "They are well, and I thank you. And Mrs. Washington?"

"She is quite well. It is kind of you to ask."

We exchanged further pleasantries, an interchange which made me feel physically ill as I attempted to maintain a pretense of respecting such a two-faced liar. Nevertheless, after a suitable amount of time,

I eventually asked the question that mattered most to me: "Have you thought of any post for me, Your Excellency?"

Washington replied with enthusiasm, "Yes, indeed, a post of honor. I would like you to command the left wing of my army." This represented half of all Washington's soldiers—three full divisions. The command included both cavalry and light infantry.

It was a disaster for my plan in dealing with the British. I had told André I would secure West Point. My cheeks reddened, my smile evaporating. Saying nothing, I merely looked down at the back of my horse's mane, unable to meet Washington's eyes.

"Well, General? What say you?" As he asked, his horse stomped its feet uncomfortably in response to its master's obvious irritation.

Without gazing up, I mumbled, "I fear my injury would leave me incapable of performing my duties to Your Excellency's satisfaction."

Without touching his reins, Washington guided his horse closer to mine and said in a gentle and consoling tone, "My dear sir, this is the most coveted position in the army. You need not charge the hill yourself anymore. You've more than proven your bravery. What I need is your mind, your leadership, and your loyalty."

I looked into his unblinking ice-blue eyes, but could not hold his earnest gaze—I feared he was trying to probe my soul and read my thoughts. Eyes downcast, I once again repeated, "You overestimate me, General. My heart may be willing, but my body is wanting."

I could feel Washington's stare upon me. Exhaling, he said with concern rather than command, "If you would be kind enough to join me back at headquarters, I would be grateful to discuss this matter with you further." With that, he turned his horse and trotted away.

I returned to camp and told as many officers as I could that I was unfit for an active command and that West Point was the best place for my broken body. Later that night, I limped into His Excellency's headquarters with a greater fervor than my injury warranted. We sat alone after dinner. He patiently prodded, embarrassed, harassed, and argued with me in a vain attempt to change my position. He bluntly indicated that the years of political wrangling and infighting should not have sapped my martial spirit so badly that I would settle for an inferior command. I was unbending that my wound required an assignment in the rear.

In this situation, one might wonder if I felt despair or had second thoughts at finally being offered the position I had always wanted. The answer is unequivocal—no.

I had already committed myself to reunifying the country under the British. More importantly, I knew that Washington's current claims of loyalty meant nothing. He would cast me aside again if it were politically expedient. He had done so when he repeatedly overlooked me for promotion, when he delayed my trial, and most of all, when he censured me. I *knew*, with every fiber of my being, that I was done fighting for those either unworthy or uncaring of my sacrifice. I remember thinking as I was listening to him, *The Revolution is lost, you arrogant fool—and you lost me with it. Revenge, victory, and reward shall be mine.*

Undeterred, Washington issued orders on August 1, placing me in command of the left wing of the army.

Peggy learned of my promotion while at a dinner party in Philadelphia with the financier Robert Morris. She became nearly hysterical, saying that it was a mistake, and that I had been given the command of West Point. When her friends tried to explain that command of the left wing of the army was far more important than West Point and that she should be well pleased, she remained disconsolate.

When I saw the order, I rode to Washington and once again explained that I was unable to withstand the physical rigors of command in the field. I could see pity in the general's eyes. He acknowledged that my injuries were more severe than previously understood. Reluctantly, on August 3, Washington issued new orders, providing, "Major General Arnold will take command of the garrison at West Point."

Committed fully to my plan, Peggy and I began to convert as much of our property as possible to cash, even transferring money to London through friends in New York. My goal was to leave nothing behind when I returned to the king's service.

Chapter 73

West Point, NY - August 9, 1780

O nce I reached West Point, communications with André became increasingly difficult. To make matters worse, I could no longer consult with Peggy, whom I'd been required to initially leave behind as I took my posting. Nonetheless, I was not totally without avenues to the outside world—and one oppressively hot evening, finally, a message from André came through.

Totally alone, I sat sweating in my office. Before I could read, I was startled by the sound of hail, as large as musket balls, striking the home. I looked out the windows and marveled at a sky crisscrossed with ferocious lightning. The world seemed to tremble as I decoded André's delayed message.

I would receive the full £20,000 as promised from the British. This amount was roughly equal to my entire net worth, including all debts owed to me. To receive this full amount, I would need to turn over West Point, along with three thousand prisoners and the fortress's artillery and equipment. I viewed this proviso as a trifle. The hapless soldiers under my command would be easy prey for Royal Navy marines.

My mission in hand, I reintroduced myself to a wealthy local landowner named Joshua Hett Smith. We had met briefly when I was in Philadelphia, and I had stayed at his home earlier in the year during a visit to West Point. The pompous lawyer lived in a large white home called "Belmont" near Stony Point. He was not trusted fully by either the Americans or the British. Nevertheless, General Howe, the American who had previously commanded West Point, had used Smith as part of his network of informants in the surrounding area. Smith's name was the only contact Howe had passed on to me as I assumed my new post.

I invited Squire Smith to my headquarters and plied him with wine and compliments, hoping he would disclose all American spies behind British lines. I met with little success. The thin-blooded American aristocrat knew nothing—Washington was a stickler for compartmentalizing and limiting access to his carefully built intelligence network. Nevertheless, I sent letters off to senior generals, including the Marquis de Lafayette, seeking to discover all American spies in the area to protect myself from discovery and weaken their network when the British assumed command of West Point. Unfortunately, I did not receive any useful information.

I deliberately selected the abandoned and furnished mansion of loyalist Colonel Beverly Robinson as my residence. The prior commander had recommended a house nearer to the fort. The rambling Robinson house was two miles south and across the river from West Point, but crucially it had its own dock. It was surrounded on two sides by mountains and dense forests, and set a mile back from the Hudson with no view of the river. For me, this was ideal, as it could not be observed by any American fortifications.

I confided with no one regarding my plans. Indeed, I sent my longtime aide David Franks to Philadelphia to get Peggy and our baby to join me at my new command. I also sought the assistance of my old aide from the Northern Department, Lieutenant Colonel Richard Varick, who had resigned from the army and was studying law in Hackensack, New Jersey. He accepted the position as my writing aide, but I also kept him in the dark as to my true goals.

As I set up my headquarters, Colonels John Lamb and Jonathan Meigs met me at the door. Although half of Lamb's face had been blown away in the assault on Quebec, he had recovered and was the ranking artillery officer at West Point. Meigs had led my division on the march to Quebec and was charged with fortifying the hills to prevent a land invasion. I knew both gentlemen to be able soldiers. I was concerned that they would only further fortify and improve West Point's defenses, undermining my goal of weakening the fort. My solution was to bury Varick in paperwork and distract Lamb and Meigs as much as possible, preventing them from improving the fortifications.

All three men objected to my orders. This quickly came to a head on August 12, when I ordered two hundred of the fifteen hundred soldiers we had positioned upriver to cut firewood. Meanwhile, I wrote almost constant correspondence to Washington and his staff seeking increased supplies. I ordered ten thousand rations be removed from the fort's cellars and moved over to my mansion by barge. Varick confronted me, indicating that if the British ever attacked, the provisions would be in the worst possible place. I ignored his objections.

At the same time, I discreetly sold off barrels of pork, rum, and hams for cash. When Franks protested, I told him this was a reimbursement for monies owed me by Congress. Varick was unable to hold his tongue when a loyalist ship captain arrived to purchase barrels of food that I sold for gold. I freely admit that such actions would have been improper had I remained in the Continental Army—but I was "leaving," so I did not care.

I recognized the importance of having men loyal to me alone under my direct command. As such, I set up a personal guard of one hundred picked men. The strongest were selected as oarsmen on my thirty-foot barge, allowing me to move quickly up and down the Hudson—ostensibly to inspect forts, but I also recognized the importance of having an efficient way to exit in the event my plans were discovered.

I took perverse satisfaction when I learned of the defeat of the American army in Camden, South Carolina, where my nemesis Gates had panicked in the face of the British and been caught 180 miles from the battle. Hopeful that Gates's failure could turn the tide and break the back of the American patriots, I wrote André, "I have accepted the command at West Point. The mass of people are heartily tired of the war and wish to be on their former footing. The present struggles are like the pangs of a dying man, violent but of short duration." Central to my plan, as a British general, I would secure a quick victory, ending this unpopular war and reuniting the wayward colonies with the mother country. I saw not only military victory, but knighthood in my future.

Communication with the British remained a daunting challenge. Varick was becoming increasingly suspicious of my attempts to establish lines of communication with New York. I told him that I was working on corresponding with an American agent inside the state, hence the need to establish contact with messengers going across enemy lines. My hope was that this ruse would keep Varick at bay long enough to permit the British invasion and prevent the discovery of my plans.

I believed a final meeting with the British was required to coordinate the strategy. While I wanted an emissary of General Clinton's to come and meet with me behind the American lines, Clinton demurred and demanded the meeting be held on neutral ground between the two lines near the Hudson, where British ships could stand by. Clinton proposed to send his representative under a flag of truce. I realized this was insanity—if I met a high-ranking British officer under a flag of truce, I would fall under immediate suspicion.

I wrote a letter to André proposing we meet secretly at Dobbs Ferry on the night of September 11 to make final arrangements for the surrender of West Point. This covert meeting in neutral territory was necessary, but I also knew it was tremendously dangerous. André had headed north on the sixteen-gun sloop HMS *Vulture* and awaited my arrival.

On the morning of September 11, I approached our meeting spot in my barge. We quickly hit a complication—André had not informed these officers that an American general was to meet British officers under a flag of truce. Several British gunboats patrolling the river saw us and began to open fire. Shells raked the water around us, and my unarmed boat narrowly escaped to the western shore, where we remained undercover for nearly nine hours until sunset. I was forced to retreat to West Point and swore my crew to silence. I informed Lamb that I had been on an inspection tour downriver, then wrote a frantic letter to André emphasizing that his gunners had nearly done me in, and trying to arrange another meeting.

When Peggy and my son Neddy embarked upon a trip from Philadelphia, I was anxious to see them as soon as possible. We met at Joshua Smith's home on September 14—overlooking Haverstraw Bay, it was a good distance from any patriot camp, hidden off in the trees, but near a secluded beach, a perfect spot for a secretive rendezvous. I decided to take the unwitting Smith into my confidence—albeit partially— and told him that I would be having a secret meeting with a British spy working for the Americans. I asked that the meeting take place at his home. Smith readily agreed to assist me in my plans.

Having secured Smith's cooperation, I proceeded with my family back to my home near West Point. On the way, I received news that George Washington and his staff would be arriving on their way to meet French generals. If properly coordinated, the capture of both the fort and Washington could effectively decapitate the Continental Army, ensuring British victory—and catapult me to success in both countries.

Back at our temporary home, I sat at the midday meal on September 17 when a letter was handed to me. With my officers surrounding me, I had no choice but to share its contents. Colonel Beverly Robinson was writing under a flag of truce, seeking to correspond with the occupier of his home about matters relating to his property. The house that he had owned was the one I had selected as my headquarters. I realized immediately that the letter was actually an attempt by André to communicate with me and set up a meeting. When Colonel Lamb saw the letter and Robinson's name, his already badly scarred face reddened and distorted—he insisted that I should have no contact with the traitor and disclose the letter to General Washington.

The next day, Franks and I crossed the river at King's Ferry to meet Washington, Knox, Lafayette, Hamilton, and their staff at Smith's home for dinner. The Marquis de Lafayette indicated that a French squadron under, Count de Guichen was expected any day on the coast. Aware of my request that I meet Robinson, the Marquis joked, "General Arnold, since you have a correspondence with the enemy, you must ascertain as soon as possible what has become of Guichen."

I felt myself flush at the accusation, and whether it was the wine or that the statement had struck too close to home, I barked, "I beg your pardon, General, but what precisely are you insinuating?" I locked my eyes hard on the diminutive boy.

Peggy Arnold with child
Painting by Sir Thomas Lawrence.
Courtesy of the National Archives 11-SC-92575

Blanching at my challenge, Lafayette looked to the others in confusion. I suddenly realized I had overreacted. Everyone was looking at me with surprise as Lafayette said, "No, no, my dear General. I meant only to make a jest. I sincerely apologize if I have offended you." He bowed from his chair, his palms up in supplication.

The table turned to me as one. I could see Washington's disapproving straight-mouthed stare from the corner of my eye as I answered, "It is I who should apologize." I bowed in return from my chair. "I am afraid the joke was lost in translation." With that, I tried to force a smile. My internal voice screamed, *You idiot!*

After a few moments of silence, the affable Henry Knox poked the fellow at his right. "I supposedly speak the same language as this fellow Hamilton, but half the time I don't understand what *he* is saying!"

The tension broke at once—Washington laughed, and everyone followed suit. To my great relief, the dinner ended without further blunder.

Afterward, Washington and I strolled down to the Hudson. My limp was pronounced, and I moved slowly, but Washington was patient and showed no signs of irritation as he shortened his long strides. When we reached the river, he pulled out a telescope to examine the HMS *Vulture* at anchor. As Washington studied the ship, which no doubt contained Major André, I attempted to casually bring up the issue of Colonel Beverly's request. Washington had known Beverly before the war, so I hoped he might be willing to entertain an exchange.

He shook his head as he collapsed the telescope and turned to me. "Our acquaintance was in the past. You will have nothing to do with my former friend." With that, he walked away. My only solace was that his instructions were both verbal and private. No one else would know I had been barred from meeting Robinson. Washington would be leaving for Hartford, and I would again be the service officer in the area.

I returned to my headquarters and composed a letter to Robinson, which my aide Richard Varick read. He commented that my letter was too friendly to be sent to an enemy. I rewrote the letter in a more stiff and formal fashion. However, what he did not know was that I included a second, hidden letter requesting a meeting on September 20 on board the HMS *Vulture* under a flag of truce. I wrote, "You may depend on my secrecy and honor, and that your business shall be kept a profound secret. I think it will be advisable for the HMS *Vulture* to remain where she is until the time appointed." I went on in a postscript: "I expect His Excellency General Washington to lodge here on Saturday night next, and will lay before him any manner you wish to communicate." Obviously, my goal at this point was to not only surrender the fort, but hopefully to capture the leadership of the Continental Army in one fell swoop. I understood the date of the attack was set for September 23.

Chapter 74

Belmont, Smith Home, Stony Point, NY – September 20, 1780

T hings were happening very quickly. I used Smith to my advantage by telling him that he was meeting Colonel Robinson and might also be introduced to a man named "Mr. Anderson," who could be of service to the Cause. I asked him to row out to the British ship, pick up Robinson, and bring him ashore to meet me in Smith's house, emphasizing that this was a secret which he should share with no one. Smith was thrilled and honored to be included in an opportunity to serve his country.

However, the dolt did not apprehend the urgency of his task and failed to arrange for rowers to transport him in a nighttime rendezvous with the British vessel. Rather than press the issue, he sent word to me that his efforts had been delayed and went to bed. Washington was on his way, André and Colonel Robinson were offshore on the HMS *Vulture*, and I needed a meeting to finalize our plans to capture Washington and turn over West Point. Time was running short.

WEST POINT

ROBINSON HOUSE
ARNOLD'S HEADQUARTERS

N

5 Mi

ANDRÉ'S ROUTE

KING'S FERRY

STONY POINT

PINE'S BRIDGE
SMITH TURNS BACK

SMITH'S HOUSE

HUDSON

ARNOLD AND
ANDRÉ MEET

TELLER'S POINT

VULTURE

RIVER

NORTH CASTLE

NEW YORK

ANDRÉ
CAPTURED

TARRYTOWN

TAPPAN
ANDRÉ IS HANGED

West Point Meeting & Escape

SEPTEMBER 1780

Chapter 75

Belmont, Smith Home, Stony Point, NY – September 21, 1780

Concerned that my plans were unraveling as a result of Smith's incompetence, I saw no choice but to take the lead to facilitate the meeting. I located a boat and had it brought to his home.

On the night of September 21, I rode to Smith's house, near the place the HMS *Vulture* was anchored. When I arrived, I found a letter from the ship's captain that had been brought to shore, ostensibly complaining about the behavior of some American troops. Nevertheless, I immediately recognized the exquisite handwriting of Major André, discreetly emphasizing that he remained on the HMS *Vulture* until our meeting.

Smith was resistant when I informed him that the boat would be rowed out at night. He explained in his high and grating voice, "You see, General, these sorts of exchanges happen all the time during the day. A flag of truce is flown prominently on a boat which goes out to a British man-of-war. Information and goods can be exchanged, mail and messages shared. On rare occasions, individuals are allowed to cross the line."

I hid my irritation—I well knew of such exchanges—and took on a conspiratorial tone. "See here, Smith. I am sure you are aware that the Carlisle Commission's attempt to end the war has failed. It is my charge to act as an emissary to bring this unhappy conflict to an end." Reaching down and placing my hand on my lame leg, I said, "I have fought many battles for my country. There is a time for war, and a time for peace. The sooner this conflict is brought to an end, the better. I tell you this in the strictest confidence." Leaning in close, I whispered, "General Washington has asked me to contact Mr. Robinson to engage in a mission that could result in resolution on favorable terms."

Smith's eyes widened and his mouth hung open as I continued with my tale. "I have come to you because you are both a lawyer and an individual with the sophistication and understanding necessary to discreetly handle these matters. Let me be clear—you can never acknowledge this information, even to General Washington." I made this statement so he wouldn't accidentally say something to Washington or anyone else that might arouse suspicion. Frankly, the injunction made no sense, but I was pleased to see Smith knowingly and vigorously nod in agreement as I continued, "A time will come when all will recognize our joint efforts to serve our country. I quite simply ask you to trust me. We must go to the ship in the middle of the night to recover an individual with whom I can engage in these important discussions. I need to know I can count on you."

Smith stammered, "Of course, General. Of course. I am honored you are including me in this important mission. I will not share this with anyone and will find men to row out to the ship tonight."

As he began to stand, I reached out, grabbed his arm, pulled him a little closer, and murmured with a sharp edge, "I mean it, Joshua, you cannot tell anyone about this. Our lives and the country's future depend upon it."

His face turned crimson with fear and excitement as he answered, "As I say, I will tell no one and will find someone immediately. Thank you, sir." As Smith scampered off, I sat back, confident in both his naive earnestness and his discretion.

Smith tried to hire two tenant farmers to row us out, but they were so reluctant that he brought one of the men before me as the sun was setting. The dirt-covered and shabby farmer shifted uncomfortably and looked down at his cap, which he twisted in his large hands. "Beggin' your pardon, General, but it is late at night and I am tired. I don't think I could row out tonight."

I could feel my ire rising. *My plans might be thwarted by this peasant.* Nevertheless, I said gently, "Aren't you a patriot, Mr. . . . ?"

I looked at Smith, who interjected, "Samuel Cahoon."

"Don't you want to serve your country, Mr. Cahoon? You know who I am?"

Still looking down at his hat, Cahoon nodded in agreement.

"Well, how about it. Will you help me? Will you help your country?"

Clearly trying to avoid the work, Cahoon inquired, "Where will we be goin' out on river?"

I pointed to the ship. "To the HMS *Vulture*. I need you pick up an individual and bring him back."

Now he vigorously shook his head. "General, meetin's are durin' the day. If we wait till mornin', it will be safer and I won't be so tired. Besides, as likely as not, 'em redcoats will shoot first and ask questions later. It ain't safe near 'em at night."

I could feel my patience giving way. Leaning in close, I growled, "Damn it, man, it won't be a *secret* if every bloody fool on the river can see the meeting occur. This is a *secret* meeting. It has to happen tonight."

"Well, I'm real sorry, General, but I'm too darned beat to do the round trip. The current's also pushin' against us, you know."

Smith, clearly sensing my exasperation, said, "General, perhaps his brother can assist us." When I nodded agreement, he and Cahoon left the room.

Moments later, Cahoon was back, but without the brother. He stammered, "My brother . . . Joseph . . . you see, his wife . . . well, she is a formidable woman . . . and she says no. She says he can't go and I can't neither. Beggin' your pardon, General, sir."

Genuinely losing my temper now, I smashed the table hard with my fist. "Christ's blood! You will do as I say, or as the Lord and Congress are my witness, I will have you put under guard and flogged within an inch of your miserable life. You need to stop fearing your brother's wife and start fearing me, by God."

Smith bolted from the room and reappeared a few moments later, this time with the second brother. A half step behind Smith, Joseph seemed even more reticent and addle-minded. I decided I needed to balance the vinegar of my threats with some honey. In a gentler voice I said, "Listen, boys. Why don't you help yourselves to some rum. That will make the trip easier. I know flour is hard to come by, and I will give you fifty pounds for your efforts." As I was speaking, Smith was already pouring generous glasses of rum and handing them to each man. Both took prodigious gulps.

While Joseph kept drinking, Samuel, the marginally brighter of the two, paused and said, "Fifty pounds of flour for each of us?"

I once again found my anger rising. Before I could answer, Smith chimed in, "Sure, boys, sure. You heard the general. This is an important mission. You want to serve your country, right? A little flour and helping the Cause—why, that's a good night's work, eh?"

As he spoke, Smith amicably put his hand on each man's back and topped off their glasses. Stepping back, he gave me a conspiratorial wink and nod, then turned to his new "friends" and said, "All right, boys, down to the river you go." Unwilling to part with their full mugs of rum and still somewhat petulant, they nevertheless shuffled away.

I painfully made my way over uneven ground to the shore, where I watched Smith get onto the boat and take the rudder. The tipsy Cahoon brothers rowed the boat out to the menacing HMS *Vulture* with sheepskins around the oars to muffle the sound. They quickly disappeared into an impenetrable night.

Smith later shared with me all that occurred. Apparently, André had not briefed the sailors on the HMS *Vulture*, as they challenged the approaching boat with curses and oaths. Finally, at 12:30 a.m., Smith and the Cahoons were eased alongside the ship. Smith was then yanked from the boat, accused of being a "rebel rascal," and dragged in front of the ship's captain, Major André, and Colonel Robinson. André had put a large overcoat over his red uniform, so Smith thought only Robinson was an officer.

I had provided Smith with a letter and pass to be shown to the men on the ship. I'd explained that he would take a designated individual to a "place of safety" for our meeting. It became clear to Smith that André, a.k.a "Mr. Anderson," wanted to go ashore and meet me. Apparently, Colonel Robinson was not "feeling well" and thus was sending Mr. Anderson in his stead. Seeing there were only two men rowing the boat, Robinson offered to have the boat towed by an armed barge, but Smith objected, indicating that would be an infringement on the flag of truce.

Chapter 76

Hudson River, Near Stony Point, NY –
September 22, 1780

I mpatient, I had moved down from Smith's home into a grove of fir trees providing the ideal cover. I alternately shuffled down to the lakeshore or sat on a stout log, biding my time. I repeatedly thought I saw the shadow of a boat moving across the river, only to realize it was a wave or a reflection.

The weary, and now slightly hungover, oarsmen struggled for almost two miles against the tide as they returned to the beach near Smith's home. As is the nature of things, when my mind was wandering and I wasn't paying attention, they finally arrived around 2:00 a.m. I heard the unmistakable sound of a heavy wooden boat grinding onto a rocky shore. A few minutes later, a slightly out-of-breath Smith announced, "Colonel Robinson refused to come, sir." Resting his hand on his knees from the exertion, he looked up and inquired, "I hope that is all right, General. Mr. Anderson was quite insistent he should come in his stead."

Struggling to keep my composure, I replied evenly, holding my hands behind my back, "That is fine, Smith. Please send him up here, and be good enough to wait at the boat while Mr. . . . . Anderson"—*I nearly said André*—"and I have our discussion."

Smith turned on his heel, nodded, and began walking down the hill, shouting uncomfortably loudly over his shoulder, "As you say, General. I will fetch him straight away." I knew that standing amongst the trees in the middle of the night in late September was no place to have a substantive discussion with André, but such were the exigencies of war.

Less than a minute later, I heard the sound of feet crunching up the path. Covered in almost impenetrable darkness, only André's ostentatious white-topped boots were visible. I could faintly see the silhouettes of both him and Smith standing before me. In a voice far too loud, Smith said, "I brought Mr. Anderson as you instructed, General."

I answered in a quiet but firm tone, "Thank you for all your assistance, Mr. Smith. Mr. Anderson and I need to speak in private. I am sure you understand." Even in the darkness, I could still perceive his disappointment and reluctance to leave. When he did not immediately move, I said again, "We will come down to the shore to get you when we have completed our discussions. Thank you again, Mr. Smith—that will be all."

With an audible sigh, Smith answered, "Of course, General. Please let me know when you are done."

Major John André
Engraving by J. K. Sherwin.
Courtesy of University of Michigan William L. Clements Library

Turning to André, I saw him bow in the dark. "Mr. Anderson." André nodded in return as Smith shuffled off.

I was somewhat ill at ease in meeting André, whom I knew that Peggy had felt some affection for during his stay in Philadelphia. I had expected to be discussing matters with Colonel Robinson, who was more of a kindred spirit, rather than a highborn British officer. We stood silently on wet grass. The moonlight was blocked by a large pine tree, leaving us in deep shadow. My eyes, accustomed to the night, could perceive his stiffness. As seconds went by with nobody speaking, his head cocked slightly upward; he seemed, despite his airs, unsure about what to do next.

As is my nature, I took command and bowed. Removing my hat, I said, "Major André, Mrs. Arnold sends her compliments."

I detected a slight shuffle of feet at my words, but he recomposed himself, removed his hat, and bowed, albeit noticeably less deeply. "Thank you, General. Please send her my warmest greetings. She is a remarkable woman. You are a fortunate man."

His timidity increased my resolve. André was at least ten years younger than me. I was a major general and he was a mere major. In a matter of days, I would be a brigadier commanding him in the British Army.

Having taken his measure and dispensed with pleasantries, I moved to the issue at hand. "Major, I was promised £20,000. Let me be clear— if I do not receive this promised sum, this entire episode will come to naught."

Negotiation was my stock-in-trade, whether for barrels of rum, medicines in London, or my fair compensation. I had my wits about me enough to observe, even in the dark, André's involuntary behavioral clues. When I finished speaking, I noted that he took a half step back and shifted uncomfortably. "I do not have the authority to offer such a large sum." Then, he reached up and rubbed his hand over his mouth. I knew he was lying. He mumbled, "Perhaps I could convince General Clinton to part with £6,000."

I then took a full step forward and pointed my arm back to the boat.

"Be on your way. Stop wasting my time. I have great responsibilities to my family and have taken tremendous risks. You do not understand what I have endured or what I can bring to the table. Godspeed, off you go, sir."

André put his hands up as if to both stop my approach and beg to stay. He responded a little louder, I suspect, than he intended, "No, no, General. I am sure we can reach an accommodation. I need better information to convince General Clinton that you are deserving of a larger sum."

I bristled. "My dear Major, you stand at the gates of West Point. I have unlocked gates for your men to walk through. If you act with alacrity, you even stand the chance of capturing General Washington and his staff. What, pray tell, could I have done to be more 'deserving'? This Revolution is a house of cards that Washington has stacked together. Without him, there will be an immediate collapse."

Leaning forward, André entreated, "Promises will not suffice. I need specifics. What is the exact condition of the fort and its defenses? How many men are present, and how will we overcome the fortifications?"

"Well then, let's go through them. I will show you how to overcome the soldiers, shatter the depleted defenses, and give you the specific route to capture the fort and mayhap General Washington."

With that, I pulled out a set of carefully drawn plans, which we both struggled to see in the moonlight. "There is a table of land on the west shore where troops can be landed. You will be at the rear of Fort Putnam and overlooking the whole parade of West Point. From this commanding eminence, you will control the field. I have arranged the garrison so there will be little or no opposition."

André moved in close to look at the map. The smell of perfume was overwhelming—this man was indeed a fop. Fortunately, the dark hid my disgust as I continued, "Damn it, man, there is at least a chance that you could capture Washington, his brilliant aide Alexander Hamilton, the Marquis de Lafayette, and General Henry Knox."

I took his stupefied silence for what it was: a man suited to the salon, not planning how or where men will die. "See here, André. I have placed men at Fishkill and other distant locations. There are just over three thousand of my worst men left to guard the fort. When I know you are going to attack, I will send an urgent request for Washington to send reinforcements, and ask for his personal leadership. Given his aggressive nature, I think there is a better than even chance we can capture him."

I desperately wanted to sit down. My leg was throbbing as bone shards drove into my leg muscles. I'd remained upright longer than I had for many months. I directed André to a nearby downed log, where we continued our conversation in a businesslike and less combative manner. "Well, what say you? Am I 'deserving' now, Major? Will you and General Clinton honor your promise?" The pain in my leg put an edge in my voice that I did not intend, but it had the desired effect.

"I'm very sorry, General, to have offended. Of course, I want to assure you that while I don't have the authority to unilaterally make this decision, I have been granted some latitude by General Clinton. I will do everything in my power to see that your request is met, especially given what you have presented this evening."

Satisfied, and with the discomfort of my leg easing, I returned to the map. "Well, the devil is in the details." I then walked him through the plans in detail, elaborating on the best way for the British to proceed.

The predawn light revealed André as an elegant young man with delicate features and an aquiline nose. A mere boy, he was unaccustomed to the rough-and-tumble world of combat. I was a thickset, swarthy New Englander with generations of Anglo-Saxon strength, both physical and mental. Yet I knew we shared one characteristic: ambition. Handing over West Point could end the war. As importantly, we both stood a chance of changing history and reaping the benefits from it.

After two hours of talking, we were interrupted by Smith, who noted that the time was nearly 4:00 a.m. I told him, "Please take Mr. Anderson back to the *Vulture*." He and André walked down to the boat and woke the Cahoons.

The brothers steadfastly refused to make another trip, as the tide was coming in strongly against them. In no event would they be able to make it to and from the boat before sunrise. The pair insisted they were "fatigued" and simply would not go. I quickly realized that no combination of threats and rewards would change their mind. They promised to return at dusk and extracted a promise of more flour.

Neither André nor I were especially concerned about continuing our discussions an additional day. We both expected the HMS *Vulture* to remain at anchor and easily accessible. In any event, I wanted to go over additional paperwork with André in better conditions than a dark and dingy wood. Daybreak found me in a fine mood, anticipating both revenge and significant reward. We resolved to go to Smith's home, some four miles to the north, and continue our conversation. Smith returned to his home on a wagon carrying the Cahoons, and lent André his horse.

As André and I proceeded on our mounts toward Smith's home, we encountered American sentries who recognized me, came to attention, and saluted. André became very ill at ease when he saw the American soldiers. He had thought he was on neutral ground between the British and American lines. After we passed the sentries, I assured him that he had nothing to worry about, as I was the officer in titular command. I took André to Smith's house, where he went upstairs and removed his heavy blue greatcoat.

What followed next was almost disaster. Without warning, Smith barged into the room and was stunned to realize that his guest was wearing a British officer's uniform. "What the blazes?" he stammered. "This man is a British officer. I understood we were meeting an emissary."

Dumbstruck, face flushed, André turned to me for help. I shuffled toward Smith, my hands open and patting the air. "Calm down, my dear fellow. Mr. Anderson is indeed an American citizen from New York. He merely borrowed this uniform to facilitate traveling on a British ship. This is all being done for the benefit of the Cause. These are delicate matters. I am sure you understand."

Incredibly, the gullible Smith accepted my story. "Certainly. Obviously, Mr. Anderson cannot leave my home in this garb." Turning to André, who had also recomposed himself, Smith bowed slightly and said, "I apologize for my reaction, Mr. Anderson. I will see breakfast is made and will be brought up. I would ask that both of you do not allow anyone in my home to see Mr. Anderson in his uniform."

André spoke with newly found confidence. "Of course, Mr. Smith. You may rely upon us." With that, Smith left the room.

The spy turned to me and stifled a laugh. "Where in heaven's name did you find that man?"

I grinned and quipped, "The fool doth think he is wise."

"At least he is *our* fool," André said, sitting down and beginning to relax.

"Amen to that."

An hour later, our breakfast was interrupted by the sound of explosions coming from the river. An American officer named James Livingston had been surprised to see the HMS *Vulture* floating so close to West Point. Taking two small four-pound cannon, he decided to take shots at the British ship. For the next two hours, Livingston and his crew took potshots at the HMS *Vulture*, with six of their shots piercing the ship's hull and several others fouling the rigging. As fate would have it, a splinter from the rigging hit the captain of the HMS_*Vulture* in the nose. In response, the captain ordered the ship to drop out of the range of the American guns.

André and I rushed to the second-floor window in Smith's home. Puffs of smoke could be seen from the shore, followed by the report of cannon fire. Dots on the horizon showed longboats attempting to pull the HMS *Vulture* out of the range of American guns. Eventually under sail, it moved back to safety toward New York.

André began to pace. "Dear God. What are we going to do? Can you find out where the *Vulture* stopped? Perhaps we could move further south and meet her?"

I said in a soothing voice, "Of course, Major. We will have no trouble tracking her. I will receive reports on where she is located." What I did not say was that now that this incident had occurred, gunboats and telescopes would be watching her day and night. I knew that the best route home for the major, from the moment of the first report of cannon fire, was to go by land.

I tried to distract André by picking up the plans I had brought to our meeting. "See here, André—I have included so much detail in these plans that they will be absolutely essential for a smooth taking of the fort. You should bring them with you and conceal them on your person."

My plan worked. He became animated and rapidly shook his head. "No, General. My instructions were quite clear. I am to remain in uniform, and under no circumstances am I to be carrying any incriminating documents. To do so could brand me as a spy."

Sitting back in a chair and lifting my leg on a stool, I replied, "It is your decision, Major, but you have come all this way. Do you really want to leave behind so much detail to assist General Clinton in the assault? Do you really want to risk forgetting something? You can always destroy the papers if it looks as though there is any chance you will be caught." I held out the papers as I spoke.

André glided over, took the papers from me, and stared at them, lost in thought. I knew he would take them, so I sat silently as he came to his own conclusion. "Just so, General." He sat down, removed his boot and his stocking, and placed the plans under his foot. He replaced the stocking and stomped his boot into place, then looked up with a boyish grin and said, "That should do."

I nodded in agreement.

With victory not only in our grasp, but literally underfoot, André's anxiety was in an instant replaced with zeal. I decided to broach the subject of the method of his return. "Major, even if the *Vulture* comes back, it will be under constant surveillance. Finding men willing and able to row out to the ship will be problematic. I do not think, whether day or night, that can be done safely. In any event, we don't know if your ship is going to come back any time soon. This is a very time-sensitive operation—that is, General Washington is going to come to inspect West Point. Our opportunity to capture him and his staff hangs in the balance. The only viable alternative is for you to proceed over land. Mr. Smith can take you to the very cusp of the British lines."

André, who had been standing looking out the window at the empty river, suddenly flopped into a chair. With a pathetic theatrical flourish, he put the back of his right hand to his forehead and whined, "I honestly don't know what to do, General. I know the safest thing is probably to wait for the *Vulture*. However, *Audentis Fortuna Iuvat.*" He raised his nose impossibly high and translated, "Fortune favors the bold."

You prancing coxcomb. You assume I am a mere provincial who does not speak Latin. At that moment I was grateful for the compulsory reading at Dr. Cogswell's school. I nodded in agreement. "Virgil." I was pleased to see the surprise on his face. Pointing out the window, I continued, "You too are cast on a foreign shore. Are we to be as brave as the Trojans?" I shuffled over to him, spinning a chair to be placed directly across from where he was sitting. "This is *your* opportunity to be bold. This is *your* moment. Sitting and waiting is not our fate. We are men of action, aren't we, Major?" I honestly didn't believe he was, but perhaps he did.

Finally, looking up, André nodded in agreement. "Yes, you are right, of course, General."

Slapping my right leg, I exclaimed, "Damn fine! I will write you passes that will make your return through the lines a certainty."

I then wrote out a pass for André: "Permit Mr. John Anderson to pass the Guards to the White Plains or below if He Chooses, He being on Public Business by my Direction. B. Arnold M Gen." Confident that a pass signed by me would get André through the lines, we agreed that as soon as he returned to New York, the British attack could begin.

I wrote a second pass, just to be safe, that allowed Smith and André to go out to the HMS *Vulture* if that possibility occurred: "Joshua Smith, Esq. has permission to pass with a Boat & three hands & a flag to Dobb's Ferry on Public business & to return immediately. B. Arnold M Gen." Finally, I wrote a pass for Smith in the unlikely event he needed to cross the British lines: "Joshua Smith, Esq. has permission to pass the Guard to the White Plains, & to return, being on public business by my direction. B. Arnold M. Gen."

Handing André the passes, I said with a confidence I genuinely felt, "I am in absolute control of this military district. Both my rank and reputation are beyond reproach. If you show these passes to anyone, there is no danger. You will be perfectly safe." André nodded in agreement as he put the passes in his pocket.

Having calmed the major down, we needed Smith to take him across the lines. I knew that there were limits, even to Smith's stupidity. He continued to fixate on André's military uniform. I once again patiently explained that Anderson had borrowed it from a British officer and was wearing it out of vanity. We both agreed that he would need to remove the uniform if he were to cross British lines. Smith agreed to loan André clothes.

Leaving Smith downstairs, I walked back up to André's room with a plain beaver bowler-type hat with a wide circular brim, a frayed purple jacket with gold-laced buttons, and some boots. Handing them to him, I said, "If you are going through the lines, you will need some clothes. Mr. Smith has been kind enough to lend you something to wear."

André looked shocked. "General, my orders are quite clear, I am not to remove my uniform. This is what protects me as a prisoner of war and will allow me to avoid being treated as a spy."

"What did we just talk about? You are not a god-damned spy, but you are never going to get through the lines in a British uniform." Throwing the clothes on the floor in front of him, I allowed my voice to rise: "You said it yourself. *Audentis Fortuna Iuvat.* Well, how about it? Are you going to sit here and wait as success passes you by? If you are going to fulfill your destiny, you cannot do it in a British uniform."

In a final act of impotent defiance, André proclaimed, "Well, I'm wearing my boots."

As I turned to walk out of the room, I answered without looking back at him. "Fine, keep your damn boots, but change your clothes."

I met André and Smith at the bottom of the stairs. Both looked confident and relaxed. I knew that André had the plans to West Point, which assured the successful taking of the fort as well as represented a concrete manifestation of my efforts to be shared with General Clinton to guarantee my reward.

I advised the men that with the recent exchange of gunfire, the area would be rife with American patrols, and the HMS *Vulture* had likely returned to New York. Looking both of them over, I said, "Gentlemen. You have my passes. Good luck to you."

Relaxed, André beamed. "Thank you, General, and to you too."

As Smith walked me down to my barge, I emphasized the importance of this secret mission to the Cause. I asked that he guide our guest back to British lines. I sincerely believed André's success in escaping was assured. He was an experienced British spymaster and should have had no trouble getting through the lines. Little did I know, he was as big a fool as Smith.

As I traveled upriver, I reflected on the meeting. *I can see how Peggy might have found André amusing. Still, he is nothing more than a prancing staff peacock. A sycophant, comfortable in halls filled with strutting politicians or generals who lead from the back. This poltroon has never seen death, heard the screams of dying, felt smoke burn his lungs, or looked down at his own blood staining the ground. No. This is the worst sort of scoundrel. He came to gain promotion through my act of bravery. I will use him, but we are not and will never be "brothers in arms."*

I felt myself giddy at the prospect of success as I approached my headquarters at the Beverly Robinson house in the late morning of September 22. Not only would my enemies, like Reed, be sentenced to a traitor's fate, but my future with Peggy was unlimited. I could see the king making me an earl and awarding lands in America—maybe Washington's famous Mount Vernon, or Jefferson's Monticello. We would make a grand tour of England, welcomed and hailed by all. I smiled at all that awaited us—all my sufferings reversed.

It is strange how, as the years go by, my mind takes descriptions given by others to make me believe I was somewhere I wasn't. So it was for the widely recounted story of André's next few days.

Following my advice, Smith, his slave, and André set out after dark. At about 9:00 p.m. the men were overtaken by Major John Burroughs, with whom Smith had a pleasant conversation. Three miles later, Smith paid a call on Colonel James Livingston at Fort Lafayette; Livingston had led the barrage against the HMS *Vulture* that morning from Teller's Point. André was becoming increasingly agitated by Smith's attempting social progress, rather than heading south in earnest. Smith explained that he tried to maintain a relaxed and jovial appearance to put the major at ease, as well as mislead anyone that ran into them.

They then encountered Captain Ebenezer Boyd, who was not so friendly as the other men had been. Stepping forth, he challenged, "Who goes there?"

Smith said, "Friends."

Boyd glanced at André and said, "You seem very uneasy."

Smith interjected, "My name is Smith, and I am on an important mission for General Arnold. Here are my passports. We are on a business of public service of the highest importance, and you will be answerable for our detention for one moment."

The captain admonished the men to go no further, as they were approaching a no-man's-land controlled by neither the Americans nor the British. Roving gangs known as "cowboys" (loyalist-leaning thugs) fought for territory and loot against gangs known as the "skinners" (rebel-leaning thugs). Smith hesitated, unsure what to do. André wanted to proceed, but the captain suggested they stay and wait until morning. Reluctantly, the men went to a nearby farmhouse to spend the night.

Chapter 77

Tarrytown, NY - September 23, 1780

I t was a cool and foggy morning as they set out on the road before dawn.

Anxious to get going, André awakened before Smith and even helped the servant saddle the horses. Once moving, the major became more relaxed as they approached British lines. The group was, once again, stopped at an American checkpoint manned, by New York militia under the command of Captain Foote, who also allowed them to continue relying on my pass.

As the fog began to burn off, they turned off toward Pine's Bridge, where André saw an American coming toward him—Colonel Samuel Blachley Webb, who had been a prisoner in New York when André was there and likely knew his face. Webb seemed to be staring at André as they passed, but he rode on.

André began to converse freely with Smith as they discussed music, painting, and poetry. They stopped for breakfast at a farmhouse near Cat Hill, but Smith was afraid to go any further south toward British lines. He explained that André was only about two and a half miles from the nearest British outpost, then took his leave and headed to my headquarters to report to me. In fact, the nearest British were over fifteen miles away.

Still, the major should have had no trouble. If stopped by patriots, all he needed to do was to show the pass I had signed, and they would have let him through—as had already happened on numerous occasions. If stopped by loyalists, they would at worst take him into custody and bring him to a nearby British unit, thus safely returning him to the British lines. Either way, his success was inevitable.

He continued south through a nowhere land infested with loyalist cowboys and rebel skinners. About 9:30 a.m., he was just a half mile from Tarrytown and the safety of the British lines when he was stopped along the Old Post Road. Three men—John Paulding, David Williams, and Isaac Van Wart—crouched on the side of the road where a bridge crossed a small stream known as Clark's Kill, near a huge tulip tree. Whether these men were cowboys or skinners was unclear to André. He slowed his horse from a canter to a walk as he approached the trio blocking the road.

Quite reasonably, André believed that the leader of the three men, a giant twenty-two-year-old named John Paulding, was a loyalist, as he wore the green-and-red uniform of a Hessian Jaeger. André could not have known that Paulding had only escaped four days earlier from a British jail in New York and was still proudly wearing the uniform to advertise his escape to his comrades and perhaps entrap fools like the major.

His large hand reaching out and grabbing the bit of André's horse, Paulding intoned, "You are in a hurry. Where are you bound?"

Instead of showing the pass, which would have guaranteed his survival, André blurted out, "Gentlemen, I see you belong to our party," gesturing toward the tall man's Hessian coat.

Paulding responded evenly, "What party is that?"

"The lower party," André answered, meaning the lower or southern part of the state occupied by the British.

"We do. My dress shows that."

André said with relief, "Thank God, I am once more among friends. I am glad to see you. I am an officer in the British service. I have now been on a particular business in the country, and I hope you will not detain me."

The men stared up at André, saying nothing. André, perplexed by the silence and sensing danger, pulled out his gold watch, the sure sign of a British officer. "And for a token to let you know I am a gentleman . . ."

Paulding cut him off. "Get down."

André tried to take control. "I must warn you. You are interfering with General Clinton's business, Crown business . . ."

"Get down!" Paulding repeated with a voice tinged with ice. "We are not of the lower party. We are Americans. What is your name?"

André's face went pale, and he said as he dismounted, "God bless my soul. A body must do anything to get along nowadays." Trying to regain himself, he pulled out his pass and handed it to Paulding.

"The truth is, I am not a British officer. I said that because I thought you were British. That Hessian jacket you are wearing . . . I was just being careful, you understand. My name is Anderson. I am an American on an important errand for General Arnold at West Point."

After scanning the pass, Paulding answered politely, "Please don't be offended. We mean no harm, but there are bad people all around here—Tories and traitors. We have to be careful."

"Of course," André answered as he attempted to get back on his horse.

"Not yet, Mr. Anderson." Paulding pointed to the woods. "You need to come with us, here among these trees."

Now, panic bubbling in his voice, André responded, "You listen to me. General Arnold sent me to meet the American agent at Dobbs Ferry. You are headed for serious trouble if you don't let me continue on now!"

Without a word, Paulding nodded to his companions, who each took André by the arm and led him into a clump of trees. In a calm and professional voice, Paulding said, "Just a little search, Mr. Anderson, just to be sure. Please turn out your pockets." After looking at his pockets, Paulding directed his men to search the boots and britches.

André shouted angrily, but with increasing panic, "You are wasting your time. You are wasting your time!"

When nothing was found in his boots, Paulding had the men check his stockings. Van Wart pulled down the knee-length hose on the right leg and turned to Paulding. "There is something in this one."

Paulding instructed, "Try the other one."

Van Wart immediately held up more papers.

Looking at the documents, Paulding said to his men, "These are all about West Point—how many men, how many guns, and where. One is about meeting our generals . . ." Paulding now, eyes blazing, turned to André. With a tone that revealed a man comfortable with violence, he said, "This here paper mentions General Washington! Where did you get these papers?"

André stammered, "From a man I met on Pine's Ridge. I didn't know him. I am to deliver them to an agent at Dobbs Ferry."

Paulding now leaned toward André and growled, "This is not a pass from Arnold. It is a forgery, isn't it?"

Without meeting Paulding's eyes, André replied, "No."

Turning to his men, Paulding said, "This man is a spy! At least I think he is." Williams and Van Wart nodded in agreement. Paulding barked, "Get dressed. We will take him to the dragoons at North Castle. Let them figure it out."

Sighing heavily, André pleaded, "Gentlemen, I am certainly not a spy. I am delivering these papers back with some vital intelligence to—"

Paudling snapped, "Get dressed."

As he pulled on his shirt, André turned to Paulding. "I can't explain all this to you. It is a secret, but if you'll just let me ride off, you will be doing a great service for your country. When I reach where I am going, you will have a reward. A large reward, which I will send to any address you name."

Williams chuckled. "Will you give us your horse and saddle too? How big a reward? A hundred guineas?"

In desperation, André responded quickly, "Yes, yes, a hundred guineas. Sent anywhere you would like, but the horse I'll need to get where I am going. I'll leave it for you at Dobbs Ferry. I promise solemnly."

Nodding at Williams, Paulding ordered, "Tie his arms behind his back."

"All right! All right!" André pleaded. "Make it any sum, anything reasonable, say a thousand guineas! I'll write a note—one of you can take it to a spot in the city to a certain party, and he'll pay you the money. When the money gets here, you let me go."

"In the city? But you just said you were an American," Williams answered.

Desperate, André replied, "I am not allowed to explain any further. A thousand guineas! I'll give you an address."

"Sure," laughed Van Wart, "Then his friends will follow us back here and we will be done for!"

"A thousand guineas. Just send one man in and keep me here for you . . . All right, I'll make it five thousand . . ."

"Not for ten thousand," Paulding said quietly. "Put him on his horse and make sure the ropes are tight, boys."

After allowing André to put his clothes back on, the three sentries began the trek twelve miles north to the headquarters of Lieutenant Colonel John Jameson at North Castle, New York. As he was led away, André grumbled, "I would to God you had blown my brains out when you stopped me."

Chapter 78

Robinson House, West Point, NY –
September 23, 1780

Meanwhile, back at my home, at the evening meal of September 23, Joshua Smith arrived after dropping off André in the morning. I was desperate to know about the major's status. After Smith had briefed me privately in my study, I had little choice but to ask him to join us, despite the complaints of my aides. Unfortunately, he began boasting to the members of my staff what a great job he had done for me on a "secret mission."

Everyone stared at him in stunned silence. The conversation sputtered like a dying candle. Peggy broke the silence by asking for butter and was informed by a servant that there was no more.

I said with forced levity, "Bless me, I forgot the olive oil I bought in Philadelphia. It will do very well with salt fish." When the servant brought the oil, I commented, "That oil cost me eighty dollars."

Smith chuckled loudly. "You mean eighty pence."

Varick's face glowed red, outraged by the insult to the Colonies' worthless currency. He yelled, "You are mistaken!"

The table erupted in accusations, with Varick and Franks yelling at Smith. I attempted to calm my aides, who were clearly looking to provoke Smith into a confrontation. Peggy shrieked in desperation, asking them to stop. Everyone quieted down in response to Peggy's pleas. The rest of the meal was eaten in total silence, broken only by the sounds of chewing salted fish.

When the meal ended and Smith had left, I asked Franks and Varick into my office. I realized that if I was going to maintain an appearance of normalcy, I could not allow my military family to misbehave at the table.

To say nothing would be out of character. In any event, regardless of my future and planned actions, such behavior was intolerable. Thus, with genuine fury and frustration, I turned on Franks as the men entered my study. I slammed the desk. "By God, Franks, I have had enough of you. If I asked the devil himself to dine with us, then the gentlemen of my family should be civil!"

Franks did not back down. He leaned toward me and almost shouted, "If Smith had not been at your table, sir, I would have sent the bottle at his head."

Varick then tried to interject, with little enthusiasm. "General, the blame for any insult to Mr. Smith should not be placed at the feet of Mr. Franks, but rather at mine."

Before I could respond, Franks snapped, "I have observed, General, that of late, you view every part of my conduct with an eye of prejudice. I beg discharge from your family." With that, he bowed and walked out of the room.

Varick, now apparently emboldened by Franks's decision, turned on the offensive. "General, Mr. Smith is a damned rascal, a scoundrel, and a spy. You must guard your reputation from him. He is ungentlemanly to both you and Mrs. Arnold."

In a different situation, I might have reacted more strongly to the misbehavior of my two subordinates, but I needed to hold my temper, so I said in measured tones, "I am always grateful to be advised by gentlemen of my family, but I will not be dictated to by them. I believe I possess the prudence to evaluate the situation, and I am aware of circumstances of which you are not."

Varick bowed in acknowledgment and left the room. Within the hour, he submitted his resignation. I responded to both men that the entire matter would be put behind us and that I would have nothing further to do with Smith; that seemed to temporarily mollify them. I knew I did not have much time before things would be brought to a head.

As I would later learn, while I was enduring an acrimonious dinner, André was being delivered to the American post by his three captors. The commander, Colonel John Jameson, did not know what to do with the prisoner. The pass from me appeared genuine, but why would this man be heading for British territory with plans to West Point in his socks? Jameson was hesitant to accuse me of anything, but he couldn't let this prisoner go. He decided to send a notice to me that a prisoner had been captured with incriminating papers. He also sent the papers to George Washington, including the actual documents in André's possession and a description of the circumstances of his capture. Messengers rode through the night, one toward my headquarters and the other to find Washington.

André persisted in asserting that he was acting on my instructions and encouraged the hapless Colonel Jameson that he should be turned over to my custody, as I was the ranking military officer in the area. If this occurred, it would give us time to permit André to escape when he was delivered to me. The witless Jameson agreed and ordered André sent to me at Robinson House, along with a letter describing the circumstances of his capture.

Unfortunately, after André left camp under escort to be taken to my headquarters, Major Benjamin Tallmadge arrived at Jameson's camp. The twenty-six-year-old Tallmadge was the head of the American spy network and quickly realized that Anderson (a.k.a. André) must be a spy, and he suspected my involvement. I had previously written a letter to Tallmadge indicating that I expected John Anderson to come through the lines to see me on a private matter. Tallmadge convinced Jameson that it was a mistake to send "Mr. Anderson" to my headquarters, and ordered an express rider be sent to overtake André's party and return him to North Castle. Regrettably for me, Jameson acceded to Tallmadge's request, and André was brought back. Upon his return, the British major underwent close questioning from the able Mr. Tallmadge. He confessed his role as a British officer, but did not initially disclose my involvement.

I later learned that, in fact, Major Tallmadge had argued that not only should André/Anderson be returned to North Castle, but that I should be seized and held prisoner until General Washington arrived. The timid Jameson compromised by only ordering the recall of André. If Tallmadge had been listened to, I would have been held and captured with no chance of escape.

Chapter 79

North Castle, NY - September 24, 1780

The day began as it ended: with a steady rain that slackened only as darkness fell. André, recognizing that he would likely be treated as a spy, wrote a letter to Washington, explaining that he had been "betrayed" and placed in the "vile condition of an enemy in disguise within your post." Again, he did not disclose my identity.

The messenger seeking to find Washington had returned, unable to locate the commander. Jameson, now having a confession from André with the assistance of Tallmadge, included the confession in the packet to be sent to Washington, who was now believed to be somewhere in the New York highlands.

While I was fortunate the letters to Washington had been delayed, I was unlucky that the courier charged with delivering Jameson's initial letter to me at Robinson House had taken his time, deciding to wait until the morning of September 25 to deliver the letter. In an even more bizarre twist, as the letter was en route to me, Smith traveled up to Fishkill to have dinner with General Washington. Meanwhile, Varick and Franks were in open rebellion while I played for time, expecting the HMS *Vulture* and Washington to arrive and my trap to be sprung. I still had no idea André had been captured.

Chapter 80

Robinson House, West Point, NY –
September 25, 1780

M ajor Franks did not come to breakfast in protest, and Varick claimed a fever, staying in his room. Peggy proceeded with furious preparations for General Washington's arrival, anticipating his staff for breakfast. Captain Samuel Shaw and the Marquis de Lafayette's aide, James McHenry, carried word that the general would be late. Peggy, fatigued by her travels and preparations, decided to stay in our room with the baby and rest until Washington's arrival.

At 9:00 a.m., as I sat downstairs with Washington's aides, eating breakfast, a Lieutenant Solomon Allen, rain soaked and covered with mud, arrived with an express message from Colonel Jameson, in command of North Castle. Typically, Varick or Franks would have met the courier and reviewed the correspondence. Fate was kind to me, as my officers were both indisposed, and the message was brought to me at the table.

Sir,

I have sent Lieutenant Allen with a certain John Anderson taken going into New York. He had a pass signed with your name. He had a parcel of papers taken from under his stockings, which I think of a very dangerous tendency. The papers I have sent to General Washington.

I tried with all my might to control the blood rushing to my face. I feared everyone in the room would hear my heart pounding as I absorbed the implications of the letter, which began to rattle in my quivering hand. In an instant, I realized I had to leave the house. I stood and excused myself with more haste and less poise than I would have wished.

I moved to the bottom of the stairs and was met by Franks coming out of his room. I snapped, "Mrs. Arnold is ill. Please call for Dr. Eustis and get my horse ready. Please inform General Washington that I am going to West Point to inspect and will return in about an hour."

Franks began to protest, but I interrupted, "You have my orders, sir. Off you go." With that, I pointed toward the back of the house. When he was out of sight, I went out the front door and stood there for a second to compose myself.

I turned and went back inside, limping up to Peggy's bedroom. She was asleep. I strode across the room and shook her awake with an unaccustomed vigor. As she startled to consciousness, my face inches from hers, I blurted in a panicked whisper, "Washington is on his way. André has been captured." Her eyes became as wide as saucers as she absorbed what I was saying.

Stepping away, I began grabbing incriminating letters and documents and throwing them into the fireplace. I kept talking as I lit the fire: "Somehow the plans I gave to André are in the process of being delivered to Washington." Peggy merely stared at me, mouth agape. Not waiting for a response, I shuffled around the room, pulling items for my journey and tossing papers into the flames. "Washington will be here any moment, and I will be arrested as a traitor." In response, Peggy, who had sat up in bed as I spoke, flopped back onto her pillow, covering her face with her hands.

It was ten o'clock in the morning, and at that exact moment, there was a knock on the door. Peggy and I froze, our eyes locked. From behind the door, Franks said loudly, "His Excellency is nigh at hand."

I turned to Peggy and said, "I must go. You must tell Washington you know nothing."

There was no time for discussion, no chance for an emotional embrace or separation. She merely nodded in agreement, and I turned and left.

When I got outside, given Franks's insolence, I was not surprised that a horse was not ready. Tied up in front was the bedraggled gelding that Lieutenant Allen had ridden to deliver the message to me. Without hesitating, I untied the horse and swung up onto the saddle with more grace than I had been able to muster since Saratoga. I rode the steed at a full gallop to the river. Blocking my way were four men of Washington's personal guard. I was about to reach for my pistol when the men saluted and stepped out of my way. Giving them a hurried, and I hoped casual, salute, I proceeded on.

Rather than taking the gradual switchbacks down to the river, I went headlong down a precipice straight to the river and my barge. At the river, I jumped off my horse, again without the usual stab in my leg. My eight bargemen were standing about. I barked, "Up you go, boys. We are going downriver, and be quick about it." They started moving, but not fast enough, so I added, "I'll give two gallons of rum if you can get me to Stony Point and back in time to meet General Washington."

Once we were out into the open water, I checked my satchel to ensure that my pistols were fully loaded and ready to be used in case I met any resistance. While they were furiously pulling on the oars, I said, "See here, I have an important mission for General Washington. We need to get out to the *Vulture*. Once I meet with them, I will go back to General Washington and update him. Put your backs into it, and you will be rewarded as promised and have the thanks of both myself and His Excellency." I felt the pleasing surge as the boat picked up speed in response.

It is difficult, even now, to fully articulate the tide of emotions that engulfed me as we moved down the river. My brilliant plan, which would have led not only to the fall of West Point, but also to the capture of the leadership of the Continental Army, lay in ruins.

I did not know, or at that time care, about the fate of the supercilious Major André. With each stroke down the river, I was aware that my prospects of being greeted as a hero by either the British or the loyalists were being left in my wake. Running from a fight was never part of my countenance, and leaving Peggy and our child behind was heartbreaking, but I saw no rational alternative. My only recourse was to hold the British to their promises of funds and a command. If I could not savor victory, at least I could enjoy the taste of sweet revenge.

I waved a handkerchief, and we were allowed to approach the HMS *Vulture*. As the captain and Colonel Robinson greeted me, my bargemen were suddenly and keenly aware of my changed allegiance. I turned to them with the confidence of a soon-to-be-minted British general. "If you join me, my lads, I will make sergeants and corporals of you all. And for you, James, my coxswain, I will do something more."

The coxswain's response was disappointing and immediate: "No, sir! One coat is enough for me to wear at a time." The other men nodded in agreement.

Irritated, I responded, "So be it—you are now prisoners of the Crown, who I am sure will not treat you as gently as I have."

Robinson shuffled uncomfortably and leaned over, whispering something in the captain's ear. The captain nodded, and to my surprise intoned, "You boys are released on parole." He flicked his hand toward the boat. "Off you go. Make it quick."

The men scuttled over the gunwales, and the sound of rowing could be heard as I turned back toward the captain, who had already walked away. Only Robinson remained.

As I tried to control my irritation at the release of the prisoners, Robinson directed me to the captain's cabin, where we could converse in private. We sat across from each other at the small, empty table. I noted Robinson had dispensed with the usual pleasantries of offering me food or drink. "What do you have to report, Mr. Arnold?"

I stiffened at the lack of military title; nevertheless, I continued evenly, "André has been captured."

At that moment, the captain entered the cabin. We both stood, and Robinson snapped, "By God, he's botched it. They have André."

The captain looked at me, wide eyed. "How can that be? We returned to our original position after your troops opened fire on us!"

Remaining calm, I said evenly, "Obviously, those were not my troops. I would not have authorized the firing. Nevertheless, seeing that your ship had retreated under fire, I didn't have confidence that you would return." Their rudeness, in my view, justified my implicit attack on their lack of courage for withdrawing.

"Well, where in God's name is he? You didn't bring him back to the ship, so what the bloody hell did you do with him?" a glowering Robinson replied.

We were all now standing feet apart, none of us inclined to back down. What infuriated me was the notion that I was somehow responsible for their spy André. "First of all, André was the one who arranged the meeting. Second, he could not return to the ship when it became clear that you did not have the will to withstand fire. Thus, as a result of your actions, we were forced to improvise an overland route to British lines. Finally, through his own incompetence, he was apparently captured."

Robinson, with fear in his eyes, said in almost a whisper, "Please tell me he was in uniform when he was captured."

Are you a complete fool? Do you think someone in a British uniform can simply pass through American territory unmolested? Not hiding my frustration with the stupidity of the question, I answered, "Of course not. He would not get two feet in a British uniform. We gave him an alternate disguise with impeccable papers to get him through the lines. Evidently, André still managed to get himself caught."

With that, Robinson collapsed into a chair, his head in his hands. "Dear God . . . he was out of uniform. Was he captured with anything? Any evidence?"

"I gave him the plans to West Point."

Removing his hands from his eyes, the captain and Robinson exchanged a look as Robinson murmured, "They are going to hang him. We must inform General Clinton immediately." They nodded and left me standing alone in the cabin.

Peggy and the newspapers described what happened after I left. Thirty minutes after I exited my headquarters, Washington arrived. After being told I had just left for West Point, he and his staff decided to have a quick breakfast without calling for my wife; then Washington was rowed across the river to the fort with his staff (except for Colonel Hamilton, who stayed to do paperwork), to complete his inspection and meet me. To the general's surprise, there was no formal greeting for him when he arrived at the fort; there should have been a thirteen-gun salute and soldiers standing at attention. Washington later said that "the impropriety of Arnold's conduct when he knew that I was to be there struck me very forcibly, and my mind misgave me, but I was not the least idea of the real cause."

Colonel Lamb noticed the commander in chief standing at the muddy riverbank unattended. When he ran down and bowed. Washington demanded, "Is General Arnold not here?"

Lamb responded diffidently, "No, sir, he has not been here in two days, nor have I heard from him in that time."

Washington responded, "This is extraordinary." Exchanging puzzled glances with Knox and Lafayette, he continued, "We were told he crossed the river and we should find him here. However, our visit must not be in vain. Since we have come, although unexpectedly, we must look around a little to see in what state things are with you."

As Washington walked through West Point, looking for me and inspecting the fort, he discovered my handiwork. Over the next two hours of inspection, Washington saw that the barracks were falling down, the earthworks were half completed, the guns were neglected, and the soldiers were out of position. The fort was ripe for attack.

Peggy later told me of her brave actions that followed at our home while Washington was at the fort. Richard Varick, still claiming a fever, was resting on a settee downstairs when suddenly he heard a shriek from Peggy's room. When he arrived upstairs, he saw her raving and distracted, her hair disheveled about her neck. Two maids were attempting to return her to her room. She was returned to the bed wearing only a thin nightgown.

Seizing Varick's hands, with wild eyes, she exclaimed, "Colonel Varick, have you ordered my child to be killed?" Peggy jumped out of bed and fell on her knees while begging him to spare the baby. Varick unsuccessfully attempted to raise her to her feet. She cried, "I have been left alone," and "I do not have a friend left here."

Varick answered, "You are not alone. Franks is returning with the doctor. General Arnold will soon return from West Point with General Washington."

Screaming with her hands in her hair, she shrieked, "No, General Arnold will never return! He is gone. He is gone forever!" She pointed to the ceiling. "There, there, there, the spirits have carried him up there, they have put hot irons on my head." Peggy reluctantly allowed them to return her to her bed.

Hamilton, working on Washington's correspondence downstairs, could not help but hear the screams of my distraught wife. When he went upstairs to look, he found her clutching her baby and accusing everyone of trying to murder her child. Hamilton went downstairs and returned to his work, but was concerned about Peggy's behavior.

At approximately 4:00 p.m., Washington returned to Robinson House from his inspection. He retired to a bedroom for an afternoon repose.

Shortly afterward, Colonel Jameson's messenger arrived with the long-delayed letter to Washington concerning the capture of André. As was his duty, Hamilton opened the packet and realized its significance, especially in light of my behavior and absence. He knocked on Washington's door and brought in the papers before the half-dressed and bootless commander in chief. Washington had Hamilton summon the Marquis de Lafayette. As Lafayette entered the room, the shocked general asked, "Whom can we trust now?"

Washington ordered the young Alexander Hamilton and James McHenry to go after me. The rest of the staff began to see to the defenses of the fort.

They quickly realized I had escaped by boat. With me out of reach, Washington took command and redeployed his men, anticipating a British attack. He called for the best soldiers from New Jersey, Connecticut, and Massachusetts and put Nathanael Greene in command of West Point.

When Peggy heard Washington's voice downstairs, she left her room and repeated her hysterics in the hall, claiming there was an iron on her head and only General Washington could remove it. Varick responded by returning her to the bedroom and bringing Washington, saying, "Here is General Washington."

Once again, as the general entered the room, the profoundly disheveled Peggy screamed, "This is not General Washington."

Varick responded gently, "I can assure you, Mrs. Arnold, this is indeed His Excellency."

She shrieked again, "No, this is not General Washington! That is the man who is going to assist Colonel Varick in killing my child!" Washington stood stiffly at the edge of the bed, trying to understand the chaos spinning around him as Alexander Hamilton tried to comfort Peggy. She was dressed in a loose-fitting nightgown, which increased Washington's discomfort. He ordered a blanket brought to cover her. Washington, Lafayette, and Hamilton left the room, convinced, along with my aide Varick, that Peggy knew nothing of my treachery.

As the story began to unfold, on Washington's orders, Joshua Hett Smith was torn from his bed by soldiers, dragged at bayonet point to Robinson House, and tossed at the feet of the general. Smith was frozen by Washington's steely gray eyes. His Excellency growled, "You are charged with the blackest treason against any citizen of the United States."

Confused and terrified, Smith sputtered, "Treason? Treason for what?"

Washington erupted, "Sir, do you know that Arnold has fled? The Mr. Anderson, whom you piloted through our lines proves to be Major John André, the Adjutant-General of the British Army, now our prisoner?"

Groveling at Washington's feet, Smith pleaded, "Your Excellency, I did what General Arnold told me to do. He said he was acting on behalf of the Cause. I am a loyal citizen. I am no friend to the British. I would never have done otherwise, but in my nation's service. You must believe me, sir." Grabbing Washington's ankles, he continued, "He said it was a secret mission that you endorsed and would lead to peace. I never knew who Mr. Anderson was. I beg you, sir."

Unmoved, Washington pressed, "Unless you confess who your accomplices are, I shall suspend you from a tree!"

Smith's penchant for gab suddenly served him well. He explained in great detail everything that happened, and it quickly became evident that he was merely a pawn in my grand plan. Nevertheless, Washington had him thrown in jail in the interests of prudence.

Chapter 81

HMS Vulture, Hudson River, NY –
September 25, 1780

As I headed south, I wrote Washington,

Sir:

The heart which is conscious of its own rectitude cannot attempt to palliate a step which the world may censure as wrong. I have ever acted from a principle of love to my country, since the commencement of the present unhappy contest between Great Britain and the colonies. The same principle of love to my country actuates my present conduct, however it may appear inconsistent to the world, who very seldom judge right any man's action.

I have no favor to ask for myself. I have too often experienced the ingratitude of my country to attempt it. But from the known humanity of your Excellency, I am induced to ask your protection for Mrs. Arnold from every insult and injury that a mistaken vengeance of my country may expose her to. It ought to fall only on me; she is as good and as innocent as an angel, and is incapable of doing wrong. I beg she be permitted to return to her friends in Philadelphia, or come to me, as she may choose. From your Excellency, I have no fears on her account, that she may suffer from the mistaken fury of the country.

I have to request the enclosed letter may be delivered to Mrs. Arnold, and she be permitted to write to me.

I have also to ask that my clothes and baggage, which are of little consequence, may be sent to me. If required, their value shall be paid in money. I have the honor to be with great regard and esteem, your Excellency's most obedient humble servant.

Benedict Arnold N.B.

In justice to gentlemen of my family, Colonel Varick and Major Franks, I think myself in honor bound to declare that they, as well as Joshua Smith, Esq. (who I know is suspected) are totally ignorant of any transactions of mine that they had reason to believe were injurious to the public.

Smith had been my dupe. I had tricked Varick and Franks. Nevertheless, I did not want my actions to fall unfairly on them. I had proceeded on an honorable course to end the senseless conflict. While they viewed matters otherwise, I knew that if I did not make an attempt to clear their names, they would experience the same unfair treatment at the hands of the radicals as I had faced by Reed and others. I hoped my letter would do more for them than anyone had ever done for me. I did not mention André in the letter, as I still prayed somehow his identity might not be fully known and some unknown positive result might be derived.

When the HMS *Vulture* docked in New York, I exited in the uniform of a British general. Rather than men flocking to my banner as I planned, the newspapers were filled with the capture of Major André and his treatment. Indeed, General Clinton was frantic to see the return of his young aide. He seemed uninterested in speaking with me, except to inquire as to André's condition. I trod through the streets, ignored by civilians and British alike. I came to realize that if André died, my plan would die with him.

I initially had absolutely no fear that André would be executed. Prisoners were regularly exchanged, and Clinton held many important rebels at equal or greater rank than the foolish young major. However, the Americans were clear that André would suffer the same fate as Nathan

Hale. Any man caught out of uniform and holding incriminating documents behind enemy lines would be hung.

I wrote a letter to Sir Henry Clinton explaining what had occurred:

> Thinking it much properer that he should return by land, I directed him to make use of the feigned name of John Anderson, under which he had, by my direction, come on shore ... he was invited to a conversation with me, for which I sent him a flag of truce, and finally gave him passports for his safe return to your Excellency.

From my purely military sense, I was perplexed by everyone's fixation on André. Even if no exchange occurred and André was, albeit regrettably, hanged, the British had exchanged a major general for a mere major. The British were still "ahead." This was, after all, war.

While, under the Articles of War, Washington could have hanged André outright as a spy, he instead ordered a trial be conducted before a panel of high-ranking generals. The papers reported the court-martial was started and completed on September 29 at the Old Dutch Church in Tappan, New York.

André made little attempt to save himself and admitted that he was meeting with me to obtain confidential information behind enemy lines. His main argument was that he was a spy by accident and had always intended to meet me on the HMS *Vulture*. He had crossed enemy lines at my insistence and traveled in disguise against his will. While the judges were charmed by him, they were also unanimous in their decision: "Major André, adjutant general of the British Army, ought to be considered a spy from the enemy, and that, agreeable to the law and the usage of nations, it is their opinion he ought to suffer death."

Washington announced the next day that André would die by hanging at five o'clock in the evening on October 1. Recognizing his fate was sealed, André asked Washington that he die by firing squad rather than a hanging. The former was a soldier's method, the latter a criminal's.

I do not doubt that Clinton desperately wanted to trade me for

André, but he knew if he did so, the British would lose all credibility with any Americans who deserted or switched to the British side. At Clinton's urging, I wrote a somewhat threatening letter to General Washington:

> If, after this just and candid representation of Major André's case, the board of general officers adhere to their former opinion, I shall suppose it dictated by passion and resentment. And if that gentleman should suffer the severity of their sentence, I shall think myself bound by every tie of duty and honor to retaliate on such unhappy persons of your army as may fall within my power. I have further to observe that forty of the principal inhabitants of South Carolina have justly forfeited their lives (for conspiring with patriots). Clinton could not in justice extend his mercy to them any longer if Major André suffers, which in all probability will open a scene of blood at which humanity will revolt.
>
> Suffer not an unjust sentence to touch the life of Major André. But if this warning should be disregarded, and he should suffer, I can call heaven and earth to witness that your Excellency will be justly answerable for the torrent of blood that may be spilled in consequence.

The decision to kill André was merely a final vindictive step of men who, by their actions, had driven me from the army. To address any concern that I was placing my own life above André's, I proposed to Clinton that I be permitted to go and surrender myself in exchange for the major. His reply was, "Your proposal, sir, does you great honor, but if André was my own brother, I could not agree to it." Nevertheless, I was scorned and unfairly held responsible for both André's death and Washington's cruel treatment of him.

André wrote extensive letters to family and friends. The entire unhappy event was covered in detail in the New York papers. Washington did agree to delay the execution to noon on October 2. That morning, André's servant, Pierre Raune, arrived under a flag of truce to bring André a clean British uniform. André had breakfast brought to him from General Washington's table. He then shaved, tied a ribbon in his long black hair, and put on his full regimentals—a gold-laced scarlet coat of a British staff officer, faced with the popinjay green of the Fifty-Fourth Foot, with buff breeches, a waistcoat, and highly polished boots.

Turning to his guards, he smiled and said, "I am ready at any moment, gentlemen." As he exited the stone house where he was held, a fife and drum played the Funeral March. Turning to an American officer, André said with practiced élan, "Your music is excellent."

Washington did not attend the execution in apparent fear that he would reconsider his decision to order André hanged. André's only falter occurred when he saw the gallows instead of a firing squad and said, "I am reconciled to my death, but I detest the mode! I have a mother and sisters who will be very much mortified."

He was then asked whether he had any last words. André said to the large crowd in a strong and clear voice, "I have nothing more to say, gentlemen, but this: I pray you to bear me witness that I meet my fate like a brave man." The hangman then reached to put the rope over André's head—before he could do so, the major grabbed it, placed it around his neck, and drew the knot tight. He then reached into his pocket, took a handkerchief, and tied it over his own eyes. He took a full breath and nodded that he was ready, murmuring, "It will be but a momentary pang." When the wagon moved from under his feet, he died instantly, his body swinging in a broad arc as the crowd gave out a collective gasp.

It was reported that when the news reached Henry Clinton, he moaned, "The horrid deed is done. Washington has committed premeditated murder, he must answer for the dreadful consequences. I feel beyond words to describe André's death, but I cannot reproach myself in the least."

All I can say is that André was a fool, but he died well.

EPILOGUE

London, England - January 6, 1801

A man is still young when he feels like a boy and a man at the same time. The weight of responsibility and time presses out the boy, leaving behind the husk that is an old man. For some, that happens early. For a lucky few, it never happens. For me, it was the moment André's neck snapped. At that instant, the future, with its youthful optimism, was squeezed out of me, leaving only the bitter man that I have become.

Despite André's death, I did not give up. I had formulated a brilliant plan to cut New England off from the rest of the colonies, capture Washington, and turn the tide of the rebellion. What quickly became clear was that both the Colonies and the British were against me. Everyone was lamenting the execution of the bumbling André and blaming me for his folly.

I was still entitled to my promised compensation. The British had implicitly agreed to a minimum indemnity amount. Clinton arranged for me to receive only £6,000 and expenses. I resolved to bombard him with requests for full payment and reports on how to attack American forces. Clinton, whenever I was in his presence, refused to meet my eye. It was apparent that I was a constant reminder of both the plot's failure and the death of his favorite adjutant.

My fellow British officers were never friendly and failed to treat me with due respect as a new "general." I was also told that many British officers refused to serve under my command. I did manage to put together a semblance of a loyalist unit. I presented plans to General Clinton, but I was never given a truly independent command. I also wrote letters to the king presenting my strategies and demands for payments; both were ignored.

Peggy was forced to leave Philadelphia. My sister Hannah took my seven-year-old son, Henry, back to my New Haven home, where my other boys, Benedict (thirteen) and Richard (ten) waited in fear. They too were driven out. We were all ultimately reunited in New York.

On November 30, my oldest son, Benedict, was commissioned as an ensign in the Sixteenth Regiment of the British Army. Richard and Henry were also added to the rolls of my provincial regiment as lieutenants, entitling them to payment even though they were not in uniform yet and far too young to fight.

Washington and his spies tried to have me kidnapped, but I avoided their clutches. I led an expedition up the James River to Richmond, forcing Thomas Jefferson to abandon the city, where I captured large numbers of supplies and munitions and destroyed the rest.

I returned to my home state of Connecticut, where I raided New London, a town not far from my birthplace. I gave strict orders that only military targets were to be attacked. My men faced stiff resistance and suffered high casualties in the assault. Enraged loyalist soldiers technically under my command killed surrendering rebels, and much of the town was burned to the ground, for which I was unfairly blamed. I returned to New York, where I was criticized by rebels for the death and destruction and by General Clinton for the significant British casualties.

Notwithstanding my unhappy military service, our life in New York was pleasant, and Peggy gave birth to our second child. In December of 1781, after the defeat of General Cornwallis, I was recalled to London. I took the children, Peggy, and Hannah to our new life in England.

Initially, Peggy and I received a warm welcome by the king and Secretary of State Germain. We were invited as honored guests to Whitehall and the Court of St. James. Peggy was a palace favorite. However, with the victory of the Whigs in 1783, the war was abandoned, and I fell out of favor. To add insult to injury, I never received the full amount of money I was promised.

Once in England, I changed my family motto from *Mihi Gloria Cessum* ("The glory is mine to the end") to *Nil Desperandum* ("Never despair"). Despite the many challenges I faced, I have lived by that motto to this day.

London, England – January 6, 1801

I attempted to obtain a position in India. I engaged in land speculation in Canada. I tried shipping in the West Indies. I even acted as a privateer during the French Revolution. But here I sit, most of my fortune lost. My reputation sullied, I am subject to abuse by unscrupulous men given license to mistreat, trick, or betray me. The law and society have offered me neither protection nor solace.

As I ponder my life in the fullness of time, I am convinced that honor left me no alternatives in service of my country. If a bullet had finished me at Quebec or Saratoga, I would have died a hero. If my plan had succeeded at West Point, I would have been lauded as the savior of my country and awarded a royal estate and title. I know I lived more honorably than my father, yet fate left for me the cruelest of honorable paths.

AUTHOR'S NOTE

B enedict Arnold did more for the American Cause than perhaps any soldier except George Washington. How then do we understand his treason?

Arnold's journey to treachery is the result of an almost inconceivable chain of tragic events. For it is truly a *tragic* story.

Certainly, his inability to get along with others contributed mightily to his challenges, but he was also tremendously unlucky. Benefactors he admired fell out of power (Schuyler) or died (Montgomery and Warren). Arnold was cursed to be surrounded by some of the most disreputable scoundrels of the Revolution, including Wilkinson, Brown, Gates, and most of all Joseph Reed. Arnold recognized these men as dishonorable miscreants, yet his basic flaw was his inability to hide his disdain or refrain from provoking them.

Arnold also did not try to adapt to the political reality of the American Revolution. Everything was, and would always remain, *personal*. With this in mind, Washington's assignment of Arnold to Philadelphia was one of the worst decisions in the entire war. General Washington dropped his most impatient and impolitic general into a swirling cesspool led by Joseph Reed. Almost any other general would have been a better choice than Arnold.

Crucially, he met the *perfect* woman to encourage him to become a traitor. Peggy Shippen Arnold was one of the few women in America who could connect her husband with the British spymaster John André. Put another way, if Arnold had arrived in Philadelphia and fallen in love with a rebel's daughter, she would not have encouraged treachery and might have counseled patience. Even more significantly, if loyalist Elizabeth DeBlois in Boston had reciprocated his affections, he might not have accepted an assignment in Philadelphia and would have avoided Reed altogether. At the very least, Elizabeth DeBlois would not have had connections with André, and thus Arnold's frustrations could not have been easily directed toward betraying his country.

Was Peggy Arnold the cause of Arnold's treachery? Absolutely not. However, fate led him to a woman uniquely positioned to encourage and actively assist in his treason.

Finally, he was in physical agony and financially vulnerable when he came under the unrelenting attack of radicals who hated him, not only because of his own actions and temperament, but because of a larger political struggle within the Revolution itself. When he was given an opportunity to strike a blow against all those who had attacked and abandoned him, he followed his natural aggression by contacting André and sealing his fate. His failure was merely the last chapter that doomed him and saved the Revolution.

BIOGRAPHICAL SUMMARIES

Ethan Allen [January 21, 1738–February 12, 1789]: Leader of the Green Mountain Boys and one of the early founders of the state of Vermont. He was captured by the British in Montreal in September 1775; held on Royal Navy ships, he was paroled in New York City in a 1778 prisoner exchange. Upon his release, he returned to Vermont and lobbied for the state's recognition and separation from the state of New York. Between 1780 and 1783, he and his brother Ira participated in negotiations with the governor of Quebec about establishing Vermont as a new British province. While he is often considered treasonous for his actions, no formal charges were ever laid against him.

John André [May 2, 1751–October 2, 1780]: Major in the British Army and head of the secret service in America during the American Revolution. The son of wealthy Huguenot parents, he was educated in both Westminster and Geneva. After entering the Seventh Royal Fusiliers in 1774 as a lieutenant, he served in the Battles of Monmouth, Brandywine, and Germantown, and he had won a promotion to major by the time of his dealings with Arnold. He was assigned to Sir Henry Clinton's staff and became his chief spymaster. Following his execution, his remains were returned to England in 1821 and given a place of honor in Poet's Corner in Westminster Abbey.

Hannah Arnold [December 9, 1742–August 11, 1803]: Never married. She followed Arnold to England and later to Canada, where she died on Prince Edward Island.

Margaret "Peggy" Shippen Arnold [July 11, 1760–August 24, 1804]: Traveled with Arnold to London at the end of 1786, and followed him to St. John in Canada in 1787. After multiple business failures, they were forced to return to London in 1791. After Arnold's death on June 14, 1801, she paid off his creditors and saw her sons rise to respectable military commands. Of her seven children with Benedict Arnold, five survived to adulthood; George Arnold became a lieutenant colonel in the Second Bengal Calvary, while William became a captain in the Ninth Queen's Lancers.

John Brown [October 18, 1744–October 19, 1780]: Attended Yale College and studied law before the Revolution. He was a member of the Massachusetts Committee of Correspondence and was sent to Montreal to meet with Canadians interested in joining the Revolution. He participated with Ethan Allen and Benedict Arnold in the taking of Fort Ticonderoga and was a supporter of Allen. Allen asked Brown to carry news of the victory to the Continental Congress;

Brown deliberately understated Arnold's involvement. He made a weak effort at the diversionary attack at the Battle of Quebec, failing to support Montgomery's and Arnold's attacks. Brown's personal attacks in a pamphlet against Arnold were widely rejected by Congress, but they had a continuing adverse impact on Arnold through the balance of the war. Brown was killed in action on his thirty-sixth birthday at the Battle of Klock's Field in Mohawk Valley.

John "Gentlemen Johnny" Burgoyne [February 24, 1722–August 4, 1792]: General in the British Army. He fought in the Seven Years' War and was commander in chief in Ireland. A member of the House of Commons from 1761 to 1792, he fought in Portugal, and is most notable for his defeat at the Battle of Saratoga on August 17, 1777. An accomplished playwright, he famously eloped with Lady Charlotte Stanley without her family's permission. Burgoyne died unexpectedly at his home in Mayfair.

Aaron Burr [February 6, 1756–September 14, 1836]: Served bravely as a captain on Benedict Arnold's trek to Quebec. He was at General Richard Montgomery's side when Montgomery was killed during the Battle of Quebec. Served on George Washington's staff, but left Washington's family to serve under General Israel Putnam. He fought bravely at the Battle of Manhattan. Promoted to lieutenant colonel in July 1777 and served at Valley Forge. Fought at the Battle of Monmouth. As a result of failing health, resigned from the army in 1779. Practiced law in New York City and served in New York State Assembly. Acted as state attorney general and was elected as a senator from New York. Elected as third vice president of the United States. After killing Alexander Hamilton in a duel on July 11, 1804, he journeyed west into present-day Louisiana. He was later accused of conspiring with the Spanish and was held for trial on treason. He was found not guilty, although it was not for lack of effort by then President Thomas Jefferson and his lackey, James Wilkinson. He died financially ruined and a political pariah in a boarding house in 1836.

Guy Carleton [September 3, 1724–November 10, 1808]: Born to an Ulster Protestant military family in Ireland. Fought at the Battle of Culloden during the Jacobite uprising, and throughout the wars of succession in Flanders and Germany. He was assigned to Canada under Major General James Wolfe and served bravely at the Battle of the Plains of Abraham, where he received a head wound; he also fought in France and Havana, and was named governor of Quebec during the American Revolution. Following his successful defense of Quebec from Arnold and Montgomery's attack, in recognition of his bravery, he was named the first Baron of Dorchester and served in the House of Lords. In 1782, after the defeat of Cornwallis in Yorktown, Carleton was named the commander in chief in North America. He returned to England, and died in 1808.

Henry Clinton [April 16, 1730–December 23, 1795]: Spent part of his early life in America while his father was governor of New York. He fought in the Seven Years' War in Germany and was severely wounded. At the beginning of the American Revolution, he was sent to support General Thomas Gage in Boston. His forces led the assault on the American fortifications on Breed's and Bunker Hills. After being sent to the Carolinas, he then participated in the main assault on New York in August 1776. After Burgoyne's defeat at the Battle of Saratoga, General Howe resigned him as commander in chief in America; Clinton was formally appointed to the post on February 4, 1778, and tried to both defeat the American forces and engage in peace overtures. He appointed Major John André as his chief of intelligence and aide-de-camp. After the surrender of Cornwallis, Clinton was replaced as commander in chief by Guy Carleton. Clinton returned to England and took a seat in Parliament. He was appointed the governor of Gibraltar, but died before he could assume the post. He was buried with honors at St. George's Chapel in Windsor Castle.

James Cogswell [1720–1807]: Graduated from Yale College in the class of 1742. He became the pastor of the church in Canterbury, Connecticut, married Martha Lathrop, and started a school for boys. All three of Cogswell's sons fought for the Americans in the Revolutionary War.

Silas Deane [January 4, 1738–September 23, 1789]: Obtained a full scholarship at Yale and graduated in 1758. Practiced law in Hartford, Connecticut, before establishing a thriving business as a merchant. Attended the first Continental Congress. He was elected to the Connecticut House of Representatives and was the first American envoy sent to France. While Deane defended claims by Arthur Lee and others that he had improperly sought reimbursement for expenses incurred, Arthur Lee's brothers, Richard Henry Lee and Francis Lightfoot Lee, denounced him. He was financially ruined through the course of the Revolution, and accused of conspiring with the British during the war. He was forced to leave America and spent the rest of his life in England. While he remained friends with Arnold in London after the war, Deane could not be seen in public with him, as that would destroy his hope of returning to America to clear his name. In 1789, he planned to return to America to regain his fortune and reputation, but died on board the ship.

Henry Dearborn [February 23, 1751–June 6, 1829]: Was captured at the Battle of Quebec; later, he was exchanged and served on Washington's staff. Fought bravely at the Battle of Saratoga and was present at the surrender at Yorktown. He served as Thomas Jefferson's secretary of war, and was a commanding general in the War of 1812. He was an original member of the Society of the Cincinnati.

Elizabeth DeBlois [Unknown]: After rejecting Arnold's advances, she planned to marry Martin Brimmer, an apothecary apprentice. Her family disapproved of the match, and her grandfather cut her out of his will. Ultimately, her mother prevented the wedding from occurring. Betsy DeBlois continued to reject Arnold's advances. She never married, and lived into her eighties. She was restored to her rightful place in her grandfather's will after her breakup with Martin Brimmer.

Roger Enos [1729–October 6, 1808]: Fought in the French and Indian War, where he rose to regimental adjutant in the Vermont militia. He was commissioned a lieutenant colonel in Connecticut's Twenty-Second Regiment at the outset of the Revolution and took part in the Battle of Bunker Hill. He joined Benedict Arnold's expedition to Quebec as the commander of the rear guard. Upon his unauthorized return, without Arnold's permission, he was acquitted, resigned his commission, and joined the Vermont militia. By the end of the Revolutionary War, he was a major general for the Vermont militia. He served in the Vermont House of Representatives and was a trustee of the University of Vermont.

David Franks [1740–1793]: At the outbreak of the Revolution, Franks was living in Quebec with his parents. He was president of the Spanish and Portuguese Synagogue of Montreal, the oldest Jewish congregation in Canada. When Benedict Arnold and Richard Montgomery invaded Canada in 1775, he joined the American Cause. He was made a major and was assigned to Arnold's staff as an aide-de-camp. Following the defeat in Canada, he joined the Continental Army and served until October 1777. Because he spoke French, he was assigned as liaison officer to Admiral Charles Henri Hector d'Estaing, commanding French naval forces supporting America. Arnold convinced him to join him at West Point. Franks was cleared of all charges relating to Arnold's treason. As a sign of his innocence, Washington had him added to his military family. Nevertheless, Franks requested and received an official report clearing his name. He was then made a confidential courier to John Jay in Madrid and Benjamin Franklin in Paris. Franks acted as vice counsel in Marseilles. Despite his long service, the Jeffersonian Republicans attacked him for his association with Arnold. He succumbed to yellow fever in 1793 in Philadelphia, dying in poverty.

Horatio Gates [July 26, 1727–April 10, 1806]: Born in England, Gates served in the British Army during both the War of Austrian Succession and the French and Indian War. He moved to Virginia and became acquainted with Washington. Upon commencement of the Revolution, Washington made him his adjutant general in 1775. He was assigned to the command of the Northern Department in 1777 shortly before the Battle of Saratoga. After Saratoga, Gates was implicated in the "Conway Cabal," an aborted attempt to replace Washington with himself. In 1780, he took command of the Southern Department, but was removed after the defeat at the Battle of Camden. He retired to Virginia after the war, but decided to free his slaves and move to New York, where he was elected to the state legislature. In a bizarre twist, after Gates's wife died in 1783, he proposed marriage to Janet Montgomery, the widow of General Richard Montgomery, but she refused.

Alexander Hamilton [January 11, 1755–July 12, 1804]: Born out of wedlock in Nevis, British Leeward Islands. Was given a scholarship by local philanthropists and sent to King's College in New York. Joined the militia during the Revolution. Became a senior aide to George Washington and his chief aide-de-camp; fought bravely at the Battle of Yorktown. Hamilton resigned his commission in March 1782, and passed the legal bar examination in just six months. He participated in drafting the Articles of Confederation, but was critical of the document from the beginning. While in New York, he founded the Bank of New York and helped restore King's College as Columbia College. He served as an assemblyman to the New York Legislature and was a delegate to the Constitutional Convention— he supported the Constitution and drafted fifty-one of the eighty-five Federalist Papers to support its adoption. He served as Washington's first secretary of the treasury and rebuilt the American credit system. Forced to resign after the Reynolds affair, he returned to private law practice. Hamilton played a crucial role in supporting Jefferson's election as president when a tie occurred, choosing Jefferson over Burr. This simmering resentment and rivalry ultimately led to the fatal duel with Burr in Weehawken, New Jersey.

Moses Hazen [June 1, 1733–February 5, 1803]: Fought in the French and Indian War with Rogers' Rangers. Was commissioned in the British Army before the end of the war and retired at half pay in Montreal. Joined the Continental Army in 1775 as part of the Battle of Quebec. Hazen led his own regiment, the Second Canadian, throughout the war, seeing action in Philadelphia and Yorktown in 1781. He was repeatedly cleared of Arnold's charges of impropriety; his counter-charges against Arnold were also dismissed. After the war, he was unable to return to Quebec, but was given a land grant in New York. He was an original member of the Rhode Island chapter of the Society of the Cincinnati, but continued to be litigious until his death.

Benjamin Hinman [January 22, 1719–March 22, 1810]: Fought as a colonel at Ticonderoga, Crown Point, and Quebec in the French and Indian War. At the end of hostilities, he was elected to the Connecticut General Assembly and continued to hold a commission as a lieutenant colonel until the beginning of the Revolutionary War. He was an active member of the Committees of Correspondence. The State of Connecticut ordered him to Fort Ticonderoga to take command from Benedict Arnold. He fought at the Battle of Saratoga in October 1777. He was elected to the Connecticut legislature throughout the balance of the war and was a member of Connecticut's delegation to the Constitutional Convention.

Robert Howe [1732–December 14, 1786]: From one of the prominent families of North Carolina; served in the militia in the French and Indian War. He was promoted to brigadier general at the beginning of the Revolution and fought for the Southern Department. Confrontational, he fought duels and was a known womanizer. After being stripped of his command in the Southern Department, he was sent to New York under Washington. He was on the panel for the court-martial of Benedict Arnold and sat as a judge at the court-martial of John André. He assisted in putting down mutinies in Pennsylvania and New Jersey late in the war, but died en route to the North Carolina House of Commons in 1786.

William Howe [August 10, 1729–July 12, 1814]: Fought in the War of Austrian Succession and the Seven Years' War. Fought in the capture of Quebec in 1759. Led the American troops at the Battle of Bunker Hill, taking command of all British forces in America from Thomas Gage in September 1775. He captured both New York and Philadelphia. After his successes in Philadelphia and New York, he was knighted in 1776. After he resigned, he returned to England, where he sat in the House of Commons and inherited a hereditary title as Viscount Howe. He resigned as a lieutenant general in 1803 as a result of poor health.

Henry Knox [July 25, 1750–October 25, 1806]: Boston bookseller. He joined the local artillery company at the outbreak of the war and quickly rose to chief artillery officer of the Continental Army. He accompanied Washington through most of his campaigns. Following adoption of the Constitution, he became secretary of war and retired to business life in 1795. He died at age fifty-six after swallowing a chicken bone that lodged in his throat and caused a fatal infection.

Tadeusz (also spelled "Thaddeus") Kościuszko [February 1746–October 15, 1817]: Born in Lithuania, then part of the Polish-Lithuanian Commonwealth. He graduated from the Royal Military Academy in Warsaw and was trained as an engineer and mathematician, then studied engineering and artillery in Paris. In 1776, he moved to North America and joined the American Revolution as a colonel in the Continental Army. He designed fortifications at West Point and Bemis Heights at Saratoga. He was promoted to brigadier general; after his return to Poland in 1784, he was commissioned a major general. He fought in the Polish-Russian War of 1792 and commanded an uprising against the Polish Empire in 1794 until he was captured. He was pardoned by the czar in 1796, emigrated to America, and wrote a will dedicating his assets to the education and freedom of US slaves. He returned to Europe and lived in Switzerland until his death in 1817. A prominent statue to him can be viewed in Lafayette Park.

John Lamb [January 1, 1735–May 31, 1800]: The son of a convicted burglar who was exiled to the colonies, he became a successful wine merchant in New York. He was an active member of the Sons of Liberty and joined the Revolution as soon as it began. He served under General Richard Montgomery and Benedict Arnold in the Battle of Quebec, where he was severely wounded and lost an eye. After he was exchanged, he returned to Connecticut and was appointed as a colonel in the Second Continental Artillery. He fought bravely with Arnold in 1777 in the battles surrounding Danbury, Connecticut, and was again wounded at the Battle of Compo Hill, overlooking the Long Island Sound. He commanded artillery at West Point, where he resisted Arnold's efforts to weaken the defenses. He served at the siege of Yorktown and was the officer of the day when Washington fired the first American cannon to start the siege. He was breveted a brigadier general in September 1783. He was appointed the collector of the port of New York and retained the post under Washington. He was dismissed by President John Adams in 1797 and accused of defrauding the government. He died in poverty on May 31, 1800.

Marquis de Lafayette [September 6, 1757–May 20, 1834]: Born to an aristocratic French family in South Central France. Moved to America at age nineteen and was made a major general. He was wounded during the Battle of Brandywine, and also fought at Barren Hill and Monmouth and in Rhode Island. He was present with Washington at West Point at the time of Arnold's treason. He returned to France to support the American Cause, then came back to America in 1780 and helped block Cornwallis's forces, leading to the victory at the Battle of York-town. He then again returned to France and was a member of the Estates General in 1789. He helped write the Declaration of the Rights of Man and of the Citizen with the assistance of Thomas Jefferson. After the storming of the Bastille on July 4, 1789, he was appointed commander in chief of France's national guard, but radical factions ordered his arrest, and he fled to the Netherlands. He was captured and held in prison for more than five years, but returned to France after Napoléon Bonaparte secured his release. After the Bourbon Restoration, he became a liberal member of the Chamber of Deputies. In 1824, at President James Monroe's invitation, he visited all twenty-four states. He supported the restoration of Louis Philippe I as king, but turned against him when he became autocratic. He was buried in Paris, but with soil brought over from Bunker Hill.

Daniel Lathrop [1712–1782]: Graduated from Yale College in 1733 and traveled to London to study medicine. He returned to Norwich to open an apothecary shop and was joined by his brother Joshua after his graduation from Yale in 1743. Arnold apprenticed for the Lathrop brothers from 1754–1761 and impressed them with his skill. They assisted him in starting a new business in New Haven. There is no indication in the record that Arnold had any significant contact with the Lathrops following his apprenticeship.

Allen MacLean [1710–December 10, 1783]: Born as the sixth baronet in Scotland, he served initially as a lieutenant in the Scottish Highlanders. In 1759, he fought under Major General James Wolfe. He then fought at Forts Ticonderoga and Niagara. After the Seven Years' War, he returned to England. By the time of the American Revolution, he was a colonel, and was sent to the garrison in Quebec to resist Benedict Arnold. He played a central role in the successful defense of the city from Arnold's siege and attack. After the Battle of Quebec, he was stationed at Fort Niagara and participated in several other battles protecting Canada. He was promoted to brigadier general and left North America. He returned to Scotland and died without a male heir.

Return Jonathan Meigs [1740–January 28, 1823]: After the Battles of Lexington and Concord, he joined the Second Connecticut Regiment and served under Benedict Arnold. He wrote a famous journal of the Quebec campaign over the Maine mountains. He was captured in Quebec and paroled. He then continued service for the State of Connecticut. He was appointed as a colonel, served with distinction in Long Island, and was awarded a sword by Congress for his heroism. After the war, he was appointed the surveyor of the Ohio Territory and acted as an Indian agent for the federal government in Tennessee. He died of pneumonia while visiting an Indian chief. His son, Return J. Meigs, Jr. was elected as the governor of Ohio and later a US senator.

Richard Montgomery [December 2, 1738–December 31, 1775]: Raised in Ireland, he studied at Trinity College in Dublin and joined the British Army. After fighting in the French and Indian War and then the Caribbean, he returned to England. In 1773, he went back to America and began farming. When the Revolutionary War began, he was elected to the New York Provincial Congress and commissioned a brigadier general in the Continental Army. He led the invasion of Canada and captured Fort St. John, then Montreal. He led the attack on Quebec City and was killed in the battle. He was the first great American general to die in the Revolution. He was ultimately disinterred from Quebec to be reburied in St. Paul's Chapel in Manhattan in an elaborate sculptured monument. He has been a frequent subject of statues, monuments, city names, and ships throughout American history.

Daniel Morgan [1735–July 6, 1802]: Served as a teamster in the French and Indian War and received five hundred lashes for attacking an officer, which resulted in a lifelong loathing of British authority. A devout Christian, he returned to Virginia to get married and farm in peace. When the American Revolution began, he created a rifle company from Virginia for which he was named commander. Known as "Morgan's Riflemen," they went to Boston after Lexington and Concord with their unique long rifles and frontier garb. Capable of shooting British officers at great range, they were an instant sensation. Washington disliked their lack of discipline and wanted to get them out of Boston. Morgan was sent with Benedict Arnold to attack Quebec. Rather than surrender to the British, he handed his sword to a French priest and was taken into custody. He was exchanged in January 1777. He fought at the Battle of Saratoga and played a pivotal role in both the Battles of Freeman's Farm and Bemis Heights. Repeatedly passed over for promotion despite his bravery, he resigned his commission and returned to Winchester in 1779. He refused to serve under Gates. When Gates fell out of favor, Morgan reentered service at the request of Nathanael Greene. He defeated the infamous Lieutenant Colonel Banastre (the "Butcher") Tarleton at the Cowpens, South Carolina, in 1781 in a brilliant double envelopment. Tarleton's forces were almost wiped out, although Tarleton escaped with his life. As a reward for his service, Morgan was given lands in Virginia. Because of failing health, he was forced to again resign. He was an original member of the Society of the Cincinnati in the State of Virginia. He was elected to the US House of Representatives, where he served a single term.

Edward Mott [June 18, 1734–January 31, 1804]: Born in New Jersey. Served in the New Jersey militia and was on the Committees of Correspondence. He was dispatched by the State of Connecticut to assist Ethan Allen in the taking of Fort Ticonderoga. Arnold and Mott met at Castleton, Vermont, and subsequently proceeded to the storming of Fort Ticonderoga. After the taking of Ticonderoga, he returned to New York and New Jersey, fighting in various skirmishes, and ultimately fought in the Battle of Trenton, crossing the Delaware with Washington and acting as a guide. He continued to fight in the New Jersey area through the balance of the war, fighting at the Battles of Monmouth and Springfield. By the end of the war, he became a recruiting officer. Following the war, he was a justice of the peace.

Eleazer Oswald [1750–September 30, 1795]: Born in England, he moved to America and became an apprentice printer and distiller. At the beginning of the war, he joined the Cause and participated in Arnold's expedition to Quebec. He was captured. After a prisoner exchange, he was promoted to lieutenant colonel artillery. He fought bravely during the Danbury raid in April 1777, as well as the Battle of Monmouth. After the war, he was involved in publishing and journalism in Baltimore, Philadelphia, and New York. In 1792, he went to France to join the French Revolution and served as an artillery colonel. He returned to New York in 1795 and died in an outbreak of yellow fever.

Joseph Reed [August 27, 1741–March 5, 1785]: Born in New Jersey, he received a bachelor's degree from the College of New Jersey (now Princeton University). He traveled to England and studied law in London. He met his wife and ultimately returned to America to start a successful law practice. He joined Washington's military family as an aide-de-camp with the rank of colonel. Washington discovered that Reed had been conspiring with his political rival, General Charles Lee, and was openly expressing doubts about Washington's decision-making. Reed returned to Philadelphia after his falling-out with Washington and was elected the president of the Supreme Executive Council of Pennsylvania. It was during this time that he had his fights with Benedict Arnold, who was the military commander of Philadelphia following the British exodus from the city. Reed supported and signed the Articles of Confederation on behalf of Pennsylvania. After Reed's tenure as president of Philadelphia ended in 1781, he returned to the practice of law. He was elected to Congress, but declined because of deteriorating health.

Beverly Robinson [January 11, 1721–April 9, 1792]: Born in Virginia, he moved his substantial businesses to New York, where there were large inherited landhold-ings held by his wife. He initially tried to remain uninvolved when the Revolution started, but ultimately entered service with the British, joining the Loyal Ameri-can Regiment in 1777, located in New York. He was forced to abandon his home in Hudson Heights. He participated actively in battles throughout the Hudson River Valley, and played a central role in acting as a contact for Benedict Arnold's treason. When the war ended, he lost all his lands in New York and was forced to move to England, receiving only a small portion of the value of the estates lost.

Barrimore Matthew "Barry" St. Leger [1737–1789]: Born to a wealthy Huguenot family in Ireland, he was educated at Eton Colege in Cambridge. He joined the British Army as an ensign and was raised to lieutenant colonel. In 1777, he was given command of the western branch of General Burgoyne's invasion force and was made a brevet brigadier. He was outmaneuvered by Benedict Arnold at Fort Stanwix and rejoined Burgoyne's forces. After the Revolution, he briefly served in Canada. He gave up his commission in 1785 as a result of diminishing health, and returned to England.

Philip Schuyler [November 20, 1733–November 18, 1804]: Born in Albany, New York, to a prosperous and aristocratic family. Schuyler fought in the French and Indian War, was elected to the New York General Assembly, and attended the first Continental Congress. As head of the Continental Army's Northern Depart-ment, he planned both the invasion of Quebec as well as the fortifications and defense for the Battle of Saratoga. He was replaced on the eve of battle by General Horatio Gates. Schuyler resigned from the army in 1779. He served in the New York State Senate, and was also New York State surveyor general. He was elected the US senator from New York to the first United States Congress, but was later defeated by Aaron Burr. He was re-elected to the US Senate in 1797, but resigned because of ill health.

Isaac Senter [1755–1799]: Born in New Hampshire, he studied medicine under Dr. Thomas Moffat. He joined Arnold's quest to Quebec; after the defeat there, he acted as a general surgeon for the Rhode Island militia until 1781. He estab-lished a private practice in Rhode Island after the war. He was the president of the Rhode Island chapter of the Society of the Cincinnati.

Edward Shippen IV [February 16, 1729–April 15, 1806]: From a long line of wealthy Philadelphia leaders. He studied law in London and was appointed a judge of the

Admiralty Court. He was elected the Philadelphia's common counsel and was appointed as the chief clerk of the Supreme Court and a member of the Pennsylvania Provincial Council. He tried to stay neutral as the Revolution started. He ultimately embraced the Revolution, albeit tepidly, especially after the treachery of Benedict Arnold. He was given an honorary degree by the University of Pennsylvania. He served as chief justice of the Pennsylvania Supreme Court, but was impeached and did not return.

Joshua Hett Smith [1736–1811]: He came from a long line of lawyers. His father and brother were loyalists, but Joshua was an active patriot and a member of the New York Provincial Congress. He served in the militia and did work with General Robert Howe, the American general in charge of West Point. When Arnold succeeded Howe, he used Smith's innocence and naivete against him. Although acquitted of treason relating to Arnold, Smith was imprisoned by New York as a suspected loyalist. He escaped dressed as a woman and joined the British. He went to England in 1783, but returned to the United States in 1801, although all his property had been confiscated, and he had lost most of his fortune. He returned to his legal practice for the last years of his life.

Joseph Stansbury [1742–1809]: Son of a London haberdasher, he emigrated to America in 1767, opening a china store. He signed an oath of allegiance to the Cause after the British left. He carried Arnold's messages over the lines to New York. Following the disclosure of Arnold's treason, he was permitted to go over to the British lines. Clinton allowed him quarters, rations, and a stipend of £2 per day in reward for his loyalty and services. In 1783, he went to Nova Scotia and then England. He was disallowed a claim for compensation. In 1785, he returned to Philadelphia and resumed his business, but did not prosper. In 1793, he moved to New York and acted as a secretary of an insurance company.

Benjamin Tallmadge [February 25, 1754–March 7, 1835]: Born in New York and Yale educated. He initially served as a schoolmaster until the Revolution. He was secretly made Washington's director of military intelligence, and successfully ran Washington's Culper Spy Ring. After he discovered Arnold's treachery, he continued to serve in Washington's headquarters until the army was disbanded in 1783. He was admitted as an original member of the Society of the Cincinnati in Connecticut and was breveted to the rank of lieutenant colonel. He was appointed postmaster of Litchfield, Connecticut, and served in the US House of Representatives.

John Thomas [1724–June 2, 1776]: Was born in Marshfield, Massachusetts, and studied medicine. During King George's War, he was appointed surgeon in Annapolis Royal in Nova Scotia with the rank of lieutenant. By the time of the French and Indian War, he had risen to colonel in the militia. After the war, he started a medical practice. At the time of the Revolution, he created a regiment of volunteers in Massachusetts. He was appointed brigadier in the Continental Army. He led a division to fortify Dorchester Heights, overlooking Boston, with guns brought from Fort Ticonderoga, forcing the British evacuation on March 17, 1776. After General Montgomery was killed, Thomas was given command over Canada. He arrived as the army was collapsing and overrun with smallpox. He caught small-pox and died during the retreat up the Richelieu River, near Chambly.

Richard Varick [March 15, 1753–July 30, 1831]: Born in New Jersey, he came from an aristocratic line of early Dutch settlers in New York. He enrolled in King's College (present-day Columbia College) in 1771, and passed the New York bar before his graduation. After eight months of private practice, he joined the Revo-lution and was appointed secretary to General Philip Schuyler. Schuyler ordered him to assist Arnold in obtaining material and personnel to build his navy to fight at Valcour Island. Because he was loyal to Schuyler, Varick was viewed as an enemy of General Gates. After the Battle of Saratoga, he returned to his law practice, but was encouraged by Benedict Arnold to be an aide-de-camp at West Point. He was cleared of all wrongdoing relating to Arnold's treachery, and was appointed by Washington to be his recording secretary at headquarters. The Varick transcriptions—some forty-four volumes compiled over two years—are a monument to his ability and skill. Washington called him a man of "fidelity, skill and indefatigable industry." After the war, he became the recorder of New York, the speaker of the assembly, attorney general, and mayor of New York City from 1789 to 1801. He was the founder of the American Bible Society and president of the New York chapter of the Society of the Cincinnati.

George Washington [February 22, 1732–December 14, 1799]: Colonel in charge of the Virginia militia in the French and Indian War. Elected to the House of Bur-gesses. Hero of the Battle of the Monongahela. Commander in chief of American forces in the Revolutionary War. First president of the Constituational Conven-tion. First president of the United States, and "Father of His Country."

James Wilkinson [March 24, 1757–December 28, 1825]: Arnold's aide-de-camp during the Canadian campaign. Later became Gates's aide-de-camp. Breveted a brigadier general following the Battle of Saratoga in 1777, he played a major role in the "Conway Cabal" to replace George Washington with Horatio Gates. Gates ultimately forced Wilkinson to resign in March 1778. Wilkinson testified at Burr's trial, after his vice presidency, that Burr was seeking to take control of portions of the Louisiana Territory. Wilkinson's perjurious testimony turned on a letter which he wrote himself, claiming a conspiracy led by Burr. Theodore Roosevelt described Wilkinson, saying, "In all our history, there is no more despicable character."

David Wooster [March 13, 1711–May 2, 1777]: Born in Connecticut. Graduated from Yale College. Served in the French and Indian War, during which he was promoted to colonel; fought in both the Battle of Carillon and the successful taking of Ticonderoga in 1759. When the Revolution started, he was in charge of the militia in New Haven. He resisted Arnold's attempts to march to Boston with supplies held in Connecticut. He ultimately backed down in the face of Arnold and his mob. He was given the title of major general of the Connecticut militia and later was a brigadier in the Continental Army under Philip Schuyler and Richard Montgomery. He assumed command of all forces in Quebec following Montgomery's death. He was later relieved by General John Thomas. Wooster returned to Connecticut and assumed command over the militia. When the Danbury raid occurred in April 1777, Wooster and Arnold attacked the British. Wooster was killed in battle along with his son.

BIBLIOGRAPHY

Arnold, Isaac. *The Life of Benedict Arnold: His Patriotism and His Treason* (HVA Press, 2019; originally published in 1880).

Bakeless, John. *Turncoats, Traitors & Heroes: Espionage in the American Revolution* (Da Capo Press, 1998).

Bellico, Russell. *Sails and Steam in the Mountains: A Maritime and Military History of Lake George and Lake Champlain* (Purple Mountain Press, 2001).

Boylan, Brian. *Benedict Arnold: The Dark Eagle* (W.W. Norton & Company, 1973).

Brandt, Claire. *The Man in the Mirror: A Life of Benedict Arnold* (Random House, 1994).

Brookhiser, Richard. *George Washington on Leadership* (Basic Books, 2008).

Brumwell, Stephen. *Turncoat: Benedict Arnold and the Crisis of American Liberty* (Yale University Press, 2018).

Carso, Brian, Jr. *"Whom Can We Trust Now?": The Meaning of Treason in the United States, from the Revolution through the Civil War* (Lexington Books, 2006).

Chernow, Ron. *Alexander Hamilton* (Penguin Press, 2004).

Chernow, Ron. *Washington: A Life* (Penguin Press, 2010).

Cushman, Paul. *Richard Varick: A Forgotten Founding Father—Revolutionary War Soldier, Federalist Politician, and Mayor of New York* (Modern Memoirs Publishing, 2010).

Daigler, Kenneth. *Spies, Patriots, and Traitors: American Intelligence in the Revolutionary War* (Georgetown University Press, 2014).

Darley, Stephen. *The Battle of Valcour Island: The Participants and Vessels of Benedict Arnold's 1776 Defense of Lake Champlain* (Darley, 2013).

Ellis, Joseph. *His Excellency: George Washington* (Vintage Books, 2004).

Flexner, James Thomas. *Washington: The Indispensable Man* (Back Bay Books, 1969).

Flexner, James Thomas. *The Traitor and the Spy: Benedict Arnold and John André* (Syracuse University Press, 1975).

Jacob, Mark and Stephen Case. *Treacherous Beauty: Peggy Shippen, the Woman behind Benedict Arnold's Plot to Betray America* (Lyons Press, 2012).

Kelly, Jack. *Valcour: The 1776 Campaign That Saved the Cause of Liberty* (St. Martin's Press, 2021).

Koke, Richard. *Accomplice in Treason: Joshua Hett Smith and the Arnold Conspiracy* (The New York Historical Society, 1973).

Lea, Russell. *A Hero and a Spy: The Revolutionary War Correspondence of Benedict Arnold* (Heritage Books, 2008).

Lefkowitz, Arthur. *Benedict Arnold's Army: The 1775 American Invasion of Canada during the Revolutionary War* (Savas Beatie, 2008).

Lengel, Edward. *General George Washington: A Military Life* (Random House, 2007).

Lundeberg, Philip. *The Gunboat Philadelphia and the Defense of Lake Champlain in 1776* (Smithsonian Institution, revised and expanded 1995).

Lynch, Wayne. "Arnold in Command at Bemis Heights?" *Journal of the American Revolution* (November 14, 2013).

Lynch, Wayne. "Debating Arnold's Role at Freeman's Farm," *Journal of the American Revolution* (September 12, 2013).

Lynch, Wayne. "Grading British General Benedict Arnold," *Journal of the American Revolution* (August 2, 2013).

Malcolm, Joyce Lee. *The Tragedy of Benedict Arnold: An American Life* (Pegasus Books, 2018).

Martin, James Kirby. "Benedict Arnold: Natural Born Military Genius," *The Journal of the American Revolution* (March 14, 2016).

Martin, James Kirby. *Benedict Arnold, Revolutionary Hero: An American Warrior Reconsidered* (New York University Press, 1997).

Meigs, Return Jonathan. *Journal of the Expedition against Quebec: Under Command of Col. Benedict Arnold, in the Year 1775* (reprinted by Wentworth Press from private printing in 1864).

Morpurgo, J. E. *Treason at West Point: The Arnold-André Conspiracy* (Mason/Charter Publishing, Inc., 1975).

Murphy, Jim. *The Real Benedict Arnold* (Clarion Books, 2007).

Nelson, James. *Benedict Arnold's Navy: The Ragtag Fleet That Lost the Battle of Lake Champlain but Won the American Revolution* (McGraw-Hill, 2006).

Palmer, Dave. *George Washington and Benedict Arnold: A Tale of Two Patriots* (Regnery Publishing, 2006).

Pearson, Michael. *Those Damned Rebels: The American Revolution as Seen Through British Eyes* (Da Capo Press, 1972).

Philbrick, Nathaniel. *Valiant Ambition: George Washington, Benedict Arnold, and the Fate of the American Revolution* (Viking, 2016).

Randall, Willard S. *Benedict Arnold: Patriot and Traitor* (Quill/William Morrow, 1990).

Randall, Willard S. *George Washington: A Life* (Holt & Company, 1997).

Ronald, D.A.B. *The Life of John André: The Redcoat Who Turned Benedict Arnold* (Casemate Publishers, 2019).

Sale, Richard. *Traitors: The Worst Acts of Treason in American History from Benedict Arnold to Robert Hanssen* (The Barkley Publishing Group, 2003).

Sarbin, Theodore, Ralph Carney, and Carson Eoyang. *Citizen Espionage: Studies in Trust and Betrayal* (Praeger Publishers, 1994).

Sheinkin, Steve. *The Notorious Benedict Arnold: A True Story of Adventure, Heroism, & Treachery* (Roaring Brook Press, 2010).

Thompson, Ray. *Benedict Arnold in Philadelphia* (Bicentennial Press, 1975).

Trees, Andy. "Benedict Arnold, John André and His Three Yeoman Captors: A Sentimental Journey or American Virtue Defined," 35 *Early American Literature* 246–278 (University of North Carolina Press, 2000).

Van Doren, Carl. *Secret History of the American Revolution* (Haddon Craftsmen, 1941).

Van Vlack, Milton. *Silas Deane: Revolutionary War Diplomat and Politician* (McFarland, 2013).

Walsh, John. *The Execution of Major Andre* (Pallgrave, 2001).

Wilson, Barry. *Benedict Arnold: A Traitor in Our Midst* (McGill-Queen's University Press, 2001).

Zambone, Albert. *Daniel Morgan: A Revolutionary Life* (Westholme Publishing, 2018).

Zoller, Greg. *Benedict Arnold, the Fighting General: For the Love of My Country* (Greg Zoller, 2020).

EXTENDED AUTHOR'S NOTES

Prologue

Arnold never wrote his personal history, and no diary exists. Indeed, Peggy Shippen burned most of his and their private letters after his death.

Chapter 1

Historians universally describe the duel with Captain Croskie as having occurred in a port in the "Bay of Honduras." In maps of the period, this is an area bordered by the east side of the Yucatán Peninsula and Belize, with Honduras to the south. The story widely recounted the duel occurring on a nearby island. Belize Town was founded in 1638 and was a central trading post for the English as a source of mahogany (a product we know Arnold shipped). While technically Spanish territory, it was dominated by British shipping. It is also one of the few British ports with easily accessible nearby islands. Based upon the foregoing, I have selected it as the likely location of the duel.

Chapter 2

Arnold is described as being of middling height, which at that time would have been approximately five feet five inches tall. Others have described him as a head taller than average. Most say he was not exceptionally tall, but was powerfully built.

Some authors have recounted stories of bad behavior by Arnold as a youth. Indeed, early biographies describe Arnold's "earliest amusements" as snatching baby birds from their nests in order to maim and mangle them, while also strewing broken glass in a nearby schoolyard so children would cut their feet coming in and out of school.[1] Arnold is also described as leading a gang of other dissolute young men, who absconded with gunpowder and fired cannons without permission, and went into a waterfront shop, stealing barrels to make a bonfire. He is also cited as picking a fight with the larger and stronger constable.[2]

---

1 *See* Malcolm, *The Tragedy of Benedict Arnold* xiii, citing Jared Sparks, *The Life and Treason of Benedict Arnold* (1835); *see* Carso Jr., *"Whom Can We Trust Now?"*, 150–51 and 156–58 (author opines that these stories were a cautionary tale to children to behave or "end up like Benedict Arnold").

2 *See e.g.* Randall, *Patriot and Traitor*, 29; Flexner, *The Traitor and the Spy*, 7.

Many recent Arnold biographers question these stories of bad behavior by the young Arnold: "Just about every one of these stories was invented after Arnold had turned traitor and fled the country, mostly by people who openly disliked the man. The truth is that we have almost no confirmed details about his childhood or what he was really like."[3] The reconsideration of these after-the-fact attacks on Arnold's childhood behavior began with a book by his relative, Isaac Arnold, in 1880.[4]

Many biographers also present an unflattering portrayal of Benedict Arnold during the French and Indian War. In particular, they assert that Arnold repeatedly abandoned the Lathrops without permission and in turn deserted his post once he arrived with the army.[5] Once again, these stories may be apocryphal, invented after Benedict's treachery, foreshadowing his later misdeeds, or the result of simple errors in the enlistment rolls. For example, there was an individual named "Benedick" who may have been confused with Benedict Arnold.[6] Professor Martin, and other historians, take issue with the after-the-fact and unsupported assertion of Arnold's misdeeds during the war.[7] Regardless, it is inconsistent with his attitude during his tenure with the Lathrops to desert them, and flies in the face of their later generosity.

Chapter 4

Here again, unsubstantiated stories about Arnold have become part of his biographical history. One tale involves Hannah being courted by a French dancing (or dueling) master. The story goes that Arnold disliked the suitor and drove him off with the assistance of his friend, even shooting at him to dissuade his advances.[8] Some stories even have Arnold later dueling with the suitor in the West Indies and wounding him.[9] This story was based upon "after-the-fact" claims by locals who wanted to portray Arnold in the worst possible light following his treason, and lack any contemporaneous historical support.[10]

Post-treason statements need to be taken with a grain of salt; however, it does

---

3 Murphy, *The Real Benedict Arnold*, 9.

4 *See* Arnold, *The Life of Benedict Arnold*, 21.

5 *See* Randall, *Patriot and Traitor*, 32–33; Van Dorn, *Secret History of the American Revolution*, 145; Wilson, *A Traitor in Our Midst*, 6; Arnold, *The Life of Benedict Arnold*, 24; Lea, *A Hero and a Spy*, 3.

6 *See* Murphy, *The Real Benedict Arnold*, 18–19.

7 *See* Martin, *Benedict Arnold, Revolutionary Hero*, 27–29; citing Martin, "Benedict Arnold: Natural Born Military Genius"; *see also* Brumwell, *Turncoat*, 25; Palmer, *George Washington and Benedict Arnold*, 40; Flexner, *The Traitor and the Spy*, 7–8; cf. Malcolm, *The Tragedy of Benedict Arnold*, 34.

8 *See* Malcolm, *Tragedy*, 50; Morpurgo, *Treason at West Point*, 54; Flexner, *The Traitor and the Spy*, 12; Jacob and Case, *Treacherous Beauty*, 59; Sale, *Traitors*, 20; Lea, *A Hero and a Spy*, 4.

9 *See e.g.* Randall, *Patriot and Traitor*, 40.

10 *See* Murphy, *The Real Benedict Arnold*, 24–25; Arnold, *The Life of Benedict Arnold*, 27.

seem clear that Arnold had a reputation for cheating "every man with whom he had any dealings."[11]

There are no surviving records demonstrating an ongoing relationship between the Lathrops and Arnold following his indenture. As was the case for many people, following his treason, it is likely the Lathrops would have burned all correspondence and disclaimed any relationship. Nevertheless, the lack of any indication of connection is further evidence of Arnold's failure to establish and maintain meaningful connections with people, resulting in social isolation.

Chapter 5

The duel in Belize is completely consistent with the rules for gentlemanly comportment in existence at the time.[12] Croskie was not Arnold's only duel. Arnold brought a defamation lawsuit against a Captain Fobes, who spread a rumor that he had fought a duel with a man named Brookman over a prostitute and/or a claim that he had venereal disease. Arnold likely dueled with Brookman, but it certainly did not relate to the disposition of a prostitute, and there is no indication he had venereal disease.[13]

His willingness to stand and confront those who slandered him, as well as face men on the field of honor, improved both his standing and his reputation as a brave and honorable man. At least one historian posits that this pattern of personal attacks against Arnold may stem from "a quick temper, and a sea captain's sense of entitlement."[14] Regardless of the cause, this unfortunate pattern would continue throughout Arnold's entire life.

Chapter 6

Arnold's first wife was named Margaret and also went by "Peggy." To avoid confusion, I have only referred to his first wife as "Margaret."

We do not have any paintings or descriptions of Arnold's first wife. However, paintings of Peggy Shippen Arnold show she is full-figured. I have taken the liberty of describing his first wife, Margaret Mansfield Arnold, as having the opposite physique.

Post-treason accusations included assertions that Arnold impregnated Mansfield, forcing a "shotgun" marriage. The timing of their first son's birth belies this scurrilous accusation.[15] Arnold and Margaret do appear to have had a loveless marriage; or at the very least, Margaret did not write Arnold as he begged her to do.

---

11 *See* Brumwell, *Turncoat*, 34–35.

12 *See* Randall, *Patriot and Traitor*, 44–45.

13 *See* Palmer, *George Washington and Benedict Arnold*, 61–62; Murphy, *The Real Benedict Arnold*, 37–38.

14 Murphy, *The Real Benedict Arnold*, 39.

15 *See* Brumwell, *Turncoat*, 29–30.

Chapter 8

It is more likely than not that Deane and Arnold were also accompanied by Roger Sherman and Colonel Eliphalet Dyer on the carriage ride to Philadelphia.

The *Oxford English Dictionary* cites the first use of *yin and yang* as 1671. It is very likely, and indeed possible, that a merchant and intellectual like Deane would have been aware of the term.

Arnold saw the Revolution as an opportunity to restore his family's tarnished reputation and obtain personal glory. In fact, it was the worst thing that could have happened to him. Indeed, as one historian noted, "In virtually any other era, Benedict Arnold would have continued to prosper at the trading business he had clearly mastered. He would have accumulated a fortune and probably donated enough to have public buildings, institutions of higher learning, or possibly even a city named after him."[16]

Chapter 12

Historians widely report that Arnold was given £100 in cash.[17] There is a great deal of crossover between the Continental currency in dollars and British pounds throughout the Revolution. Wherever possible, the specific nature of the currency that was described in the historical record is used.

Fay's would later become known as the "Catamount Tavern" after a displayed stuffed mountain lion.[18]

Chapter 13

Arnold and John Brown were likely related and may have known each other. However, nothing in their interactions indicates anything but immediate hostility.

Chapter 15

The exact verbiage of the interchange between Allen and the commander of Fort Ticonderoga varies from author to author and source to source, but all agree on the basic storyline.[19] At least one author contends the profane Allen said something more akin to, "Come down here, you damned old rat!"[20] While the specific colorful

---

16 Wilson, *A Traitor in our Midst*, 16–17.

17 *See* Randall, *Patriot and Traitor*, 86.

18 *See* Nelson, *Benedict Arnold's Navy*, 31.

19 *See generally* Flexner, *The Traitor and the Spy*, 45–46; *see* Nelson, *Benedict Arnold's Navy*, 33–34.

20 Palmer, *A Tale of Two Patriots*, 89; Malcolm, *The Tragedy of Benedict Arnold*, 90–91; Lea, *A Hero and a Spy*, 19.

language of Allen's purported statements is in doubt, all agree that Arnold behaved in a more "gentile manner."

A review of the correspondence at this time does demonstrate how utterly dishonorable Ethan Allen was in the aftermath of the taking of the fort. In a letter to a friend on May 11, 1775, Allen admits that "Colonel Arnold entered the fortress with me side-by-side." Yet, in reports to the newspapers in Massachusetts and to Congress, no mention is made at all of Arnold's involvement. Indeed, Colonel James Easton, Allen's ally, wrote an article in the *New England Chronicle* which actually inserts Easton into every action at the taking of Fort Ticonderoga that was performed by Arnold. Easton does not mention Arnold at all.[21]

Chapter 16

Most authors describe the sloop (renamed the *Enterprise*) located in St. John as the HMS *Betsey*[22] or the HMS *Betsy*.[23] Other authors call it the HMS *George*[24] or HMS *George III*.[25]

Despite Arnold's kindness to Allen when they met on the lake and his willingness to assist Allen in returning to Fort Ticonderoga, Allen nevertheless always blamed Arnold for his failure and hardship in the attack on St. John. Mott, Easton, and Brown all backed up Allen's false assertions.[26]

Arthur Lefkowitz correctly notes, "It is amazing how quickly Arnold managed to estrange himself from officers."[27] Easton, Mott, and Brown all loathed Arnold.[28]

Chapter 18

Arnold had repeatedly asked for a replacement at Ticonderoga.[29] Thus, his outrage about being replaced by Hinman is perplexing. Hinman had vastly greater military

---

21 *See* Lea, *A Hero and a Spy*, 20–31.

22 Nelson, *Benedict Arnold's Navy*, 53; Bellico, *Sails and Steam in the Mountains*, 116.

23 Lundeberg, *The Gunboat Philadelphia and the Defense of Lake Champlain in 1776*, 6; Malcolm, *The Tragedy of Benedict Arnold*, 92–93.

24 Randall, *Patriot and Traitor*, 103–104.

25 Darley, *The Battle of Valcour Island*, 43; Lefkowitz, *Benedict Arnold's Army*, 12.

26 *See* Murphy, *The Real Benedict Arnold*, 56.

27 Lefkowitz, *Arnold's Army*, 11.

28 *See* Randall, *Patriot and Traitor*, 121.

29 *See* Lea, *A Hero and a Spy* (May 14, 1775, letter to Massachusetts Committee of Safety), 55–57.

experience and had fought bravely in the French and Indian War. By any measure, Hinman was a more experienced and accomplished military officer than Arnold in the summer of 1775.[30]

Chapter 19

While Arnold wished to have the polish and sophistication of Schuyler, his manners could not match the general's. Arnold was described as "indelicate . . . his language was ungrammatical and his pronunciation vulgar."[31]

Chapter 21

"Arnold's detailed planning, knowledge of European military tactics and strategy, and disciplined military persona greatly appealed to Washington."[32]

Chapter 22

Deane was not likely in Boston during this time; rather, he exchanged correspondence with Arnold, Washington, and Church regarding Arnold's expenses.

Chapter 23

Interestingly, it appears Washington was the driving force for putting Morgan under Arnold's command, not a request by Arnold. Morgan's six restless rifle companies in Cambridge in 1775 were wreaking havoc. Sending Morgan with Arnold would put the riflemen to good use while lessening their adverse impact in the camps surrounding Boston.[33]

At least one historian lists 1,150 men and four women in Arnold's expedition.[34] The four women who accompanied the expedition were wives of men in the ranks and served the important purpose of washing and mending clothing and acting as nurses.[35] "There is a legend about a fifth woman on the campaign, described as a beautiful Indian princess named Jacataqua. She is one of the characters in Kenneth Roberts' popular novel *Arundel* about the Arnold Expedition. The legend is that Jacataqua was the descendent of a distinguished Abenaki sachem (chief) who lived on Swan Island. She is supposed to have taken up with 19-year-old Aaron Burr during the expedition and, if the dubious story is true, Jacataqua was the second of Burr's alleged famous

---

30 *See* "Biographical Summaries."

31 Kelly, *Valcour: The 1776 Campaign That Saved the Cause of Liberty*, 15.

32 Daigler, *Spies, Patriots, and Traitors*, 148.

33 *See e.g.* Lefkowitz, *Benedict Arnold's Army*, 48.

34 Ibid., 41.

35 Ibid., 51–52.

mistresses. His first lover is mentioned as being Dorothy Quincy, who was John Hancock's fiancé when she met Burr."[36]

Burr was "already a scholar, ladies' man and charismatic character. He was a product of the New Jersey upper class, the son of the president of Princeton College. Although his father died when Aaron was young and he was raised by an autocratic uncle, Burr inherited his father's academic bent. Aaron first attended Princeton at age thirteen. He was just five and a half feet tall, but energetic and talented."[37]

Coburn had actually promoted the Maine to Quebec route to the American high command and may have brought the Montresor map to Washington's attention, not Arnold's.[38]

<hr/>

Again we see the varied descriptions of currencies used. Arnold is described as having given a local Frenchman "two silver dollars" to nurse John Henry back to health.[39] However, Arnold's records of his expenditures are all recorded in pounds.[40]

One of Arnold's men on the expedition described their colonel as follows: "Our commander is a gentleman worthy of the trust reposed in him; a man, I believe, of invincible courage, of great prudence; ever serene, he defies the greatest danger to affect him, or difficulties to alter his temper; in fine, you will ever find him the intrepid hero and unruffled Christian."[41]

"Based on what is known about the financing of the Arnold Expedition, we can summarize that Arnold was carrying the modern equivalent of $615,000 in paper money issued by the Continental Congress to pay his officers and men and to purchase goods and services while he was in American territory, as well as a money chest containing the equivalent of $115,000 in today's currency in coins. In addition to the paper money and cash, Arnold had with him an unknown dollar amount in bills of exchange with which to make large purchases from merchants when he reached Canada, plus his personal credit and/or the personal credit of his officers, who would guarantee payment against their own wealth and honor."[42]

<hr/>

36 Ibid., 52.

37 Wilson, *A Traitor in Our Midst*, 55.

38 Lefkowitz, *Benedict Arnold's Army*, 26.

39 *See* Martin, *An American Warrior Reconsidered*, 139–140.

40 Randall, *Patriot and Traitor*, 187.

41 Arnold, *The Life of Benedict Arnold*, 70.

42 Lefkowitz, *Benedict Arnold's Army*, 37.

Chapter 24

Some authors believe the "Dark Eagle" story is fiction, first created by George Lippard in his 1876 book *The Legends of the American Revolution, 1776*. It is notable that such an important and interesting story did *not* appear in Isaac Arnold's *The Life of Benedict Arnold: His Patriotism and His Treason* (1880). I have included it, as it is widely recounted, but I share doubts about whether it occurred.

Chapter 25

Barry Wilson analyzes the invasion of Quebec from a Canadian perspective. He notes that numerous factors augured against the Quebeckers taking sides when the Americans invaded. In particular, the lack of literacy made it difficult for the Americans to disseminate their pamphlets effectively. Moreover, the American anti-Catholicism, while disclaimed by Washington and Arnold, was still well-known. As Wilson notes, "the Quebeckers had no intention of going off to be killed either for the English or the American Cause. The Americans were ostensibly in favor of freedom while privately denouncing French Catholics' language and religion. As one Quebec nationalist and journalist later explained, 'We had to choose between the English of Boston and the English of London. The English of London were further away and we hated them less.'"[43] More concretely, the British had passed the Quebec Act (1774) which allowed the Catholic Church to continue and the use of French civil law. While the British Parliament was in the process of passing the "Intolerable Acts" punishing the rebellion in the colonies, it was treating the Catholic French-Canadians with every consideration.[44]

If bad weather had not pinned down Arnold's force, they might have been able to take the city before the arrival of crucial British reinforcements.[45] Further bad luck for an already unlucky campaign. Professor Flexner posits that if Arnold had immediately attacked, he might have breached the walls of Quebec, as the British had left the huge gate open and its fasteners were out of order at that time. Indeed, even the next day, Arnold's troops marched unopposed up the bluffs to the Plains of Abraham.[46]

Chapter 27

It is worth noting the audacity of Arnold as compared to Wolfe during the French and Indian War. "When Wolfe led his troops to the Plains of Abraham, his fleet, consisting of twenty-two ships of the line, completely commanded the river, while Arnold had crossed in frail bark canoes and landed his soldiers by stealth, the St. Lawrence being absolutely controlled by British men-of-war. Wolfe had an army of thousands of

---

43 Wilson, *A Traitor in Our Midst*, 97–100.

44 *See* Malcolm, *The Tragedy of Benedict Arnold*, 118.

45 *See* Martin, *An American Warrior Reconsidered*, 143–144.

46 Flexner, *The Traitor and the Spy*, 84.

well trained, well equipped, well armed veterans, while the Americans did not exceed six hundred effective men—and these in rags, bare-footed, worn with fatigue, armed with damaged muskets, and without artillery; yet, with these few men, and relying on the friendly feeling of the people within the city, and of the Canadian militia, Arnold determined, if possible, to provoke a sally and an attack by the garrison, as Wolfe had done."[47]

As was so repeatedly the case for Arnold, those who admired him either died or fell out of favor. Such was the case for General Richard Montgomery. As Montgomery wrote to Arnold's other benefactor, General Schuyler, on December 5, 1775, "I find Colonel Arnold's corps an exceedingly fine one. Immune to fatigue and well accustomed to cannon shot, there is a style of discipline among them much superior to what I have been used to see in this campaign. He himself is active, intelligent, and enterprising."[48]

Chapter 30

There is some disagreement over whether Morgan and/or his men made it over the second barrier. In any event, he did not progress far before being surrounded and captured by the British. While Morgan and Arnold believed that the attack on Lower Town could have been successfully pressed had Morgan not been forced to pause by his officers, a review of the remaining British defenses and an understanding of the topography demonstrate there was little chance they would have made it up the steep hill from Lower Town to the city's even more formidable defenses at the top of the citadel.

With Arnold's reassignment to Montreal, America's efforts to capture Quebec and bring Canada into the united colonies came to an end. From that point on, the Americans would be on the defensive in Canada.[49]

Chapter 32

The question remained why so many subordinates later became avowed enemies of Arnold, including Wilkinson, Brown, Easton, and Hazen. General Palmer posits, "Arnold's hard-nosed and hard-charging attitude could weigh heavily on subordinates whose slowness or timidity often brought forth his anger. Most of them recognized the tongue-lashings for what they were—forceful outbursts made in the excitement of the moment, passionate outpourings to prod men to action. Some, however, with

---

47 Arnold, *The Life of Benedict Arnold*, 77.

48 Lea, *A Hero and a Spy*, 94.

49 *See* Malcolm, *The Tragedy of Benedict Arnold*, 141.

egos more susceptible to bruising, harbored a lingering resentment of such preemptory treatment. The longer Arnold remained in command, the longer grew the list of affronted officers."[50] Jack Kelly describes Arnold as "blunt, often tactless. He did not suffer fools. His meteoric rise ignited envy from many directions. He neglected to groom the egos of older men—Moses Hazen was eight years older than Arnold, Enoch Poor five years older. Nor did he offer these veterans of the French and Indian War any deference they expected for their experience."[51]

◄────►

The statistics for the failure of the Canada campaign are daunting. Of the eleven thousand soldiers sent to Canada, more than half vanished. Some were certainly killed by the enemy, but disease and desertion represented the lion's share of the losses. Moreover, of the 5,200 men who returned, almost 3,000 were incapacitated by disease.[52]

Chapter 33

Arnold misperceived Gates as his friend and a worthy general. Gates "has been severely criticized by military historians, who usually describe him as an unimaginative detail hound, overly attached to defensive tactics and without a good grasp of military strategy, despite his many years in the army; they generally award him high marks for vanity, ingratiating tactics, scheming, and unscrupulousness, but only mediocre marks in military matters."[53]

Chapter 34

Skenesborough, New York, was named after Major Philip Skene. A British soldier, he returned to England at the outbreak of the Revolution. He later returned to America and was captured, but was exchanged and allowed to return to England. He returned to America under General Burgoyne's campaign and was part of the surrender of Burgoyne's army. After the Battle of Saratoga, he once again returned to England, where he died in 1810. As the Skene name had fallen into disrepute, the town was renamed Whitehall after the Revolution.

A number of authors use different terms to describe the same type of boat. The term used at the time was *gondola*. The name *gondola* was derived from a New England

---

50 Palmer, *George Washington and Benedict Arnold*, 153; *see* Martin, *An American Warrior Reconsidered*, 213–214.

51 Kelly, *Valcour*, 81.

52 Ibid., 42.

53 Cushman, *Richard Varick*, 44.

"gundalow," which was used to transport farm produce on the rivers.[54] I have adopted *gondola*, as was consistent with the term at the time.

While Schuyler ultimately engaged Arnold to construct the fleet, Schuyler had begun preparing to build a fleet as early as January 1776.[55] Indeed, Schuyler deserves much of the credit for beginning the process of collecting the materials necessary for constructing the fleet. Ultimately, it was Schuyler's eye for logistics and his political connections to obtain supplies, coupled with Arnold's remarkable leadership and design ideas, that made the fleet possible.[56]

Chapter 35

Professor Flexner asserts that there may be some truth to Hazen's comments that Arnold made a profit out of the plunder of merchants in Montreal and St. John. Wilkinson, who would later betray Arnold in favor of Gates, asserted years later that Arnold had purchased goods from owners with personal IOUs—forcing merchants to sell at a loss. While Wilkinson and Hazen are less than reliable witnesses, Arnold engaged in similar activities while commanding Philadelphia. As Flexner notes, "Such behavior was not unusual; eighteenth-century army officers used their official power for private gain as commonly as municipal politicians do today. Furthermore, Arnold, habituated to being in business for himself, tended to confuse his private and public affairs; he had used his personal credit in Montreal to buy supplies for his soldiers. Perhaps he felt he had the right to pay himself back."[57] Claire Brandt, who is highly critical of Arnold generally, is far more skeptical of assertions that Arnold engaged in bad behavior as part of the Montreal campaign: "Did Arnold steal the goods on which the lives of his men depended? It is difficult to imagine that he did. He cherished his men's respect almost as much as he cherished his shiny new image as America's Patriot-Hero. The fact that he was later proved capable of larceny does not mean that he was guilty of it in 1776."[58]

Complaints about the hardships of service made by Arnold to Gates were quite common among officers in the Continental Army. Schuyler, for example, was constantly reminding people of the great sacrifices he made for his country.[59] Nevertheless, Arnold's statements at this time do represent some of the early indications of his growing frustration with his poor treatment and show his lack of political skill.

Arnold's complete loss of control at the court-martial goes to the very core of his

---

54 *See* Lundeberg, *The Gunboat Philadelphia*, 16; Darley, *The Battle of Valcour Island*, 39.

55 *See* Lea, *A Hero and a Spy*, 112–147.

56 *See* Kelly, *Valcour*, 35–39.

57 Flexner, *The Traitor and the Spy*, 98.

58 Brandt, *The Man in the Mirror*, 97.

59 Nelson, *Benedict Arnold's Navy*, 275.

political inflexibility. As J. E. Morpurgo notes, Arnold's "only failing was one that he did not recognize his complete inability to tread the paths of diplomacy. Even when he was on the just side in a debate, somehow he put himself in the wrong by arrogant behavior or intemperate comment."[60] "Arnold was poor at politics because he refused to recognize it as a game. (Persons who are incapable of laughing at themselves are seldom good at games.)"[61]

Chapter 37

Benedict Arnold in his letters and maps during that time used the term *Valcour Isle*. I have restricted the use of the modern term *Valcour Island* to the maps and notes.

Chapter 38

The fifty-four-year-old Waterbury was a fellow Connecticut mariner and a past friend of Arnold.[62] Arnold's criticisms of Waterbury were largely after-the-fact and resulted from Waterbury's subsequent attacks on him.[63] While Waterbury was certainly less aggressive than Arnold, he was initially an asset to the small fleet. He had extensive maritime experience, had fought in both the battles of forts St. George and Ticonderoga during the French and Indian War, and served honorably under Montgomery during the first attack on Quebec.[64] Indeed, on the eve of the Battle of Valcour Island, on October 10, 1776, Arnold wrote to Gates, "You may depend I shall do nothing of consequence without consulting Genl Waterbury & Colonel Wigglesworth, both of whom, I esteem judicious, honest men & good soldiers."[65]

Crucially, the British had a four-to-one advantage in total number of guns, and in poundage (that is, the total weight of shot capable of being projected by both fleets) they had a two-to-one advantage.[66]

There is disagreement concerning which vessel served as the hospital ship. Willard Randall says the *Liberty* acted as the hospital ship.[67] Nathaniel Philbrick more recently identifies the hospital ship as the *Enterprise*.[68] James Martin and others

60 Morpurgo, *Treason at West Point*, 74.
61 Brandt, *The Man in the Mirror*, 101.
62 *See* Kelly, *Valcour*, 69.
63 *See* Lea, *A Hero and a Spy* (February 26, 1777, letter from Waterbury to Gates), 203–205.
64 Ibid., 152.
65 Ibid., 182.
66 Darley, *The Battle of Valcour Island*, 71.
67 Randall, *Patriot and Traitor*, 301.
68 Philbrick, *Valiant Ambition*, 49.

AMERICAN VESSELS AT THE BATTLE OF VALCOUR ISLAND

Name	Type	Commander	Armament (no. of guns; weight of shot) – Tonnage	Crew	Disposition
yal Savage	schooner	Hawley	4 6s; 8 4s – 70	50	Burned by British
Revenge	schooner	Seaman	4 4s; 4 2s – Unknown	35	Escaped to Fort Ti
nterprise	sloop	Dickenson	12 4s – 70	50	Escaped to Fort Ti
ew Haven	gondola	Mansfield	1 12s; 2 9s – 123	44	Burned in Ferris Bay
rovidence	gondola	Simonds	1 12s; 2 9s – 123	44	Burned in Ferris Bay
Boston	gondola	Sumner	1 12s; 2 9s – 123	44	Burned in Ferris Bay
Spitfire	gondola	Ulmer	1 12s; 2 9s – 123	44	Sunk on escape
iladelphia	gondola	Rue	1 12s; 2 9s – 123	44	Sunk in battle
onnecticut	gondola	Grant	1 12s; 2 9s – 123	44	Burned in Ferris Bay
Jersey	gondola	Grimes	1 12s; 2 9s – 123	44	Abandoned
New York	gondola	Reed	1 12s; 2 9s – 123	44	Escaped to Fort Ti
Lee	cutter	Davis	1 12s; 1 9s; 4 4s – 48	65	Abandoned
Trumbull	galley	Warner/Wigglesworth	1 18s; 2 12s; 2 9s; 4 6s – 123	80	Escaped to Fort Ti
Congress	galley	Arnold	2 18s; 2 12s; 4 6s – 123	80	Burned in Ferris Bay
ashington	galley	Thatcher/Waterbury	1 18; 1 12s; 2 9s; 6 6s – 123	80	Surrendered

als: 15 vessels   **88 guns, 645 lbs.**

BRITISH VESSELS AT THE BATTLE OF VALCOUR ISLAND

Name	Type	Commander	Armament (no. of guns; weight of shot) – Tonnage
nflexible	Man-of-War	Schank	18 12s – 204
Maria	Schooner	Starke	14 6s – 129
Carleton	Schooner	Dacres	12 6s – 96
hunderer	radeau	Scott	6 24s; 6 12s; 2 howitzers – 422
yal Convert	gondola	Longcroft	7 9s – 109
unnamed	gunboats	various	28 various, from 24s to 9s – 40
unnamed	longboats	various	4 various – 50

als: 29 vessels   **89 guns, approx. 1,023 lbs.**[69]

---

undeberg, *The Gunboat Philadelphia*, 30; Darley, *The Battle of Valcour Island*, 64–66. Waterbury was second in command f the fleet and Wigglesworth was in third command. Both leaders had captains to handle their ships; Thatcher and Warner espectivly contend that the schooner *Liberty* was not present because it was on a run for supplies for Fort Ticonderoga.[70]

Carleton was criticized for the repeated failure of the HMS *Maria* to engage, and some would even say for his cowardly role in the fight.[71] Jack Kelly, in a recent and detailed recount of the battle, notes, "With the heavier British vessels out of the contest, the two sides were almost evenly matched in firepower. But the British had several advantages: their heavy cannon had the power to break open a hull; their new bronze pieces fired balls more accurately and at a greater velocity than American cannon; and their gunners had greater skill at loading and aiming their guns. Yet as the afternoon wore on and the gun duel continued, the amateur American artillerymen continued to hold their own."[72]

Arnold was highly critical of Waterbury's decision to strike his colors, yet Waterbury was in an untenable position and viewed himself as abandoned by Arnold and his fleet.[73]

Chapter 39

As is often the case with Benedict Arnold, stories were embellished after his treachery and reported by later historians, including the assertion that Lieutenant Goldsmith was left behind and burned alive as Arnold was exiting the ship.[74] Indeed, some even assert that Arnold had abandoned thirty sick and wounded men and allowed them to burn in the abandoned ship. Eyewitness accounts support Arnold's version and not the slanderous post-treason reports.[75] Most recent scholarship has Goldsmith killed outright before the ship was abandoned.[76]

Chapter 40

While most criticize Carleton's decision not to press the attack, he was keeping in mind the past history of the fort. General James Abercrombie made a rash attack at Ticonderoga in 1758 without adequate artillery support. He suffered grievous casualties and was repulsed. Carleton no doubt wanted to avoid a repeat of that defeat.[77]

70 Martin, *An American Warrior Reconsidered*, 270; Nelson, *Benedict Arnold's Navy*, 320; Darley, *The Battle of Valcour Island*, 64.

71 *See* Kelly, *Valcour*, 170–171 and 209.

72 Ibid., 182.

73 Ibid., 201–207.

74 *See e.g.* Randall, *Patriot and Traitor*, 316; Bellico, *Sails and Steam*, 157–158.

75 Kelly, *Valcour*, 210.

76 *See* Ibid.; *see* Darley, *The Battle of Valcour Island*, 8.

77 *See* Kelly, *Valcour*, 228.

Chapter 41

"For the outcome of the Revolutionary War, the significance of Carleton's failure to penetrate the Hudson is hard to exaggerate. . . . Among historians, even Arnold's bitterest critics have been obliged to acknowledge his crucial role in helping to preserve the cause of American liberty in its darkest hour. Such verdicts are all the more telling because they are uttered through gritted teeth."[78] "The little American navy on Champlain was wiped out; but never had any force, big or small, lived to better purpose or died more gloriously, for it saved the Lake for that year."[79]

Washington warmly greeted Arnold during the planning of the attack on Trenton. Arnold's enthusiasm for taking the offensive and this hero's welcome are likely what started the fissure between him and the jealous Gates.[80]

Arnold's exuberance for the Cause and willingness to expend his own money were demonstrated when Congress was slow to provide funds; he personally paid the cost of John Lamb and Eleazer Oswald's founding an artillery battalion in New Haven.

Chapter 42

Arnold had little hope with young Ms. DeBlois. A socialite and snob, this highly educated young woman was repulsed by a self-taught and self-made general in charge of a rabble army. Despite Arnold's attempts to refine his speech, he would always be a rough-cut sea captain (and sometime smuggler) from Connecticut.[81]

←—◦◦◦—→

Washington's support may have been particularly unhelpful in securing Arnold's promotion. Congress wanted to demonstrate its independence and primacy over the military. Arnold's close relationship with Washington gave Congress an opportunity to rebuff Washington indirectly by ignoring his recommendations. It is also possible that the activities of John Brown, Easton, and Hazen—and to a growing extent Horatio Gates—all contributed to undermining Arnold's chances, especially when his only champion was being willfully defied by Congress.[82]

Arnold could have simply resigned when he was not promoted—as Hannah was begging him to do—and returned to Connecticut. Indeed, all his troubles that followed likely would have been avoided had he followed the example of John Stark. Stark was a veteran of the French and Indian War who played a crucial role in

---

78 Brumwell, *Turncoat*, 75–76.

79 Martin, "Benedict Arnold: Natural Born Military Genius," citing A.T. Mahan, Alfred Thayer, *The Influence of Sea Power upon History: 1660–1783* (1890).

80 *See generally* Palmer, *A Tale of Two Patriots*, 188–189.

81 *See generally* Flexner, *The Traitor and the Spy*, 118.

82 *See generally* Palmer, *A Tale of Two Patriots*, 205–207.

the victory in Trenton. When he was overlooked for brigadier general in favor of a well-connected man with little experience, Stark resigned, stating, "I am bound on Honor to leave the service, Congress having tho't fit to promote Junr. officers over my head." Stark returned to his farm, only to later join the Revolution under the command of the New Hampshire legislature, no longer submitting himself to the unfair whims of Congress.[83] Isaac Arnold rightly notes that if Washington had possessed the power of appointment of his general officers throughout the war, Arnold's treason would never have occurred.[84] Of course, this is true at so many turning points in Arnold's life: if he had never been sent to Philadelphia, if he had received a naval command after his wounding, or if he had never met Peggy Shippen. Any one of these events would likely have kept him from committing treason.

It is worth noting that Arnold was not alone in his sensitivity about lack of promotion. In late 1777, a French officer named Ducondray was appointed by Congress as a major general and a commander of artillery. In response, the heralded Generals Greene, Sullivan, and Knox all wrote letters to Congress requesting permission to retire and resign, because Ducondray's appointment would supersede them in command. While Ducondray was not ultimately appointed, it did show the hypersensitivity of all generals during this period.[85]

Chapter 45

It was believed that many of Arnold's records were burned on the *Royal Savage*. However, a British boarding party was able to find Arnold's strongbox, which was placed in a public archive in Canada in the Jesuit library in Laval University in Quebec. "These records show a serious attempt by Arnold, not only to keep track of his expenses, but, equally important, to document that he had scrupulously carried out Congress' and Washington's instructions to pay the Canadians, not pilfer from them."[86]

Congress was not completely unreasonable in this accounting dispute. Arnold had virtually no documentation to support many of his claims. The committee did suggest a compromise where Arnold would get more than he could prove, but less than he demanded. He viewed the matter through a lens of honor. Anything less than full recovery was a challenge to his credibility and could not be accepted.

Chapter 47

Fort Stanwix is also often called Fort Schuyler.[87]

---

83 *See* Malcolm, *The Tragedy of Benedict Arnold*, 177.

84 Arnold, *The Life of Benedict Arnold*, 46; *see* Philbrick, *Valiant Ambition*, 90.

85 *See* Arnold, *The Life of Benedict Arnold*, 129–130.

86 Randall, *Patriot and Traitor*, 337.

87 *See e.g.* Brumwell, *Turncoat*, 90–91.

In the "small world" that was the American Revolution, Jane McCrea, the woman scalped by loyalist Native Americans, was the sister of Stephen McCrea, Arnold's surgeon at the Battle of Valcour Island.[88]

Chapter 48

The man Arnold used to his advantage at Fort Stanwix has been identified by many names over the years, including "John Jost Kuyler," "Hanjort Schuyler," or "Hon Yost Schuyler."[89] Hon Yost's last name was likely Schuyler, the same as General Philip Schuyler; however, there appears to be no relation, and it certainly was not the subject of any discussion in the correspondence or reporting at the time that they were in any way related.

There is some support for the contention that the use of Hon Yost Schuyler in the manner described was first proposed by Lieutenant Colonel John Brooks and then adopted by Arnold.[90]

Chapter 50

Professor Flexner asserts that, contrary to the position of most historians, Arnold did not lead the battle at Freeman's Farm and instead was with Gates at his headquarters during the entire battle. When he did leave, he was recalled by Gates via Wilkinson.[91]

Some authors describe Arnold as trapped in Gates's headquarters through most of the battle and only leaving late in the day.[92] In contrast, some have him participating actively in the Battle of Freeman's Farm, leading the repeated charges.[93] Regardless, all seem to agree that Arnold encouraged Gates to engage and challenge the enemy.[94]

Three strong reasons support the assertions that Arnold actively participated in the battle. First, the success on the battlefield required a dynamic leader, and he was the only one present. Second, it is almost inconceivable a man like Arnold could have sat by while the battle raged. Finally, the after-action reports support that Arnold played an active role in the field.[95]

The disagreement in biographies about Arnold's actions on both September 19 and October 7 are in no small part because of the duplicitous and dishonorable actions

---

88 Kelly, *Valcour*, 95.

89 Brumwell, *Turncoat*, 91.

90 *See* Lea, *A Hero and a Spy*, 255–256.

91 Flexner, *The Traitor and the Spy*, 172–173; *see also* Brandt, *The Man in the Mirror*, 133.

92 Philbrick, *Valiant Ambition*, 148.

93 Randall, *Patriot and Traitor*, 357.

94 Brumwell, *Turncoat*, 95–96.

95 *See* Arnold, *The Life of Benedict Arnold*, 174–177.

of Colonel Wilkinson and the antagonistic attitude of Gates. Both sought to undermine Arnold and laud their own tepid performances. I presented the approach taken
by more recent historians who reject the biased presentations of these two officers,
instead looking to other contemporaneous reports during these two days of battle.[96]

Chapter 51

Some contend that Gates's troops did not call him "Granny Gates," and that it was not
until his failures, long after Saratoga, that his name and reputation fell into disrepute.[97]

Chapter 52

Wilkinson and Arnold's other enemies asserted that Arnold was drunk in his cabin or
made outrageous pronouncements like "No man shall keep me in my tent this day!
Victory or death!"[98] There is little evidence Arnold drank to excess. Also, setting aside
the fact that he was residing not in a "tent" but a small cabin, there is little evidence
that Arnold violated direct orders from his superiors. Indeed, he was a stickler for military discipline. In the absence of explicit orders, it seems likely that he used impreci-
sion to his advantage. Most authors now doubt the madman "betraying great agitation
and wrath" described by Wilkinson.[99]

As Stephen Brumwell aptly notes in *Turncoat*, if the ball had struck Arnold's heart
instead of his leg, Arnold's "last moments would have offered the perfect subject for
an artist like John Trumbull, whose dramatic brushwork immortalized the death of
Arnold's friend Dr. Joseph Warren at Bunker Hill, and of his old comrade Richard
Montgomery before Quebec."[100]

Contrary to Arnold's assertions, Gates actually reported to Congress on October
12 the efforts of the "gallant General Arnold." On November 4, Congress officially
thanked Gates, Lincoln, and Arnold for their efforts.[101]

Chapter 53

Washington had a good excuse for not getting back to Arnold in the aftermath of the
battle. While Arnold was recovering, Washington had spent most of the fall dealing

---

96 Lynch, Wayne. "Debating Arnold's Role at Freeman's Farm."

97 Kelly, *Valcour*, 20, 247.

98 *See* Arnold, *The Life of Benedict Arnold*, 198.

99 *See* Brumwell, *Turncoat*, 109–110; Lynch, "Arnold in Command at Bemis Heights?" *(makes compelling
argument that Arnold was in the field following orders).*

100 Brumwell, *Turncoat*, 111.

101 *See* Brumwell, *Turncoat*, 115; Arnold, *The Life of Benedict Arnold*, 216–221.

with the "Conway Cabal." This so-called plot sought to replace the "loser" Washington with the "winner" Gates. The intrigue was ultimately defeated by Washington and his allies, but this political battle, along with the suffering of his men at Valley Forge, distracted and delayed the general in reaching out to the injured and maltreated Arnold.[102] Likewise, Arnold's assertions that he was abandoned and forgotten ignore the fact that, despite the press of the war and the travel difficulties, both Alexander Hamilton and the Marquis de Lafayette visited him during his recuperation.[103] Richard Varick also visited Arnold regularly and gave him the encouraging news of the growing recognition that he was the true victor of the battle.[104]

<hr />

The March 1778 letter from Arnold to Washington is particularly interesting because, for the first time, Arnold begins to refer to the Colonies as "your country." As Murphy notes in his book, "These words are a far cry from those he used when retreating from Canada back in 1776. . . . Benedict's goals had shifted. He was no longer invested in the Revolution as a way to restore his family name."[105]

Chapter 56

As General Palmer observes regarding Arnold's appointment as military governor of Philadelphia, "One would be hard-pressed to find a worse personnel decision made by Washington in the entire war. While it was true that the position called for an officer of high rank . . . it also required exquisite patience, supreme tact, and unusual political sensitivity, all traits conspicuously missing in Arnold's personality."[106]

The destruction of Philadelphia by the British was profound. Even Benjamin Franklin's house was stripped of valuables by Major André and other British officers. André stole a prize portrait of Franklin, which he gave to his commander, who hung it in the family's Northumberland estate until it was donated to the United States government. It is now prominently displayed in the White House.[107]

Chapter 57

Reed's relationship with Arnold must be seen in the broader context of a power struggle between the military establishment and those favoring a radical democracy. As a Washington favorite and victorious general, Arnold was a political lightning rod who

<hr />

102 *See* Martin, *An American Warrior Reconsidered*, 415–416.

103 *See* Brandt, *The Man in the Mirror*, 142.

104 Ibid., 141; Martin, *An American Warrior Reconsidered*, 404.

105 Murphy, *The Real Benedict Arnold*, 170.

106 Palmer, *A Tale of Two Patriots*, 280; *see also* Thompson, *Benedict Arnold in Philadelphia*, 36.

107 Jacob, *Treacherous Beauty*, 52.

was safer to attack than the august Washington. As Randall notes, "In effect, Arnold became the first target for critics of the far more popular but out-of-range Washington. Arnold was preaching the hard new doctrine to ruggedly individualistic militiamen who resisted his brand of monotonous military discipline. His absolute insistence on the discipline that prepared men for battle seemed hierarchical, undemocratic, and distinctively English. . . . [Reed] concentrated his fire on the visible symbol of strong central government, military governor Benedict Arnold."[108] It is sometimes difficult for the modern reader to appreciate the fear of monarchy and dictatorship. Just eighty years before the Revolution, Oliver Cromwell overthrew the British parliament and made himself dictator for life. The radicals' fears, while ultimately unfounded, were not unreasonable, given prior history. We view history through the lens of George Washington's unprecedented willingness to give up power.[109] Washington's selfless dedication to his country and willingness to step aside make him one of the most unique and transformative figures in world history.

⟶ ⟵

Arnold's transaction with Mease may not have been technically illegal, but it was certainly an egregious breach of his duty to the people of Philadelphia. While Arnold did not use public money, he used his office to buy up goods, which in turn drove up prices, creating demand to further enrich himself. This inside trading only worsened Reed's and others' perceptions of Arnold's motivations. Many historians have noted that revolutionary generals were forced to engage in entrepreneurial and sometimes questionable business practices, as they were paid in almost worthless currency and were forced to support themselves, their staff, and at times the army at their own expense.[110]

Chapter 59

There is some disagreement about whether Arnold invested or was given an interest in the ship, as well as its timing.[111] Under the rules of the time, Arnold's dealings were not technically illegal, but they were certainly unethical. He signed Skewell's original pass on June 4, one day before Congress ordered all shops and stores sealed.[112]

This book only notes a couple of Arnold's attempts to enrich himself while in Philadelphia. He also became embroiled in the *Active* matter. In early September 1778, Connecticut fisherman Gideon Olmsted and three other sailors were captured

---

108 Randall, *George Washington: A Life*, 363; *see also* Philbrick, *Valiant Ambition*, 228.

109 *See* Malcolm, *The Tragedy of Benedict Arnold*, 245.

110 *See generally* Brumwell, *Turncoat*, 140.

111 *See generally* Randall, *Patriot and Traitor*, 412.

112 Lea, *A Hero and a Spy*, 298.

by the British off the coast of Virginia and were pressed into service on the British sloop *Active*, bound for New York. One night, Olmsted and his three friends seized control of the ship, capturing fourteen British officers and seamen. A two-day struggle ensued where the British crew desperately tried to recapture the ship by forcing hatches and sweeping the deck with fire. While severely wounded, Olmsted managed to turn a swivel gun and rake the deck, killing many of the British officers and men. The British captain ultimately cut a hole through the stern of the vessel and wedged the rudder so that Olmsted could not steer the ship. Olmsted responded by starving the British out and refusing to provide them with water.

The British finally relented, but soon thereafter the ship was attacked by two Pennsylvania privateers who claimed her as a prize. A Pennsylvania judge, George Ross, declared the ship a prize to Pennsylvania, finding it inconceivable that four men could have taken the ship on their own. Olmsted appealed to Arnold in Philadelphia as a fellow man from Connecticut. Arnold agreed to bankroll the appeal to Congress and pay for the lodging of Olmsted's men and his lawyers during the process. On September 15, Congress reversed Judge Ross's decision and ordered the marshal of the Pennsylvania court to sell the sloop and cargo and turn over the funds to Olmsted— Arnold was now to receive a quarter share.

Instead of Arnold receiving a £12,000 profit as he was entitled, Pennsylvania defied Congress's order, and on January 30, 1779, Ross was ordered to take possession of the prize money and property. Despite Arnold's warnings to prevent the funds from being taken by the Pennsylvania treasury, Congress dawdled. By the time a decision was made, the matter was moot and Arnold had lost £12,000 in expected profit, as well as the cost of paying for the appeal. Olmsted fought the decision for another thirty years, and ultimately the United States Supreme Court ruled in his favor in a landmark case.[113]

◆━━◆━▸

Arnold's generosity relating to the Warren family was genuine and is often overlooked. His support for Warren's family was truly remarkable, given his stressed financial condition. He also never forgave Congress for its failure to support Dr. Warren's family.[114]

Chapter 61

At least one historian believes that the delay in the trial was the "last straw" where Arnold finally lost faith in the American cause and decided to contact the British.[115]

---

113 Randall, *Patriot and Traitor*, 416–417.

114 *See generally* Martin, *An American Warrior Reconsidered*, 426–427; *see* Arnold, *The Life of Benedict Arnold*, 216; Randall, *Patriot and Traitor*, 423.

115 *See* Boylan, *The Dark Eagle*, 164.

John Roberts was not the only Quaker that Arnold sought to protect from the radicals; his story presented here is simply one of the most compelling.

Arnolds thoughts about being abandoned by everyone except Peggy is consistent with his letters. Of course, he ignores Hannah and many of his loyal friends, such as Silas Deane.

Chapter 62

Even Arnold's wedding night was a subject of post-treason rumors and attacks. Arnold was accused of sharing bawdy anecdotes with his companions regarding the pleasures of the nuptial bed.[116]

Chapter 64

Most authors now accept that Peggy played a major role in Arnold's treason,[117] though one recent author reverts to an old and previously accepted version of her innocence.[118] Another posits that Peggy and André had planned this scheme from the beginning and that Arnold was "ripe for the plan that she and John had in mind."[119] Most believe that whether or not Peggy originated the idea of treason, she was involved in the conspiracy from its inception.[120]

Those who think Arnold acted on his own without Peggy's assistance fail to take into account that he would have had very little ability to identify Stansbury as a potential contact of André's. Peggy also had the prior friendship with the well-placed André. It was only through her contact and experience in Philadelphia that this secret messenger to André could have been identified.[121]

Chapter 65

Historians universally conclude that a sexual relationship between André and Peggy was extremely unlikely.[122] Much is made of the large Meschianza costume ball organized by André prior to the exodus from Philadelphia. However, not only was Peggy not permitted to attend the ball, but André was never going to be her escort; instead,

---

116 Brumwell, *Turncoat*, 152.

117 *See* Philbrick, *Valiant Ambition*, 239.

118 Malcolm, *The Tragedy of Benedict Arnold*, xv-xvii, 289, 326–237.

119 *See* Ronald, *The Life of John André*, 186–187, 192–193.

120 Brumwell, *Turncoat*, 168.

121 *See* Ronald, *The Life of John André*, 188; Palmer, *A Tale of Two Patriots*, 303–304; Brandt, *The Man in the Mirror*, 177.

122 *See* Daigler, *Spies, Patriots, and Traitors*, 153; Jacob, *Treacherous Beauty*, 42–43; Ronald, *The Life of John André*, at 192; Brumwell, *Turncoat*, 127.

he attended with her friend Peggy Chew.[123] Crucially, it would have been an extraordinarily bad decision for both André and Peggy to become romantically intertwined.[124]

Following Benedict's treason, Peggy's family destroyed all correspondence they had in their possession.[125] The most rational approach is to accept that the extent of Peggy's attachment to André, and whether it ever crossed the sexual threshold, can never be answered definitively, although it is improbable.[126]

Chapter 66

Jonathan Odell and others played a role in the communications between Arnold and André, which are simplified and not fully included in this book.[127] While André played his cards close to his vest with Arnold's emissary, we now know that both he and Clinton were thrilled at the prospect of engaging Arnold. After the abandonment of Philadelphia in May 1778, Sir Henry Clinton was "increasingly desperate to search for some rear-guard masterstroke."[128] Stansbury arrived in New York and made contact with a loyalist poet, Reverend Jonathan Odell. With Odell's help, Stansbury was taken to André's office at British headquarters on One Wall Street on Monday, May 10, 1779. Stansbury immediately violated Arnold's instructions and indicated General Arnold intended to offer his services to the commander in chief of the British forces. André was told Arnold's goal was either to immediately join the British Army or to cooperate on some concealed plan with Sir Henry Clinton.

In discussing Arnold's May 14, 1779, letter to Washington, Professor Flexner notes, "The interjection of 'I hope' made this sentence mirror Arnold's thoughts exactly. Was it a slip of the pen, indicating that he was not yet an accomplished conspirator; or was he warning Washington that he could not be pushed too far? Perhaps a commander who had the seeds of disloyalty in his own heart, to whom treason was a personal possibility, might have noticed the telltale words; but Washington was so firm in his own constancy that he could not doubt the constancy of a man he believed worthy of trust. His suspicions were not aroused."[129]

---

123 *See* Ronald, *The Life of John André*, 168–169; Lea, *A Hero and a Spy*, 336–337.

124 *See generally* Flexner, *The Traitor and the Spy*, 205.

125 Jacob, *Treacherous Beauty*, 11.

126 *See* Boylan, *The Dark Eagle*, 143.

127 *See* Brumwell, *Turncoat*, 170–172; Randall, *Patriot and Traitor*, 460–462.

128 *See* Ronald, *The Life of John André*, 160.

129 Flexner, *The Traitor and the Spy*, at 279; Lea, *A Hero and a Spy*, 339–340.

Chapter 67

Money was certainly a motivation for Arnold, but it was not paramount. However, once he decided to switch sides, he wanted to maximize his return.[130]

Washington placed a premium on following rules and decorum, even at the expense of his own self-interest. In contrast, Arnold saw rules as malleable impediments to his desires. Washington found it appalling that Arnold would show up and ask for assistance on the eve of a court-martial. In contrast, Arnold was hurt and shocked that Washington did not assist him in the upcoming trial—notwithstanding "proprieties."[131]

Did Arnold feel guilty about the apparent hypocrisy of his situation—showing righteous indignation in defending his honor in a court-martial, while simultaneously providing detailed information to the British that could undermine the Revolution and lead to the deaths of rebel soldiers? Most authors believe that Arnold, by his very nature, was not only untroubled by but unaware of his hypocrisy. "Arnold had never worried about the consequences of his actions. Guilt was simply not a part of his makeup since everything he did was, to his own mind, at least, justifiable. Where others might have shown, if not remorse, at least hesitation or ambivalence, Arnold projected unwavering certitude."[132]

I have shortened and simplified the extensive negotiations that went back and forth between André, Arnold, and others during this period.

Chapter 68

Arnold's exact role at Fort Wilson is the subject of much debate.[133] Some have Arnold actively fighting in the fort as depicted here.[134] At least a few authors have him not fighting at Fort Wilson, but arriving later and pulling his pistols as Reed arrives.[135] Some authors have Arnold playing a far more minor role at the encounter at Fort Wilson and arriving after Reed[136] or retreating in the face of stones thrown by a mob.[137] There is no doubt that Arnold was the subject of derision and under constant physical and verbal threat and abuse by the mob at this time. Whether he participated as actively as described in this book is simply unknown. This version of events is certainly what Arnold would have done if given the opportunity, and would not have been widely reported.

---

130 *See* Brumwell, *Turncoat*, 159–160; Murphy, *The Real Benedict Arnold*, 189.

131 *See* Philbrick, *Valiant Ambition*, 246–247.

132 Ibid., 246.

133 *See* Jacob, *Treacherous Beauty*, 116.

134 Randall, *Patriot and Traitor*, 481.

135 *See e.g.* Malcolm, *The Tragedy of Benedict Arnold*, 267; Lea, *A Hero and a Spy*, 356.

136 Philbrick, *Valiant Ambition*, 254.

137 Brandt, *The Man in the Mirror*, 184.

Chapter 69

Arnold repeatedly lied in his defense at trial. He did have a financial interest in the *Active* and had indeed speculated while closing shops in Philadelphia, and used his influence to his benefit in protecting his interest in the *Charming Nancy*.[138]

Arnold's quoted arguments at the trial have been shortened and reordered for ease of presentation. I have also not presented witness testimony which included Timothy and William Matlack, Lieutenant Colonel Alexander Hamilton, Deputy Quartermaster General and Colonel John Mitchell, and John Hall, assistant to Mitchell.[139]

Arnold's attack on those he considered unworthy and his vigorous defense of himself seem almost inconceivable given that he had already been dealing with the British for over six months, providing valuable information and negotiating his treason. However, at the most basic level, Arnold had such a strong belief in his own "rectitude" that he truly did not believe himself to be doing anything wrong and felt completely innocent of the unfair charges made against him. Indeed, he seemed capable of simultaneously holding outrage in his mind for his mistreatment and seeking vindication at the hands of the British.[140]

Chapter 70

Isaac Arnold correctly notes that the finding of no intentional wrongdoing or any "illegal" conduct makes the public reprimand a non sequitur, but clearly a political concession to the State of Pennsylvania.[141]

Even at this late stage, in early 1780, Arnold might have avoided his treachery if Washington and the Admiralty had granted his request to lead the Continental Navy. He could have brushed off the British; if they attempted to reveal his treachery, he would have simply asserted it was his own plan at counterespionage. Regardless, another unfortunate decision by Washington and Congress moved Arnold inexorably closer to treason.

Chapter 71

$9,164 equals approximately $177,177.62 in current US dollars.[142]

Arnold first began his contact with Stansbury, and in turn André, as far back as

138 *See* Flexner, *The Traitor and the Spy*, 302–303.

139 *See* Lea, *A Hero and a Spy*, 364.

140 *See generally* Brumwell, *Turncoat*, 192–193.

141 *See* Arnold, *The Life of Benedict Arnold*, 260.

142 *See* www.officialdata.org; Randall, *Patriot and Traitor*, 499. (Randall calculates the amount as $275,000 at the time of publication of his book in 1990.)

May 1779, eleven months *before* Washington's censure. Thus, it is an exaggeration to call the censure the "last straw." It simply added fuel to the fire.

Chapter 73

Arnold was familiar with Colonel Beverly Robinson. In May 1779, Robinson wrote a letter to Arnold urging him to join the loyalist cause. In many ways it summarized Arnold's feelings about the change in the Revolution and his motivations: "There is no one but General Arnold who can surmount obstacles so great as these. A man of so much courage will never despair of the republic, even when every door to reconciliation seems sealed. Render then, brave General, this important service to your country. The colonies cannot sustain much longer the unequal strife. Your troops are perishing in misery. They are badly armed, half-naked, and crying for bread. The efforts of Congress are futile against the languor of the people. Your fields are untilled, trade languishes, learning dies. The neglected education of a whole generation is an irreparable loss to society. Your youth, torn by thousands from their rustic pursuits or useful employments, are mown down by war. Such as survive have lost the vigor of their prime, or are maimed in battle: the greater part bring back to their families the idleness and the corrupt manners of the camp. Let us put an end to so many calamities; you and ourselves have the same origin, the same language, and the same laws. . . . United in equality, we will rule the universe: we will hold it bound, not by arms and violence, but by the ties of commerce; the lightest and most gentle bands that humankind ever can wear."[143] Arnold did not respond to the letter.

Chapter 75

One writer indicates that André and Smith may have met earlier when André was an American prisoner and traveling to Pennsylvania. There is certainly no indication in the record that they recognized each other.[144]

Here again Arnold's plot might have succeeded if Smith had agreed to the additional help being offered by the HMS *Vulture*. The presence of an armed barge would have expedited the meeting and likely assured Andre's ability to return to the *Vulture* after the meeting with Arnold.

Chapter 76

The unwillingness of the Cahoon brothers to row André back to the HMS *Vulture* "successfully ruined the entire conspiracy and probably changed the course of American

---

143 Lea, *A Hero and a Spy*, 331–335.
144 Koke, *Accomplice in Treason*, 20, 84.

history by their indolence and blockheaded refusal."[145] As John Walsh persuasively argues, a more experienced agent would have avoided being caught behind enemy lines. André "should simply have leveled a pistol at the two [Cahoon brothers] and ordered them to man the oars. They could have been held aboard ship and released days later, after it was all over. Or not released, as it suited the British. In the larger scheme of things during those momentous hours the fate of two plain American civilians couldn't have meant much."[146] Instead, André agreed with Smith and Arnold and returned to Smith's home without any apparent protest.

André's ambitions were no less than Arnold's, and for good reason. The night before he left, Clinton held a dinner in New York and made a final toast: "A word in addition, gentlemen, if you please. The Major leaves the city on duty tonight, which will most likely terminate in making plain John André, Sir John André, for success must crown his efforts."[147]

The dialogue between André and Arnold in the woods is conjecture. However, Arnold was an experienced and skilled negotiator, and André was not. It is reasonable to expect Arnold dominated their discussions.

The HMS *Vulture* did retreat in response to American cannon fire; she pulled back only a few miles downriver and anchored on the other side of the Croton peninsula to avoid the shelling. Eventually she returned to her original position off Teller's Point, but André had already left to proceed on an overland route to the British lines.[148]

Clinton had given André three explicit orders to protect him: (1) he was not to assume a disguise, (2) he was not to cross into American-held territory, and (3) he was not to accept any documents.[149] By the time Arnold had left André's presence, all three of Clinton's admonitions had been breached by the hapless major.

André was never a field operative. "He had risen to become Clinton's chief of staff, many officers felt he had been unfairly promoted over more senior officers. Until his capture and death, he had been seen as a foppish dandy."[150] He lacked any experience behind the line and held such a low opinion of his enemies that he engaged in sloppy intelligence and underestimated the competition.[151] Arnold was a brilliant field commander, but had no experience as a spy.[152] As a practical matter, both men were bumbling novices who were in over their heads.

---

145 Boylan, *Dark Eagle*, 201.

146 Walsh, *The Execution of Major Andre*, 76.

147 Lea, *A Hero and a Spy*, 451.

148 Philbrick, *Valiant Ambition*, 293–294.

149 *See* Jacob, *Treacherous Beauty*, 142.

150 Trees, "Benedict Arnold, John Andre, and His Three Yeoman Captors."

151 Daigler, *Spies, Patriots, and Traitors*, 153.

152 *See* Malcolm, *The Tragedy of Benedict Arnold*, 301.

Chapter 77

Paulding later admitted that "had he [André] pulled out General Arnold's pass first, I should have let him go."[153] John Evangelist Walsh presents a compelling case that André was a wholly unqualified amateur who "entirely on his own made a blundering failure of his supremely important mission."[154] "The British had final victory in their grasp, and they knew it. That chance was lost only because of André's incredibly inept performance."[155]

The exact language of the exchange at the bridge varies, but most agree on the basic interchange. The majority of historians follow the story told by André, repeated by Colonel Benjamin Tallmadge forty years later in Congress.[156] They claim the three men who caught André were nothing more than thieves who stumbled upon him and in the course of robbing him discovered the incriminating papers.[157]

This more widely accepted story slandering the three captors was the result of a calculated effort by André to rehabilitate his reputation in the aftermath of his capture, and Tallmadge's similar effort on behalf of the major, whom he greatly admired.[158] Alexander Hamilton wrote a widely distributed letter, effusive in its praise of André, that helped cement the public's view of the major as a noble gentleman sacrificed at the altar of Arnold's evil.[159] The narrative in this book closely followed the encounter proposed by John Walsh.[160] I have followed more recent scholarship which paints the three captors in better light.

Notwithstanding the later slander of André's captors, in the immediate aftermath of his capture and indeed for most of their lives, the three men were rightly viewed as heroes. A popular twelve-stanza tavern tune spread throughout the colonies, sung to "Bonnie Boy," sang the praises of the young men.[161]

Chapter 78

Smith was an apparent supporter of the Cause. However, his brother was a chief justice of the Supreme Court and an avid loyalist. His prominent loyalist brother cast a

153 *See* Boylan, *Dark Eagle*, 210.

154 *See* Walsh, *The Execution of Major Andre*, 6.

155 Ibid.

156 Philbrick, *Valiant Ambition*, 300–301; Randall, *Patriot and Traitor*, 553–554; Walsh, *The Execution of Major Andre*, 107.

157 *See* Cushman, *Richard Varick*, 72, 75.

158 *See* Walsh, *The Execution of Major Andre*, 152–171; *see also* Jacob, *Treacherous Beauty*, 151; *see generally* Brumwell, *Turncoat*, 284; Carso, *"Whom Can We Trust Now?"*, 165–166.

159 *See* Lea, *A Hero and a Spy*, 548–556.

160 Walsh, *The Execution of Major Andre*, 107–110.

161 Lea, *A Hero and a Spy*, 561–562.

shadow over Joshua Smith and, ironically, may have made him exceptionally susceptible to proving his loyalty to the Cause by assisting Arnold.[162]

Chapter 80

There are divergent historical accounts of exactly what occurred at West Point. Below
are the areas where historians diverge on what occurred.

AIDES DISPATCHED

There is disagreement about which aides were dispatched by Washington to Robinson House to inform the Arnolds of the delay in Washington's arrival. Palmer probably takes the best approach by merely indicating "two aides" were sent, but does not
identify the individuals by name.[163] Some list Hamilton and another aide (most likely
McHenry) as being sent to the home.[164] At least one author has two aides being sent
and Hamilton later joining them.[165] Even Pulitzer winner Ron Chernow has two different descriptions of who was dispatched to Arnold. In *Alexander Hamilton*, Chernow
indicates that Hamilton and McHenry were dispatched early to the Arnolds' home,[166]
whereas in *Washington: A Life* he indicates that Samuel Shaw and James McHenry
were the individuals dispatched.[167] Nathanial Philbrick follows the majority of historians identifying Shaw and McHenry as the dispatched aides.[168]

WHEN AND WHERE ARNOLD GOT THE LETTER FROM JAMESON

Most histories have Arnold sitting at the breakfast table with Washington's aide when
Jameson's note arrives.[169] However, others have Arnold getting up from the table
to meet Allen at the door and telling him to say nothing to anyone.[170] Some even
have him in the buttery.[171] Some have Arnold receiving the news from Allen in the

---

162 *See generally* Koke, *Accomplice in Treason*, 37.

163 Palmer, *A Tale of Two Patriots*, 365.

164 *See* Randall, *George Washington: A Life*, 381; Randall, *Patriot and Traitor*, 557; Boylan, *Dark
Eagle*, 216; Murphy, *The Real Benedict Arnold*, 213; Wilson, *A Traitor in Our Midst*, 159; Arnold, *The
Life of Benedict Arnold*, 159.

165 Morpurgo, *Treason at West Point*, 123.

166 Chernow, *Alexander Hamilton*, 141.

167 Chernow, *Washington: A Life*, 382.

168 Philbrick, *Valiant Ambition*, 308; Flexner, *The Traitor and the Spy*, 366; Lea, *A Hero and a Spy*,
493; Brumwell, *Turncoat*, 273.

169 *See* Van Doren, *Secret History of the American Revolution*, 345; Boylan, *Dark Eagle*, 217; Walsh,
The Execution of Major Andre, 128; Lea, *A Hero and a Spy*, 293–294.

170 Brumwell, *Turncoat*, 273; Arnold, *The Life of Benedict Arnold*, 295.

171 Sale, *Traitors*, 51; Murphy, *The Real Benedict Arnold*, 213; Flexner, *The Traitor and the Spy*, 366;
Chernow, *Alexander Hamilton*, 140.

hallway.[172] Some have him reading it privately on the porch, outside the view of the others.[173] Nathaniel Philbrick probably best states, "It is not known whether Arnold was with them at the table or somewhere else when Lieutenant Allen, after two days of marching up and down the east side of the river (first with André in his custody and now with only a message for Arnold), arrived at Robinson House."[174]

TIME OF WASHINGTON'S ARRIVAL

Even the time of day that Washington returned to the home is inconsistent among historians. Most say 4:00 p.m.,[175] but some say as early as 2:00 p.m.[176]

WASHINGTON LEARNS OF TREASON

The exact circumstances of how and with whom Washington learned of Arnold's treachery also vary. Most have Washington returning to Robinson House, retiring to his room, and receiving the dispatch from Hamilton, then having Hamilton summon Knox and/or Lafayette.[177] Some have Hamilton going over the dispatch ahead of time and bringing it to Washington.[178] Many have Hamilton bringing it to Washington's room, where they discover it together.[179] Another historian has the Marquis de Lafayette being in Washington's room as the notice arrives from Jameson.[180] Yet another has Hamilton opening the letter and meeting Washington and his party as they come up from the river.[181] Finally, one historian indicates that the notice from Jameson arrived and was discovered by Hamilton, who mounted a horse and informed Washington outside Robinson House.[182] Most have Lafayette walking into the room with Washington, shoulders slumped, saying, "Who can we trust now?"[183] "Lafayette recalled, 'I believe this is the only occasion throughout the long and sometimes hopeless struggle that Washington ever gave way, even for a moment, under a reverse of fortune; and perhaps I was the only human being who ever witnessed in him an exhibition of feeling

172 Morpurgo, *Treason at West Point*, 125.
173 *See* Malcolm, *The Tragedy of Benedict Arnold*, 317.
174 Philbrick, *Valiant Ambition*, 308.
175 *See* Ibid., 311; Malcolm, *The Tragedy of Benedict Arnold*, 321.
176 Palmer, *A Tale of Two Patriots*, 366.
177 Boylan, *Dark Eagle*, 221; Lea, *A Hero and a Spy*, 496.
178 Palmer, *A Tale of Two Patriots*, 367; *cf.* Flexner, *The Traitor and the Spy*, 371.
179 Chernow, *Alexander Hamilton*, 341; Chernow, *Washington: A Life*, 382.
180 Randall, *George Washington: A Life*, 381; Randall, *Patriot and Traitor*, 558.
181 Arnold, *The Life of Benedict Arnold*, 299.
182 Morpurgo, *Treason at West Point*, 126–127.
183 Boylan, *Dark Eagle*, 221; Flexner, *The Traitor and the Spy*, 371; Sale, *Traitors*, 53.

so foreign to his temperament.' [Washington soon recaptured control of his emotions, and] 'not a trace remained on his countenance of either grief or despondency.'"[184]

PEGGY ARNOLD'S HYSTERICS

Most historians, and subsequent history, support the idea that Peggy's hysterics were largely contrived. Peggy allegedly admitted to Theodosia Burr that she had staged her hysteria. Colonel Varick later asserted that he believed her actions at the Robinson house were "a piece of splendid acting."[185] In *Treacherous Beauty*, there is an insightful discussion about the pervasive diagnosis of "hysteria" for women of the period. The authors note that "it was never clear whether Peggy's fits were truly uncontrollable or were merely a convenient psychological weapon."[186]

Alexander Hamilton, always having an eye for public opinion, sent a letter to his fiancée which was quickly published in the *New York Post* and the *Pennsylvania Gazette*, recounting Peggy Shippen's performance, exonerating herself while making her husband all the more hated.[187] While Peggy was certainly in a perilous situation, and it did not require much to cause any reasonable person to panic, this "episode was the mother of all hysterical fits, so hallucinatory and over the top that it's difficult to believe it was a condition rather than a calculated piece of theater. And the fact that it didn't start until Washington had left to inspect West Point strongly suggests that it was a distraction aimed to give Arnold time to make good his escape. . . . She had no choice but improvisation, no weapons but her wits. And so she brilliantly took advantage of her gender expectations: The men around her were obligated to show chivalric concern for her suffering, and to avoid any rude question about her husband's conspiracy. She played her role, and they played theirs. For Peggy, the Mad Scene was a great achievement, a virtuoso performance."[188]

Many historians believe that, at the low ebb of the Revolution, the foiling of Arnold's plot reinvigorated the Cause and provided a focal point for American loathing of both Arnold and the British. General Greene's General Orders on September 26, 1780, portrayed the American attitude: "Treason of the blackest dye was yesterday discovered. General Arnold who commanded at West Point, lost to every sentiment of honor, of private and public obligation, was about to deliver up that important post into the hands of the enemy. Such an event must have given the American cause a deadly wound if not a fatal stab. Happily the treason has been timely discovered to prevent the fatal misfortune. The Providential train of circumstances which led to it

---

184 Jacob, *Treacherous Beauty*, 162.
185 *See* Brumwell, *Turncoat*, 278–280.
186 Jacob, *Treacherous Beauty*, 158–166.
187 *See* Randall, *Patriot and Traitor*, 558–560.
188 Jacob, *Treacherous Beauty*, 164–165.

affords the most convincing proof that the liberties of America is [sic] the object of divine protection."

Chapter 81

Washington earnestly did not want to hang André, so he sent a secret note through Alexander Hamilton to Clinton: "If Sir Henry Clinton would in any way suffer General Washington to get General Arnold within his power, Major André should be immediately released." Driving the point home, the letter stated, "Arnold appears to have been the guilty author of the mischief and not to more properly be the victim."[189]

Henry Knox had met André years earlier in a coincidence that only history could manufacture: "There is a charming story told—charming stories abound, concerning the ill-fated young André—about his march to internment in Pennsylvania. During the howling winter of 1775–76, André and his fellow British officers were herded into an inn near Lake George, which was already crowded with sleepers. André is said to have bedded down with a portly gentleman who, when the storm kept them both awake, initiated a conversation that lasted through the night. Upon awakening and donning uniforms, the two bedmates discovered they belonged to opposing armies. With old-world courtesy, each introduced himself. André's bedmate had been the former Boston bookseller-turned-artillerist, Colonel Henry Knox, on his way to bring the cannon captured from Ticonderoga to Washington's army besieging Boston. The two men parted cordially, destined to meet again in the Dutch Reformed Church of Tappan on a sunny autumn morning in 1780, when General Henry Knox would sit in judgment of Major John André."[190]

Epilogue

Washington gave Peggy the option of crossing the battle lines and joining Arnold in New York or returning to her family in Philadelphia. She *chose* Philadelphia. This cemented the public perception that she was a victim. This has always raised the question of whether she was implicitly rejecting Arnold, and would have ultimately chosen to stay in Philadelphia, if given the chance.

The plot had failed. There is at least a chance—and we will never know—that Peggy wanted to return to Philadelphia on a permanent basis. Fate prevented this from happening because she was expelled from the city. We see no indication that her decision to go to Philadelphia caused any consternation in her marriage to Arnold, but it does raise an intriguing possibility.[191] Flexner also raises the prospect that Peggy did

---

189 Randall, *Patriot and Traitor*, 566.
190 Boylan, *Dark Eagle*, 119–120.
191 *See generally* Jacob, *Treacherous Beauty*, 168–175.

not actually want to return to Benedict, even if she had been complicit in the treason. She was only forced to do so when she was expelled from Philadelphia.[192]

Nathanael Greene best summarized the view of the American military leadership relating to Arnold's actions: "Since the fall of Lucifer, nothing has equaled the fall of Arnold. His military reputation in Europe and America was flattering in the vanity of the first General of his age. He will now sink as low as he had been high before, and as the devil made war upon heaven after his fall, so I expect Arnold will upon America. Should he ever fall into our hands, he will be a sweet sacrifice."[193]

Some biographers claim Arnold asked to be buried in his old American uniform and even uttered, "God forgive me for ever putting on any other."[194] There is certainly no record that Arnold expressed any contrition for his treachery. Indeed, it would have undermined the fundamental nature of his existence. He believed to the end that he acted with courage and honor in his attempt to overthrow the Revolution.[195]

---

192 Flexner, *The Traitor and the Spy*, 395.

193 Lea, *A Hero and a Spy*, 512.

194 Arnold, *The Life of Benedict Arnold*, 395.

195 *See* Brumwell, *Turncoat*, 329–330.

ACKNOWLEDGMENTS

I could not research, write, and obsess about Benedict Arnold without the support of my family. My trips to strange places and purchases of often expensive books and rare maps were met with indulgent smiles. Chores neglected were readily forgiven. Most of all, my amazing wife, Andrea, gave frank and helpful feedback on my drafts. In sum, I am a lucky guy.

When I was a young man, I developed a serious condition which limits my ability to type or strenuously use my arms. My partner and friend Deb Murphy typed most of the book for me and encouraged me even as she faced challenges in her life. I will always be humbled by her kindness and support. Fortunately, Jen Egge agreed to pick up the baton and was absolutely fabulous in assisting me during the editing process and taking this book to the finish line.

Award-winning author and friend Steve McEllistrem provided truly astounding editing, proofreading, and comments. He is a brilliant writer, and I count myself fortunate to have learned from him.

Once again, I sought input from a group of accomplished, diverse, remarkable, and insightful friends who read a draft of this book and provided invaluable insight: Mike Aydt, Jim DeMay, Matt Hendrickson, Neil Kraus, and Steve Lieb. Thankfully our friendships survived my imposition on them while I benefited from their wisdom.

Isabel Lieb patiently worked with me to design the book cover and suffered through many drafts of the maps. I am grateful for her skills and insight.

I am grateful for the amazing tour and invaluable insights from Xavier Chambolle of Tours Accolade at the City of Quebec; likewise to Cédric Lapointe at the Fortifications of Quebec National Historic Site, who went above and beyond to help me understand and appreciate the fortifications as they existed at the time of Arnold's assault. James Hughto provided a vivid and detailed tour of the Saratoga battlefield while challenging my view of Arnold. James also assisted in understanding the confusing and contradictory maps of the Battle of Bemis Heights. I am grateful for the insight of Susan Evans McClure, the executive director of the Lake Champlain Maritime Museum, concerning the nature of the cannon used at the Battle of Valcour Island.

I wish to thank other family, coworkers, clients, and friends too numerous to name who provided encouragement. Any errors in the form or substance of this book are mine; the credit and thanks go to many.

ABOUT THE AUTHOR

Steve Yoch and his wife, Andrea, have two fantastic sons, who have finished college and left the nest. He graduated with honors from Boston College and the University of Minnesota Law School. He has enjoyed over three decades of practicing law in the Twin Cities and is also involved in his family's marketing business. In his "free time," he enjoys supporting the Minnesota Aurora, the new women's soccer team founded by his wife and a group of remarkable community-minded leaders.

Book Club Questions

1. What are some of the biggest myths about Benedict Arnold?

2. What surprised you about Arnold?

3. You got to know Arnold. Do you admire him? Do you like him?

4. Was Benedict a traitor because of Peggy? Was it her fault?

5. Why did he become a traitor? Was it really all for money?

6. Arnold's father became an embarrassment. How did this impact him?

7. Arnold did not succeed, but was he punished?

8. How would history be different if Benedict had succeeded?

For previous titles by Stephen Yoch, visit www.yoch.com.

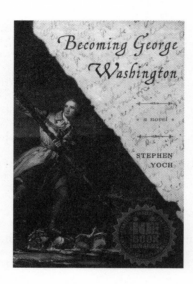

The George Washington you don't know. . .

Long before Washington was the old man on the dollar bill, he was a fatherless boy with few resources and even less education. So how did he become the most famous person in American history?

Becoming George Washington tells the story of a young man with boundless energy, bravery, and passion, who grew into a self-confident leader. At the same time, he struggled to suppress both an awful temper and his love for a married woman, Sally Fairfax. A courageous war hero, Washington rose to the pinnacle of Virginia politics. His experiences as a young man allowed him, decades later, to lead the Revolution.

This compelling historical novel reveals the person behind the famous face and how he became America's indispensable Founding Father.